# THE FAMILY ON
# PARADISE PIER

Also by Dermot Bolger

NOVELS
*Night Shift*
*The Journey Home*
*Emily's Shoes*
*A Second Life*
*Father's Music*
*Temptation*
*The Valparaiso Voyage*

PLAYS
*The Lament for Arthur Cleary*
*Blinded by the Light*
*In High Germany*
*The Holy Ground*
*One Last White Horse*
*April Bright*
*The Passion of Jerome*
*Consenting Adults*
*From These Green Heights*

POETRY
*The Habit of Flesh*
*Finglas Lilies*
*No Waiting America*
*Internal Exiles*
*Leinster Street Ghosts*
*Taking My Letters Back: New & Selected Poems*
*The Chosen Moment*

EDITOR
*The Picador Book of Contemporary Irish Fiction*
*Finbar's Hotel*
*Ladies' Night at Finbar's Hotel*

# DERMOT BOLGER

# *The Family on Paradise Pier*

FOURTH ESTATE • *London* and *New York*

First published in Great Britain in 2005 by
Fourth Estate
A Division of HarperCollins*Publishers*
77–85 Fulham Palace Road
London W6 8JB
www.4thestate.com

1 3 5 7 9 8 6 4 2

A catalogue record for this book
is available from the British Library

UK hardback
ISBN 0-00-715409-7

Trade paperback
ISBN 0-00-720730-1

Typeset by Palimpsest Book Production Limited,
Polmont, Stirlingshire

Printed in Great Britain by
Clays Ltd, St Ives plc

*For Donnacha and Diarmuid*

# Prologue

## 1941

A parched twilight began to close in around the unlit prisoner train. For over a week the *zeks* in Brendan Goold Verschoyle's wagon had jolted across a landscape they rarely glimpsed, crushed together in putrid darkness. Only those crammed against the wooden slats ever saw the small worms of daylight flicker in through the slight cracks. Little sound penetrated into the wagon either, just the ceaseless rumble of the tracks and very occasionally a more confined echo as they passed at speed through an empty station. Sometimes the long train stopped and prisoners shifted eagerly, yearning for the noise of hammers as guards untangled barbed wire coiled around each carriage and eventually opened the doors. In the stampede to relieve themselves on the dry earth outside, dignity would be forgotten as men and women squatted together under the gaze of the guards and their dogs. But more often these stops occurred for no obvious reason. There would be no sound outside after the wheels came to a rusty halt, no footsteps, no safety catches unleashed, no orders screamed for *zeks* to get down on their knees and be counted. Instead the train would remain motionless for an indeterminable period during which the *zeks* inwardly clung to dreams of water and dry bread and fresh air to replace the rancid stink within the sealed wagons.

Eventually when the wheels slowly jolted forward again nobody would speak, even the children no longer able to make the effort to cry. Yet each *zek* felt a stir of relief amidst their disappointment. Because despite the demand for railway carriages no decision had been made to liquidate them. Fresh instructions must have been issued to change direction and transport them to a different gulag or some patch of barren earth where their first task would be to erect barbed-wire fences around themselves.

Hours later when the train finally stopped for them to receive a small mug of water and several ounces of bread, there would often be another corpse to be lifted off, stiffened in an upright position from having sat cradled between the legs of the chained man behind him.

Half the *zeks* in this carriage had no idea why they had been arrested. The Polish surname of the man behind Brendan was sufficient to implicate him in a counter-revolutionary Trotskyite conspiracy. The man who died yesterday was among workers sent by Stalin to help build a railway in China, all arrested on their return as members of a Japanese spy ring. Some had endured appalling torture while others knew only cursory interrogation by overworked *troikas* who took just a few seconds to concoct random treason charges before sentencing them to fifteen years.

Brendan's position as a foreign political had become perilous in the weeks since a voice on the Tannoy in his last camp had abruptly announced Germany's treacherous attack on the Soviet Union, with guards and *zeks* equally stunned that anyone – even Hitler – could dare to defy Stalin. Since then all prisoners with German names had been killed. This train contained *zeks* who were foreigners or had been contaminated by contact with foreigners and were therefore now classified as enemy soldiers. Still, Brendan had known worse transports. The carriage might lack the luxury of those cattle wagons where *zeks* could squat over a small toilet hole in the floor, but this heat was better than the cold. Today was bearable. He had managed to fully evacuate his bowels at the last stop, had savoured his mug of water and eaten most of his bread while keeping a small chunk concealed on his person. He was hungry now but would wait until the apex of this starvation before starting to slowly chew the last hunk of black bread. To be able to control when he briefly relieved his hunger gave him a sense of power.

Only two men sat between him and the wall so that when he leaned backwards there was some support. Nobody had yet soiled themselves so that no stream of urine seeped into him and there was no stink of shit. Nobody had died as yet in this wagon today or if they did they had done so without attracting attention. Nobody had tried to steal another *zek*'s bread, with prisoners lashing out until the thief was dead. Any other theft was acceptable but even here there were taboos one could not break. No woman had been gang-raped, mainly because the carriage consisted of politicals, and true violence only occurred when the common criminals seized control of a wagon, dominating it with their brutality. This wagon was so quiet that for a few seconds Brendan blacked out into sleep and dreamed of Donegal.

The four Goold Verschoyle children were home from boarding school for Easter, reunited with their sister Eva who was considered too delicate to send away. They were bathing at Bruckless Pier in Donegal Bay. At sixteen, Brendan's eldest brother Art raced hand in hand with seventeen-year-old Eva along the stones to step off the private stone jetty and tumble

3

laughingly into the waves. Nineteen-year-old Maud swam near the shore, while Thomas, aged fourteen, stood balanced in a long-oared punt like a sentry. And Brendan saw himself, nine years of age and sleek as a silvery fish, flitting through the green water, while Mother sat sketching on the rocks and Father looked up from his Walt Whitman book to wave. Eva surfaced and shook out her wet hair before joining Mother to take up her sketchbook as well. Art plunged deeper into the water and surfaced beside Brendan. Reaching out to ruffle his hair, he asked if Brendan liked the kite he had made for him that morning. Brendan nodded his gratitude and plunged his head into the water to glide behind his beloved big brother. Opening his eyes he watched Art power through the waves and longed for the day when he would be that strong. His lungs hurt and he needed to surface for breath while Art's feet pushed inexhaustibly on.

The unexpected jolt of the train woke him as he crested the waves. Some *zeks* came out of their torpor and began to talk, wondering if they would be allowed into the air. Others shouted for quiet so they could listen for the click of rifles and the panting of dogs. Brendan discreetly checked that his bread was still there. He longed to still be asleep, yearned for the salty tang of seawater at Bruckless Pier and wanted his family to know that he was still alive. No *zek* spoke now but he sensed their terror. Because there was no sound of guards' voices, just the leisurely drone of an aeroplane approaching.

Nettles were in flower on the fringe of the small Mayo wood, with a peculiar beauty that people rarely looked beyond their poisonous leaves to see. Eva watched a Red Admiral alight on the tip of a leaf and the butterfly's colouring reminded her of the dying glow of the turf last night when she had paused, after blowing out the wick, to gaze back at the fire which moments before had seemed dead in the candlelight. Yet in the dark it had been possible to glimpse the turf embers still faintly beating like two red wings.

Eva was noticing such details now that she had the freedom to see things. Freedom seemed a peculiar word in times of war, but this was how Mayo felt to her soul after escaping from England. The freezing winter was now just a memory. In January her husband had written from barracks to describe the Thames frozen over for the first time in fifty years. Every tiny Mayo lake had been the same, with local children tramping across the ice to pull home whatever firewood they could scavenge. When the *Irish Times* carried a picture of Finns attempting to hack away the corpses of invading Russian soldiers frozen to the ground, the icy backdrop could have been any white-capped Mayo hillside.

For much of January Eva had been snowed into Glanmire Wood with her two children. Playing and squabbling, drawing pictures on the walls of abandoned rooms and singing hymns at dusk, Francis and Hazel had longed to hear another voice. One night all three heard an unearthly cry from the woods and gathered at the front door to gaze out at the snow, the unnerving wail reminding them of the banshee. Convinced that Freddie's Territorial regiment had been dispatched to join the desperate battle abroad, at that moment Eva felt sure that her husband was dead. As ever, eleven-year-old Hazel proved the level-headed one.

'It's a dog,' the girl had cried. 'Trapped out there.'

Hazel had not waited to get properly dressed, but ran into the snow with Francis following and Eva trying to keep up – more concerned for their safety in the snowdrifts than for the dog. It had taken ten minutes to locate the collie's cries and dig her out. The children carried her back to the house, refusing to change their drenched clothes until they found a blanket to wrap the starved creature in. The dog's ribs were so exposed that it seemed she would never recover. She survived though and so did they, despite the February storms that shook all of Europe as if God was moved to fury by mankind's rush to slaughter.

They had safely come through two winters to be happily becalmed in the warmth of this summer's afternoon with no wind to disturb the trees encircling their crumbling home. The Red Admiral fluttered out onto the uncut lawn where Francis lay bare-chested, intoxicated by the high-pitched warble of two goldcrests in the wood. Returning to Ireland had restored his confidence. He was king of his castle here, venturing in his canoe down the Castlebar river or tramping the bogs where his father loved to shoot, but armed only with binoculars to watch for snipe among the reeds. Eva tried to keep his education going, but he only became excited about Latin when a neighbour loaned him a study of Irish trees. Now on walks through Glanmire Wood he eagerly displayed his knowledge. The hazel, with its coppery-brown bark and dangling yellow catkins, was called *Corylus avellana*. The birch with its sticky long winter buds and winged nutlets was *Betula alba*. He even told her Latin names for absent species that he intended to plant one day. *Arbutus unedo*, called the strawberry tree because its clustered fruit was covered with tiny warts and resembled strawberries. If Francis had his way Eva doubted if he would ever leave this wood again, because here he was Adam in all his innocence, reminding her of her youngest brother, Brendan, on those long childhood afternoons when they used to bathe at Bruckless Pier.

Eva watched the collie rouse herself from the front steps and pad across the lawn to collapse beside Francis. The boy lazily stretched out his hand and the dog rolled over to expose the freckled stomach she wanted rubbed.

Eva had a list of urgent tasks to jot down, but despite having taken pencil and paper outside she was too caught up in this miraculous heat to focus on responsibilities. Hazel emerged from the stables where she had been brushing down her pony and went to fill a bucket with water as the pump handle creaked in rusty protest.

'I'm going to the kitchen,' she announced. 'I'm going to make bubbles.' But the girl paused to stare past the branches of the sweet chestnut framing the avenue. Hazel had sharp hearing but soon Eva also heard the jingle of a bicycle circumventing the deep ruts on the overgrown path. She could not prevent herself being seized by a familiar fear, a residue from her childhood in the Great War when silence would envelop Dunkineely village whenever the postmaster left his office with a telegram. Was it news of Brendan or her parents? Surely Freddie, with his club foot, would not be sent into battle, no matter how desperate the war effort. But perhaps age and disability meant nothing, with Mussolini conscripting boys at fourteen, barely older than Francis. Eva lowered her pencil and tried to pray for all those she loved whom she knew to be in danger.

Full-length drapes across the window gave the Oxford bedroom an appearance of twilight, though it was only mid-afternoon when Mrs Goold Verschoyle woke. For most of the night she had fretted about her husband's safety as he patrolled the blacked-out streets as an air raid warden. So far, Oxford had escaped the fate of Coventry and Southampton, but some nights the fires in London were so great that their glow was said to be glimpsed even at this remove. Only after hearing Tim return safely at dawn had she allowed herself to fall asleep. But there was no sign of him having come up to bed. She lay on for a moment, recalling her dream about Donegal. She could still see Mr and Mrs Ffrench crossing their lawn from Bruckless House down to the stone pier with trays of homemade lemonade for the visiting swimmers. Brendan had loved their lemonade, often prolonging his thirst so as to savour the taste. Brendan, her youngest, had been like a fish in her dream.

A constant struggle with arthritis had left Mrs Goold Verschoyle's face severely lined. Her disability was so acute that holding a pen was torture: still she refused to stop writing to British and Soviet officials. Each line represented physical agony, but she was motivated by a need to quench the greater anguish in her heart. Today she determined not to upset herself by sifting through the replies piled in the bedside drawer – curt responses expressing regret at being unable to supply any information about her missing son. Today she would make herself look well for Tim. Painfully she brushed her hair, still soft and fine like a child's. Through the open wardrobe door she glimpsed the mothballed dresses she had once worn at parties in Donegal. She put down the hair-brush on the dressing table beside a copy of *The Great Outlaw* – her favourite book about Christ – and opened a drawer to examine the small bottles of perfume she was carefully nursing there.

Selecting her husband's favourite, she rose. Tim would be pleased to see that she was not too frail to leave her bed today. He was probably sleeping downstairs so as not to wake her. But when she reached the drawing room he was not lying on the sofa. His body was slumped forward in an armchair, with a book of poems still balanced on his knee. Mrs Goold Verschoyle watched, too scared to move. It would be typical of Tim for his death – like his entire life – to be

8

so understated that the book had not even fallen from his lap.

*Show some mercy, Lord*, she prayed. *Don't take him away from me also.*

The book toppled over, striking the carpet with a dull thud. Mr Goold Verschoyle stirred slightly, looking down at the book and stooped to pick it up. He became aware of her.

'How is my darling?' he asked quietly.

Mrs Goold Verschoyle made no reply, but walked over to place her hand on his shoulder.

'I know,' he said. 'I can feel how precious this time is too.'

Tragedy declined to penetrate the Mayo wood today because it wasn't a telegram boy who emerged beneath the chestnut branches onto the lawn where Eva and her children watched. Instead it was Maureen, their former maid but now their friend and lodger. She freewheeled up to the steps, delighted with her weekly half day off from the shop in Castlebar where she worked. Her wicker basket was full of provisions ordered by Eva, with every item paid for. It was bliss to owe no money and have no fear of creditors.

Glanmire House had undoubtedly gone to seed. Cracked windowpanes had not been replaced, loose tiles let rainwater into disused rooms with walls covered in a seaweed-like vegetation. But the kitchen was dry and warm and the few habitable rooms were adequate for their needs. Just now those needs were simple.

The horror of war was ever present by its absence. This woodland silence seemed artificial, as if punctured by distant cries so high-pitched that only the dog could cock her head to stare off puzzled into the distance.

Ireland was not yet directly consumed by the conflagration, but few doubted an imminent invasion from one side or the other. While the countryside held its breath people learnt to live in limbo. For Protestant neighbours the fact that Freddie had joined the British army was sufficient to reinstate respectability after the debacle of their bankruptcy. With Freddie too engrossed in army life to press her about maintaining appearances, Eva could discreetly go native with the children, talking and thinking as they liked in the privacy of this wood. Without Freddie, Glanmire House reminded her of the freedom of her childhood in Donegal.

Hazel waved to Maureen, then picked up the bucket of water and went to the kitchen. Francis waved and rolled onto his stomach to let the sun warm his back. Maureen laid her bicycle against the steps and strolled over to Eva.

'That heat's a terror.' She flopped down. 'The chain came off my bike near Turlough and I thought my hands would be destroyed with oil.'

'Any news from the village?' Eva asked.

'Divil the bit, Mrs Fitzgerald. The Stagg boys are off to England for work, though you'd swear half of Mayo had the same idea if you saw the crowds in Castlebar Station and the train already packed from Westport. They'll be sitting on the roof in Claremorris if it gets that far with the wet turf they're burning. They say English factory owners are crying out for workers.'

Maureen kicked off her shoes and lay back to let the sun brown her legs. Eva wondered if the girl was hinting at being tempted to go. The young woman reached into her bag to produce a letter.

'I met Jim the Post and said I'd save him the cycle,' she said. 'He looked killed with curiosity wondering what might be in it.'

Both laughed before Maureen picked up her shoes and went to join Hazel in the kitchen. Eva opened Freddie's letter

with trepidation because it was true that his weekly registered one, containing her allowance, had only arrived on
Monday. As always his tone was candid, yet circumspect.
The mantra that careless talk cost lives was instilled in him,
though Eva doubted if his letters were being steamed open
by German sympathisers in an Irish sorting office. The Irish
preferred to receive news of the tightening Nazi noose by
listening to Lord Haw-Haw's bragging tones on German radio.
Even then she suspected that most locals only listened because
Haw-Haw was a fellow Connaught man and they took pride
to see a local do well for himself in any walk of life.

Typically the first page enquired after the children before
Freddie imparted his news. Eva's fears of him being dispatched
to join the fighting were groundless – for now at least. With
two million young men called up, the army needed experienced men to provide military training, and Freddie wrote
that his time spent shooting on the Mayo bogs might not
have been wasted after all. He kept his tone self-deprecating,
as if baffled at having to relay the news of being commissioned as a second lieutenant in the Educational Corps. But
Eva knew he would have impressed his superiors by being
the best shot in his reserve artillery company. Such promotion
was a dream realised, especially with his disability. Eva knew
that he would show each conscript the care he would have
taken with Francis had his son betrayed the slightest interest
in guns.

Freddie had knuckled down to army life. The routine suited
him. He would be popular once he controlled his drinking
– his Irishness being a bonus for showing that he had deliberately chosen to be involved in the war. His tales about
shooting on the bogs would be embellished for comic effect.
He wrote about missing them but at heart Eva knew that
he relished the freedom to succumb to a last drink with new

acquaintances and ease himself into each day by waking up alone. Eva knew that he would feel guilty for enjoying this sense of freedom because she experienced the same guilt here in Mayo. Neither said it, but war was providing the camouflage for them to commence separate lives. Her brother Art had been right to proclaim that they should never have married.

In the wooden dormitory hut of the Curragh Internment Camp for subversives, Art Goold rose after polishing his boots. The discipline of camp life suited him. It was the sole advantage gleaned from having attended Marlborough College. Last week yet another IRA boy had been rounded up and interned for the duration of the conflict in Europe – which de Valera and his puppet imperialist government euphemistically termed 'The Emergency'. Listening to the boy cry when he thought the other internees were asleep, Art had remembered dormitories of boys abducted at an early age to be brainwashed and brutalised into managing an empire.

The difference of course was that in this camp, guarded by the Irish army, every internee was equal. There were no prefects or fags, no casual bullying or ritualised beatings. At Marlborough you were force-fed lies, but here a chance existed for genuine discourse. Not that all IRA men had open minds: some made a hurried sign of the cross when spying him. Art was used to such superstition, but most internees had grown relaxed with him, especially as he knelt alongside them at night while they recited their rosary. They knew that Art did not pray, but he considered it essential to camp morale to show respect for their beliefs. It made them curious about his beliefs too. His description of Moscow streets socialising and how agricultural production was transformed by the visionary genius of Stalin fascinated men who had never previously travelled more than thirty miles from their birthplace. At heart they were *kulaks* who would need to be prised from their few boggy acres when the time came. But what could one expect when they were terrorised by priests with the spectre of eternal punishment. Besides, having emanated from the *Byvshie Liudi*, Art could look down on no one. Stalin had coined that term well: *the former people* – remnants of the despised tsarist class who refused to play their part in the revolution. Soviet re-education camps were full of them, with soft hands learning to handle a shovel and be given a chance to redeem themselves. The triumph of the White Sea Canal, carved from rock with primitive tools and honest sweat, proved how re-education worked. Art had been sent back to Ireland to spread the gospel and, if de Valera insisted in interning him as a communist, then this camp was an ideal environment to do that.

The IRA and the communists were not natural allies but the persuasiveness of his argument was starting to gain converts. Art had previously agreed with the IRA leadership that Ireland stay neutral. However – since Hitler's attack on Russia – Art had no option but to call on Ireland to join the fight against German fascism now that Comrade Stalin had strategically aligned himself with the imperialists. Blinded by misguided nationalist shibboleths and petty hatred of Britain, the camp leadership had grown scared of his speeches in recent weeks. But it was not about collaboration with Britain, it was about using the Allies as a vehicle to crush fascism before uniting behind Stalin to create a new world order. That was a greater prize than the steeples of Fermanagh.

This was the moment for all revolutionaries to unite and, while the IRA might find it hard to adjust, Art had shown how radical change was possible. It had not been easy. Christ only endured forty nights in the desert, but Art had spent two decades working on the docks, kipping in tenements and police cells. He had been his own judge, serving every day of his sentence with hard labour and was strong and cleansed of his former class now. But the confusing thing was that last night he dreamt about his family bathing off Ffrench's private pier and had felt no guilt in re-experiencing that life of idle privilege. Instead he had known a sense of belonging, a dangerous wave of love all the more disturbing for emanating from those he was forced to repudiate.

Art left the hut, anxious to be on time for the few internees not intimidated away from his Russian language class. But soon he realised that two men were walking alongside him. He glanced at them as they pinned his arms. They belonged to the primitive Catholic element of Republican. He was strong enough to take them on but as they turned into a space between the huts he saw a deputation awaiting him. Taking a long knife from his pocket the camp IRA commander held it to Art's throat.

'You've been court-martialled, Goold, and sentenced *in absentia.*'

'You can't court-martial me. I'm not a member of any Republican organisation.'

'You're a Protestant crackpot.'

'I'm an atheist.'

'Either way you go to hell. You're just going there sooner than expected. I've had enough. We told the governor that unless you were gone by today you'd be found with a hundred knife wounds tomorrow morning. You're his responsibility now.'

The men pinning back Art's arms shoved him forward and he started walking. Then for some unknown reason, he remembered his brother Brendan in that dream last night, swimming alongside him, trying to keep up. Art stopped, not through fear but after being overcome by *déja vu* and an

14

inescapable guilt. He lifted his head, almost as if willing for retribution to finally come through a bullet or a knife.

Mrs Ffrench crossed the lawn from Bruckless House, and reached the gravel path that led to the small pier. Years ago on a picnic there when the Goold Verschoyle family argued about whether they should call it Bruckless Pier or Mr Ffrench's Pier, Eva had insisted that it should really be christened Paradise Pier because that was what it was. But with the Goold Verschoyles gone, nobody called it Paradise Pier any more. Indeed no one ever came here, though locals knew that she never objected to people swimming there. But superstition was strong, despite everyone in Bruckless and Dunkineely being kind to her in her grief. Perhaps nothing summed up her husband's failure more than their affection for him. He had seen himself as a radical orator, a progressive torch of truth amidst their fog of ignorance. But she realised that locals had just considered him a colourful eccentric – not even regarding him as Irish. Local priests had frequently railed against the Red Menace without bothering to mention her husband, despite his years of standing up on the running board of his Rolls-Royce at public meetings to heckle the speakers and beseech people to read the communist pamphlets that she had patiently held out.

Locally their crusade had been considered so laughable that it counted for nothing. The only converts they ever made came from their own class – those marvellous Goold Verschoyle boys. Not that class would count for anything after the revolution, but it still counted for something now. This was evident from the respectful way that people had carried her husband's body home last month after he collapsed while bicycling to Killybegs to heckle de Valera at a political rally. She had warned him it was too far to cycle but petrol was impossible to obtain. Mrs Ffrench had laid him out in the study, with his maps and books and his tame birds that flew about, soiling everywhere, disturbed by all the visitors. For three days the most unlikely people came to pay their respects, farm labourers who had never previously set foot in the house. Any trouble he had caused with Art Goold Verschoyle was forgotten. But all the neighbourhood could whisper about was his funeral arrangements.

No one attended the interment but she had sensed eyes watching from across the inlet as four workmen laid her husband's body in this sheltered corner of the garden beside the pier. In Donegal only unbaptised babies and suicides were buried on unconsecrated ground. But this had been Mrs Ffrench's wish and where she would lie when her time came. There had been no prayers or speeches; just *L' Internationale* played on the wind-up gramophone. Mrs Ffrench reached the headstone and knelt to lay wild flowers. The local stone-mason had gone to his priest for advice before chiselling the stark inscription her husband chose as his epitaph: *Thomas Roderick Ffrench: The Immortality of the Dead Exists Only in the Minds of the Living.*

The silence outside the prison train was broken by indistinct sounds: the barking of released dogs, guards shouting in panic, a scramble of boots across the ground.

'The bastards,' an old *zek* muttered behind Brendan. 'They're more concerned with saving the dogs than saving us. Come back, you cowards, unlock these doors.'

The entire wagon was on its feet now, banging at the roof and wooden walls. Bursts of machine-gun fire came from above, interspersed with cries.

'Aim well, Germans,' a woman said. 'Kill every guard.'

'That's who they want,' a young man added. 'I mean, why would the Germans want to destroy us?'

'They don't,' replied the old *zek*. 'We count for nothing. They want to destroy the carriages, this rolling stock.'

Noise of frantic hammering came from inside every wagon. Brendan heard the crush of timber and knew that one set of prisoners had broken free. Their shouts turned to screams amid a burst of gunfire, but he could not tell if the bullets came from the plane or if the guards might have set up their machine guns in the undergrowth. Two men beside him hammered at the roof, being lifted up by other prisoners. They broke away a wooden slat, yielding a dazzling glimpse of blue sky. Everyone was screaming now. But Brendan was utterly still, mesmerised by the blueness above him. It was the blue of an Irish summer and crossing that patch of light was a small aircraft, departing or wheeling around for another assault. It resembled a child's plaything, a sparkling gleam in the bright air that made him catch his breath as it turned in a slow loop. Others saw it too and began to scream louder. But Brendan said nothing because he had become a boy again, standing on Bruckless Pier to draw in the bright kite that his eldest brother had made for him.

Eva looked up from her husband's letter as Hazel waltzed out from the kitchen onto the lawn in her bare feet. The girl stirred a mixture in the jug she carried, then tossed back her hair to blow the first bubble skyward, laughing as it rose and burst. Francis briefly watched, then lay back with the dog beside him.

Eva laid down Freddie's letter and, feeling a sliver of guilt at her idleness, purposefully picked up her pencil to start making the list of tasks planned for this afternoon. But Hazel's laugh made her glance up at the extraordinary way the child twisted her supple body to keep the bubbles aloft. The girl was totally immersed in this game, enjoying her triumph whenever a bubble stayed intact, laughing at the silent plop of its extinction, then starting anew with a fresh bubble stream. Nothing else existed for Hazel at this moment: no war, no bombers circling Europe's skies, no threat of invasion or nerve gas, no future complicated by adult decisions. Just these weightless globes to be savoured for the brief totality of their existence.

Eva stared down at the jotting pad, the list of tasks banished from her thoughts. It was years since she last held a pencil for any reason except to scribble down lists. Her childhood instinct to draw – dormant for so long – had unconsciously taken over. She discovered a swirling sketch of her daughter already half finished. Eva examined it with a quickening of the heart. She could draw again if she didn't think about it. Let the pen do the thinking. A second image shaped itself on the page. Of Hazel stationary this time, back arched and head held back to blow a bubble upward. Eva could see her own reflection within the girl, as if she was the same age, experiencing the same joy. The second sketch was barely finished before her fingers commenced a third. If the girl looked over, the magic would be ruined. Hazel would demand to see what Eva was doing, minutely examining each sketch. But these drawings felt as light as bubbles. At the slightest pressure her ability would burst asunder. It was like a sixth sense returning to her fingers, with the tension of adulthood banished.

Francis spied Maureen's bicycle beside the front steps. He mounted it and freewheeled deftly across the lawn. Two quarrelling birds chased each other among the trees. There was so much that Eva could add to her sketch: their crumbling house, cattle in the fields below, the crooked stable door. But there was no need to include these because Eva merely wanted to draw happiness. As Hazel spun in giddy circles she seemed like an axis, a fulcrum, a whirlpool of happiness, drawing the whole world into her on invisible threads.

The dog barked, chasing the weaving bicycle. Maureen came from the kitchen to say that tea was ready. But nobody moved as if nobody could hear. Hazel scooped into the jar to unleash a final stream of bubbles. They soared above her, rainbow-coloured in the light. This was how her family had been in Donegal, Eva realised, diving into the waters at Bruckless Pier, beautiful, impractical, living in the moment with no awareness of how short-lived that paradise would be. Hazel danced beneath the last bubble, throwing her head so far back that it seemed impossible she would not fall. Borne by her breath, the bubble rose so high that Eva had trouble following it. Maureen stopped calling and even Francis halted the bicycle to watch. The bubble balanced in midair and Hazel balanced on the grass, equally poised and beautiful until, without warning, it burst and there was nothing left. Hazel toppled backwards, rolled over to gaze at her mother and laughed.

# PART ONE

# 1915–1935

# ONE

## *The Picnic*

### *August 1915*

Eva thought it was glorious to wake up with this sense of expectation. The entire day would be spent outoors, with her family chattering away on the back of Mr Ffrench's aeroplane cart as Eva dangled her legs over the swaying side and held down her wide-brimmed hat with one hand in the breeze. Surely no other bliss to equal this.

Her older sister Maud was asleep in the other bed in the room. Dust particles glistened in the early sunlight, creeping through a slat in the wooden shutters, the thin beam making the white washbowl beside the water jug even whiter.

It was barely six o'clock but thirteen-year-old Eva could not stay in bed a moment longer. Nobody else was yet awake in Dunkineely. Soon the endless clank of the village pump would commence, but until then Eva had paradise to herself. If she rose quietly she could go walking and be home again before the Goold Verschoyle household rose to prepare for today's picnic.

Dressing on tiptoes so as not to wake Maud, Eva slipped downstairs. An old white cat beside the kitchen range lifted his head to regard Eva with a secretive look as she lifted the latch and escaped into the garden. The clarity of light enraptured her, with spider webs sketched by dew. Eva followed a trail of fox pawmarks along the curving path leading to the deserted main street, then took the lane that meandered down to the rocky Bunlacky shore. The sea breeze coming off St John's Point swept away her breath, filling Eva with a desire to shout in praise. She closed her eyes and formal hymns took flight in her mind like a flock of startled crows, with new words like white birds swooping down to replace them. The prayers that meant most were the ones which came unbidden at such moments:

> 'O Lord *whom I cannot hope to understand or see, maker of song thrush and skylark and linnet. Do with my life what you will. Bring me whatever love or torment will unleash my heart. Just let me be the person I could become if my soul was stretched to its limits.'*

Eva opened her eyes, half-expecting white birds to populate the empty sky. Instead a few bushes bowed to the wind's majesty.

As son of a Church of Ireland bishop, Father took his task seriously of instructing the boys in religion but Mother claimed that secretly he only went to church to sing. It was Mother's responsibility to instruct the girls. Yet even without Mother's Rosicrucian beliefs and indifference to organised religion, Eva knew that she would have outgrown their local church in Killaghtee, where sermons were more concerned with elocution than any love of Christ. She needed a ceremony which encompassed her joy at being alive. But if Eva did not belong with her family in the reserved top pew in Killaghtee church, where did she belong? Neither in the Roman Catholic chapel which Cook and Nurse attended nor with the Methodists in their meeting hall next door to her home. Right now this lane felt like a true church, filled with the hymn of the wind. Freedom existed in this blasphemous thought, a closeness to God that might have heralded the sin of vanity had it also not made her feel tiny and lost. Eva closed her eyes and slowly started to spin around, feeling as if she were at the axis of a torrent of colour. Behind her eyelids the earth split into every shade of green and brown that God ever created. The sky was streaked in indigo and azure, sapphire and turquoise. Prisms of colour mesmerised her like phrases in the psalms: jade and olive and beryl, rust and vermilion. At any moment she might take off and whirl through the air like a chestnut sepal. Her breath came faster, her head dizzy.

'*Can you see your child, Lord, dancing her way back to you?*'

A sound broke through her reverie, a suppressed laugh. Eva opened her eyes but the earth declined to stop spinning. A young barefoot girl grasped her hand with a firm grip, steadying her. The girl looked alarmed.

'I'm sent for the cows, miss,' she said. 'Are you okay?'

'Yes.' The world still swayed dangerously but Eva let go her hand, able to stand unaided.

'Was it a fit? My sister has fits. She's epil ...' The girl struggled with the word. 'Epileptic. They took her to the madhouse in Donegal Town. Are you mad too?'

'No. I'm just happy.'

The girl mused on the word suspiciously.

'Your father defended my Uncle Shamie in court for fighting a peeler, miss. They say you're a fierce dreamer, and your father is for the birds. Why don't you go to boarding school like your sister?'

'Mother says I am not strong enough.'

'They say your mother is a right dreamer too, miss.'

'What's your name?'

Deciding that she had already revealed too much to one of the gentry, the girl veered past Eva and moved on, viciously whipping the heads off nettles with a hazel switch. Eva felt embarrassed at being seen.

Where the lane bent to the left the sea came into view. A small sailing ship was firmly anchored in the bay, never changing position despite the buffeting it received from the waves. It was time to go home but Eva could not stop watching the boat. More than anything she wished to be like it, firmly anchored despite the wild seas of emotion she constantly found herself in.

A queue was forming at the village pump by the time Eva returned up the main street. People greeted her respectfully and she talked to everyone. Possibly because she had never gone away to school for long, the whole village had adopted her.

Eva's miserable few months in boarding school last year had convinced Mother that she was not strong enough for sports or other girls. But sometimes Eva wondered if she was kept at home to afford Mother company during the winter when Mother was affected by illnesses that Dr O'Donnell seemed unable to pinpoint. The front door of the Manor House was open and her five-year-old brother, Brendan, ran out half-dressed to chase the ducks splashing in pools along the deeply rutted street. Eva swept him up in her arms and handed him back to Nurse. The clang of the pump followed her as she walked around by the side of the house. Visitors sometimes asked how the family tolerated this constant clank, but Eva only really noticed the pump when it stopped. For her it represented the creaking heart of Dunkineely.

Her family would be up, chattering away over breakfast,

but Eva's first responsibility was to feed her rabbit in the hutch near the tennis court. Crickets communicated with each other along the grassy bank in an indecipherable bush code as Eva cradled the rabbit to her breast, savouring the special shade of pink within the white of his ears. Sitting on the grass beside the rabbit as he ate, she spied Father through the drawing-room window. His few briefs as a barrister were mainly the unpaid defence of locals in trouble. His real passion was music and Father had left the breakfast table early to work. A black cat – whom he christened 'Guaranteed to Purr in Any Position' – sat motionless on his piano as he composed. The cat loved Father, not with a dog's adoring servitude but as an equal with whom she condescended to share her space. She would sit for hours when he played – her head cocked like a discerning, slightly quizzical, music critic.

All the house cats belonged to Father. Mother's pleasure arose from holding any baby in her arms. Eva was the only baby she ever rejected, just for a brief moment after Eva was born. *Take her away*, she had ordered Nurse because – having already borne one daughter – she was convinced that she had been carrying that all-important son and heir. Mother herself had told Eva this story and though Eva never sensed any trace of rejection within Mother's unequivocal love since then, it still caused unease. Returning the rabbit to the hutch, Eva plucked some daisies from the grass bank and held them to her nostrils. The scent always conjured her earliest memory of sitting on this slope at toddling age, picking a bunch of daisies to breathe in their smell that swamped her with happiness. In her memory, Nurse sat knitting nearby, her white apron hiding a plump, inviting lap. Eva could remember longing to be on Nurse's lap and suddenly it had felt like she was already there, as if Nurse's essence – her warm skin and laughing breath – was reaching Eva through the ecstasy of inhaling the fragrance of daisies. Even now she could still recall racing towards Nurse's arms, holding out the bunch of daisies to be savoured.

'Eva, quit dreaming and come and have some breakfast! The Ffrenches are calling for us at eight o'clock.'

Maud's voice had an exasperated big sister tone as she summoned Eva from the doorway. Eva waved and went to join her family in the breakfast room. In Father's absence, Art sat in the top chair. Sixteen months younger than Eva, he was the heir whom Mother had longed for, being groomed already to take over the Goold Verschoyle lineage. Thomas sat beside him, a year younger and two inches smaller, focusing on eating his egg with the exact concentration that he brought to every task. Being the middle brother made him weigh the value of everything. Brendan was too small to care about such matters. As the youngest he took it as his right to be spoiled by everyone. Maud was organising the hamper with the cook, having baked the cakes herself last night. The servants looked to fifteen-year-old Maud for instructions, finding Mother frequently too unwell to oversee the running of the house. But this was one of Mother's good weeks and, spurred by the presence of her Cousin George, she would accompany them on today's picnic.

Everyone at the table talked about their plans for the day. All were good swimmers, though Art was by far the strongest – being nearly as fast as Oliver Hawkins who was seventeen. The Hawkins family from Herefordshire had spent all this summer at Bruckless House, two miles away. Last year a young couple, the Ffrenches, bought this isolated mansion, built by two local brothers on the proceeds of selling guns to Napoleon and pickled herring to Wellington's army. Mrs Hawkins was related to Mr Ffrench who after being commissioned into the Royal Navy had been away since January. But Mr Ffrench had returned home two weeks ago, claiming that he had insisted on his naval shore leave coinciding with Eva's end-of-summer birthday party.

Eva had laughed along with everyone else when he said this, but secretly she believed him. This final week of summer was always the most exciting, culminating in Chinese lanterns being hung in the garden for her birthday party, with charades and fancy dress costumes and singers gathering around Father at the piano. After Eva's birthday the farewells would start at the train station, with the Hawkins family returning to England, Art, Thomas and Maud going away to school and Mr Ffrench rejoining his frigate currently moored in Killybegs Harbour. But Eva refused to let this thought sour her mood as the maid ran in to announce that Mr Ffrench's cart had arrived and, within seconds, the breakfast room was full of laughing voices.

Mother entered the room with Cousin George to greet the new arrivals. Cousin George was a wise chameleon, secretly in tune with Mother when discussing the occult and yet indistinguishable from any other Church of Ireland curate when a guest preacher in the pulpit at Killaghtee church before their neighbours. His sermons were the only ones that Eva still enjoyed, although the Ffrenches never attended church to hear them – being of a religious persuasion, the Baha'is – that not even Mother had heard of. No locals minded the Ffrenches' eccentricity because nobody understood it. Grandpappy, now on his annual summer visit, declared that no such religion existed except among a handful of demented Arabs driven from Iran, and the Ffrenches would forget such nonsense once they began to procreate like decent Christians. But since Father invited them along to a picnic last autumn, the Ffrenches had become part of the family, opening up their house and shoreline garden to the Goold Verschoyle children.

The ceaseless chatter made Eva fear that today's picnic might never start. But Maud coaxed everyone out onto the street where people started to lift picnic baskets up onto Mr Ffrench's open-backed float, christened the Aeroplane Cart. Maud sat at the back with the Hawkins twins, who were the same age as her, dangling their legs and bending their heads together to gossip beneath wide-brimmed hats. Somehow twelve-year-old Beatrice Hawkins managed to perch between Art and Eva, unable to address either of them. Until ten days ago Eva and Beatrice had been the closest chums, left to fend for themselves when Maud and the twins disappeared to whisper about grown-up secrets. They had searched for nests without disturbing the eggs, taken turns to push Brendan on his scooter along the street with anxious ducks scattering or had gone walking along the shore with Art minding them. But recently Eva could not explain the friction between them, as if Beatrice was jealous of Eva having a brother so wonderful as Art and wanted to push in and play at being his sister also.

Beatrice's brother, Oliver, held the reins as the cart left Dunkineely behind. Eva saw Maud watching him furtively and knew that she had fallen in love. When they reached Bruckless village, Oliver gave Thomas the reins and went to sit among the grown-ups. Cousin George had Brendan on his knee, teaching him to shout the responses to a music hall rhyme:

*'Who goes there?'*
*'A grenadier.'*
*'What do you want?'*
*'A pint of beer.'*
*'Where's your money?'*
*'In my pocket.'*
*'Where's your pocket?'*
*'I forgot it.'*

The adults laughed, demanding an encore as the horse jangled along the Killybegs road. The Donegal hills rose to the right, arrayed in purple, with the sea to their left and beyond it Ben Bulbin screening the distant Mayo mountains. Sunlight lit the gorse, with foxgloves peeping from hedgerows. Father was maintaining that idle moments like this brought us closer to the truths of the universe, while Mr Hawkins countered that the Irish were sufficiently lazy without being given a philosophy to excuse their idleness.

Eva was relieved to hear the adults not discussing the war because today was too perfect for outside intrusions. The morning passed in a babble of voices that died away as they neared the sea, leaving just the jangle of the harness and the noise of hooves on the dusty road.

The view from the rocks beside the beach was so striking that Mother had to sketch it at once. Eva climbed up with a sketchpad to keep her company. Both looked out to sea, drawing quietly. Behind them, rugs were spread out on the sand and Maud arranged plates from the hamper as the Hawkins twins poured homemade lemonade. Father sat talking to Art while Beatrice Hawkins lay beside Art in the very spot where Eva wanted to lie when the sketching was finished. Brendan kept pestering Art by presenting seashells to the big brother he worshipped and, although Beatrice Hawkins was normally too quiet to merit notice, Eva saw that she also kept bothering Art by shyly brushing sand with her bare foot over his.

They had forgotten to bring drinking water, but Mr Ffrench climbed up towards the caves with a copper kettle to collect water from the streamlet trickling down over the glistening rocks. Father went to assist him and suddenly Beatrice Hawkins found the courage to lob a handful of sand over Art's hair. She shrieked as Art rolled over to trap her in a wrestling hold, gathering up sand that he playfully threatened to make her swallow. Then just as quickly Art rolled off the girl and picked up Father's book, pretending to ignore her.

'Oh,' Mother said quietly, distracting Eva. Her pencil went still as she stared across the waves. Thirty seconds passed before she looked at Eva with an air of casual curiosity. 'How strange. I've just seen something interesting.'

'What?' Eva asked.

'I don't know,' Mother replied matter-of-factly. 'A stone statue rose slowly from the sea to block the horizon.'

'What did it do?'

'Why nothing, dear, obviously. It was just a statue. It rose as far as its navel, then sank slowly without a sound.' Mother resumed sketching, her seascape bereft of any figure. 'It looked rather like Neptune,' she added as an afterthought. 'Or Manannán Mac Lir, the Celtic God of the Sea, the way that AE draws him in visions. Not that AE is a good draughtsman, of course. How is your sketch coming on?'

'Fine,' Eva replied, accustomed to Mother's psychic visions. They sketched away with nothing further to say. The stone figure would be their secret. It had no place in the boisterous picnic taking shape on the sands where Mr Ffrench clambered down to applause, jumping the last few feet without spilling a drop from the kettle. Eva was anxious to help Art deal with the pest which Beatrice Hawkins had become for him and, once the kettle was boiled over a fire of twigs, Mother was also happy to join the main picnic.

The meal was gloriously protracted, with interruptions as shapes in the changing clouds diverted people's attention or when they paused to hear each other's favourite quotations. Father, for once, chose not Whitman but Longfellow to share with the gathering:

> *'And evermore beside him on his way*
> *The unseen Christ shall move,*
> *That he may lean upon his arm and say*
> *"Dost thou, dear Lord, approve?"'*

Cousin George was a master diplomat, encompassing the Ffrench's strange beliefs by reciting:

> *'So many gods, so many creeds;*
> *So many paths that wind and wind,*
> *While just the art of being kind*
> *Is all the sad world needs.'*

Eva saw how this gesture impressed Mr Hawkins, who knew that Grandpappy – who avoided today's picnic by rising early to go into Killybegs – had little time for divergent beliefs, including those of his own daughter-in-law. Mr Hawkins's good mood was tempered however by Maud's hot-headed contribution to the quotations:

> *'Ireland was Ireland when England was a pup*
> *And Ireland will still be Ireland when England is done*
> *up.'*

Home Rule was anathema to Mr Hawkins and Eva sensed how the picnic could be soured by politics. Nobody disputed the absolute rightness of the war in Europe, but people held differing opinions as to what should happen in its aftermath. Father believed strongly that what was good enough for Belgium should be good enough for Ireland and so, in fighting to free that small nation, the Irish boys were fighting for their own right to self-determination. Mr Ffrench appeared less sure. Since his rapid promotion within the Royal Navy he seemed to lean more towards Mr Hawkins who called Father's attitude treasonous for a Briton. Father laughed off this comment, saying that the Verschoyles lacked one drop of English blood. They were Dutch nobles who came over with William of Orange and later married into ancient Irish clans whose ancestry he had personally traced back to Niall of the Nine Hostages.

Leaving politics to the grown-ups, Eva joined the other children bathing in the sea, with Maud delighted when Oliver Hawkins joined them. Oliver said little about the war and Eva suspected he felt differently from his father. As Art and Oliver raced each other out to the rocks, Eva lay in the waves and watched Maud secretly cheer on Oliver against her brother and Beatrice Hawkins secretly do the same for Art. At last the time came to pack away the hampers and load the cart, with Beatrice again interloping between Eva and Art. People said less on the return journey, content to relax in the evening sun.

When they reached Killybegs Harbour a coach was parked along the quay where a travelling showman was demonstrating a wireless set. Mr Hawkins gave them all money to sit among a row of people with earphones over their heads, listening to a crackle of faint voices breaking in from outside. Maud seemed indifferent amid the general gasps of wonder, but these bodiless voices disturbed Eva, breaking into her closeted world with other lives and languages. She couldn't wait to dismount from the coach but the showman had to shake Art and Thomas before her brothers removed their headphones. Art seemed distracted as they returned to the cart, questioning Mr Hawkins about every aspect of radio.

Waiting for them there was Grandpappy, a tall white-bearded old man dressed in knickerbockers appropriate to his ecclesiastical station. Two soldiers arranging their posters more prominently outside a recruiting booth respectfully nodded to Mr Ffrench, instinctively recognising his military bearing. Young women leaving the carpet weaving factory studied a poster outside the Royal Bank of Ireland advertising sailings to New York for three pounds and sixteen shillings. Grandpappy wanted to know who would ride in his pony and trap. Eva scrambled up into the trap, with Art behind her. People joked about them being inseparable during the holidays and she hated to think of him returning to Marlborough College. Eva fretted when Mrs Hawkins asked Grandpappy to wait, complaining that her old bones couldn't take the bumpy aeroplane cart, but although Beatrice longed to join them she was too shy to follow. The old man took Art on his knee, allowing him the reins.

Eva might be Grandpappy's favourite but in time Art would be his heir after Father, with the Manor House perpetually indentured by law to be passed in trust to the eldest son of the eldest son.

On a bend with fields falling away towards the sea, a flock of sheep halted them, crowding through a crude gateway from the lands of Mr Henderson, a local farmer. Frightened of the pony, they shied into the ditch. A sandy-haired boy of Art's age darted after the sheep, fiercely waving a stick. Welts formed a mottled pattern down his thighs. His bare feet were brown with dust and his face had a pinched hungry look.

'Gee-up!' Grandpappy encouraged Art to take control and urge the pony forward. The boy lowered his stick to stare at Art. For a moment Eva saw them observe one another, each boy intensely sizing up the other. Then Grandpappy flicked the whip and the pony jogged past, scattering the sheep.

'Why does he have no shoes?' Art asked, as if their staring contest had only now brought home this everyday disparity.

'What would he need shoes for?' Grandpappy laughed. 'His feet are as hard as the hob.'

'He wasn't born with hard feet.'

'He was born poor. He looks a strong lad who'll do well for himself if he works hard. He won't be left standing at the Strabane hiring fair when his time comes. Tyrone farmers know the measure of everything from horseflesh to boys. He'll find a good master.'

'Better a farm than the Glasgow mills,' Mrs Hawkins said.

She and Pappy fell silent, but something troubled Art. The reins went loose, the pony slackening as if sensing a lessening of authority. Eva looked behind to spy the aeroplane cart encountering the sheep.

'What if he doesn't want to stand at a fair like an animal?' Art asked.

'That's how life is ordained.' Mrs Hawkins broke into a verse of *All Things Bright and Beautiful*:

> *'The rich man in his castle,*
> *The poor man at his gate,*
> *He made them high or lowly*
> *And ordered their estate.'*

'Stop the cart,' Art said with sudden fierceness. 'He's my size. I want to give him these shoes. It's stupid that I own five pairs and he has none.'

Pappy laughed, wrapping Art in a bear-hug till the boy ceased to struggle.

'You're a good boy, but you must harden yourself or be fooled by every beggar and three-card-trick-man on the street. He'll have shoes when he earns them. It's how the world works. You'll have men under you one day. Firm but fair is how to win respect, not by throwing away your possessions.'

36

Distant laughter rose behind them as Father joked with the boy who managed to harry the sheep into an enclosure. Brendan was asleep, being rocked on Mother's lap. Eva envied Art his place on Grandpappy's knee, like she envied him the status she would have enjoyed if born a boy. Art was her special friend, but since Beatrice Hawkins started talking too much or going silent in his company, Eva had been disturbed by a recurring dream. In it Art was bound in a dungeon with Eva advancing on him, holding the terrible steel contraption she once saw a farm boy carry. When Eva had asked what it was the boy snapped it shut and smirked, 'To castrate young bulls, miss, and put a halt to their jollies.' Eva did not know what castration meant until Maud, who knew everything, said it was 'to cut off the slip of a thing men make such a fuss about'. This dream mortified her because she could never hurt Art. Shivering, Eva reached guiltily across to ruffle Art's hair. He loosened Grandpappy's bear-grip enough to smile back, although she saw how he was still upset.

Dunkineely village was deserted when the pony cantered past MacShane's public house. Mr MacShane emerged and said that a shoal of mackerel had swum into the inlet at the Bunlacky jetty. Grandpappy whipped the pony so as not to miss the excitement. The lane was crammed, with people lining the rocks beside the tiny jetty as the trap came to a halt. Youths had only to cast fishing rods in the waves to instantly haul out more silvery bodies. Women waded into the water using turf creels to capture the fish battering senselessly against each other. Barefoot children outdid one another in savage bravado as they killed the gasping fish with stones. Grandpappy laughed with approval, urging Art to dismount. Eva watched her brother join in the orgy of slaughter, blood and fragments of gut staining his shirt. The air was festive, pierced by warlike shouts of *Take that, you Hun*. Finally the aeroplane cart arrived and Beatrice Hawkins watched Art spatter a mackerel's brains with as much admiration as if he were harpooning a whale. Father noticed Eva sitting very still beside Mrs Hawkins. 'Run along home,' he said quietly, 'and tell Cook we're having mackerel for supper. I'm sure the Hawkinses can be prevailed upon to stay. Aye, and tell her we'll be having mackerel for breakfast, lunch and dinner all next week too.'

Eva had seen Art fish with Father and even helped them to kill sea trout out on their small boat. Sea fishing had felt noble but now she couldn't bear to look back in case she saw Art hold up the dead mackerel amid the slaughter for Beatrice to admire. Eva ran home to give Cook the message, then went to her room. Her perfect day in paradise felt ruined. Pressing her face against the cool sheet on her bed, Eva closed her eyes but kept visualising a floundering shoal of mackerel. They refused to die, wriggling furiously with their battered heads. Fish eyes stared up, having got separated from scaly bodies. They became the eyes of dead soldiers in the war that Eva hated people discussing. She had always loved the taste of mackerel but knew that she could never bear to bite into their oily flesh again.

Maud entered the room, kicked off her shoes and threw her hat on her bed. She flopped down. 'Come on, Eva,' she said. 'The Hawkins girls are staying and Mother says we can play musical bumps. Surely there's some way to persuade Oliver to join in. My word, it has been such a day.' She stopped and looked across. 'What's wrong, Eva?'

'Nothing.'

'You look like you've been crying.'

'Haven't.'

'Cook says we'll have a feast.'

'What is she making?'

'Fish, you goose. Get changed. It will be such fun. Father says we can use the gramophone.' She sat up to observe Eva closely. 'Shall I call Mother?'

'I'm all right.'

'I think I will.'

Maud went out, leaving the door open. Rising, Eva poured water into the white basin to wipe the smudge of tears from her eyes, then walked towards the window over-looking the street. The carpet ended a few feet from the window, the floorboards cool on her soles. The window-pane soothed her forehead. She felt so small suddenly in that long room, imagining the lonely winter months of soli-tary lessons ahead. Sketching for hours by the Bunlacky shore, reading to Brendan or sitting with Mother while she read books of sermons sent from London. Each Tuesday Mother would engage in planchette with her psychic friend, Mrs O'Hare – both women calmly attempting to decipher spirit messages, with the table moving beneath their outspread hands. But despite such loneliness it was better than the horrors of the bustling school dormitories to which the others would return.

A sound betrayed Mother's presence.

'What's wrong, Eva?'

'Nothing.'

'That's not true. Normally you would be the first down-stairs on such an evening. We don't have secrets, you and I.'

'It's too terrible.'

'Nothing is terrible if you share it.'

Eva meant to describe the mackerel, but the streaks of blood on Art's shirt on the jetty became confused with his tortured body in her dream. 'I keep having nightmares where I hurt Art terribly. I must be the worst sister in the world.'

Mother stood behind Eva who was unable to turn and face

39

her. The woman did not place a hand on her shoulder but Eva sensed the comfort of her presence.

'You're a Virgo,' Mother said calmly. 'All Virgos have a touch of that. I'm to blame for telling you I wanted a boy before you were born. But your dream might not be about Art. It could be the memory of unfinished business from another life or a vision of something to come. And even if it is about Art we're not to blame for our dreams or for being complex. You want life to be black and white, but we all have two sides. Just because we each hide one side from strangers doesn't mean we should hide it from ourselves. Everyone is jealous. Look at me, crippled with arthritis. Some days I'm jealous of you dancing around, unaware of the wonder of being able to move without pain. You're allowed to feel jealous, Eva. You're allowed to be anything that's part of you once it doesn't take over. Now is your secret so terrible?'

'Don't tell Father.'

Mother laughed. 'Us women need a few secrets, because God knows men keep enough. I'm jealous of your hair too. Let me comb it, then away downstairs. You need to be out more with other children. Maybe I've been wrong to keep you away from school. But you've always been so delicate that I was worried you might not cope.'

'I don't want to go to school,' Eva said. 'I love life here.'

'You're lonely in winter,' Mother replied. 'Still, it's too lovely an evening for worries.'

She brushed Eva's hair in comforting strokes, tilting her head slightly and smiling at Eva until her daughter smiled back. Eva looked around to spy Art in the doorway, concerned at her absence.

'The fun is starting,' he said, 'but it's not the same until you come down.'

Taking Eva's hand, he drew her from the room. On the

stairs they passed Nurse carrying Brendan who had woken up. The small boy put out his hand to Art, delighted when his big brother squeezed it. Eva looked back at Mother who smiled as she watched them descend towards the excited voices in the drawing room. Grandpappy had gone to rest but the other men were emerging from a pre-dinner drink in Father's study. Eva noticed that Oliver had been allowed to join them.

'Your AE is a menace with his anti-recruitment talk,' Mr Hawkins was complaining. 'It was bad enough him siding with Larkin's union during the Dublin lockout two years ago. He would do better sticking to painting fairies than meddling in politics.'

'AE is entitled to his opinion,' Father replied. 'Not that the King or Kaiser will pay him any more heed than the Dublin employers did. They were determined to break the workers and had the Roman church behind them.'

'Your church too,' Mr Hawkins pointed out. 'Larkin is a communist. What support could AE gather for such a black-guard?'

Remembering Mother's reference to AE, Eva imagined an army of stone figures rising from Dublin Bay, summoned by the bearded mystic whom Mother regarded as a friend.

'What is a communist, Father?' Art asked, alerting the men to their presence on the stairs.

'A thief,' Mr Hawkins retorted, 'who would murder you in your bed and divide your possessions among every passing peasant.'

'Somebody who thinks differently from us,' Father interjected quietly.

'True,' Mr Ffrench agreed. 'Perhaps Christ was a communist.'

'Really, Ffrench!' Mr Hawkins was aghast.

'I don't think he was,' Father said. 'Christ asked us to live

41

selfless lives for love of our fellow man and the promise of our reward in the next life. The communist offers no such reward. His world will not work because we are the flawed children of Adam. The communist may proffer an earth without God, but he cannot create an earth without sin. Our chief sin is greed and that is the worm which would devour the communist's clockwork world.'

'Larkin would devour your world too,' Mr Hawkins argued. 'Hand in hand with the Germans, he would murder every Irishman of property, with your cousin acting as his scullery maid.'

'Countess Markievicz knows her own mind,' Father replied mildly.

'She's a traitor to her class,' Mr Hawkins declared, 'consorting with dockers and slum revolutionaries? Is this the mob you would put in power if we gave you Home Rule?'

'Mr Larkin wishes to murder nobody,' Father argued. 'He simply wants children not to sleep nine in a bed.'

'And I agree with him,' Mr Ffrench interjected. 'Is it so wrong to want children to have bread?'

'And shoes?' Art asked.

'Yes, shoes too,' Mr Ffrench agreed.

Mr Hawkins bristled. 'You're too free with the talk you allow in this house.' He pointed into the study. 'I never though to hear such comments allowed by someone with that portrait over his desk.'

Eva glanced in at the dark portrait of Martin Luther whose stern eyes followed her whenever she entered Father's study.

'Any man who pinned a thesis of ninety-five points on a church door invited discourse,' Father replied, unflappably. 'Come, Hawkins, let's not quarrel.' He smiled at Art and Eva. 'You children run along before you forfeit your forfeits.'

Maud fretted in the drawing room, impatient at their

dallying and upset because Oliver had been commissioned into the ranks of the men. Beatrice Hawkins was anxiously awaiting their presence too. The carpet was rolled back and six cushions placed on the waxed floor. Gas jets hissed as Nurse came down from Brendan's room, having been coerced into playing records on the gramophone. Dance music began as the children waltzed around the cushions, never straying far lest they lose the game. Nurse lifted the needle and the music stopped. Maud and Thomas were first to sit down, each laughingly bagging a cushion. The three Hawkins girls fell in unison so that Art and Eva were left battling for the last cushion. But Eva spied Art's almost indecipherable feign as he slipped, ensuring that she got to the cushion first.

'Forfeit!' the others shouted gleefully.

'What is it?' Art asked.

Maud glanced towards the door, ensuring that the adults were beyond earshot. She sneaked a look at Nurse. 'You must kiss the person you like best,' Maud commanded – her favourite forfeit, the one she longed to play on Oliver. Eva blushed as Art glanced at her, certain of being chosen, yet dreading the public spectacle. Then, to her astonishment, he strode towards Beatrice Hawkins to surprise the girl with a kiss. Beatrice stared at Art as if nobody else was present and Eva suddenly sensed that she was losing her brother. Then the others laughed as Beatrice blushed in embarrassed delight. Art turned to Nurse, smiling.

'More music,' he commanded. 'Let's dance. Let's all dance.'

They danced on in the August twilight. Art was now being so attentive to Eva that she made herself forget the way he had kissed Beatrice. It grew so dark outside that their reflections became visible in the windowpanes. There was something comforting about seeing her world there, exactly as it should be, with bodies whirling about. Still she was glad when Cook knocked on the door to announce that supper was ready because it hastened the time when the Hawkins family would be leaving and she would have Art to herself.

Mother sensed that something was wrong as soon as the cooked mackerel was placed before Eva. Gently she suggested that Cook might find something else for her. People at the table were too busy trying to be heard to pay much attention. Father had yielded his normal seat to Grandpappy who seemed to agree with Mr Hawkins on most issues concerning politics. Oliver Hawkins spoke little but Eva saw how he often glanced at Maud. Art finished eating and asked to be excused. Eva waited a few moments then followed him out to the old coach house where he and Thomas had constructed a den. He was busy at a table with bits of tube and wires.

'Are you feeling okay?' she asked. 'Would you like to do something?'

Art looked up. 'I will later. I just want to see if I can make a wireless.'

Brendan appeared in the doorway, having sneaked out of bed in hopes of being with his oldest brother. He was fascinated by anything Art did and pleaded to be allowed to help with the complex arrangements of wire. Eva left them there, knowing that soon Thomas would join them to question each decision with his impeccable logic, becoming even more determined than Art to construct this contraption. She knew that she would not see Art for the rest of the night, with the boys locked away, fixated by crackling siren voices as they attempted to construct their wireless set.

Returning to the house she found that the adults and the girls had moved into the drawing room. The front door was open and several local people had wandered in, attracted by the sound of the piano. Eva liked how people always spilled into the Manor House. There was old Dr O'Donnell from Killaghtee House, waylaid on his way home from a sick call, and two soldiers home on leave who clapped loudly when Maud finished her party piece. Eva took a window seat in the crowded room as Father sang the tone poem for violin and orchestra in his still unperformed *Tir na n-Og* symphony:

> '*Far, far away, across the sea*
> *There lies an island divinely fair*
> *Where spirits blest forever dwell*
> *And breathe its radiant enchanted air.*'

Everyone applauded, taking pride in this local composition. A hush came as Mr Ffrench took Father's place at the piano. This striking young officer was still a novelty in Dunkineely and few people had previously heard him sing. Mr Ffrench announced that while travelling with the Royal Navy he had encountered strange men, but none as unusual as the hero of Mr Percy French's song, *Abdullah Bulbul Amir*. He commenced the opening bars, then stopped to stare at Eva.

'What are you sketching, Eva?'

'You.'

Mr Ffrench beckoned Eva forward. She felt embarrassed, unused to anyone except Mother paying attention to her sketching. Heads craned forward to await the officer's opinion. He considered her drawing in a silence that seemed to last for ever.

'Well, Eva, do you know what this officer thinks?'

'No, sir.'

'That you will be a true artist when you grow up. Let no one steer you from that path. Can I keep this?'

Eva nodded, too overcome to speak, and returned to her seat, watching as Mr Ffrench began to play, with no sheet music in front of him, but an unfinished sketch balanced on the holder instead. She longed to get back the drawing, to sketch in Mother and Father and all the other faces in the crowded drawing room as Mr Ffrench smiled at her, then began to sing in a wondrous voice. People demanded an encore and it was midnight before all the party pieces were performed, with the visitors departing into the night, calling their farewells as the cart moved off along the dark street.

Eva and Maud had hot milk and bread in the kitchen before being sent to bed. Eva was glad to go, but Maud felt that she should be allowed to stay up with the adults who would talk late into the night. The wooden shutters blocked out any moonlight. Both sisters lay quietly, awaiting Mother's final visit. Eva gazed up at the picture of a young girl kneeling beside a bed in prayer. She could not remember a time when this picture had not hung on her wall. She listened for Mother's shoes on the creaky step near the bend of the stairs. The door was ajar, gaslight filtering in from the corridor. Mother ascended the stairs and Eva heard her soft voice in Art's room before she pushed their door fully open. Framed in the light she looked beautiful in her dark grey hostess gown. She sat for a time on each bed. There was no hugging. She never took them on her knee for cuddles. Instead they sensed the aura of her love as she quietly asked each daughter if they had enjoyed their day. Mother's fingers played with Eva's hair while they talked, braiding imaginary plaits as a faint fragrance filled the air. It emanated from the hand lotion Mother always rubbed into her palms after gardening. She wore no make-up or perfume, just this scent as her fingers stroked Eva's hair for a final few seconds before she said goodnight and the door closed.

Maud turned over, quickly falling asleep. Eva lay awake for a while, still able to smell Mother's hand lotion. It had been a perfect day after all and there was still her birthday to come. The story about being rejected at birth for being a girl seemed less scary now. She fell asleep, filled with warm milk and bread and knowing that she was truly loved.

# TWO

## *The News*

### *Easter 1916*

Last night the maid had gone out walking and saw the lights of a German submarine rising from the dark sea at St John's Point. She ran back to the house, hysterical for her country and her virginity, calling out for Mr Tim. Mr Timothy Goold Verschoyle had cycled out along the Bruckless road to watch the lights approach, stopping Dr O'Donnell on his way home from a sick call to tell him how he'd been mistaken for the vanguard of an invading force. On the deserted road the two men had laughed but tension lurked behind their good humour because for once the maid's hysterics might have contained an edge of truth. The declaration of martial law in Dublin City and environs did not extend to Donegal, where life appeared normal. But amidst the constant bushfire of rumours about an armed insurrection in that city there was so little confirmed news that nobody was certain what to believe any more.

On Monday some bizarre class of Republic had been proclaimed in the capital by a handful of desperadoes. In some accounts the insurgents were utterly isolated, but in other reports they were holding Dublin until German reinforcements arrived. Whatever was happening, Mr Tim knew that his cousin, Countess Markievicz, would be at the centre of it, in James Connolly's Citizen Army. Last year in the *Irish Times* there had been a photograph of her in a fantastical military uniform, marching at the head of a group of young men who resembled boy scouts more than volunteer soldiers. Mr Tim had supported the Irish Volunteers who were founded to demand Home Rule from Britain, especially as that force threatened no offensive action but existed merely as a counterweight to the unionist militant Ulster Volunteers who were pledged to resist at any cost Westminster's plans to grant Home Rule. When the Great War started, the Irish Volunteers leadership had declared it to be the duty of young men to fight against Germany to show how Ireland valued freedom and would deserve the reward of self-government within the Empire when peace came. Republican zealots like the Countess had broken away from the Irish Volunteers to form a small splinter force, but it possessed so little support that nobody took them seriously. Indeed her conversion to Catholicism had caused more scandal in the family than what, until this week, had been seen as amateur theatrics of militaristic posing.

Mr Tim did not know how many others had joined the Countess in this shocking fiasco in Dublin. He was just glad that all his family would soon be safely gathered in the Manor House. Maud was the last to arrive, having gone to spend three days with a schoolfriend in Londonderry before the trouble broke out. Thankfully the trains were running and she would now be in Dunkineely, being escorted home by Art. Art had decided to meet the train alone and tell Maud the news. Mr Tim regarded his eldest son's offer to do this as a sign that he was adjusting to the role and duties of an heir. With the sudden death of Grandpappy in January, Art was now just one heartbeat – Mr Tim's heartbeat – away from inheriting the family home. Art was growing up. Mr Tim could see a difference when he travelled home at the end of each term from Marlborough College. This Easter he had brought back two school chums who had not previously set foot in Ireland and were alarmed by the startling events in Dublin. Still they were decent chaps, familiar with the rituals of bad news. They had played tennis with Eva and Thomas this afternoon, then slipped off for a swim at Bruckless Pier to let the family be alone when Maud reached home. Having changed trains at Strabane before boarding the narrow-gauge service that chugged along the coast from Donegal town to Killybegs, Maud would be expecting her siblings to crowd the tiny platform at Dunkineely in welcome. The sight of Art standing alone would disconcert her because she had the quickest brain in the family.

Mr Tim kept watch at his window, wanting to be the first to greet her. He saw them approach along the main street in silence, Art carrying Maud's case. Leaving his study, Mr Tim opened the front door. The street was utterly quiet, like it always went after the postmaster left his office holding a telegram. This had nothing to do with their news, but ongoing events in Dublin had created a strange atmosphere, with people saying little and little way of knowing if they meant what they said. Maud's eyes were puffy but she had not cried as yet.

'I'm all right, Father,' she announced before he could utter a word. 'It's not as if I knew Oliver Hawkins well. We only met for the first time last summer.'

'You were fond of him all the same,' Mr Tim replied.

'He was a boy that any girl would be fond of. When did you hear the news?'

'Last week. Mrs Ffrench told us he was reported missing

in action. I didn't want to write to you at school. I thought
it best to wait until you were here.'

'I don't see why . . .' Maud looked away, anxious lest she
betray her emotions. 'Oliver sent me the odd letter from the
army, but only I think so he would have some girl to write
to, like other boys in his outfit. Nothing was ever . . .' Maud
looked at her father. 'Still you were right not to write. So
many girls get news about their brothers and cousins. You
see them cry for days, with other girls crying as well, caught
up in hysteria. Last summer Oliver's parents thought he was
going back to school from Donegal but he had other plans.
He told me he was going to enlist on his last night here. I
wanted to talk him out of it, but it seemed so gallant.'

'There's nothing gallant in war.' Mr Tim glanced at Art,
anxious to make his son understand. At thirteen he was tall
and broad enough to pass for sixteen. Last month a fifteen-
year-old boy, who lied about his age to enlist, was executed
for cowardice in France. Art possessed a rebellious streak
but, with his accent, no recruiting sergeant would dare sign
him up as trench fodder.

'Nothing gallant even in Dublin?' Maud asked.
'Outnumbered a hundred to one? The family I was staying
with kept talking about the pro-German traitors fighting in
Dublin. I wanted to say they were pro-Irish and I was related
to one of them. But you know what Ulster Protestants are
like. Have the rebels a chance, Father?'

'A chance of what?' Mr Tim asked. 'It would be laughable
if people were not being shot dead. Every second Dublin family
has a son in France. The only people who rose with them
were the slum hordes looting shops.'

'I should visit Mrs Ffrench,' Maud said. 'She must be upset
about Oliver.'

'The poor woman has lost both brothers in this war already,'

Mr Tim replied. 'She has aged so much worrying about Ffrench, who is seeing plenty of naval action. He's quite the rising star but she just wants him safely home.'

'How is Eva?' Maud asked.

Mr Tim smiled. 'Eva is Eva. Yesterday she decided to aid the Dublin rebels by climbing into a tree and writing a poem for them.'

The front door opened and Maud's mother stood waiting to comfort her daughter. Father and son watched them embrace and disappear indoors. Glancing down the empty street Mr Tim felt a disconcerting sensation of being watched. He went inside where his son followed him into the study.

'Are your two chums back yet?'

'Last night one wanted to know where we kept the guns. He couldn't believe that we don't have a single one in the house.'

'I've always hated shooting. However if they want to go hunting birds I'm sure we can arrange it with a neighbour.'

'He meant guns for protection.'

'Protection?' Mr Tim smiled. 'What does he expect, our neighbours to rush the house? Still I shouldn't laugh. This trouble in Dublin is disconcerting. Such madness, with Irishmen already dying every day in France.'

'Maybe that's the problem. They're dying in the wrong land.'

'The problem, Art, is that they are dying at all. War solves nothing and cleanses nothing. It just leaves more bitterness waiting to spill over again.'

'The fighting in Dublin is different,' Art argued.

'In what way?'

'No one is forcing them to fight. There is no officer to shoot anyone who turns back. That's one of the tasks they prepare the older boys for in school. That and being first out from the trench with a drawn sword to spur on your men to follow.'

'You like your school, don't you?' Mr Tim probed. 'I mean you're popular, you have good chums.'

'Some times I feel totally at home there. Other times I think I don't fit.'

'Being Irish can make you feel that.'

'It's not being Irish.'

'What is it then?'

'I don't know.' Art struggled for the words. 'One to one I like most chaps there. Even the teachers are good eggs when not being jingoistic. But ... sometimes when they are all gathered together ... I find myself hating them. I hate their superiority, the sense of their absolute right to rule.'

'The English have that,' Mr Tim agreed. 'Even our friend Mr Hawkins – poor man – is unshakeable in his self-belief. But they cannot be blamed for being what they are, any more than a fox can be blamed for being a fox.' His father paused. 'Maybe there's something else you hate?'

'What?'

'Maybe you see the same qualities buried inside you. I mean no offence, but when asked to describe what we least like in people we often end up inadvertently describing ourselves.'

'I'm not like my fellow students,' Art stated angrily.

'I know. But maybe deep within yourself you see a seed which, if not careful, might one day make you become like them. They will all find jobs ruling the Empire when this war ends. If that is what you want then doors will also open for you. Ffrench went to a poor school, yet see how well he is forging ahead. Imagine what you could do with your contacts.'

'Is that why you sent me to Marlborough? What you want?'

'I wanted to give you the best education I could afford. After that I merely wish you to be happy. I disappointed my father, our cousins too. They wanted me to achieve things. One said that I was a lotus-eater, lacking ambition, hiding away in my own little paradise here. But my ambitions were different from theirs. Perhaps I am inventing excuses and I have been a failure, but only on their terms. Because I never accepted their right to put their ambitions on my shoulders, I have no right to place my ambitions on yours. I'm merely saying that you may be afraid of being contaminated by the outside world. My days in Oxford were the loneliest time in my life. Young men boorishly drinking in societies. Grandpappy claimed that I ran away and I needed to toughen up to survive in the world. But I didn't want to toughen up because something inside me would have died. You're different. You have steel. Find your own path and stick to it.'

'What if you don't like my path?'

Mr Tim stared at the brooding portrait of Martin Luther. 'The one thing I wish to give all of you is a conscience. If you trust to your heart you will not go wrong, no matter how others may judge you. Go and see if your chums are back. I want to finish something before I dress for dinner.'

Art left Mr Timothy Goold Verschoyle alone. Upstairs Maud would be crying, comforted by her sister and mother. Thomas would be glad all his siblings were home because he seemed happiest when they were all together. Brendan was probably reading in his den in the coach house. Of all his children Brendan was the one Mr Tim knew least about. He spent many evenings walking with the boy, but it was never fully clear what Brendan felt. Being so young, he made the others seem grown-up. Opening a drawer, Mr Tim took out new lyrics for the latest song cycle he was composing. The villagers though his music remarkable. Neighbours often said how

54

much they enjoyed hearing the sound of his piano filtering out onto the street. But no orchestra had yet played a single composition. Music companies returned his compositions with polite notes of refusal. But still he pressed on, motivated by a desire to bring beauty into this world or, maybe at a subconscious level, to feel some vindication in succeeding to prove his cousins wrong.

In Dublin now rebels were fighting behind barricades, with buildings shelled and slum dwellers looting amid the corpses of horses and soldiers. Boys trapped on barbed wire in no-man's-land in France were screaming for comrades to end their agony with a bullet. Rats grew fat on corpses. Young Oliver Hawkins's body might never be found. Mr Tim remembered how handsome Oliver had looked last summer. What must it be like to lose a son? He prayed that this war would end before his boys were old enough to be drawn in and that the Dublin madness would end without too many deaths. Scrutinising the lyrics he wrote this morning, they seemed a feeble pastiche of his favourite poets. At heart he knew this cycle would fare no better than the others, but still he worked on, knowing that these imperfect songs were the only poultice he could offer the world.

# THREE

## *Four Thousand Lamps*

### *December 1917*

Local Catholics had such long memories that Mrs Ffrench was careful not to betray any hint of proselytism about her activities. Older people still cursed the visiting Protestant clergymen who had tried to steal souls during the famine by offering soup to any starving wretch lured into attending their church services. Last year a Dublin Protestant was sacked after his Catholic employers discovered how he served tea each Sunday at the *Free Breakfasts for the Poor* Protestant Missionary Charity. Mrs Ffrench thought that it was easy for her fellow Baha'is in America to advocate Baha'i children's parties as vehicles by which children of different social classes might learn to intermingle and be gently taught the truth, but in this remote part of Donegal any form of preaching was dangerous. Her husband might not think so, because Commodore Ffrench feared nothing. But, with the Bolshevik unrest in Russia, his leave was cancelled and, without him, their house felt empty and the winter hills desolate.

Still, with a war on it was unpatriotic to look glum. There was much that a woman could do. Last week Mrs Goold Verschoyle had hosted a Red Cross musical evening, attended by many young officers from the warships anchored in Killybegs Harbour. Mrs Ffrench had invited several to dine in Bruckless House, impressing them by her knowledge of Northern Russian ports. Not that Commodore Ffrench ever divulged naval secrets, but his last letter had been filled with a boyish excitement about his latest mission. The northern route into Russia was always important as a line for supplies to be ferried into the ice-free port of Murmansk and sent on by rail to St Petersburg. However it had been an unglamorous naval backwater until the recent revolution in Russia, when it now became vital to prevent Murmansk and Archangel falling into the hands of the dangerous Bolsheviks who had seized power. This was the moment of destiny which her husband had been waiting for. Over dinner the officers had agreed that if he could help to fight off the Bolsheviks and hold these ports he would return a hero.

When the Tsar abdicated in February nobody suspected that the Bolsheviks would seize power – indeed few people, including Mrs Ffrench, knew much about them. But the world was out of kilter in these days of incessant bloodshed, with nothing predictable. The Dublin rebels – booed off the streets last Easter, with James Connolly and the other leaders executed – had recently been welcomed home from internment camps like returning heroes instead of hooligans who had levelled their own city. Mrs Ffrench was glad to have a Baha'i spiritual master like Abdul-Baha to make sense of these changes. His instruction was to spread light and human fellowship through every class and creed she came in contact with.

This was her intention behind today's party. Every child from Bruckless and Dunkineely was invited. The attendance – smaller than she hoped for – was a curious mix, with prosperous Protestant children who were used to enjoying her gardens mingling uneasily with a few local poor Catholics.

The better-off Catholic tradesmen had kept their children away. They liked the notion of their offspring taking refreshment with the gentry on her lawn, but not if they had to mix with their own lower social classes.

At first there was little mixing, as Protestant children formed one clique and the Catholics another, too ill at ease to enjoy themselves. She suspected that some Catholics had never attended any type of party, let alone an afternoon one. For a terrible moment she even envisaged a fight breaking out, a miniature re-enactment of the riots in Moscow. The servants were thinking this too, from the way they whispered to each other, but then the arrival of Eva Goold Verschoyle put everyone at ease because children from all creeds were comfortable with her.

Although Mrs Ffrench told people that every child was always welcome at Bruckless House, few ever called. Yet she never visited the Goold Verschoyle household without seeing village urchins wandering freely about the tennis court or sitting with Eva in the old coach house, taking turns to use her paints and brushes, laughing with their hands streaked in watercolours. Eva quickly became the centre of the party now, not even conscious of how she drew the children into the games she suggested. Perhaps it was her size, with many children towering over her. Or maybe it was her aura. At fifteen, Eva was older than her years in some respects, yet far younger in others.

Soon Mrs Ffrench found herself peripheral to her own party, a bystander who would love to swing a four-year-old girl around like Eva did or have toddlers cluster about her skirt while she told stories. She kept trying to mingle and talk to each guest but a glass wall existed with the village children that she could not break down.

Still, she loved the sounds of laughter and was delighted

at having risked holding the party outdoors during the few hours of winter sunlight. There was real Baha'i happiness by the end as children relaxed with each other. Village children waved as they walked away in clusters, with the Protestants being collected in ponies and traps. Finally only she and Eva were left, excitedly discussing the party on a sofa in the library while, outside, serving girls cleared away the mess on the lawn.

She offered to have her man drive Eva home, but Eva insisted that she loved the two-mile walk in twilight. Mrs Ffrench knew that she would be safe because something about the child's innocence suggested that Eva could not be hurt so long as she never left Donegal. Eva sympathised at how lonely Christmas would be in Bruckless House with Mr Ffrench away and asked would the Hawkins family ever come back to visit.

'I suspect not, dear. Bruckless holds too many memories. These days a lot of ghosts sit on empty chairs at dinner. It would be hard for them not to keep seeing Oliver in their minds swimming down at our pier.'

Mrs Ffrench stopped, surprised by her tears. Grief was a sly thief always waiting in ambush. She had thought she was over the worst of the anguish at losing her two brothers, but last month's news that her sister's husband had also been killed had brought back her dreams of blood. When she woke some nights now she was afraid to touch the sheets, having dreamt that they were saturated in blood. She hated the three-card-trickery of these insidious dreams. In them she could be back with her brothers in their nursery, watching them play with boxes of tin soldiers. Next moment they would be wading through barbed wire and foxholes where dying men screamed, still only boys holding their tin soldiers, oblivious to danger. Then they would become her own unborn sons walking towards the German guns, not hearing her screaming to warn them until they were shot and fell. She always woke with a start from such dreams, her hand instinctively reaching down between her legs where she bled every month whether her husband was home on leave or not. Five years of marriage, stained by unwelcome blood. The Commodore had devised a code so that she could send him news after each visit home. They had names chosen if it was a boy or a girl and a locked room set aside to be a nursery. At thirty-one she was still young enough. When his victory at Murmansk was achieved, he would come home for them to try again, as often and with as much passion as it took. To compensate for all the deaths, her first child would be a boy.

Mrs Ffrench became aware of tears also in Eva's eyes.

'Don't mind me being silly, dear.' She put her hand on the young girl's arm.

'Sometimes I blame myself for Oliver dying,' the girl said. 'You see, Mrs Ffrench, I didn't want his family to come back because of Beatrice. I wanted to keep Art to myself. It's just too terrible how I got my wish.'

'You can't blame yourself, child. Thousands of boys are slaughtered every week. Men will have to answer to God for this one day, but you have nothing to answer for.'

Something about the wide-eyed fifteen-year-old reminded Mrs Ffrench of herself at that age. Eva would also be a seeker after truth. Mrs Ffrench remembered how isolated she had felt as a girl until she stumbled by seeming chance upon a reference to Abdul-Baha and his beliefs. Now she knew that The Master had been guiding her life on a quest to find a man sufficiently open to embrace her beliefs. Her conversion of the Commodore meant that there were now four Baha'is in Ireland. She wanted to thrust copies of *World Fellowship* and other Baha'i publications into Eva's hands but each seeker needed to find their own path. Instead she decided to let the girl share The Master's work in a different way.

'Will you help me light my lamps?' she asked, knowing that Eva loved this task.

'Yes, please,' the girl replied.

Dusk had set in already. The lamps could not be seen from the road where they would attract attention but any walker by the pier would see them shine in eleven windows. This was a vital task and some nights Mrs Ffrench woke, fearful that one might have burnt out while she slept.

The greatest moment of her life was travelling to London this spring to meet Abdul-Baha in person. She could still see the Master's piercing eyes as he announced that she could cause the illumination of all Ireland if she lit four thousand lamps in one year. Mrs Ffrench had broken this down to mean eleven lamps to be lit on three hundred and sixty days and just eight lamps on the last five nights. Initially she felt foolish, knowing that the servants considered her behaviour odd, but recently they seemed to understand because they smiled when passing her each evening, as if silent conspirators. She took it as a sign that the Master was right. If the lamps were having this effect in her home, then perhaps they were spreading harmony in other houses across Ireland without her knowledge. The maids knew to fill each lamp full of oil but never to light them. That was her strangely comforting task. But tonight she let Eva help, walking from room to room through the empty house.

Finally the task was finished and Mrs Ffrench saw her guest to the door, knowing that Eva would pause on the lawn to count each lamp that beckoned to her and to Ireland and across the seas to where her husband knew that they were being lit. Eva said good night and Mrs Ffrench had to resist a impulse to embrace her. The thought of all the marvellous

Goold Verschoyle children being home for Christmas filled her with hope. She would carefully choose presents for each one, making sure that they knew her door was always open. Sometimes she imagined a fantasy where young Brendan was trapped here by a snowfall and she was able to mind him for some days until the road cleared.

Mrs Ffrench stood in her doorway until Eva was out of sight and there was nothing for it but to close the door. Lizzy, the parlourmaid, was descending the stairs. Mrs Ffrench smiled to put her at ease.

'That was a good day, Lizzy.'

'It was indeed, mam.'

'The party went well.'

'Yes, mam. Will there be anything else, mam?'

'No.'

The girl hesitated. Mrs Ffrench suspected that some servants, including Lizzy, might feel happier in a house where the mistress never addressed them except with an order.

'Have you the lamps lit, mam?'

'Yes, Lizzy.'

'We do the same for you, mam.'

'What do you mean?' Mrs Ffrench was puzzled.

'If we're passing the church, the other maids and me always light a candle for you. That's what us Catholics do for special intentions. All of us are praying that when the Commodore comes home things will go well for you and it will be a boy.'

Mrs Ffrench was momentarily too shocked to speak.

Suddenly aware that she had been too forward, the maid went to apologise, then realised that this could only make matters worse.

'I light my lamps for a different reason,' Mrs Ffrench replied icily.

'Yes, mam. I wouldn't know, mam.'

'Your Master and I . . .' Mrs Ffrench stopped in time, shocked that she was explaining herself in front of a servant. 'That will be all, Lizzy.'

'Yes, mam.'

The girl curtsied and scurried away. Mrs Ffrench entered the library that was in darkness except for the lamp in the window. They would be whispering about her in the kitchen like they always whispered. She had tried to create a household where servants were not in dread of their mistress, but she had never envisaged that they would feel pity for her. She hoped that no maid would come in to stoke the fire. She wanted to be alone. She had never felt so utterly alone. Mrs Ffrench took a deep breath. This war would pass. Her husband would return from Murmansk as a hero, having fought off the menace of Bolshevism. Her bed linen would be stained with blood, only this time good cleansing blood from her labours in childbirth. She would welcome every wave of pain, every push that it took. She would be made whole then, she would illuminate Ireland and her child would illuminate her life. The Master had ordained this ordeal to test her faith, but she would be strong and learn to be patient. Rocking herself softly back and forth, Mrs Ffrench waited for her true life to begin.

FOUR

# The Motor

*Donegal, August 1919*

Maud was surprised at the ease with which she discovered the location of the remote cottage being used as a temporary headquarters by the local IRA commander. A mark of how the villagers trusted the family was that it only took Art five minutes to emerge from the smoky gloom of MacShane's public house with directions and a respectful warning that he might be found with a bullet in his head if he did not keep his mouth shut. But it had not gone unnoticed how the family had so far declined to contact the constabulary about last night's incident, which had begun when Brendan announced at dinner that he could see men moving about in the coach house. They had all watched from the window as four armed strangers pushed the family's battered Ford across the yard to the gate, then cranked up the starting handle, climbed in and drove off.

Father had placed a hand on Maud's shoulder when sensing her about to intervene. Last year his cousin the Countess became the first woman ever elected to the British House of Commons. She refused to take her seat however, setting up an illegal assembly in Dublin with other Sinn Fein MPs instead, which proclaimed the right of its volunteers to use arms. Donegal had seen little of this new lawlessness, but remote police barracks were being attacked, and there had been raids on Big Houses by masked men seeking weapons.

Locals knew that Father didn't hold a gun licence, so last night's raid was confined to the outbuildings. But Maud was determined to recover the motor. Father had no idea about this expedition but Father rarely bothered to use the motor, whereas, since finishing school, Maud had become at eighteen the first female in Donegal to drive. Learning was not easy, because Father, himself an infrequent driver, had been nervous about teaching her. But after Art was given permission to drive the motor, there had been no way in which Maud was going to be forbidden. Now, having fought for that right, she was simply not going to simply see their motor stolen. She did not wish to bring Art, but after divulging the address he had refused to let her cycle up into the hills alone.

Although she thought she knew the area, Maud would have been lost by now except that Art had a mental map of every sheep track for miles around. The sixteen-year-old rarely paused for bearings, but cycled up the negotiable parts of the steep track and carried his bicycle over stretches potholed beyond repair. By now they were probably being watched. The IRA lookout would think them picnickers at first, only growing alarmed as their destination became clear. Maud knew that she was taking a huge risk and their informant in the village might be in danger too. Yet all she could think about was the damage surely inflicted on the motor when it was driven up this rough boreen. Branches on both sides must have destroyed the paintwork.

Art stopped to scan the hilltop where, beneath a clump of trees, there was the entrance to a cottage.

'Do you think they're really there?' he asked.

'They will have seen us coming for miles.' Maud looked back down the steep hill. Having left Dunkineely fuelled by righteousness, she was now apprehensive, sensing that the respect she was accustomed to might be absent in this new world of desperadoes. Would they be locals whose faces she knew, or strangers? Which would be the most dangerous? It was whispered that flying columns rarely stayed under one roof for more than a few nights. Their chief weapon against the army was inconspicuousness, the ability to blend back into the local populace. So few motors existed in Donegal that using one would be a death warrant for such a column, making their movements easy to track. But perhaps it had been stolen for use in a one-off attack.

'You stay here,' Art said. 'This is men's work.'

His remark banished uncertainty from Maud's mind.

'You stay,' she retorted. 'This is for grown-ups.'

In the end they raced each other up to the farmyard. Only when they swung through the gate did the two armed men stand up. It was hard to see their faces beneath the caps. Maud knew they would not shoot her, but Art might be a different matter. She tried to control her fear and dismounted, speaking authoritatively.

'I want to speak to whoever is in charge.'

'What are you doing here?' a man snapped back.

'I will speak only to whoever is in charge.'

'He's off about his business,' the older man replied.

'I'll wait.'

'Aye, you'd better do that.'

They lowered their guns, reluctant to aim at a young woman and a boy. Maud was relieved that Art stayed silent, because Marlborough College had eroded any trace of an Irish accent. He nudged her elbow, nodding to a hastily constructed turf rick beside the cottage, which could not conceal the car parked behind it. The men glanced at each other, uncertain of what to do.

'Would you be Miss Goold Verschoyle?' the first one asked.

'I am,' Maud replied.

'Step inside the cottage like a good woman and bring the young master with you. Who told you where to find us?'

'We followed a trail of broken branches. It would be easy enough for the military to do likewise.'

'What have you told the military?' the man demanded.

'We told them nothing.' Art spoke for the first time. 'We're all Irishmen together.'

The men said nothing, looking amused.

'We don't need to tell them,' Maud added quickly. 'A motor car is a big object. It will be as hard for us to hide the fact of not having one as it is for you to hide the fact that you do.'

'That's what I told him,' the first man hissed to his comrade. 'The damn yoke is a stone around our necks.'

'That's enough.' The second man nodded towards the cottage door. 'Step indoors and if there's any sign of the military you'd best run for it like us because they only start questioning when they're finished shooting.'

A small fire provided some light in the gloom of the cottage. The thatch was discoloured, the whitewash long faded. An elderly couple stood up as they entered and silently beckoned for them to take the two chairs, ignoring their protestations. The old man went outside and Maud heard low voices through the doorway before the youngest volunteer mounted Art's bicycle and set off down the rutted lane. The old woman was making strong tea for them, tasting of peat. She paused to take a bottle of clear liquid from the mantelpiece and added a sup of illicit whiskey to Art's cup. Then she disappeared, leaving brother and sister alone.

Being close did not prevent Art and Maud from frequently quarrelling. They were both so strong-willed that conflict was inevitable – especially if Eva was not present as peacemaker. Now however they were united by unease, each wishing they had come alone to prevent the other being exposed to danger. But neither had been willing to be left behind and allow the other to act as *de facto* head of the family.

It would be some hours before the others realised they were missing. Mr Ffrench was expected back from naval service at any time. Mother would think that they had cycled over to Mrs Ffrench who found the strain of awaiting her husband's final homecoming very difficult. Father would be in his study, preoccupied with deciding what to do. Last month a respected police sergeant had been shot dead in front of his children in Donegal town. Father was among the small attendance at his burial, with local mourners warned off. Perhaps this had attracted the IRA's attention. Maud didn't know who had ordered the theft of their motor, just that worse trouble might ensue if Father felt obliged to report it.

Eventually they heard the bicycle's return. Maud thought that the volunteer had gone to notify his superior, but she was mistaken because, as if watching out for the bicycle, the old man re-appeared in the doorway with a wind-up gramophone which he placed on the stone flags near the fire. The volunteer entered, breathless, carrying a bag over his shoulder.

'You'll be a while waiting yet,' he panted. 'We thought these might pass the time for you.'

Maud had no idea where he had found the records but they included several very scratched Protestant hymns. The old man put one on and smiled at Maud, with his wife momentarily appearing to claim her share in this gesture of hospitality.

'That's lovely,' Maud said. 'I could listen to it all day.'

'You might have to,' the volunteer replied grimly. 'I'll be outside, mam, if there's anything you'd be needing.'

The hymns sounded strange in this dark, smoky cottage. Perhaps some Protestant family in the hills had left them behind when they packed up and left, grieving the loss of a son in France. The second time Maud played them Art joined in the singing, his clear voice soaring over the crackling record as she began to sing too. Each record was played five times before she heard voices outside. The new arrival had a strong Cork accent. Maud felt suddenly petrified. The Donegal men's hospitality could have been a ruse to keep them here so that they could be held as hostages to secure the release of Republican prisoners. Art rose, ready to face whoever entered, but Maud remained seated, reciting a quiet prayer. The stranger was a tall stocky man, possessing a confident authority. He laughed and kicked the gramophone lightly, knocking the needle to the end of the record.

'Hymns?' he said. 'You'd swear we were at a funeral. Now, what's this about a motor car?'

'It belongs to my family.' Maud stood up. 'What possible use could you have for it?'

'Sure, if I told you that I'd have to shoot you.'

'Please. I need it for my mother. She has terrible arthritis. She can only get around if I drive her.'

'You?' The man laughed louder. 'Don't tell me they let a wee slip of a thing like you behind a steering wheel?'

'They let a slip of a thing into the House of Commons, only my father's cousin wouldn't take her seat.'

The man nodded, as if Maud had scored a point. 'But they also say you have an uncle an Orangeman who would burn every Catholic out of Belfast.'

'My father is a Home Ruler, on the same side as you.'

'To hell with Home Rule,' the man said. 'Home Rule was

a bone thrown from the English table to keep the Irish dogs gnawing away quietly. This struggle is about freedom . . . a Republic.'

'Hear, hear.' Art spoke for the first time.

The man eyed up Art. 'Did you say something, sonny?'

'I've argued this same point with my father who's a pacifist. But for me it's full independence or nothing.'

'Glad you think so.'

'I do more than think. I offer you a fair trade. Give my sister back her motor car and you can have me. I wish to volunteer my services for the Irish Republic.' Art ignored Maud tugging at his sleeve, anxious to shut him up. 'I have received comprehensive training in how to use a rifle at boarding school.'

'Bully for you.' The Corkman sat down, amused. 'What exactly would the Irish Republic do with your services?'

'Are you insinuating that I'm a coward?'

'I'm suggesting that you stay out of what doesn't concern you.'

'Of course it concerns me. I want what you want.'

'What exactly is that?'

'Freedom for us all.'

Maud could no longer contain herself. 'Sit down for God's sake, Art, and stop being an ass.'

Art turned, annoyed. 'Stay out of this. I'm sick of other people mapping out my life for me.'

'Listen to your big sister, sonny,' the Corkman said. 'Run off and join a circus if you want, but you're misinformed about our fight. It's not about freedom *for* you, it's about freedom *from* you. The best way you could help Ireland's freedom is to pack up and return to where you came from.'

'Where exactly is that?' Art was so furious that the two volunteers appeared in the doorway with their rifles.

'England.'

'More Irish blood runs through my veins than through yours. My father can trace our family back to Niall of the Nine Hostages. Can your father do that?'

'My father was too busy trying to earn an honest wage. That's more than you parasites have ever done.'

Maud was no longer interested in the motor. She simply wanted to get Art safely out of this cottage. Of late he frequently took notions, but rarely as dangerous as this. Was it his way to rebel against Father who was shocked by each bullet fired on either side in this Irish conflict? She wanted to speak, but any interruption would only further inflame her brother.

'So what constitutes an Irishman now?' Art demanded.

'An Irishman is someone with Irish blood in his veins and in his father's and grandfather's before that.'

'Where does that leave the half-breed Patrick Pearse?' Art retorted. 'His father was indisputably an Englishman. At least my distant ancestors had the decency to be Dutch.'

The Corkman rose and took a pistol from his holster. 'Don't ever take Pearse's name in vain,' he hissed. 'I fought with him in Easter Week. He was a true Irishman.'

'I am not saying he wasn't.' Art was calm, exuding an unconscious superiority in the face of the man's anger. 'It's your definition that excludes him, not mine.'

The commander turned to the volunteers. 'Give them their blasted car and shoot them both if they turn back.' He looked at Maud. 'Take this child away and put him somewhere safe, miss. Let this be a lesson. Property required by the Irish Republican Army will be requisitioned in the name of the Republic. Any collaboration with the army of occupation will be seen as an act of treason. You understand?'

'Yes.'

71

'How can it be an act of treason if we're not even Irish?' Art queried. 'I suppose you call my father's cousin a foreigner too.'

The commander replaced his gun, calmer now. 'You're sharp, sonny. If debating points were bullets you'd have killed me long ago. But the Countess gave up everything. Could you do likewise? Revolution is not a half-way house. Your accent would be a liability to any flying column. You'd stick out, like a motor car. Stay in your own world. We leave this cottage tonight and won't be back. If you reveal where you found this car the roof will be burnt over the old couple's heads. Such a thing would not be forgotten. The peelers have just abandoned the barracks that I had planned to attack with your car tonight. They probably got a tip-off. Go home and keep your mouth shut. And tell them to do likewise in the pubs of Dunkineely.'

'Nobody said a word to us,' Art said quickly.

The commander escorted them out to the yard where the old couple silently stood. 'If I had to shoot every loose-tongued Irish fool, I'd have no bullets left for the British.'

The car started at the second attempt. Art loaded their bicycles into the boot while the volunteers stood back as if expecting Maud to crash into the gate. Only after she drove into the lane did her hands start shaking.

It was dark as they descended the rough track and she steered cautiously, knowing how easy it would be to snap an axle. Father would be angry when he discovered the risk they had taken, but Maud could now convince him not to contact the police. Art stared ahead in silence.

'Did you really want to volunteer?' she asked.

'No,' he replied, though Maud knew he was lying. 'I was merely winding up the blither. Can't say I'd fancy the type of country he would build.'

'I'm not sure he will get the chance,' Maud said. 'The Prime Minister can flood Ireland with troops.'

'True. There's no way these fools can win. I'm just not sure they can be beaten either. Don't mention my offer to Father.'

They drove on in silence because the dark world beyond the windscreen felt different now. Maud wondered if the Corkman's story about the barracks was a ruse. Perhaps some poor man had been driven in this motor to a remote spot last night, shot and his body dumped? She would spend hours scrubbing the upholstery, yet the motor would never feel like it fully belonged to her again. At the bend beside Bruckless House a Crossley Tender was parked, with a party of British soldiers blocking the road. A local man was being searched, his hands raised as a soldier roughly kicked his feet apart. The man looked up, relieved that there were witnesses to his search. A sergeant stopped the car and put his head in the window.

'And where would you two lovebirds be heading?'

'This is my brother,' Maud replied, tersely.

'Is it necessary to search the man like that?' Art asked.

'I assure you it is.' The sergeant relaxed upon hearing Art's accent. 'The Shinners would shoot loyal citizens like you in your bed.' He called back. 'That will do. Let him go.' Watching the local man cycle quickly away, he turned back to the car. 'Can't say I like this posting. At least in France you knew who the enemy was. It must be hard for you, barely able to trust your own servants.'

'I trust everyone in my village,' Maud replied.

'What village is that?'

'Dunkineely.'

The sergeant whispered softly, 'We've heard rumours of a car stolen in Dunkineely.'

'Was it reported stolen?'

'We get reports in many ways.' His manner was brisker. 'Where have you just come from?'

'We were out taking the air.'

'What if I don't believe you?'

'Are you calling my sister a liar?' Art demanded.

'I want to know your exact movements. I'm keen to encounter a certain party of men. I have a little silver present for each of them.'

'We met nobody today,' Maud said.

'For God's sake, miss, whose side are you on? If they take your car today it will be your house and lands tomorrow. The savages won't leave you with a roof over your heads.'

'Please move your lorry,' Maud replied. 'I want to go home.'

'And I want to know where you've been.'

'What is the problem here, sergeant?' Two figures emerged from the driveway of Bruckless House. The soldiers raised their rifles, then lowered them, sensing Mr Ffrench's military bearing as he stood beside Dr O'Donnell. The sergeant saluted.

'Just carrying out our duties, sir. Keeping the peace.'

'Go and keep it somewhere else so. And don't salute me, I'm a civilian.'

'Sorry, sir. It's just obvious you were in the services.'

'We all make mistakes.'

'The Commodore has returned from service off Murmansk this evening,' Dr O'Donnell said mildly. 'We can vouch for these young people. Kindly let them pass.'

'Damned hard luck about the withdrawal of the expeditionary force from Russia, sir,' the sergeant addressed Mr Ffrench. 'I hear the Bolsheviks are savages.'

'On the contrary,' Mr Ffrench replied, 'the Bolsheviks are men of principle, which is more than can be said for the

White Russians we were shoring up, for whom I could not give a horse artillery hoot. Our retreat was bliss for me.'

The sergeant searched Mr Ffrench's face as if this was a black joke that he was missing. His tone stiffened.

'I lost a cousin there, at the battle on the Ussuri River.'

'I'm sorry to hear that,' Mr Ffrench replied. 'Good men died needlessly. I made it my business to write to their widows.'

'He was just twenty-two,' the sergeant said. 'He fought bravely. His kids will be proud of him. What did you do?'

'I fought my best to ensure that as few of my men as possible died. I don't have children yet to be proud of me. If I had I might have been truly brave for their sake and joined the Bolsheviks to fight for the liberty of all men.'

The sergeant looked at his men who were all watching this encounter, then, very deliberately, he spat and gave the order to board the truck. He climbed in without speaking. Headlights lit up the dark road as it pulled away. The darkness was more intense after it was gone.

Mr Ffrench approached the car.

'My word, you pair have got so big. Come down tomorrow and we'll have a picnic on the pier like old times. Maybe you'll give the doctor a lift as far as Killaghtee church.'

Mr Ffrench sounded relaxed and jovial, but Maud wondered if when she woke tomorrow she would suspect that his conversation with the sergeant had formed part of a bizarre dream. Mr Ffrench shook their hands, then strolled back up his avenue. The doctor got into the back seat and Maud drove on.

'Is Mr Ffrench feeling all right, Doctor?' Maud asked.

'I'm afraid that diagnosis is out of my league,' the doctor replied. 'Our neighbour appears to have embraced a new faith. He has spent the evening preaching the benefits of communism for all mankind. I have not heard such ardour since travelling medicine men used to pontificate on the virtues of their elixirs at fair days, curing everything from croup to baldness. In Mr Ffrench's favour he makes no claim that communism will cure either. A few weeks' rest should sort him out. Ffrench always took up hobbies with enthusiasm. Reading between the lines, it seems that he was relieved of the command of an assault on Archangel. It was given to a well-connected young English officer whom the Admiralty were keen to blood. I put Ffrench's zeal down to pique, but we old doctors are a cynical breed. Here will do fine, Maud. I'm glad you recovered your motor.'

Maud stopped to let him out.

'How did you know it was missing?'

The doctor laughed. 'Who doesn't know? Good night.'

Brother and sister drove on and entered the village. Two men leaned on the low windowsill at MacShane's pub to watch the car go by. One gestured a silent greeting. Only after they passed however did Maud wonder if it was actually a greeting or had his fingers been cupped in the shape of an imaginary revolver. She didn't know. Indeed, as she turned into the lane to the coach house Maud realised that there was little she was truly sure of any more.

# FIVE

## *The Boat*

### *Donegal, August 1920*

Nobody else called this the Fairyland Road, but in her mind Eva never referred to it by any other name. It was a rough track over bogs and rocks that cut the trip to Killybegs by two miles. Sometimes at dawn she loved to sketch here, knowing there would be no traffic and rarely another person to disturb her. But it was barely passable to cycle on as she had discovered with Jack this morning, going to the Killybegs Regatta when they struggled to lift their bicycles over exposed rocks where the track had vanished. Still, she was happier to travel independently rather than be squashed between her boisterous brothers in the battered motor with the roof tied down with rope.

This morning, Mother had seemed perturbed at allowing the recently demobbed twenty-two-year-old New Zealand officer to accompany her alone down this isolated track. But – as if to encourage Eva's growing friendship with Jack – her brothers and, more reluctantly, Maud, had all expressed a fierce determination to travel by motor.

Jack looked slightly comic now, as his long legs struggled to cope with Maud's small bicycle, but the family was lucky to have two bicycles left. Eva dismounted as they reached another outcrop of rock. Her wicker basket was crammed with eggs purchased from an old woman who resembled an amiable witch and kept eggs for sale in a chamber pot under her box-bed in a tiny cottage near the road. Cook would be glad of them for tonight's regatta party. Jack also dismounted to offer Eva a hand, but she blushed and said that she would manage. Twice already she had taken his hand at awkward parts of the track and twice he seemed hesitant to let it go.

They discussed the afternoon regatta in Killybegs where crowds had lined the harbour walls. Eva explained how British submarines based there during the war had created great local excitement. She was careful when mentioning the war, having never ascertained how Jack received his injuries which required such a lengthy recuperation. Two months ago Father had acceded to a request from an army friend that the family might take in Jack for some rest before he undertook his long return voyage to New Zealand. Luckily Cousin George had been leaving after a summer visit, so it was agreed to offer the young officer his room. When asked to inscribe the visitors' book on his last day Cousin George had listed an entire alphabet, with his Q & R causing particular hilarity. *Q is for all the impossible QUESTIONS discussed at dinner. R is for the RESULT: indescribable babble.*

The New Zealand officer was initially bewildered by the Goold Verschoyles's indescribable babble on the night he arrived. Mother – engaged in 'table turning' with her psychic friends in the drawing room – had suggested that Father play a march on the piano to see what the spirits did. As Eva had answered the front door and led Jack into the room, the table started to move by itself in time to the jaunty music while Mother's friends with outstretched hands linked across it, needed to stand up to keep pace with its swaying. Father was impressed, although her brothers' disbelief remained unaltered. But that night Eva and Maud had been more preoccupied with their new arrival than with any occult manifestation.

The sisters had expected a pale invalid, perhaps mildly deranged like several local ex-soldiers who had been exposed to nerve gas and were prone to fits. But apart from a slight limp, Jack seemed in perfect health. Eva did glimpse a scar down his leg on the first occasion when Jack accompanied Art and her to the pier beside Mr Ffrench's house. The tide had been in, with high waves washing over the stones as they splashed down the pier to jump feet first into the sea. The water was deep and exhilarating, so intensely cold that for several seconds after each jump Eva feared that she would never surface again. But excitement kept her warm as she repeatedly clambered out to do it again, suddenly conscious of how tightly the bathing suit clung to her eighteen-year-old body.

She had never imagined that anyone could jump higher than Art, but after several timid attempts, Jack suddenly charged through the spray to launch himself forward with a roar that scared Eva because she instinctively knew this was how he had been trained to bayonet German soldiers. Jack never uttered such a yell again as if his leap off the pier had exorcised some terrible vision trapped in his heart. But afterwards Eva never used her nickname for the pier again as if the sight of his muscular body had altered her innocent vision of paradise.

Indeed, Eva never really thought of him as a British soldier until the night, soon after his arrival, when loud knocking disturbed the house. Father was away. Eva and Maud had looked down to see armed men outside. The IRA guerrilla campaign was ongoing, with hardened British auxiliaries ransacking villages and shooting bystanders in reprisals. Little of this had filtered into Dunkineely since their motor was stolen, but Maud understood the danger and had whispered for Eva to wake Jack and smuggle him out the back door. Eva had often visited the spare room when Cousin George slept there, but to enter it with a stranger in the bed felt different. Jack's shoulders had been bare and for a terrible moment Eva feared that he was naked. Jack woke once she touched his arm. His hand covered her fingers as he gazed up in a cryptic way she could not understand. He seemed unsurprised at her presence.

'Armed men are here,' Eva had whispered. 'They may have come for you.'

'Turn your back.' Eva heard him slip into his trousers.

He went to his window to look down at the coach house and she touched his sheets that retained a warm scent of sleep and dangerous masculinity. Jack had reached back for her hand, his touch exciting and excusable in the context of leading her onto the dark landing. She had wanted him to hurry down the back stairs but he leaned over the banisters to watch Maud open the door and Mother exclaim: 'Oh, do put those guns down, I can't stand guns.'

'Sorry, mam,' Eva had heard a man reply. 'Lower the guns, lads. We're after bicycles. We need two.'

'Then only two of you come through,' Maud had said with such authority that only two men entered the hallway and were led by Maud down towards the kitchen. Jack drew Eva back into his room to watch the men remove bicycles from the coach house and mount up with rifles on their backs before cycling beyond a ring of light cast by the paraffin lamp which Maud held aloft. Eva had detached her hand from Jack's grasp as her sister re-entered the house.

'That was a spot of excitement, what?' Jack had said quietly.

'Was your bicycle taken?'

'No.'

'If it ever is I'll happily carry you around on my shoulders. Good night, Eva.'

For one moment they had stood so close in the moonlit bedroom that Eva half-feared and half-hoped Jack would kiss her. He might have done so had she not turned to run bare-foot back to the safety of her childhood bedroom.

No such sanctuary was now available on this rock-strewn track however as Eva remounted her bicycle, checking that none of the eggs wrapped in newspaper was broken. Jack was behind her, so close that her back was colonised by goosepimples. Eva was intently aware of his breath and could almost feel his fingers though his hand was inches away. She knew that he was about to touch her shoulder and couldn't decide if she wished him to. She was used to school pals of Art who played tennis in white flannels and brought her for bicycle rides. But their prime focus had always been Maud who was prettier and more mature, well versed in accepting and deflecting their attentions with a confidence Eva felt that she could never master. At twenty, Maud had fully supplanted Mother as head of the household. She trained the maids and issued instructions, while Mother gardened and attended to her bees in an enormous black-veiled straw hat. Eva would understand Jack being besotted with Maud, but he seemed to have chosen her instead, to Maud's thinly concealed surprise. Eva turned to face him, suddenly bold.

'Slowcoach,' she laughed. 'I'll race you to the crest of the hill and beat you too.'

Eva began to pedal furiously, knowing that with his limp he might have trouble catching her at first but would soon gain ground. She glanced behind and slowed down, for the sake of the eggs. Jack was laughing, straining in the effort to catch her and Eva realised with a shock that she loved him. Yet she loved him most at moments like this, when she could feel Jack's love without him being able to reach her, when his love made her feel grown-up without forcing her to fully become an adult. Eva waited till their wheels nearly touched, then pedalled faster, loving the wind in her hair, the scent of heather and distant view of Donegal Bay. Mother had insisted that Art wait for them where the track rejoined the Killybegs road, but just now Art seemed as far away as New Zealand. Everything felt distant in the exhilaration of this chase – the regatta they had left, this evening's house party, the unrest in Ireland and the aftermath of war that brought Jack into her life.

Since the night the bicycles were taken, the IRA never returned and even die-hard Republican villagers accepted that Jack had nothing in common with the Black and Tans in Crossley Tenders who often invaded the main street. Indeed Jack had even allowed himself to be lined up and roughly frisked by drunken British soldiers without revealing his former military rank. His only contact with any ex-officer was with Mr Ffrench, who steadfastly refused to answer to his naval title when dealing with British squaddies, though he seemed to enjoy it when local people affectionately addressed him as 'Commodore'.

War had changed the Ffrenches. Mr Ffrench's favourite topic at dinner now concerned how the White Russians were a decadent dictatorial class and his pride at having done everything short of being court-martialled to aid the revolutionary Bolshevik victory. But such dinner parties were infrequent, because relations between Father and Mr Ffrench seemed strained compared to the days when they wandered for miles on his aeroplane cart. The Verschoyle children still enjoyed the run of Bruckless House and pier, often helping

Mr Ffrench in his new passion for making handcrafted wooden cabinets. But Father argued with seventeen-year-old Art over all the time he spent in Ffrench's study, lined with maps of Russia and where a tame jackdaw flew freely about since having his wing mended by Mrs Ffrench. Father never criticised the communist tracts that Art and Thomas often brought home from Bruckless because he believed in open discussion. But Eva sensed his difficulty in dealing with some of the assertions Art had started raising.

Not that Eva paid attention to their political arguments, because lately all her attention was focused on Jack and most of his attention on her. As they cycled now she knew that she would not be able to keep ahead of Jack for much longer. This chase that she had initiated worried her because it had to lead somewhere. Jack was riding abreast suddenly, both bicycles wobbling dangerously on the narrow track. He reached across to grasp her handlebars and she had to brake, slipping slightly in the dust. She halted, suspecting that several eggs had cracked. He was beside her, his hand gripping her bicycle. Eva wondered what acts that hand had committed during the war and what it might do alone with her now.

'You caught me,' she said.

'Have I?'

Eva knew suddenly that he was not going to kiss her. Jack's eyes were serious. She wanted to kiss him, purely to stop him saying whatever he meant to say because Eva sensed that it was about to change everything.

'I'm going away,' he announced soberly.

'Where?'

'New Zealand obviously. At least I have written to my doctor to say that I'm ready for the voyage . . . if I wish to go . . . if there's nothing to keep me in Ireland. That is what I need to know. Is there?'

'Of course,' Eva replied blindly. 'We all love having you.'

'Do you?'

Eva blushed, not wanting to admit what she felt, even to herself, because it meant having to leave so much behind. 'Yes. I only ever had younger brothers before.'

She knew that the words were wrong, not what Jack wished to hear or she wanted to say in her heart. Maud would know the right words.

'I'm not – I don't want to be – your brother,' Jack said firmly. 'Is that all you're seeking? A big brother?'

'It's more than that,' Eva insisted. 'I like us being together. I love when we lie in hayricks and you read me poems like Father, only different.'

'I'm not your father either. Look at me.' His voice was quiet, his hand steadying her bicycle. 'Is there anything you might like us to do that does not involve your precious family?'

'I liked the midnight picnic last week when we all sailed out to the Green Island,' Eva admitted shyly. 'I liked it when I decided to swim alongside the boat and you dived in and swam beside me. Just us two in the water.'

She wanted to add how she had liked touching his bare shoulder on the night the IRA came. She liked how he shook his wet hair when climbing from the water at Bruckless Pier. She liked the accidental glimpse she had caught of him drying his naked body by the shore, unaware that she could see through the trees.

'I liked us being in the water too,' Jack said. 'Just a few inches between us and nobody able to see in the moonlight. That sort of moment might make a man not wish to return to New Zealand or make him bring somebody with him. You'd love New Zealand, Eva. It's bigger and more beautiful than here. And there's no trouble, no armed gangs, just people getting on with life. Childhood doesn't last for ever. What do you want?'

'I don't know,' Eva replied, scared. Mother frequently scolded her for spending too long in her studio, dreaming about the future instead of actually planning it. Jack sighed.

'None of your family know what they want. Look at Art.'

'What about him?'

'This place is like the Garden of Eden and he will inherit it all, but instead you'd swear he was in the Garden of Gethsemane. Especially with that renegade Ffrench filling his head with nonsense.'

'Mr Ffrench is nice,' Eva protested.

'It's easy for Ffrench to entertain notions without children to pass his wealth on to. I want children and want to work hard for them. Do you want children, Eva? I don't mean this year or next, with you being so young and having seen so little. I mean in time.'

'Yes,' she replied, because he had qualified the question so it did not threaten her. But she hated Mr Ffrench being crit-icised, like she hated the arguments always simmering now at family gatherings.

'I'm glad you said that.' Jack's hand moved from the handlebar to grip her fingers alarmingly. 'Give me hope and I'll stay. I'll have the slowest recuperation in medical history. Even at the risk of an IRA bullet I'd walk barechested across Donegal if I stood a chance with you. Do I?'

'I've said I like you,' Eva replied.

'What does that mean?' Jack pressed.

'Art will be wondering what's keeping us.'

'He knows damn well. He may be an apprentice saint, but he's no fool.'

'What do you want from me?' Eva was desperate to escape, yet made no effort to free her hand.

Jack took a deep breath, trying to be patient. 'Nothing you don't want to give. Your mother says you're not ready and

I know it would be better if we met in a few years' time, but we haven't got that luxury. I don't know where I'll be then and you don't know what type of country you'll be living in if the house isn't burnt over your heads.'

'They wouldn't burn our house,' Eva protested. 'They know us.'

'You don't know them.' He paused. 'Listen, we can't talk with a chaperone waiting over the hill. You loved swimming out to the island, didn't you?'

'Yes.'

'Then do it again tonight. I'll borrow Ffrench's boat. He doesn't believe in private property any more anyway. Meet me on the Bunlacky shore at midnight and we'll have our own picnic on the island.'

'That sounds magical,' Eva said. 'Can I bring Art?'

'For God's sake, Eva.' Jack put his hand to her cheek and made her stare into his face. 'Stop playing at being a child. I want us to visit the island alone as man and woman, if you want that too. Do you understand?'

'Yes.' But Eva didn't want to understand. She wanted to remain poised on the cusp of this new world without having to leave the safety of her old one.

'Not that I'd do anything improper,' he added. 'You know I'm a gentleman. I just need us to talk alone with none of your family having seances or political debates or playing polkas or simply being so damned cheerful. I need a sign that you understand and return my feelings. I'm willing to wait if there is hope but I'll not be played as a fool.'

A shout disturbed them. Art had grown impatient and come to check on them. Jack quickly released her hand. His fingers had not been rough but Eva still felt their touch and knew that she was blushing. She waved to Art, with a gaiety she didn't feel.

'Are you okay?' Jack asked quietly.

'I'm fine,' she whispered.

'So, should I steal Ffrench's boat or not?'

'I'll bring my bathing costume. You can sail and I'll swim the last stretch.'

Eva mounted her bicycle to pedal up the slope towards the safety of her brother. Jack followed more slowly. Both dismounted when they reached Art so that they could unhurriedly walk home together with Eva in the middle, between the two men she liked most in the world after Father. Jack was less frightening in company. He was in wonderful form as they sang and swapped snatches of poetry. If Eva had a choice she would have continued walking like this for ever, but that was a child's wish and, glancing at Jack, she knew that she was a woman.

The house was packed when they reached home and the drawing room carpet had been taken up for dancing. Mr Barnes, manager of the Royal Bank in Donegal town, had transported the Goold Verschoyle family silver from his vault despite his misgivings about taking such a risk in these times. His three sons were here and the eldest boy was playing tennis against Maud in the garden. Through the window Eva watched Maud gracefully return a volley with one hand holding down her straw hat. Thomas talked to Mr Barnes in the grown-up way which came naturally to him, while ten-year-old Brendan raced in and out of the open front door pursued by a clutch of village children in a game that Eva couldn't fathom but would have loved to join in. Male voices came from Father's study and Art joined the men there like poor Oliver Hawkins had been allowed to do the summer before he died. Mr Ffrench was also in there with the rector whose son always attended their musical evenings and sang *I Love Thee, Come Forth Tonight*.

The kitchen would be dangerous territory, with the flustered cook complaining that in any other house the mistress would have some notion about how many were likely to arrive for dinner. Mother would be trying to soothe her, with Mrs Trench, the gardener's wife, also there to help. Maud sometimes whispered that Art was sweet on Mrs Trench's only daughter, but Mr Trench – a man of few words – had once announced that he would twist the neck off any boy seen near her. Art's social position would not save him from Mr Trench's temper if he were over-familiar with the girl. Thinking of this made Eva wonder where Beatrice Hawkins was now. The Great War had changed everything. Tonight's gaiety would be tinged by absences. Eva and Maud often lay awake discussing the dozen young men from nearby Protestant families butchered in France and Belgium, with Mother despairing that so few eligible locals remained for her daughters to consider marrying. Eva wondered how long a boat took to reach New Zealand and what it would feel like to be a bride. The possibility would have been exciting were it not suddenly tangible.

She went to answer the front door where two local women wearing shawls stood with a donkey cart loaded with whiting, herrings and sprats, looking to sell them at two pennies a plateful. Eva explained that tonight was a special dinner. As the women moved off, she checked the basket on her bicycle and found that only two eggs were broken. Carefully she removed them while Brendan ran through a flock of geese to offer to ride her bicycle around to the coach house.

Eva braved the chaos of the kitchen to give Cook the eggs. The babble there was too much for her, so she slipped out to her studio where she could think.

It was seven o'clock, five hours until midnight. It would be impossible to talk to Mother all evening and, even if she could, Eva wouldn't know what to ask. She longed to knock at Father's study and ask to speak to him alone because Father understood her, but Eva was too shy to seek advice from anyone about anything so personal.

Eva's parents were used to her wandering off for walks at night to sketch in the moonlight or simply sing with joy where she could not be overheard. With so many people arriving tonight nobody would miss her or Jack. She imagined cold water soaking into her bathing costume, the sway of dark waves, the white splash of oars. She would need to change back into her clothes when they reached the island, having to render herself naked under a bathing robe before slipping every item of apparel back on. Jack would be kindling a fire with his back to her, aware that she was briefly naked and knowing that when she sat next to him a tang of salt would still linger on her lips if he kissed her. He would definitely kiss her on the island with no one else there. If she allowed him, he would touch her through her clothes in places where Eva had never been touched. Surely it would be the most fleeting of touches because he was a gentleman who wished to marry her and would do nothing that might lessen his respect. Perhaps he would just want to talk or read her poetry.

The coach house was deserted. The family had divided the building into separate dens. Being fascinated by science, Art and Thomas had constructed a laboratory in the part furthest from the kitchen, from which explosions were occasionally heard. Nearby Maud had set up a weaving shed, after visiting local weavers to master the loom. Maud's den was also the editorial address of *The Dunkineely News*, the family newspaper established by Maud to record the advent of summer visitors. A flight of rickety steps led to the small loft that Eva used as a studio for painting. Brendan generally flitted between dens, anxious to be with his brothers but knowing he would be teased less by his sisters. He considered the back seat of the motor as his private den. This was parked in the main coach house, and Art and Thomas were summoned to discuss engine problems whenever it refused to start.

Eva climbed the stairs to her studio where she could be alone, except for the mouse behind the skirting board whom Eva had trained to come out and accept food from her hands. Jack was the only visitor to her studio with the patience to sit still long enough for the mouse to emerge. Jack seemed content to sit for hours and watch her paint. At first Eva was too self-conscious in his presence, but she had grown so accustomed to him being there that she found it hard to paint without Jack at her shoulder.

She picked up a paintbrush but put it back, wishing she had socks to darn because she found darning a soothing occupation. Footsteps ascended the wooden stairs and she prayed it was not Jack. It was Brendan, wearing the comical oversized hat that he loved.

'What are you doing?' he asked.

'Just dreaming.'

'I bet you'll be a famous artist when you grow up.'

Eva laughed. 'I doubt it.'

'I'll stand by the door in tails and top hat greeting the crowds pouring into your first exhibition.'

'I prefer you wearing that hat. What will *you* be?'

'A world famous traveller. Foreign correspondent for *The Dunkineely News*, sending dispatches from Killybegs and Kilimanjaro. I'll recruit a tribe of pygmies to land at Bruckless Pier and march on Dunkineely to put Art and Thomas in the stocks with people ordered to empty chamber pots over their heads.'

Eva smiled. 'What have they done now?'

'Thomas won't let me into the attics to dress up.'

'For what?'

'The dancing, silly. Maud has decided we should wear fancy dress tonight. She says you must go as Becky from *Vanity Fair* and she is dressing as a damsel from a harem, whatever that is. Will you help me to find a costume and stop the others from teasing?'

Eva took his hand, which felt so small after Jack's, and left the studio. She envied Brendan being the magic age of ten, just like he envied Eva her grown-up status. At ten she had seemed old compared to her brothers, but, as the youngest, Brendan would always seem young. They crossed the yard, swinging their arms and singing. She knew that the others had not really barred him from the attics, especially Art with his deep sense of justice, but Brendan was sensitive to every slight, convinced that his brothers patronised him no matter what he did. Normally Eva loved to dress up but this evening she found it hard to focus on anything except the slow approach of midnight. Maud had opened a trunk of clothes belonging to Grandpappy's late wife who had been locked away in an asylum for the incurably insane. Grandpappy had never encouraged visitors, claiming that she recognised nobody, but Eva used to hate imagining the old woman stranded in a ward of strangers.

Maud was dressed in bright silks, set off by a rich Persian cummerbund. She had found a pageboy outfit that Brendan only agreed to wear on condition that he could keep on his favourite hat. For Eva, Maud had a high-waisted, full-skirted pale green satin dress, which had probably not been worn for decades. Normally Eva liked to make her own choice but this evening she didn't argue, even allowing Maud to put up her hair with a ring of silk rosebuds after they returned to their room.

'You're quiet,' Maud observed, finishing Eva's hair. 'Did anything happen on the cycle back from Killybegs?'

'Like what?'

'You tell me.' Maud looked down. 'You're blushing.'

'Am I?'

'Jack is daft about you. I heard him tell Father and Mother.'

'What did they say?'

'That you couldn't be rushed, you didn't really understand such things yet. But you do, don't you? You must do what you alone want in your heart. But a man cannot be put off for ever either. You could lose him.'

Eva knew this. But there was so much else she could lose. She felt safe in Donegal where she understood this peaceful world and it understood her. Jack didn't just bring the horror of war into their lives by occasionally shouting in his sleep, making Eva long to comfort him, he also brought home the encroachment of adulthood. There was no doubt but they made a wonderful couple, matched in everything except experience. He loved nature like she did and would happily lie out in the fields while Eva recited Tennyson or Whitman. But change was everywhere. This autumn Art would enter the University of London. A suitor could snatch away Maud at any moment. Watching Father check the windows at night Eva knew in her heart that they could wake to find the house in flames. That was why she loved to stop time in paintings. But life refused to work like that.

The maid's voice called from the landing that Maud was urgently needed to sort out seating arrangements. Left alone, Eva examined herself in the mirror. The Victorian dress made her seem older, the piled up hair emphasising her slender neck. She closed her eyes to imagine Jack's hand caressing it. Then the dinner gong broke her reverie. At Maud's chest of drawers she put rouge on her face, then walked downstairs to greet people, sensing Jack watching her every step.

By a miracle they all fitted at the table. Some neighbours disapproved of such mayhem but Eva loved the informality where Cook was applauded and people struggled to make themselves heard. Across the table Jack caught her eye and Eva knew that he thought she looked beautiful. Normally she would have brought down her autograph book to ensure that everyone inscribed a clever remark or fragment of poetry. At last year's regatta party Mr Barnes's eldest son had inscribed a poem:

> *If the wicked old world was swept away*
> *Like dust from your studio floor,*
> *And only those parts of it made again*
> *That were good and fair and pure;*
>
> *And if the re-making was given to me,*
> *I'd begin with Donegal,*
> *And your studio out in the stables*
> *Would be the first of all.*

But the treasured autograph book belonged to her old life and she would have felt childish bringing it to the table now.

As befitted dangerous times, there was no talk of politics, with even Mr Ffrench and Art respecting Father's wish. Afterwards people crowded into the drawing room, where the rector's son produced a fiddle to accompany Father on the piano. They launched into old-time waltzes, English folk dances like *Sir Roger de Coverley* and then, when the room was warmed up, riotous Irish set dances like *The Walls of Limerick*, with people eager to teach Jack the steps. Eva noticed that he never danced with her, anxious not to spoil the moment when they would finally be alone in the boat. At eleven o'clock, the dancing halted to let people deliver their party pieces. Maud was first, singing the *Skye Boat Song*. Eva saw Jack slip away and knew that he was about to cycle to Bruckless House to untie the small boat by the pier.

Maud's song finished and old Dr O'Donnell sang *Eileen Alannah*, with eyes only for his smiling arthritic wife. The minute hand on the mantelpiece clock picked up speed as more songs followed. Father played a piece by Liszt and Mother who was tone-deaf said, 'That's lovely, Tim,' as she always did whether he played Beethoven or *Pop Goes the Weasel*. Mr Barnes insisted that Father play a composition of his own and the room was still as he began to sing:

> 'Far, far away, across the sea
> There lies an island divinely fair
> Where spirits blest forever dwell
> And breathe its radiant enchanted air.'

The familiar words followed Eva as she slipped unnoticed upstairs. Her room was moonlit, her bathing costume in the drawer. She chose a robe and long white towel, took the band of silk rosebuds from her hair which tumbled down, and then, as an afterthought, washed the rouge from her face. The kitchen was empty when she desperately wanted someone to find her. But nobody came to stop her lifting the latch and slipping into the yard, past her dark studio and around onto the main street. She stopped across the road to look at the open drawing room window where family and neighbours were gathered. The dancing would soon recommence. The noise of a Crossley Tender's engine in the distance suggested troops were about. The street was deserted, with locals cautious of venturing out. Jack would be waiting at the Bunlacky shore. It was dangerous to leave him alone, in case patrolling auxiliaries mistook him for a rebel. Yet she couldn't bring herself to move from the scene in the window. Footsteps came down the lane she had just left. Eva recognised the hat before hearing Brendan's lilt: *'Who goes there? A grenadier. What do you want? A pint of beer . . .'*

He spied her and stopped. 'Where are you going?'

'Swimming.'

'It's midnight.'

'I know. Do you want to come?'

'I've no costume.'

'You can stay in the boat and explore the island?'

'What boat?'

'It will be an adventure, our secret.'

Even as she held out her hand Eva knew that she was making a terrible mistake. But she couldn't stop herself. All the way down the Bunlacky road she kept intending to send Brendan back at the next bend, but she swung his arm and let him sing, until on the final bend she hushed him.

'What's wrong?' the boy whispered, sensing her tension.

Eva didn't reply, but walked on, clutching her bathing costume to her breast, feeling so small in the moonlight as she struggled to decide what she wanted. She reached the rocks and spied the boat below, with Jack smoking as he waited. He stood up, tossed the cigarette into the waves and held out a hand which halted in midair as the boy appeared behind her.

'Hello, Jack,' Brendan called. 'Are we going on an adventure?'

Jack didn't reply. He looked across the dark waves and Eva knew that he simply wanted to row away. But the boy had already run down the crude stone steps and Jack swung the boat around so that he could clamber on board. The young officer put a hand out to help Eva get in, then immediately released his grip. He seemed taut like a coiled spring, saying nothing. Yet Eva knew that he was not angry, merely disappointed and more annoyed with himself than with her. Without Brendan she would never have come this far. She would have hesitated on a bend on the Bunlacky road, lacking the courage to continue. Yet now she was here Eva wished that the boy was gone. She wanted them to sail alone to the island, with Jack's back turned as she stripped out of this ridiculous Victorian dress to don her bathing suit. She wanted all this when it was safely out of reach, because Eva knew that they could not simply let the child off. Jack had set her a test which she failed. Brendan's clear voice filled the air: '. . . *Where's your money? In my pocket. Where's your pocket? I forgot it.*'

The child lay back, trailing his hand in the water. 'This is more fun than the party. Can we do it again tomorrow, Jack?'

'Not with me, sonny. I'm New Zealand bound. I'll swing this boat around now and leave you both on dry land.'

'But it's great fun having you here,' the boy protested. 'Must you really leave?'

'I'm afraid so.' Jack altered course effortlessly to steer them towards the shore. He was a superb sailor. Eva imagined the pair of them sailing across a New Zealand lake. Only in this fantasy she was older and wiser and he had built a cabin with high windows to allow her to paint by the lakeside. She closed her eyes and tried to keep imagining these things, because she knew that when she opened them he would be regarding her with quiet disappointment. 'I'm off in the morning,' Jack added. 'I was never one for long farewells.'

Eva opened her eyes and stared at him. She wanted to say so many things that she didn't possess words for. She wanted to explain that she was just not ready. She wanted to be someone older than herself, yet she longed to be ten years of age again.

With a thud the boat bumped against the jetty. Eva wanted the comforting touch of a hand. She reached out in the moonlight and held one tight, never wanting to let go. Brendan glanced at his sister and whispered, 'You're hurting my fingers.'

With great courtesy, Jack held the boat steady while she got out.

'I'm sorry,' she told him.

'Don't be. The fault is mine.'

Eva longed to say more but the young officer had already set his back to her and began to row away along the dark shoreline towards Bruckless Pier.

# SIX

# *The Docks*

## *London, August 1922*

All night Art had been arguing with university friends about Italian politics in Fletcher's rooms near Blackfriars. Fletcher was not of like mind to the others: he saw nothing wrong in truckloads of Il Duce's fascists storming into Milan to end the communist-led strike there with the black-shirted thugs tearing down the Bolshevik flags hanging from the town hall. Fletcher could not understand why Art took such matters so seriously. To him, Mussolini was a clown who would never achieve power, just as Lenin would not hold onto it for long with famine in Russia. Fletcher would have been happier discussing Johnny Weissmuller's new world swimming record or playing *I Wish I Could Shimmy Like My Sister Kate* on his gramophone, because, to him, university was merely a lark. Tragedy had set Fletcher's future in stone, no matter what he studied. With the death of his eldest brother on the Somme, he was set to inherit the family estate. University was a chance to escape from home and discreetly make hay in this unburdened limbo before he came into his inheritance.

Watching him, Art wondered would Thomas possess this

same air of haunted gaiety if he had died in battle. So many chaps at the University of London carried a guilty look at having come into their inheritance not by birth but by an elder brother's death, that Art had learnt to recognise them. The peculiar thing was that they often mistook him for one of their number as if he too was cursed with the stain of underserved wealth. Yet the more he studied politics the more he realised that he was like them. All that distinguished him from his siblings was a fluke of birth, a throw of the dice yielding him absolute access to wealth while the others were left to scramble for minor bequests. Past generations had ensured that this was a chalice he could not refuse. Short of dying, Art had no means of breaking that cycle of indenture.

Yet Art argued now with his college chums that surely to God – if there was a God – the Great War's slaughter had overturned all previous rules and conventions. Crippled beggars on the London streets were daily reminders that any pretence of innocence was gone. For the Great War to mean anything it had to herald the advent of a new era. Freedom was not about one Kaiser defeating another, it was about granting people the liberty to be truly themselves.

Before the Bolshevik revolution the bulk of humanity had sleepwalked through life, unaware that they could possess total power if they merely looked up from their chains. Every day the imperialist press repeated lies about millions starving in Russia because they were afraid to report what was really occurring there. But once ordinary British workers understood this truth, they would emerge like risen Christs from the tomb, liberated from the inbred fear of their alleged betters. Last year the miners had suffered on strike without the country rising to back them and today it was the engineers' turn to be locked out. But once the Communist Party was fully organised across Britain a day of reckoning would come.

Fletcher laughed at Art's intensity and rang the bell for his manservant to fetch more stout. The others agreed with Art's assertion that the Labour Party had become lured away from its revolutionary roots and was now merely a cloak and dagger ally of imperialist expansion. But Art sensed the hollowness of their convictions. They were flirting with radicalism, like their fathers on Grand Tours of Europe once flirted with exotic dancers. Typically short-sighted, they regarded Lenin's revolution as too foreign to impinge upon their world. These student discussions were not about genuine revolution, but simply a chance for the privileged idle to enjoy a brief *frisson* of danger by pretending to be different from their parents. After college they would drop such notions and take up golf and banking, fattening out into premature middle age. Art lost patience with their play-acting and was about to leave, when the manservant returned and sought him out with a sympathetic look.

'Begging your pardon, Mr Goold Verschoyle, but I thought you should know the news from Ireland. I'm afraid your Michael Collins has been shot dead in an ambush.'

The room went quiet, the others studying his face. They had no interest in the civil war raging in Ireland since the peace treaty was narrowly accepted and British troops had withdrawn. The treaty had divided the country, with the majority of people sick of war and anxious to accept the partitioned Free State which the treaty offered. But Art could not imagine any compromise on a full Republic being accepted by such men as the IRA commander who had once returned the family motor to Maud in the Donegal hills. In the ensuing split he surely sided with the diehards like de Valera and the Countess who were now fighting against Michael Collins and his fellow treaty negotiators whom they accused of betraying the dream of a Republic. Art had initially been excited by this civil war, seeing parallels with the power vacuum in Russia in which Lenin seized authority. But de Valera was no true revolutionary. Art still hoped that both factions might weaken each other sufficiently for a communist takeover, but – with the union leader Jim Larkin sidelined in an American jail – there was nobody of sufficient stature to lead such a coup d'état. Art's enthusiasm for the IRA had never recovered from his encounter with that Cork commander. It left him feeling occluded from all sides in recent years, as the conflict grew increasingly bloody. The Troubles had taken a toll around Dunkineely, not just in occasional killings and reprisals, but in the way that people came to be judged purely as being on one side or the other. At times in Donegal he was made to feel a foreigner, whereas in London he was viewed as a totally Irish outsider.

Having delivered his news, the manservant slavishly waited for a morsel of acknowledgement.

'That is shocking,' Art said. 'Thank you for letting me know.'

'They shot him like a dog, sir. Mr Collins claimed that when he signed the peace treaty he was signing his own death warrant and he was right.'

'Thank you, Jenkins,' Fletcher interrupted. 'That will do.'

'Yes, sir.'

The man placed four bottles of Imperial Russian stout on the table and left. Fletcher leaned over to refill Art's glass. 'Damned bad news,' he said. 'I liked Collins. He was a murderer but one you could do business with. My sister developed quite an attraction to his picture in the papers when he came to London for the peace talks. The whiff of danger I suppose. You know romantic girls. These must be worrying times.'

'Yes.' Art sipped his stout, surprised at how moved he was

by this news. Dunkineely would be shocked, even those who felt that Collins had sold out the Republic. He longed to be among people who understood this contradiction. His sister Eva had recently enrolled at the Slade Art School, but she was sleeping in a London girls' hostel where he would not be welcome at this late hour. Besides, though he loved Eva more than anyone in his family, she was too vague to fully understand what was happening.

He finished his stout and rose to leave, glad to descend into the night air. Collins had been a strong man, a Catholic reactionary, yes, but still a man of both action and thought and he was to be admired. Crossing Queen Victoria Street, Art found himself humming *The Soldier's Song*, the illicit anthem sung by rebels during the Easter Rising. The tune attracted a policeman's attention. He approached Art, then took one look at his expensive clothes and passed by with a surprised nod.

Art knew that if he had been poorly dressed it might have been a different story. He cut down sidestreets, being well-versed in long night walks from Donegal, heading towards Wapping where there were early morning pubs for dockers. Other Irish people might be there, fellow countrymen with whom he could discuss the news. The first pub door he tried was locked, although lights were on inside. He knocked but the drinkers ignored him. It was the same at the next one but when he reached the Thames he fell into step with two young Mayo men, Liam and Tomas, near Tower Bridge Wharf. When he offered to buy them a drink they laughed, claiming that he must be desperate for a cure. Still they knew exactly where to go.

The pub shutters were down to keep out the night. Casual dockers inside were having a pint to steady their nerves before commencing the struggle to find work. More afflicted drinkers sat among them, crippled by alcohol, hands shaking so badly that they could barely lift a glass to their lips. Art bought drinks and then a second round as the three Irishmen discussed Collins's death and the grip that his new Free State army was gradually gaining over the country. Neither Liam nor Tomas was educated, yet Art felt happier in their company than with the students in Fletcher's room. Here there was a sense of real life being lived. More Irishmen joined them, distraught at the news, glad of Art's company and opinions. He bought a final round of drinks, including a whiskey for an elderly English carpenter who initially refused Art's offer because he had not eaten a meal for several days. The man was seventy-four and told Art he had always found work until his health recently began to fade. Some older stevedores still took him on, knowing that he was a good worker, but most were scared of having a dead weight on their hands. He was a veteran of the 1889 Dockers' Tanner strike and had been among the first crew two years ago who refused to load coal onto the *Jolly George* when that ship was due to sail with arms against the Bolsheviks in Russia.

The group drank up, hurrying out from the pub now onto the dark quayside where the casual hiring was about to commence in a large iron-barred shed. Dockers permanently employed by the big firms brushed past them, knowing that they were guaranteed work. But for the men around Art it was a case of hoping that smaller ships had docked in the night and needed casual workers to unload them. Men emerged from other pubs and nearby streets, a swarm pressing into the shed where stevedores selected workers from the crowd. Art stood beside Liam and Tomas who didn't know the stevedores and so found it hard to get noticed. This was capitalism at its most ruthless – men reduced to units of labour, hired for the shortest time then discarded when they grew old. Repeatedly the old carpenter pleaded with the stevedores who shook their heads. Art was impressed at how the other hungry men, while focused on their own plight, sympathised with him. This was a world Art knew little about, but he might learn more here than from a day in university.

He began to raise his hand amongst the clamouring throng as things started to look desperate for the remaining men. Liam and Tomas were amused at first, then hissed at him to stop messing. He ignored them, fighting his way forward to eventually attract the attention of a burly stevedore.

'What the hell do you want?'

'A day's work. You're hiring, aren't you?'

'I'm hiring men. This isn't some sort of student lark.'

'I'm as strong as any man you're taking on.'

'You're big all right but your hands are as soft as a baby's arse. Now piss off.'

The other men regarded Art with none of the measured sympathy they felt for the old carpenter. They stared at him coldly, like he was trying to mock them. Was it solely his accent and clothes or was there another difference that he was unaware of? Perhaps the proletariat was harder to join than the bourgeoisie. From an early age the proletariat was trained to ape their so-called betters, whereas the rich were trained to largely ignore the existence of workmen and servants. He could not recall the names of all the maids who worked in the Manor House when he was a boy but all of them would remember him.

The stevedore glanced at a shabbily dressed young man with huge shoulders standing behind Art.

'Ready to burst a gut?'

The young man mutely nodded and the stevedore nodded too. Art noticed how their interaction was entirely based on appearances. Only five words had been exchanged. Men behind Art pushed aggressively forward and he moved back to where he was less intrusive but could still observe these rituals. The stevedore chose his crew and there was an anguished murmur, although someone amongst those left claimed that there was another ship yet to be unloaded. Art went to join Liam and Tomas at the entrance to the shed, though he sensed that their camaraderie had cooled since leaving the pub.

'Swap shirts,' he said to Liam.

'Are you daft?' The Mayoman laughed.

'It seems a fair exchange.'

'You won't be saying that, being eaten alive by his fleas all night,' Tomas joked. 'Talk sense, man.'

Art ignored Tomas. 'Do you want this shirt or not?'

Liam licked his lip nervously. 'What's the catch?'

'None. I'll swap you my shoes, trousers and all.'

'Jaysus, is it to be standing in the nip you both want?' Tomas asked. 'I'm not staying around to be a laughing stock.'

But Tomas didn't move and Art recognised the greed in his eyes. He was jealous that Liam had been asked. Liam sensed this too and he agreed to the swap as much to gain an advantage over his companion as to get the clothes.

Both of them went down a narrow dank alley smelling of piss between two warehouses. They undressed, first exchanging shirts and then trousers, anxious that no garment touched the filthy ground. Liam's boots were too tight for Art, and Liam would slide about in his shoes but the Mayoman did not complain. Liam craned his neck, trying to inspect himself in his new outfit.

'Well? Do I look like a gentleman?'

'Yes,' Art lied, though the way in which Liam held his body resembled an awkward servant in fancy dress. 'Do I look like a docker?'

'No.' Liam was suddenly aggressive, feeling that he had been made a fool of. 'You look like the gobshite you are. Now piss off and stop following us.'

The Mayoman stalked off to rejoin his companion and Art watched them leave, knowing that there was a new friction between those two friends. Collins's death had been quickly forgotten in the acquisition of a good shirt. This was the corrupting influence of possessions. It was easy for Art's college friends to discuss Marxist theory but the Ffrenches had shown that it was possible to live out your convictions. As yet he was not in a position to follow them to Russia but this morning was a first step. He wondered if Mr Ffrench dressed like this in the Moscow furniture factory where he and his wife had now been working for the past three months. They were sharing a large room there with three other couples, in a big house seized from a bourgeois family. Ffrench had described in his last letter how quickly you grew accustomed to restricted space. He did not know how he ever put up with the waste of rooms in Bruckless House which lay empty for the IRA to burn for all he cared. True life for the Ffrenches had only started since their move to Moscow. Fellow workers welcomed them and Mrs Ffrench loved how children from all the different families ran about the room, climbing onto her knee as easily as onto their mothers' laps. Ffrench urged Art to ignore imperialist propaganda. Life under Lenin was the greatest adventure in history and the Ffrenches, like other foreigners flocking there, were privileged to be allowed to play a small role within it.

Art had sworn to join them one day. He could visualise arriving in Moscow, with Mr Ffrench embracing him at the station like a true father because – although this was awful to say – Father, who supported the new Free State, felt like a stranger.

Art walked back out to join the men at the dockyard gates

and thought about Collins's body lying in its blood-soaked uniform. The deputation that Collins led to Downing Street to negotiate the treaty had looked more like civil servants than revolutionaries. Nothing would change in Ireland, no matter which faction gained final power. The priests would rule, urging the new government to grind the poor with the same iron grasp. A degree in murder was no substitute for a degree in political theory. The new government would look like Liam, aping their former masters in clothes that didn't fit them. The only true revolutionary was the Countess who was still enduring prison and hunger strikes, having given up everything to live in the slums with Dublin's poor. True freedom was not freedom to acquire colonies or possessions but the freedom to be liberated from such burdens.

Art re-entered the shed where a stevedore was scanning the remaining crowd.

'I need twenty strong men. No layabouts. Stand still so I can bloody well see you.'

Art noticed the elderly carpenter and walked towards him. The other men let him slip through their ranks, not seeing him or paying any heed but Art felt that he was being seen properly for the first time. Not as a Goold Verschoyle or public schoolboy or university student but as flesh and blood on a par with all humanity. The carpenter did not recognise him and only looked up, baffled, when Art began to speak.

'Do you know this stevedore?'

'For years.'

'Say I'm your son and I'll work beside you all day. I've strength enough for us both if you show me what work needs to be done.'

'I don't understand what you're at, sir?'

'Don't call me "sir". I'm after a day's work like you. Help me get in and I promise to fetch and carry for you all day.'

Ten men had already been chosen. The carpenter nodded, weak with hunger. As he pushed forward, Art followed, bending down to pick up some mud and smear it through his hair. He kept his soft hands in his pockets where they could not be seen. The stevedore looked down at the carpenter and shook his head.

'If I could do you a favour, Andy, I would. But I need muscle for this job.'

'My son is with me,' the carpenter called back. 'He's a mute but built like an ox. Look at him. We're a team. We'll do the work of three men between us.'

The stevedore stared at Art. The appraisal was brutal and honest, like a gaze at a horse or a boy at an Irish hiring fair. 'Lost his tongue, eh? Could be worse, he might have lost his prick.' The stevedore nodded curtly. 'Let's hope he's half the man his father once was.'

The old carpenter pushed eagerly in through the gates at the end of the shed and Art followed into a new world, a university of toil where he had so much to learn.

# SEVEN

## *The Exiles*

### *Donegal, Easter 1924*

There were no lamps in the windows of Bruckless House when the horse and cart bumped over the small stone bridge leading onto their property. Since arriving back in Ireland yesterday Mrs Ffrench had grappled with the wild hope that somebody – the Goold Verschoyle girls or one of the servants who had been laid off a year ago – might have placed eleven lamps in eleven windows to welcome them. But there was no such illumination, merely the damp rain that so frequently settled around this isolated house which she had been longing to see for weeks – or months if she was truly honest.

She could not tell when her husband's zeal had begun to weaken. Perhaps only in the cramped Moscow hospital where they realised there was little likelihood of him receiving proper medical attention for the terrible arm wound received in a factory accident. Poor medical conditions were not the fault of the Soviet authorities but of the belligerent European capitalist powers still trying to blockade the revolution into submission. The Moscow doctors were heroic in the loaves and fishes miracles they performed with such limited supplies – not that the medical orderly who took her husband's details

109

would have appreciated this metaphor from a discredited religion. Every comrade citizen had been heroic even when they did not appear to be so and violent squabbles broke out between families trying to commandeer every inch of space in the room where they all ate and slept. Even the children's heroism was undiminished by their inability to stop crying with hunger. Heroism existed in the very air on the streets, in revolutionary banners and endless workplace meetings, in the orchestra which entertained her fellow workers in the furniture factory by playing a new style of music, composed collectively instead of being imposed by the tyrannical will of a single conductor.

If heroism alone could have healed the gash in her husband's arm that threatened to turn septic they would still be in Moscow, walking through crowded streets at dawn to commence long factory shifts, whispering in English at night so that people sleeping nearby could not understand their intimate endearments. Their Russian was poor, but had slowly improved. They did not understand what the medical orderly had said to them until he made the shape of a saw through the air and they realised he was warning them that Mr Ffrench's arm might be amputated. That was the first time she cried in Moscow, although she had wished to cry on many nights when the noise and cold and hard floor kept her awake, when she was forced to overhear strangers break wind or furtively make love despite having too many children already huddled like rats beneath piles of rags. When she had watched a husband beat his wife while other families ate supper as if this monstrous behaviour was unworthy of comment or intervention. When the Secret Police came to take one father away for reasons that nobody knew and were careful not to speculate about. When she woke some nights longing to be back in her old bed in Ireland with clean sheets and the other decadent bourgeois trappings they had rejected. Yet throughout all this she had been strong and supported her husband in his enthusiasm to embrace this new order.

But it had been too much to contemplate the notion of a half-qualified foreigner sawing through her husband's arm with a dirty implement and the pair of them returning to that crowded room where she would need to physically fight for the space to nurse him and make bandages by tearing up whatever small amount of her clothes had not mysteriously vanished. Mrs Ffrench had cried that day on a dirty bench in the hospital and nothing Mr Ffrench could say had been able to penetrate the terrible grief that opened up inside her. Perhaps she had been a bad wife to show her feelings like that and was weak in not supporting her husband and the revolution. But behind the tears was the terrible fear that he would die during the operation, leaving her alone in that city which stank of hunger and terror, with nobody to protect her except the God whom she could no longer even mention.

Lenin had died in January but her god was not dead. She could not have uttered such blasphemy in Moscow, but she knew it was true because here at last was Bruckless House and her husband still had both arms intact – even if his left hand would never regain full power. God had steered them safely back home. It was God's voice she had heard in the hospital when her husband announced quietly over her tears that his wound was a job for his old naval surgeon friend, Geoffrey. When she reminded him that Geoffrey would hardly leave his Harley Street practice for Moscow, Mr Ffrench had patted her arm with his one good hand and said that if Harley Street refused to come to them, they would simply have to go to Harley Street.

The driver stopped the cart at the front door of Bruckless House. Two figures stood there whom Mrs Ffrench had despaired of ever seeing again. Art Goold Verschoyle stepped forward with Eva. Mr Ffrench shouted a greeting and suddenly there was laughter and welcoming smiles and the driver was helping her down onto the overgrown lawn and she did not mind the rain or cold but longed to kneel and kiss the damp earth. She hugged Eva. How could she ever have found Donegal dull? How could she have been so eager to pack up and start again in Russia with nothing but the unuttered hope that a fresh start might make her body finally yield to her husband's seed?

The cases unloaded by the driver contained nothing from Moscow but new clothes purchased by her in London while the Harley Street doctor treated her husband. Not that Geoffrey had done more than merely examine the job done by a doctor in a private Helsinki hospital after they managed to get themselves onto a train to Petrograd and cross into Finland. Mr Ffrench had kept assuring her that, having freely entered Russia, they were equally free to leave for a short time. She had tried to believe him and not seem scared by the constant inspection of their papers and how soldiers patrolling the railway system shouted at them. But her husband's arm had oozed pus and he was in such distress that the patrols had let them proceed – less for humanitarian reasons, she suspected, than because they didn't want to be responsible for an invalid.

In Helsinki they wired their bank in London and contacted the British attaché. Soon Mr Ffrench was in hospital and a new fear replaced Mrs Ffrench's previous concerns. She had started to dread her husband's recovery. Helsinki felt strange but it had no slogans on walls or agents of the All-Russian Extraordinary Commission for Combating Counter-Revolution and Sabotage seeking out class enemies. On her first night alone in her hotel bedroom she realised that she had been constantly terrified during the previous six months. Now that she had escaped from Russia she did not know if she would have the courage to ever go back.

She had dreaded Mr Ffrench announcing his intention to return to Moscow and reclaim their corner of that pigsty room. However he had kept postponing this decision because it was vital to be able to fully contribute to the new order and he feared being a dead weight who would drag down production targets for their comrades in the furniture factory. Besides he had affairs in Britain to put in order and people should be told at first hand about how exhilarating life was in the new Bolshevik state. Mrs Ffrench had agreed with everything her husband said, unable to decode what was going on in his head. All she could do was trust that, unbeknownst to him, her spiritual master, Abdul-Baha, was guiding her husband's hand. She had decided it prudent not to force him into confronting any decision. Such careful passivity on her part got them to London and now to Donegal where the mayhem of the Irish Civil War seemed halted and tonight at least everything seemed like it had always been.

Eva Goold Verschoyle shyly released her hand from Mrs Ffrench's grip as Art eagerly questioned her husband in the doorway.

'How was Moscow? You have to tell me everything!'

Mr Ffrench gripped the boy's shoulder joyously. 'My dear boy, it is everything we dreamt of, the most just society on this earth. Mankind hasn't known a fresh start since the Garden of Eden. But in Russia the old rules are gone and the people, not their masters, are shaping the new order. Come inside and I'll tell you everything. Is there nobody about? I wired for your father to reinstate some servants.'

'You did?' Art sounded surprised. 'I fought with Father,

saying that he must have misunderstood the telegram. I mean, what would you want servants for?'

Mr Ffrench laughed. 'What would I want them for? Dear boy, do you know the size of Bruckless House? It would be an injustice to only have two people living here. The important thing is to fill the house with life. Obviously *servants* is a reactionary term, but you can imagine what Papist clergy would say if I advertised for worker comrades to share my home.'

'You mean you're looking for local people to live here with you.'

'Obviously. They will have the full run of their quarters and we shall have the run of ours.'

Mrs Ffrench watched the boy consider this. In truth he was a boy no longer. Eva's tiny figure still lent her a girlish look, but Art's shoulders had broadened out, making him look tough and strikingly good-looking. He reminded her of her brothers lost in the war. Once on a Moscow street she was convinced that she had seen her two brothers side by side ahead of her in the jostling crowd. For a moment she had let herself believe that they had not gone missing in action but simply wandered off from the terrible trenches to find their way to this new land. The hope was ludicrous, but she had been unable to stop herself pushing through the crowd, elbowing strangers and being cursed at until she touched one of their shoulders. Both men turned, neither remotely resembling her brothers now she could see their faces and she had felt their eyes undress her, taking in her manic look and the fact that she was foreign. They had looked hungry, as everyone did in Moscow, but strong and when they addressed her she knew immediately that their remarks were lewd, suggesting that they would be willing to share her body. She had run away and never told her husband what happened.

Mrs Ffrench entered the hallway of Bruckless House and almost cried to see a wood fire burning in the grate. Art and Eva had been busy, with another fire burning in the study. Returning home as a girl from her first term in boarding school, she could remember how small the rooms in her childhood home seemed, but after Moscow the opposite was true of here. Previously she had paid little attention to the size of this study, but now she realised that it was bigger than the awful room where she had been forced to sleep with the squabbling families. Sitting down on the sofa she surveyed its fantastic dimensions. She almost wished for the Goold Verschoyle children and even her husband to be gone so that she could explore each room and luxuriate in the extraordinary space. This physical greed shocked her. She was never greedy before, dutifully sublimating her needs and dreams to those of her husband. But just now she experienced an almost sexual thrill at the thought of cradling the brass doorknob of each bedroom, at pressing her palms against the huge uncracked windowpanes and placing her cheek to the cold mahogany of her dressing table.

Eva's questions about Moscow were discreet enquiries compared to Art's frenzied interrogation of her husband. The boy had studied Moscow street maps and knew more about the city's layout than Mrs Ffrench had learnt in seven months of living there. He wanted to know every detail of the crowds at Lenin's funeral and quizzed her husband about Comrades Zinoviev and Stalin and Trotsky and Kamenev as if Mr Ffrench had spent his days at internal party congresses instead of manufacturing poor-quality tables and chairs.

'The failure of the communist revolt in Germany was a blow to Trotsky's prestige,' Mr Ffrench was saying. 'It shows that the spread of the revolution will be slower than expected because Germany is ripe for change and yet the reactionary

115

forces dug in. If our German comrades had won the day all of Europe would rise with us but there is talk of Russia needing to stand alone for a while longer.'

'But surely Moscow won't abandon the rest of us?' Art argued. 'What is the point in mankind taking one step forward and then simply stopping?'

'Who mentioned stopping?' Mr Ffrench replied. 'Moscow cannot be a wet nurse to everyone. It is up to us who live here to fan the flames of revolution.'

Art went quiet and even Eva ceased to prattle on about the scraps of local gossip that Mrs Ffrench had been enjoying. There was a subtext in her husband's remark, a Rubicon quietly crossed, a declaration she had not dared to seek from him. Hope surged inside her in direct opposition to Art's baffled disbelief.

'What do you mean by *us*?' he enquired. 'Surely once you recuperate you will return to Russia. I understand your desire to come back here and recover your strength, but . . .'

'Desire did not enter into it,' Mr Ffrench interjected. 'It was necessity. Because I could seek medical treatment elsewhere it would therefore have been a selfish, counter-revolutionary act to deny a comrade treatment by clogging up a Moscow hospital. Medical supplies are crucial, as are able-bodied workers. My arm will never fully recover. The revolution is no rest home for cripples. Do you think I wish to be a parasite in Moscow, living off the sweat of my fellow workers? Mrs Ffrench and I had no desire to ever return to Donegal. Crossing into Finland was the hardest chore we ever did. I curse my disability for dragging Janet away from an environment where I saw her blossom with such happiness and purpose. But personal feelings cannot be allowed to rule. What is vital is that we each contribute to the maximum of our potential. I was shocked in London to read appalling propaganda in the capitalist newspapers. Janet and I have decided that for now our place in the revolution is here where we can counter lies and bear testament to the amazing society that we were privileged to witness and to which one day we will hopefully return. Here we can serve a purpose which you can help with too. The Irish peasants imagine that they have undergone a revolution, but they've just swapped one master on horseback for another. We can show them the truth – and do you know the great thing? They will listen to us because even in my short time back I see that the old respect remains for people who speak with authority. They don't look up to this new Johnny-Come-Lately Free State government trying to lord it over them. Oh, no doubt there will be fireworks with their priests waving sticks and shouting threats from the far side of the bridge leading onto my property but they can't stop us telling the truth to those who will listen.'

Mrs Ffrench saw Art trying to shape a question, but no words came because the boy needed to believe in her husband. What did she believe? She watched her husband grow so animated that soon Art was caught up in his enthusiasm and asking questions again about the factory and the workers' debates. Both she and Eva stopped talking so that they could listen too, because his version of Moscow was so wonderful that it felt like a poultice on her mental scars. It was simpler not to argue or even contradict him in her mind because maybe he was telling the truth and she had been too preoccupied with her own petty concerns to appreciate the wonder of revolution.

The children had brought food and it felt like a picnic to share it out by the fire in the study. The mantelpiece clock had long stopped and she had no idea what time it was when the young Goold Verschoyles left. But it was too late to do anything except retire to the main bedroom where the sheets felt damp. Her husband was asleep within minutes and she knew that he would not wake. She slipped from bed and walked from room to room, trying to reclaim all this space and make it feel that it belonged to her. But she felt uneasy, as if hordes of strangers might arrive at any moment to stake a claim to the kitchen or the locked room overlooking Donegal Bay that had been once intended as a nursery. She longed to immerse herself in a bath but knew that she could never scrub herself clean. Closing her eyes she could still smell in her pores the stink of foul breath and unwashed clothes in that Moscow room. So why was it that she could not hear the voices of the children who had clambered onto her knee to stare at her like a curio? She could not feel their fingers that had gripped hers, hoping that she might produce a morsel to feed them. Why was it that the single experience she treasured seemed to be erased from her mind, so that all she could hear was silence as she wandered from room to room, barefoot in her thin nightgown?

# EIGHT

## *The Studio*

### *Donegal, August 1924*

The more that Eva drew, alone in her studio, the less she could hear of the raised voices from the house. Her fingers shook, giving the elfin figures a slightly blurred outline. She had intended painting in oils today but once the shouting started she reverted to using this sketchpad on her knee, hunching over it to make herself as small as possible. She longed to escape and sketch wild flowers in the hedgerows, but was reluctant to leave her studio and cross the courtyard where the angry clash of voices would be impossible to ignore. Eva hated these arguments and the terse silence that followed them. During the fragile suspension of hostilities her brothers and Cousin George would individually visit the studio, ostensibly to comfort her, but each would start to justify their case, anxious to convert her into an ally.

Eva had no wish to take sides in the quarrels that had raged all summer. The Free State's civil war was over, with de Valera's Diehard Irregulars defeated. But just as an uneasy normality settled over the new nation they found themselves in, a civil war had commenced in the heart of her family. Friends and relations who visited earlier in the summer had helped to paper over the fault lines by dragging them back into a childhood world of tennis and picnics on the strand. These visitors inscribed amusing notes of thanks in the visitors' book and carefully avoided politics like an unmentionable family illness. So perhaps Father was foolish to invite Cousin George to stay for Eva's birthday party because Cousin George knew Art and Thomas too well to allow for any pretence. As a true Verschoyle he was as headstrong as they were. To him the family's reputation was being indelibly eroded by Art's wilful madness in embracing communism, which he considered to be a cancer gradually infecting them all. Such lunacy might be all right for pagans like the Ffrenches, but his uncle was always too soft in allowing inflammatory discussions at the table.

If Eva was forced to listen to George she knew that she would be swayed by the power of his argument but Art's impassioned defence would equally convince her in turn. Her beliefs were more obscure and less dogmatic than either point of view. Although influenced by Mother, Eva found it hard to believe in the occult world as passionately as she did. Seances – with desperate women holding photographs of slain sons – seemed a form of voyeurism, making her as uncomfortable as these political arguments. This was why she locked herself away in her studio when the quarrelling started – not to avoid venturing an opinion, but to avoid favouring one family member over another. Ironically her silence seemed to lend weight to her opinions, with the others frequently appealing to her as if she were a judge who, when she finally spoke, could attest to the rights and wrongs of their dispute.

The voices grew louder as Eva crouched over her sketchpad, focusing all her attention on the tiny figures she was conjuring. They had wings and asexual bodies, flitting like bees around blooming foxgloves growing in a ditch. Her fingers were steadier now and she sketched the ditch with intense concentration. After some time Eva ceased to hear the arguing voices and initially thought that this was because she had managed to block them out. Then she realised that hostilities had paused. Soon the first petitioner would arrive to solicit support – George or Thomas, who generally sided with Art while maintaining his own slant on things, or Father, weary of trying to see both sides. By now Mother would have retreated to her bedsitting room to read the few books from the Rosicrucian Order in London which made it past the censorial new Irish post office, or some volume sent to her by Madame Despard – the elderly English suffragette who had settled among the Dublin poor and shared Mother's interest in theosophy. Eva closed her eyes, allowing the sketch to become saturated with colour. She could visualise the ditch she had drawn from memory, with a tumbled-down, dry-stone wall. But, try as she might, she could not believe in the fairy figures. That childhood belief had died in London along with any belief in her ability as an artist. Art school had stripped her of illusions.

It did not seem like eighteen months ago since she had spent an autumn and winter sleeping in the tiny cubicle of a London hostel for shopgirls, with a sprig of Donegal heather beneath her pillow. Mother had considered London as the ideal tonic to lure Eva down from the ivory tower of this studio where she had locked herself up to secretly mourn the loss of her young New Zealand officer. It was only after Jack left that Eva fully understood her feelings. By then it was too late because no girl could write and ask for such a proposal again: Eva had constantly painted and destroyed portraits of him, grieving alone in this studio. Her obvious distress more than her talent made Mother enrol her in the Slade Art School. Eva had felt like a princess in a fairy tale, forced to plait her hair into a rope and descend into those bustling crowds to try and start a new life.

Her brief time in London was good in every respect except for painting. What slender spark of talent she possessed was quickly extinguished under the glare of her tutors at the Slade. The more they tried to teach her the less she found that she could paint. She discovered that she had more in common with the shopgirls in the hostel than her chic fellow students. Their cosmopolitan sense of surface gloss and parroting of the tutors' techniques to create deliberately grotesque compositions made her retreat into herself. By comparison her paintings seemed naive, the childish work of an Irish country simpleton.

But back then Eva was certain that there had to be a purpose behind her stay in London, beyond avoiding the increasing vicious conflict in Ireland. When Art had visited her in the hostel between university lectures, Eva used to show him her poems urging the rebels to *fight, fight, fight for what is right, right, right!* But, in truth, at the age of nineteen in London her patriotic bursts were outweighed by her preoccupation with a different search for independence, the struggle to find a religion to which she might truly belong.

Converting to Catholicism like the Countess did after the Easter Rising was never an option. Instead the Christian Scientists had been Eva's first port of call. While shopgirls gossiped about boys outside her cubicle she had studied the Christian Scientist bible, absorbing their mantra that no life, truth or intelligence existed in matter alone. Next she spent long afternoons in a High Church where women wore blue robes and their elaborate rituals, though beautiful to watch, made her wary. She needed something simpler and more direct. She tried a Jewish synagogue and, after that, sampled every religion in London for pleasure and interest. Yet no matter how comfortable she felt, an intuitive inner voice warned: 'Move on, don't mistake this stepping stone for a summit.' In the end she felt herself to simply be a child of the universe, blown about like a sycamore sepal at the creator's will. That wind had carried her back to Donegal as the civil war spluttered to a smouldering halt soon after Michael Collins's death.

Eva glanced up from her sketchpad now, having become so absorbed in drawing that she had been unaware of a presence in her doorway. It was Brendan but Eva felt she had stepped back in time because he wore the comical hat that he used to love. At fourteen-and-a-half, it made his face seem younger. His serious expression recalled the days when he would visit her, upset because his brothers kept excluding him from their schemes.

Eva smiled. 'Where did you find that hat?'

'In the attic. Mother must have put it away.'

'She was always threatening to burn it,' Eva said. 'But I like it on you.'

'I'll take it with me so.'

'It would give the boys in school a laugh, but I doubt if you'll be allowed to wear it.'

'From now on I wear what I like.' There was no rebellion in Brendan's voice, just the quiet resoluteness that was in his character. He was not prone to Art's passionate oratory or a stickler for logic like Thomas. Indeed, he rarely ventured opinions aloud but once he made up his own mind about something nobody could alter his beliefs.

'What do you mean?'

Brendan's tone was apologetic, anxious not to offend. 'I'm rather tired of all these rows, aren't you? The fact is I won't be returning to school. I have decided to make my own way in life. I just announced the fact and, you know, for the first time I saw both Cousin George and Art lost for words. I can't see why they are so surprised. Plenty of chaps my age have been earning their keep for years. Art and Thomas talk the good fight, but still cling to the privilege of a university education. Well, wild horses wouldn't drag me back to Marlborough. Not one chap there knows a thing about life or could manage without ten servants. What's the point in being educated for a world which, as Mr Ffrench rightly says, will soon be swept away?'

'Does Mother know?' Eva asked.

'You understand, don't you?' Brendan's voice faltered, anxious for approval.

'Does Mother know?'

'Well, I didn't rightly know myself until it came to me as I listened to them argue. I want a proper job making something, not pen-pushing in some corner of the Empire. I want to become an engineer. Marlborough doesn't teach you anything useful like that.'

'Will you go to Dublin?'

'Don't be silly.' Brendan smiled to show that he meant no offence. 'In Dublin I'd still be the youngest Verschoyle brother. I want to be known only for myself. I hardly know a soul in London, so that's where I'll go. One cannot wait for life to come to you like a gentleman caller. You must go out and confront it.'

They both turned as Thomas entered the doorway.

'This is entirely Art's fault,' he announced.

Brendan shook his head. 'You're obsessed by Art, Thomas. Maybe it comes from being next in line. Being the last born means that I can simply be my own man.'

'You're the one obsessed by him,' Thomas retorted. 'Idolising him since you were a baby and you're hardly more than a baby now. A pet hamster has more chance of surviving in the wild than you have of finding a job in London at your age.'

124

'I'm old enough.'

'I'll give you a fortnight before Father has to pull strings to get you re-admitted to your warm school dormitory. Don't be stupid, Brendan. You don't need to renounce wealth because you and I won't inherit anything to give up anyway.'

Thomas went silent as footsteps ascended the rough steps. Father had to duck his head to enter.

'Is this a meeting of the Verschoyle Party Congress?' His mild humour disguised his obvious distress.

'It will break Mother's heart if Brendan doesn't return to school,' Thomas said bitterly. 'Though, even then, she won't bring herself to criticise her golden boy Art.'

'I've never heard her criticise any of her children,' Father replied. 'No matter how hard you all hurt her. Cousin George is about to leave. He says he won't stay to be insulted by the names Art has called him.'

'Art means no harm,' Eva pleaded.

'That doesn't mean he won't cause it.' Father looked around. 'I heard what you said about inheritance, Thomas. I will try to leave you all something. But it cannot be this house which I only hold in trust for Art and which is legally entailed to his son after him.'

'You know that weeds will grow through broken windows here before Art will accept it,' Thomas replied sharply.

'I know he is young. I know that you see life differently at twenty-two and thirty-two.'

'Art will never change.'

'Why should he?' Brendan asked. 'I don't want inherited wealth either. I want to establish my own worth.'

'You will return to Marlborough and stay there until your sixteenth birthday.' Father's voice was quiet but firm. 'After that you'll be a child no longer. Hopefully you will finish your education and make something of yourself. That will be your decision. All I request is that you obey me for the next eighteen months.'

'Why should I?' Brendan's voice was not aggressive. It contained an innocent openness that Father also possessed.

'Because you are a gentleman, it will please your mother and because I will never ask anything of you again. I shall never walk away from any of my children, no matter what you do. Should you choose to walk away from me I will not stop you. But take something with you while I'm alive and you still can. Take jewellery or the family silver if you wish before Art gives it away to a beggar.'

'I won't steal from my brother,' Thomas replied.

'Art doesn't own this house yet. Steal from me.'

Thomas looked down awkwardly. 'I'll see George,' he said 'Maybe I can twist his arm and persuade him to stay for Eva's party.'

He walked out. Brendan fingered the hat he had removed when Father entered. 'I give you my word to return to Marlborough until my sixteenth birthday,' he said. 'I make no promises beyond that, but you know it is not in my character to break my word.'

'Define *character*,' Father asked.

Brendan pondered. 'Character is what you are, what you do every day.' He blushed slightly. 'I'd better see Cousin George too in case he leaves.'

Father watched his youngest son descend the steps and shook his head in wonder. '*Character is what you are, what you do every day*. If only dictionaries were as clear and noble. He's a noble boy, you are all noble, but I worry about whether I've prepared any of you for life out there.'

'We'll be fine,' Eva assured him. 'I just hate seeing you look so frightfully upset.'

'Do I? Maybe I don't understand what's happening any

more. I've never harmed anybody in my life. I've given my services freely to defend neighbours in court and gave them land behind our house to hold a market every Tuesday. I address every man equally – Catholic, Protestant or dissenter – yet my eldest son thinks I should feel guilty for simply existing.' He looked at Eva. 'What terrible crime does Art feel I've committed? I've only ever wanted to mind your mother and for you all to be happy. We were happy once, weren't we?'

'We still are,' Eva insisted. 'Let's go on a picnic tomorrow, all day. It would be lovely.'

'It would. But then unfortunately we'd have to come home again.'

Down in the yard Maud's voice called up to them both.

'Dinner shall be in half an hour,' she announced, 'and we shall be sitting down together in peace.'

'Has George left?' Eva asked, going to the doorway.

'I confiscated his bag in the hall and ordered him to give up his nonsense,' Maud said. 'I raided the wine cellar and shall have Art and George playing chess peaceably before the evening is out.'

'You're a marvel,' Eva said. 'Is there any chance of a picnic tomorrow?'

'We'll sail out to the island where I shall personally drown every annoying male in the family.'

Father laughed as Maud marched back to the kitchens. 'Your sister is a marvel,' he said quietly, 'but you are one too.'

'I'm not.'

'You're a marvellous shape still emerging with slow wing-beats into the light. Too far away for me to judge the outline of what you will become, but I know it will be truly wondrous.' His hand strayed into his pocket where a small edition of

Walt Whitman was kept. 'We've half an hour before being summoned to the next congress on world affairs. What about a walk?'

Eva smiled and closed the studio door behind them. 'Just you and me.' She took his hand and squeezed it.

'A quick bid for freedom.'

Eva released his hand as they entered the lane. Demonstrative shows of affection were not in their character. Passing the village pump, they took the lane to the Bunlacky shore, saying little because little needed to be said between such soul mates and friends.

# NINE

# *Not a Penny off the Pay*

## *London, 1926*

Brendan intended being utterly true to his word. Mother would be upset but Father would respect how he honoured his vow. In recent months he had been careful to make no reference to his decision when talking with the other chaps. Eighteen months ago he was vocal about his plans and was ragged because of them. Now he had not even mentioned that his sixteenth birthday occurred this week. Naturally, his two best schoolchums knew his intentions and envied him, but both had too much to lose to follow his example. Being eldest sons, they needed to think about more than just themselves.

Brendan knew that his family loved him, but if he had not been born, little would be different in their world. The last born was always counted as a blessing, but generally counted as little else.

Still Brendan would not wish to swap places with Art or Thomas. Older teachers at Marlborough still paused in the corridors to ask about Art and shake their heads, almost as if sympathising with a bereavement. They recalled Art with affection, even if he had constantly queried every issue with them but they also spoke as if he had perpetually borne a heavy weight on his back. Brendan was not as clever as Art but he sensed their relief at Brendan's cheerful spirit. He had actually enjoyed his time at Marlborough, making friends and being generally respected as a good sort. Therefore this morning when he made an excuse before assembly and requested permission to see the nurse in sickbay, he felt no resentment towards any person in the school. They were simply misguided, unaware that they belonged to a world shortly about to be eclipsed.

Packing his small suitcase while the other boys and the staff were in assembly, he calmly walked down the deserted driveway. He did not run because he was not running away: he was simply leaving to start his own life. It felt somewhat dishonourable to fabricate a lie about feeling ill, but Art had once said that a degree of subterfuge was occasionally justified if oppressive forces were ranked against you. If Brendan was spotted he would be dragged back and probably receive the cane. The school would only release him if Father wrote to give his consent, but that would mean the decision being Father's and not his, and it was unfair to place Father in such a bind.

This was his choice alone, to start a new life at the very moment when Art's predictions of class warfare were coming true. For the past six days a general strike had gripped Britain, to the consternation of his teachers. Five years ago the coal miners had stood alone and been defeated. But this time the other unions were striking in solidarity with those miners locked out after refusing to accept a savage pay cut and the imposition of another hour onto their working day. Events had escalated at midnight last Friday when printers in the *Daily Mail* refused to print an editorial entitled *For King and Country* denouncing the Trades Union Congress's plans as a revolutionary act of treason. Brendan's housemaster had gathered the pupils to hear a message on the BBC from the Prime Minister urging the nation to keep steady and remember the maxim that peace on earth came to all men of good will. Brendan had wanted to stand up and shout a truer maxim: the workers united would never be defeated. But his teachers and classmates would not have understood because Marlborough taught only Latin, Greek and complacency.

Brendan paused at the end of the avenue to look back at the imposing buildings which gave the impression that nothing would ever change. But in Ireland he had seen how quickly change could come – with a new flag, a new state and a sense of not quite belonging.

The disadvantage of starting a new life on the cusp of revolution was that Brendan could not be sure how far he would get. The railway workers were striking, but a crew of middle-class scab volunteers was maintaining a skeleton timetable. It would be difficult to evade capture if forced to spend hours waiting on the platform. But, when he reached Marlborough Station, a Special Constable sworn in to protect the strike-breakers said that a London train was due in twenty minutes.

Brendan had decided to still wear his school uniform for now because he looked less suspicious in it. A scab volunteer with the look of a merchant banker staffed the ticket office. He possessed the same eagerness as the other volunteers operating the station – oversized schoolboys being allowed to play with a life-sized train set. This quality was most apparent in the driver and the engineer when the train finally arrived from Bristol and they cheerily greeted the passengers of their own caste boarding the first class carriages. Brendan might have found something comic about these little Englanders clinging onto their rotten class structures if they were not blacklegs. He purchased a first class ticket because he would seem less conspicuous among people who spoke like

him. Two businessmen occupied the compartment he entered.
One nodded jovially.

'What's this, young man? Skipping term?'

'Called home. A family illness.'

The man nodded with practised sympathy. 'Bad show. Still
at least you will get home. Three days ago the blackguards
had closed down the whole rail network. But their grip is
weakening. They've misjudged the resolve of the British people.
I'll give them another two days at most, then I hope they
lock up the ringleaders.'

Brendan did not argue because he was not yet free to do
so. The train was taking for ever to leave, with some fat scab
making an elaborate show of waving his flag as if seeing off
an ocean liner. The boy watched the platform, expecting
teachers and prefects to rush after him. But the train was
moving now, the wheels seeming to chant, '*free-dom, freedom*'. The businessmen both read the government propaganda ragsheet and paid him no heed. The print unions were
refusing to print any newspaper except *The British Worker*,
produced by the strikers themselves. Yesterday Brendan's
form master had confiscated a copy of *The British Worker*
which Art had managed to get to him, saying that if Brendan
wished to know the truth he could read the government-
printed *British Gazette* in the library. Brendan had not argued,
because by then he already felt that his school days were over.

His class would be doing French now. He should be past
Reading Station by the time they realised he was not in the
sickbay. Then it would be on to Maidenhead, Slough and
Ealing. As a communist he felt guilty at being on a train
driven by a scab, but speed was essential. This was the greatest
adventure of his life. He felt like Toad of Toad Hall escaping
from prison. The chaos of the strike would aid his chances,
the police being too busy to look for a schoolboy.

He would not be dragged back to face the cane. They would wire Father who would release Brendan from the school's care. The headmaster might be disgruntled but teachers would simply shake their heads and dismiss him as being as mad as his brother.

The businessmen in his carriage glanced uneasily out as the train entered Hungerford, as if expecting strikers to storm the platform. But only a handful of well-dressed passengers waited there with Special Constables visible at the exits. It was impossible to see if rail workers protested outside the station. This was the thing about boarding school, the outside world could end and you might never be told. He knew that the army had been called out in South Wales and Yorkshire and that in Glasgow, mobs had forced public vehicles off the road. Brendan strained his eyes as the train moved away, yearning to glimpse his first striker and feel part of this momentous occurrence. An elderly couple had entered the compartment, the old lady smiling at him. The four adults began to discuss the strike, the mayhem in the country loosening the usual reserve between strangers. The lady's daughter had volunteered her services to help sort mail in the post office. Her grandson, an Oxford undergraduate who had abandoned his studies to enlist with the hastily established Organisation for the Maintenance of Supplies, considered the whole affair to be a grand lark.

Brendan only half listened to their nonsense about the strike crumbling. They were leaving Wiltshire behind. He took down his suitcase from the rack, not opening it until he was alone in the corridor. Choosing another jacket to wear, he held the Marlborough College blazer in his hands for a moment, staring at the crest. Then he lowered the window to lean out. He loved trains, loved their freedom and the exhilaration of the wind against his face as he let his school blazer billow behind him for a moment before releasing it. He laughed, imagining the shock of passengers in the carriages behind when they saw it sail through the air. Glancing back he saw it land in a bush and gave a yell of delight, knowing that nobody would hear above the noise of the engine. Stepping away from the window, he closed it and patted down his hair, then retook his seat. The lady smiled at him again, having obviously been told his white lie about a family illness.

The mood in the compartment grew apprehensive as the train reached Paddington Station. The platform was clear but pickets jostled against a line of police outside the entrance at Eastbourne Terrace, abusing emerging passengers. A crude hand-painted banner proclaimed the coal miners' demands: '*Not a Penny off the Pay, Not a Minute on the Day.*' Brendan tried to tell one of the protesters that his own brother was among the strikers and he had come to support them.

'Is he now? And so what does he do then, this brother?' the man demanded, and Brendan realised that he didn't properly know the answer himself. A Special Constable hurriedly moved him along as the protester called him 'a lying bloody toff'. The crowd carried Brendan out on the London streets, a Dick Whittington wandering towards Regent's Park, savouring every glimpse of life around him. He didn't mind getting lost because this seemed the best way to encounter his new home, to learn his bearings from scratch and gradually implant each alley and side street into his brain. He had visited London before but never alone. Brendan was too excited to be scared. Here were the names he had studied on maps in the school library: Primrose Hill to the north, St John's Wood to his west, to the southeast, Russell Square and beyond it Holborn.

Art's address was in Camden Town, on a lane so small that no map in school showed it. Brendan would get there in his own time, not needing to take any of the scab buses that occasionally passed because nobody could chase him now. Crossing Regent's Park he emerged at Gloucester Gate humming *Bye Bye Blackbird*. Many shops were closed with pickets standing outside them, but he was shocked to see creeping signs of normality elsewhere. The *British Gazette* had trumpeted about Grenadier Guards in armoured cars forcing through a convoy of a hundred lorries from the docks to the Hyde Park depot, claiming that this had broken the strikers' will and assured London's vital supplies. But Art's scribbled note on the confiscated copy of *The British Worker* had insisted that the strikers would not let this breach re-occur.

Brendan studied the faces of picketing comrades, wanting to speak to them. Yet he knew that his clothes and accent would be a barrier. How had Art overcome this? Since graduating from university his eldest brother had shown no inclination for any profession, but – according to a relation who sometimes encountered him – spent his nights mixing with earnest young men selling socialist newspapers around public houses. Art's letters hinted at various manual jobs – the more backbreaking the better – but employers were suspicious of his accent and invariably found a reason to sack him, normally claiming that he was attempting to ferment dissent.

When Brendan reached the end of Parkway he sought directions to Art's flat. Yet it was Art himself that he found first. A crowd had gathered at the corner of Camden Road where a blackleg bus was being blocked to prevent it moving off. Some people were encouraging the nine strikers who sat on the cobbles. More, however, shouted abuse at them. Here at last was a revolutionary act, thought Brendan, but his attention was taken by a small girl on the pavement who looked frozen in her short skirt even though the afternoon was warm. Hunger lines and shadows under the eyes made her look old as if she had already seen more of life than he ever would. She stared with palpable terror at one of the strikers, probably her father, linking arms on the cobbles as if expecting the bus to drive over him, leaving her alone to starve among strangers. Brendan saw the strain on every face now, including the passengers – some of whom slipped off the bus while others sat tight-lipped and defiant. A whistle heralded the arrival of a police squad. These were no Special Constables but seasoned Bobbies who did not wait to ask the protesters to move. Batons came out and they struck the first striker before he had time to rise. He fell back among his comrades, blood coming from his forehead. The small girl screamed and Brendan reached out to touch her shoulder reassuringly. A woman among the crowd pulled the child away, claiming that he had tried to snatch her. For a moment both the protesters and police glared at him, each man becoming a protective father. Then he was forgotten as the strikers rose and tried to defend themselves. Women screamed and the volunteer bus driver raised his hands to his face as a stone crashed through his windscreen.

Brendan's attention became fixed on one protester, the only man who did not seem panicked. He remained in position before the bus, staring defiantly ahead amidst the melee. His cloth cap was pulled low and his clothes ragged, but Brendan knew that jaw and those defiant eyes. An aura seemed to protect him from the blows overhead. Here at last was the struggle Brendan had left school for, being played out at its most raw. It afforded him the chance to step from the pavement and sit down beside his brother as Art's equal at last. Brendan kept telling himself that at any moment he would do so, but then a space cleared in the affray and a policeman glanced down at Art, baffled by the calm way he sat awaiting his fate. He aimed a blow and Art fell forward unhurriedly, sprawling onto the cobbles with blood seeping from his head. This blow activated the crowd's sense of injustice. There were shouts with people pushing forward as the police started to make arrests. The bus driver was screaming, holding his eyes as he sat covered in shards of glass. Nobody remained on the bus. The woman holding the small girl hurried her away.

Amid the confusion Brendan saw two men lift Art and drag him into the shelter of the crowd. They moved quickly, anxious to get him to safety. One looked back at Brendan who followed. He lifted a threatening fist. Brendan slackened his pace but kept them in his sights as they hurried down a side street. They knocked at a house and were admitted. The door closed as Brendan approached. It reopened as he reached it and the man who had raised his fist grabbed Brendan's jacket and flung him against a wall.

'What do you want, you little police snitch? Lead the coppers here and I swear I'll come after you. I never forget a face and I'll break your legs. Understand? Now get the hell away.'

'That's my brother,' Brendan said. 'I want to see him.'

The men peered at Brendan. 'Say something.'

'What?'

'Anything. Say "proletariat".'

Brendan swallowed, being choked by the man's grip. 'Proletariat.'

The grip was relaxed. 'That's his favourite bloody word and I never heard anyone else make such a bloody mouthful of it as you. You must be his brother. Get in before the cops come.'

They entered a narrow hallway stinking of damp and boiled cabbage. He opened a door and Brendan saw an attractive girl of eighteen cleaning the wound on Art's head.

137

'You okay, Verschoyle?' the man asked.

Art grimaced, but nodded.

'Leave his skull alone for a minute, sis. He has a visitor.'

Art looked up to see Brendan holding a suitcase. He shook his head, annoying the girl who scolded him for not keeping it still.

'What are you doing here?' Art demanded. 'You've run away from school, haven't you? You bloody fool.'

'Why am I a fool?' Brendan was aggrieved.

'Because they'll blame me in Donegal for this as well. They'll say I encouraged you.'

'I didn't think you cared what anyone thought?'

'Of course I care. You're my baby brother.'

'Well, you're wrong. Firstly, it has nothing to do with you, and secondly, I did not run away. I walked at my own pace. I gave Father my word to stay until I was sixteen. I am now a free man.'

'You're a child. They'd never forgive me for harbouring you.'

The girl lifted a bloodstained rag away from the wound and surveyed it. 'Not too deep. You're lucky. It was one soft baton or you have one hard head. Has your brother really run away from a posh boarding school? Funny, my ambition was always to run away *to* one.'

'As what?' her brother laughed, lighting a cigarette. 'A cleaning lady?'

'I have brains, you know, though God knows I must have lost them to start helping out your ragtail socialist friends. Are you saying I couldn't hold my own in a class of posh bitches? I'd knock them dead. Now give me a ciggie.'

Art smiled at Brendan. 'This is Ruth Davis. She's been running a virtual field hospital in this kitchen all week.'

Brendan nodded, slightly bashful under her gaze, then

attacked Art. 'Did I ask you to harbour me? I've asked nothing of you, though I'll take a bed for a few nights until I get sorted. Anyway, why send me pamphlets if you wanted me to believe in nothing? You opened my eyes and now what do you expect me to do? Stay in school and become a minion of the Empire?'

Art nodded, respecting his brother's intensity. 'All right. It's inbred in me to feel responsible. What will you do?'

'Live. All my life I've been sheltered. But I've never felt more alive than today. I want to dance.'

Art grimaced slightly and smiled. 'Forgive me if I don't waltz with you. My head is slightly sore.'

Satisfied that she had stemmed the bleeding, Ruth began to apply a makeshift bandage to Art's head. 'I'll dance,' she said. 'Any Saturday night. I like a man who dances. The problem with revolution is that there's too much talk and not enough dancing.'

'I saw you being hit,' Brendan confessed to Art. 'I wanted to join you but I was too scared.'

The girl snorted. 'You'd too much sense, more like.'

'Leave it out, Ruth,' her brother hissed.

'It's my kitchen, I'll say what I like.'

'Your time will come,' Art assured him. 'Today's battle was lost. There was no point in joining in.'

'There'll be another one tomorrow.'

'No.' Art went to touch his head and Ruth gently slapped his hand away. 'The workers are being betrayed. Ever since this strike started the Trades Union Congress have been seeking a compromise. They can't see that this is our chance to galvanise the proletariat into one huge push forward. If it happened in Russia it can happen here. But the lackeys are already looking for a way to capitulate. The miners will wind up standing alone again.'

'What would you have us do?' Ruth said. 'The strike is crumbling. If the TUC don't back down, ordinary workers will simply leave their unions. A compromise must be found.'

'I don't believe in compromise,' Art insisted.

'That's because hunger is a novelty for you.' She tilted his head to tie the bandage.

'If we lose this strike,' Art said, 'the revolution in England is finished before it has even begun.'

'Maybe I don't want a revolution,' Ruth snapped. 'I want a wage that lets me fill my belly and go out dancing at weekends with a good-looking fellow like your brother. If you want every girl in London to join your revolution then produce a hundred bashful lads like him.' She laughed teasingly. 'I believe he's blushing. What's his name?'

'My name is Brendan,' Brendan said, annoyed that his cheeks were red.

'You're probably not used to girls in boarding school, Brendan. You might not know one end of us from the other. Are you sticking around London or tramping off to Russia like your brother?'

Brendan stared at Art. 'Are you going to Russia?'

'If there's nothing to fight for here. I want to see it for myself like Ffrench did. But I'll introduce you to people before I go.'

'I'll give him the guided tour,' Ruth teased. 'Parts he didn't even know existed.' She inspected her handiwork. 'I think you'll live with that thick skull of yours. Now scarper out the back way before my father comes in.' She looked at Brendan. 'You are a bloody fool. Go back to school and learn sense. He'll lead you astray.'

Brendan smiled. 'Maybe I want to be led astray.'

'You have my address.'

Brendan held her gaze so that it was she who blushed. 'What age are you?' he asked.

'Eighteen. Old enough to know not to cradle snatch.'

'I climbed out of my cradle long ago.'

'You needn't think of climbing into mine. Still, you have nice manners and clean nails. I always knew I'd meet a man one day with clean nails. Keep your brother out of trouble until he gets home at least.' She turned to the man who had let Brendan in. 'Joe, give Art the loan of a cap: his own is covered in blood.'

They climbed over the scullery yard wall and dropped into an alleyway, with Art unsteady on his feet. Joe went to the corner and waved, indicating that no police were about.

The cap covered Art's wound and once they merged back into the crowds there was nothing suspicious about them beyond the contrast in their dress.

The broken glass had been swept up and blood on the cobbles was the only sign that an altercation had occurred. A bus passed unhindered. The *British Gazette* was right after all in that the strike was crumbling. But correct about nothing else. Maybe this strike was not the decisive moment but a dress rehearsal like the 1916 Rising had been in Dublin.

Art was sombre, but Brendan did not know how to be downhearted. He could remember being carried on Art's back along the stones on Mr Ffrench's pier and it felt good now to stride beside him through these London streets, two grown men and comrades, desperadoes avoiding the law.

Art stopped at a doorway and led the way up four flights of stairs to a tiny attic flat. He indicated the patch of floor that was the only place where Brendan could sleep, then asked Brendan to excuse him while he lay on the bed. Brendan knew that his brother's head was throbbing, although Art did not complain. Art turned his face to the wall and Brendan sat quietly on his suitcase so as not to

141

disturb him. Tomorrow he would write to Father and begin to make plans. But for now he just wanted to sit and stare out of this attic window at the London streets that seemed to stretch away for ever like the infinite possibilities of his future.

# TEN

# *The Turf Cutters*

*Donegal, 12 September 1927*

Mr Goold Verschoyle had not set foot in the police headquarters in Donegal town since the day in 1919 when he
went to pay his respects to the Royal Irish Constabulary
sergeant shot dead by the IRA in front of his children. The
crest and uniform had changed since then, but the Free State
civic guard sergeant who knocked on the Manor House door
was a similar decent type to his slain predecessor. It was hard
to believe that he had been a guerrilla desperado hiding in
the hills less than a decade before.

Civil war hatred still simmered and remnants of the
Diehards had assassinated the Vice-President of the Free State
Executive two months ago as he walked home from Mass.
Special courts had been established in response to this atrocity,
but generally there were few signs of trouble and none in
Donegal until Art returned home two days ago for his sister's
wedding and met up with Mr Ffrench.

To minimise the attention that his presence would attract,
the sergeant had left his bicycle at the Dunkineely barracks.
Mr Goold Verschoyle was grateful for his discretion because
the Manor House was crowded with wedding guests, with

more staying nearby at Hill's Hotel. The sergeant explained the situation in a low voice and Mr Goold Verschoyle thanked the man for directly approaching him, although aware that this diplomacy would also ensure a lift and so save the sergeant a long cycle up into the hills. The sergeant declined his offer to wait inside the house, saying that he would return to the local barracks.

Mr Goold Verschoyle entered the morning room where his wife sat. Thankfully, Maud had returned home to ensure that the wedding progressed smoothly but his wife remained stressed, not least due to her worries about the suitability of Eva's suitor who was currently reading the *Irish Times* in a deckchair in the garden, unaware of being observed from their window. The local children who had been playing on the tennis court when Mr Goold Verschoyle went to answer the front door were gone.

'Your future son-in-law has a worrying temper,' his wife announced quietly. 'He flew into a frightful rage when the children disturbed him. He doesn't approve of us allowing the locals free rein. I'm not quite sure he approves of anything we do. Isn't it terrible, Tim? I'm handing my daughter into the hands of a man whom I like less the more I see of him.'

'He loves Eva,' her husband said. 'Love goes a long way.'

'He was not thinking of love when he drove such a hard bargain with his solicitor for the marriage settlement.'

'At least he takes an interest in money,' Mr Goold Verschoyle replied, rather half-heartedly. 'Sometimes I wish that at least one of our children did. I have to go out in the motor.'

'Now?' Mrs Goold Verschoyle turned. 'Why?'

'Some things to sort out. I'll get Thomas to drive.' He didn't want to say more and she knew not to coerce him into white lies.

He was relieved that his future son-in-law had not heard the sergeant's knock. The rest of his wedding party were out shooting. He called Thomas and the boy, now a Trinity student, knew from his expression that there was trouble. They got the car and drove to the barracks.

Dunkineely was suspiciously quiet and he knew that people had retreated indoors to get a better view of what was occurring from behind their curtains. The sergeant waited in the doorway with his local counterpart. Mr Goold Verschoyle was relieved when only one of them climbed into the back of the motor, which suggested that arrests were not being considered, at least for now. The local civic guard stood watching the car drive out of sight. Mr Goold Verschoyle knew that once they were gone, doors would open with local people emerging to speculate about what was happening.

Thankfully, the local policeman would feel it beneath his station to gossip. Mr Goold Verschoyle admired this unarmed force – which the locals called the *Garda Síochána* – who had taken possession of the RIC barracks while the civil war was ongoing and slowly won people's respect. Since de Valera had ordered his supporters to bury their weapons, sandbags no longer fortified the barracks. Police life had settled into a routine of summonses being served for petty offences and the cat-and-mouse game of trying to stamp out illicit whiskey-making. Thankfully the sergeant in the car was no promotion seeker looking for the attention of his Dublin masters. Maybe the fact of having seen so much fighting made him anxious for common sense to prevail.

Summer had once been the highlight of Mr Goold Verschoyle's year, with his family returning from boarding schools and friends joining them for picnics, but now he dreaded having all five siblings under one roof. Last Christmas was marked by rows between Art, Thomas and Maud over

Brendan leaving school. His youngest son looked remarkably happy since settling in London where he worked by day, studied electrical engineering at night and already seemed to possess more friends than Art. At Easter the rows had been about Art selling family heirlooms to donate the proceeds to the newly-founded Communist Party of Ireland which Mr Ffrench supported. Since their time in Russia the Ffrenches were evangelical in their praise of Comrade Stalin's redistribution of wealth, with Mr Ffrench cursing his misfortune at being forced to leave Moscow to receive the medication which Imperialist doctors withheld from their Bolshevik brothers.

Mr Goold Verschoyle didn't know if it was Ffrench who had lured Art out this morning or if it was Art who was a bad influence on his neighbour. Although Art had sworn to be on his best behaviour, Thomas – who also visited Bruckless House last night – said that they had ignited each other's passions when discussing a letter in the *Donegal Democrat* from Mr Henderson, a local big farmer. Henderson's letter accused the Free State government of Bolshevik sympathies in the compulsory provisions in the new School Attendance Bill. He demanded that these provisions not be applied to children of agricultural labourers because taxpayers' money was wasted by keeping them in school until fourteen and it hindered the supply of cheap young labour. Henderson paid the worst wages of any Donegal farmer, allowing his men just twenty-nine shillings a week to keep their families alive.

Art had left home early this morning and his father would not have known his whereabouts if word hadn't reached the sergeant about two men being seen in the fields urging farm workers to join the Transport Union.

The sergeant was too shrewd to discuss their mission as Thomas drove up lanes so deeply rutted that Mr Goold Verschoyle wondered if the axle might break. Instead he talked about old cures his grandfather had sworn by and which he still believed had great merit. That the lick of a dog's tongue provided great healing for a cut and a cobweb placed over it helped to freeze the blood. Whenever they passed men working in the fields, Thomas would stop and the sergeant got out to talk to them before giving Thomas fresh directions. Eventually they had to abandon the car and take to the bog on foot. They heard the commotion long before they saw anyone. Eight of Henderson's men must have been sent to cut turf, but work was suspended while the labourers pelted wet sods at the crude bothy hut where Mr Ffrench and Art had taken shelter. The turf workers stopped as the sergeant approached. Sods littered the bothy entrance. An old man had piled a pitchfork with smouldering straw as if planning to smoke out the two men. He dropped the straw and two younger labourers sheepishly stamped on it. The sergeant was brisk.

'What's happening here, men?'

The workers were quiet. Few were willing to look Mr Goold Verschoyle in the eye, especially those he had defended for free in court. One man who still held a turf sod dropped it with a shake of his head. 'Begging your pardon, Mr Tim, and no disrespect on you or your family, but we were mightily provoked. They came at us from nowhere with rigmarole and blasphemy. We were only trying to protect our souls.'

'I know, Seanie. There's no harm done.'

'There will be if they ever come back,' a second man said, emboldened now. 'I'd sooner take soup in church than poison my soul listening to their talk. There'll be hell to pay when the priest finds out. Father Danaher is a hard man and he'll make out we were up to something.'

'Aragh, we were up to nothing beyond mischief,' a sandy-haired young man interrupted. 'And what were they saying

– only what we're never done blathering about ourselves? That we're paid lousy, that Henderson is a bag of guts who treats his cattle better than us, that after a life of work all that will await us is the County Home.'

'That's enough,' the old man with the pitchfork said.

'You've said it yourself often enough, Seanie.'

'What we say amongst ourselves is a different class of matter entirely to what we have to listen to. I already spend half the year working in Scotland. There'll be no work left for me here at all if Henderson finds out what's been happening on his land.'

'Who says it's *his* land?' Art emerged from the bothy hut with Mr Ffrench who looked rather shaken. 'You are the men who work it and your fathers before you. Why are his sons fat and your sons in rags?'

'My grandfather worked this same land for your great-grandfather,' the old man replied, 'and he made Henderson look like a decent Christian. You've no rights to this land any longer, so you can stop your notions of bossing us about.'

The sergeant intervened, urging the labourers to move away. 'It would be better for you all to let the gentry sort this out while you clear up those sods before Henderson flays the marrow from your bones.'

Mr Goold Verschoyle approached Art, reasoning in a low voice. 'Your sister is getting married tomorrow. Half the village is calling in tonight. You swore there would be no trouble for her sake.'

Mr Ffrench interrupted. 'We were causing no trouble, Tim, merely telling these men what their rights are.'

Mr Goold Verschoyle eyed him coldly. 'This is between me and my son, Ffrench. You are not part of my family and I curse the day I was foolish enough to take you into our company.'

'That's not fair,' Mr Ffrench protested.

'Neither is life, as you're fond of pointing out. Is it fair that you brought mayhem into our lives by poisoning the mind of *my* son and heir? What do you intend leaving him?'

'That's your problem, Father,' Art said. 'Can you not see the reactionary way that money has warped your brain? I don't wish to be left things I have not earned. Do you ever look beyond your nose?'

'Perhaps I can't afford to, with five children to consider, including a daughter being married tomorrow.'

'To a fool, to the narrow-minded product of a fatally diseased class. He's highly unsuitable for Eva's temperament and you know it.'

'I know that he proposed and it was Eva's decision alone to accept him. I also know that her pool of eligible men was considerably reduced by the reluctance of many families to be associated with us since your little spell in an English jail following the General Strike.'

'Say what you will, but, as her eldest brother, I do not approve.'

'If you love her then why are you out here making us the talk of Donegal?' Thomas demanded, and pointed at Art's companion. 'With this hypocrite.'

Art squared up to his brother. 'Ffrench is a good man.'

'Is he?' Thomas refused to step back so that it looked like they were about to strike each other. 'Then why has he more servants mollycoddling him now than before he went away to Moscow?'

'Not servants! Fellow workers!' Mr Ffrench interjected. 'If I did not employ them they would be forced to emigrate to Scotland. I see no reason to be attacked for keeping Irish families at home.'

'You're a fairground attraction,' Thomas said bitterly. 'Along with the crab apple stalls and quacks selling cures for rheumatism. With your unfortunate wife forced to hand out leaflets to any illiterate who stumbles into her path.'

'Leave my wife alone,' Mr Ffrench hissed, incensed.

'And you do the same to mine,' Mr Goold Verschoyle said, shocking both his sons into silence.

'What exactly are you insinuating?'

'That your recent attentions are neither appreciated nor returned. Your hobbies may stray from cabinet-making to acquiring sons by proxy, but my good lady wife shall not be your newest fad to covet.'

Mr Ffrench bristled. 'Except that I am an officer I would strike you.'

'Except that I am a pacifist I would have horse-whipped you years ago.'

'Gentlemen, gentlemen!' the sergeant who had kept his distance intervened. 'Mr Goold Verschoyle, please, my point in bringing you here was to avoid trouble. If there are disputes between the gentry haven't you got high walls to settle them behind? I was counting on you to show some example.'

Mr Goold Verschoyle became aware of the labourers observing proceedings from a distance. Their anger at Art was defused by amusement at the notion of the quality publicly quarrelling. He was shocked by his own lapse in behaviour, even though he had been observing Mr Ffrench's attempt at over-familiarity with his wife for months now. He needed to take control and keep these events quiet until the newlyweds drove away after the celebrations tomorrow. At least it was better for the two brothers to argue out here in the open, rather than in front of Eva's future in-laws.

He looked at Art. 'Will you come home? And cause no further trouble until your sister is married?'

'I didn't start trouble. I simply came here to speak with these men.'

Mr Goold Verschoyle turned to the sergeant. 'I take it there will be no charges.'

'That depends on how far away your son is willing to travel after the wedding.'

'Am I to be banished?' Art demanded. 'What sort of a Free State is this?'

'One where you were free to have your say with these men.' The sergeant glanced back at the scattered sods near the bothy door. 'And they were free to give you their reply. Be a decent man and go home because they don't want you out here. And maybe after the wedding you'd take yourself off to Dublin where it would not be my responsibility to lock you up for disturbing the peace.' He looked over Art's shoulder. 'Oh, merciful God, look who's coming.'

Mr Goold Verschoyle followed his gaze and saw Henderson stride across the bog with his two sons. All three carried shotguns. The labourers shifted uneasily.

Henderson fired a warning shot in the air, then saw the sergeant and held up a restraining hand to prevent his sons doing likewise.

'You're trespassing,' he roared. 'Every man of yous is trespassing! Are you going to stand there, sergeant, with your gob hanging open? Arrest them, you hear me! They've little enough right to still remain in Ireland and damn all right to be on my land.' He addressed his labourers. 'And you lot needn't think I don't know you've been plotting against me, organising communist meetings on my time and my land. Do you think the sun shines out your arses and you can't be replaced? I'd have a queue of men here in the morning ready to do your jobs with no whining. I'm giving every name here to the priest.'

'I'm handling this, Henderson,' the sergeant said.

The farmer snorted. Everyone knew that he had been a de

Valera supporter until de Valera deserted the IRA Diehards and started his own party, Fianna Fáil. Henderson's most venomous attacks in the *Donegal Democrat* letters page were now on de Valera for being a turncoat who legitimised the Free State and abandoned the Republican ideal by taking the oath of allegiance and leading Fianna Fáil onto the opposition benches in the Irish parliament. However his true ire was reserved for men like the sergeant who had sided with the new state during the civil war. 'I'll go to someone with authority,' he sneered, 'not a jumped-up quisling traitor!'

'And what did you do during the war with England, Henderson?' the sergeant retorted. 'If you want your idle lumps of sons to do something useful they could carry down the bed you hid under when I was fighting the British in the hills.'

'I never sold out to the British in no treaty,' Henderson roared.

'That didn't stop you selling their troops stringy, over-priced turnips. You'd sell souls to Cromwell if he passed this way.'

'Hold me back,' Henderson roared, 'or your Free State quisling uniform won't be enough for you to hide behind. These foreigners are trespassing. Will you arrest them or not?'

'The gentlemen are just leaving,' the sergeant replied, with studied calmness. 'I must ask you to hold your tongue or the only arrest here will be for breach of the peace.'

'Are you threatening me in front of my own men and a pack of communist Freemasons?' Henderson raised his shotgun, infuriated by the sense that he was being made to look foolish.

'It's not the first time I've looked down the barrel of a gun,' the sergeant said, 'and so little has changed that some mornings now I wondered why I bothered. If our Saviour was born in a stable on your lands, Henderson, He'd pray for Calvary.' He turned. 'If you'd follow me now please, gentlemen.'

Mr Goold Verschoyle walked beside the sergeant with his two sons following in silence and Mr Ffrench behind them. He sensed Henderson watching them and heard his frustrated roar at the workmen. 'God blast you! What are you pack of lazy bastards doing standing there? There's work to do and you can stay an extra hour to finish it.'

They reached the car. The sergeant got into the passenger seat beside Thomas, while Art sat in the back between his father and Mr Ffrench. They drove in a terse silence before Mr Goold Verschoyle leaned forward.

'Thank you for the way you handled that, sergeant.'

'It will be bad for your family if Henderson poisons the new priest into denouncing your son from the pulpit. You are well respected here. That could change.' He looked at Art. 'Do you want this for your parents?'

'Did you think of your parents when you were fighting in the hills?' Art replied.

'No. My only thought was for an Irish Republic. The roof was burnt over their heads twice and I thought it worth the sacrifice because they would be revered for their suffering when we won. But my father never lived to see that. The second time he lost everything he turned his face to the wall. The British were watching the cottage – or the ruins of it – hoping to catch me if I was lured into visiting him when he was dying.'

'Do you regret fighting?'

'If we did nothing we regret, there'd be no point in being young. One day you will regret making a holy show of yourself just now on that bog. I regret that I never quite knew exactly what I was fighting for. We were idealistic, with a vision of freedom, but you can't feed a family with a vision. We imagined that there would be a new tomorrow where everything would be different, but young people think that in every generation.'

'You were right to fight,' Art insisted. 'Lenin said: *Not a single problem of the class struggle has ever been solved in history except by violence.* Your problem was in mistaking the enemy for an occupying nation when it was really an oppressive class.'

The sergeant shook his head. 'My problem, sonny, is that every morning from my window I see the children of the murdered RIC sergeant who once sat at my desk. His sons are growing up to become the spit of the man I looked up to when I was a boy.'

'Did you kill him?'

The sergeant coldly stared at Art. 'That's a question that maybe a man could ask another man in fifty years' time or a son could ask his father on his deathbed. But, seeing as you ask, the answer is no. However, every day I see the man who did and the sergeant's children see him too. That's in the past. I'm pledged to uphold the law, not question it. In my first month in this uniform I had to arrest workers who blockaded Henderson's farm in protest at their conditions. Aye, and lock up a Dublin bigmouth from the Transport Union trying to organise them. I didn't like doing it because I didn't fight for the likes of Henderson. But I did it because it was the law and, as revolutionaries go, we were the most conservative revolutionaries in the history of this planet. So I'll lock you up just as quick for disturbing the peace if you open your stupid gob around here again.'

'Then you'll have to lock me up,' Mr Ffrench insisted. 'I

remain true to my beliefs and refuse to be silenced. So don't think you can intimidate me.'

'I wouldn't bother trying,' the sergeant said. 'I look into your eyes, Mr Ffrench, and see a man who imagines he is a revolutionary. I look into the eyes of your young friend and see someone who imagines he is Jesus. If the lad insists on looking for nails for his own cross then I'm going to make sure he doesn't find them in Donegal.'

They sat in momentary silence as Thomas navigated a bend where most of the road surface had been washed away.

'You all think me a hypocrite.' Mr Ffrench spoke quietly. 'Especially you, Thomas. Maybe you're right, but maybe that's not such a terrible thing. If we are born under any star sign it is the sign of contradiction, with our nature pulling us in a dozen ways at once. Some days I want to return to Russia, but I won't do so because my wife was unhappy there, surrounded by children when life has blessed us with none. Maybe the revolution was too big and new for an old sea dog like me to learn or maybe I still dream of building a New Jerusalem in these hills.' He looked past Art towards Mr Goold Verschoyle. 'You ask what I intend to leave Art, Tim. He seems to reject all that you wish to leave him, yet he has inherited your character, your absolute sense of right and wrong. What I would wish to leave him are the contradictions we need to acknowledge within ourselves to make the necessary compromises by which we each live.'

The sergeant glanced back at Art. 'Does your sister still like Protestant hymns?'

Art looked up, surprised. 'Were you in that cottage years ago?'

'My brother cycled for miles to find those gramophone records. The cottage was burnt out afterwards, though we knew it wasn't you who gave the old couple away.'

'What happened to the IRA officer in charge?'

'He died in the civil war in a Longford wood. Free State lads who worshipped the ground he walked on pleaded with him to come out and drop his revolver. He charged at them, screaming threats and waving his gun. They'd no choice but to shoot. Afterwards they found a pile of bullets among the trees where he emptied the pistol in advance. They never told the priest in case he refused to bury him as a suicide.'

'He was a brave man,' Art remarked.

'He was a bloody fool.' The sergeant turned back. 'If he had waited another two days he would have read de Valera's order to surrender. He achieved nothing, like you achieved nothing today. Henderson will sack every one of those labourers. They'll starve or have to make new lives for themselves in Scotland.'

'But they did nothing,' Art protested. 'They refused to listen to one word we said. They even attacked us.'

'That doesn't matter. His authority was challenged, his ownership of the land. He'll sack them to show you who is master around here now. He sees you as an interfering Protestant still trying to tell him what to do with it.'

'The bastard.'

'Finish your sentence, sonny. The bastard upstart.'

'That's not what I mean.'

'Maybe not, but every time you open your mouth that's how it sounds like. Go away and let him think that he's won. Then just maybe he won't do it.'

'Don't worry,' Art said. 'Very soon I plan to be in Moscow.'

'That's what you keep saying,' Thomas taunted, 'but you never get around to going.'

'Stop the car!' Art demanded suddenly.

'That's typical.' Thomas braked. 'The first home truth and you walk off in a sulk.'

'I'm not walking anywhere. Wait.' Art climbed out and scrambled up the hillside to where a clump of purple wild flowers grew. He gathered up a huge handful, then returned to the car. 'Eva will love these, they'll brighten up her room.' He looked at Thomas. 'What's keeping you? We have a sister getting married, you know.'

They drove on, dropping Mr Ffrench off at the entrance to Bruckless House and leaving the sergeant at the barracks in Dunkineely. The three of them were alone then, saying little because nobody wished to breach the truce they were determined to observe for Eva's sake. The back garden was empty when they parked in the coach house, but Eva came out from the kitchen, looking so happy and exhilarated that all three men shared an identical fear for her future.

'Where were you?' she asked. 'You all vanished. People have already started to call in. It's all so exciting!'

'I was getting you wild flowers.' Art presented them to her. 'Take some with you when you leave tomorrow so that when you wake up as a married woman you can look at the vase and think of Donegal and how we love you.'

Mr Goold Verschoyle watched his three children enter the kitchen, with Eva dwarfed between her two brothers. He felt drained but these days he always felt this way. He did not want to contemplate the loneliness of life here when Eva was gone. Disaster had been averted, for now at least. Pulling himself together, he practised a smile and walked indoors to greet his neighbours.

# ELEVEN

# The Two Fredericks

## Donegal, 13 September 1927

From the moment she woke at dawn on the morning of her wedding and saw Art's gift of wild flowers, Eva longed to go walking along the narrow lane to the Bunlacky shore. But she could not vanish, even during this half-hour before anyone else woke. Now that she was virtually a married woman, Eva had responsibilities. She stared at the empty bed where Maud once slept and recalled the excitement of her sister's wedding three months ago, with guests squeezing Eva's arm and saying how much they looked forward to her own big day. The weeks since then had been thrilling, but she would have still loved the chance to spend some final moments as a girl wandering by her beloved shore.

No doubt she would often return to Dunkineely, but things would feel different when this room no longer belonged to her. Marriage changed you and changed how people perceived you. This was obvious in the way in which Maud held herself and the increased respect shown to her. Being a married woman was different in more ways than just in the night-time business that girls whispered about. It was about waking up every morning to share joys and concerns as you charted life together.

There could be no greater adventure and Eva looked forward to savouring every aspect of it, because she truly believed that opposites always attracted. When she next woke up, she would still be herself and yet would have become someone different, equal in status to her mother and sister.

These two weddings would complete her parents' duty towards Maud and Eva. Frequently over the past five years they had rented houses in Dublin so that suitable young men could help the sisters disembark from trams in the ruins of O'Connell Street and be escorted to the Abbey Theatre. Eva had been thrilled one night to notice William Butler Yeats appear at a side door during the curtain raiser, his white shock of hair visible as he scanned the near-deserted auditorium in what seemed a mystic trance. It took her pragmatic escort to point out that, as the theatre's business manager, Yeats was simply reconciling the number of patrons present with the box office returns.

This summed up Eva's problem. Her escorts were generally too pragmatic – focused on working their passage through the closed hierarchy within the Protestant fraternity of Dublin firms – and Eva was too free-floating and fanciful to prove more than an exotic diversion in their quest for practical wives. Maud enjoyed more suitors, although her fiercely independent thinking shocked some potential mothers-in-law and scared off young men who preferred women on pedestals rather than on platforms. Still, in an age of upheaval, Maud's steely character was valued.

Last spring Father had arranged for Eva to visit galleries in Italy and Germany in the hopes of resurrecting her ambition to be an artist, but inwardly she felt lost with no clear vision to sustain her as the clock ticked into her mid-twenties. Therefore when two suitors undertook the long trek to Dunkineely to visit the sisters last summer, Eva had sensed

a chance to grasp at something tangible and uncompli-
cated. Today, her wedding would complete that transfor-
mation.

Eva rose from bed, stripped off her nightgown and filled
the basin with cold water. She would bathe properly later
before the fuss commenced about her dress. She washed slowly
now, closing her eyes to imagine a hand touching her breast
tonight for the first time. Her eyes quickly reopened when
the hand she suddenly envisaged belonged to the New Zealand
officer who had once courted her. This upset Eva because
she loved her husband-to-be and he loved her. They shared the
same dreams and would be happy together, so why did
she have to remember Jack on this morning? It was nerves,
she decided.

A knock came to the door and she slipped back on her
nightgown before saying, 'Come in.'

Agnes, the young chambermaid, entered with a tray. 'I
brought you a cup of tea. I knew you'd be awake, Miss Eva.
I could barely sleep myself with the excitement. Cook is
banging away at the pots and pans downstairs, planning
enough breakfast to feed a regiment. How are you?'

'I'm fine, Agnes.'

'I believe that Master Thomas will play the bagpipes in
his kilt all the way from the church back to the house for
the wedding breakfast. The whole village will be cheering.
Have some tea before the world lands in on top of you. Did
you think I should bring . . .' The girl stopped, knowing that
the title *Miss Maud* was now incorrect. '. . . the newlyweds
up something?'

'Let them lie on.' Eva imagined Maud and her husband
entwined in the bed where Jack had once slept.

'Aye, I will. I just wanted to say good luck to you and say
that we'll all miss you sorely about the place.'

The girl seemed near tears as she left the room before Eva could reply.

The house would seem empty with both daughters gone. Mother and Father were lucky in being perfect company together, constantly chatting and still fascinated by each other. But Art rarely visited and trouble followed when he did. Mother could not bear to think ill of her son, while Father generally restrained his comments to observing that each man deserved the right to make his own mistakes. The only brother who seemed genuinely happy last night was Brendan, despite him being a source of friction between the others. Eva prayed there would be no rows today. Her brothers had sworn to do nothing to disrupt proceedings and she knew that they would keep their word because they loved her.

Eva opened the shutters to survey the empty main street. Chinese lanterns still hung in front of the house after last night's party when almost every soul in the village had called to examine the presents and wish her luck. Local farmers came in Sunday suits along with visitors from as far as Ardara. Even Mr Henderson, who rarely seemed friendly, had knocked on the door and apparently spent half an hour passing on his good wishes through Father in the study, though he was too shy to do so in person among the crowds in the drawing room. Most Protestants present had stayed aloof from any political discussions, beyond agreeing with the Pope's pronouncement that, having survived another assassination attempt in Rome, Il Duce enjoyed divine protection. Sensing Art about to deliver a counterview, Maud had interrupted the discussion by placing on the gramophone a copy of *Ain't She Sweet*, which a guest had brought from London. Eva's happiest moment had been when Phil Floyd, the local sweet-shop owner, presented her with a cone-shaped twist of paper brimming with sweets, like the ones she had bought from him as a child with her pocket money.

A child crossed the street now with a bucket and the pump's clank heralded the new day as people started to appear. Samuel Trench emerged from the Manor Lodge to cut the flowers he was carefully tending for the wedding. His daughter would help today in the house. Eva wondered if Art remained sweet on her. Such secret infatuations seemed part of child-hood whereas marriage was a sober business. She knew this because of the time it took Father to hammer out a marriage settlement with her husband-to-be and his solicitor from the Dublin firm of Moore, Keily and Lloyd. Eva did not know the details, but both parties had seemed content when the brandy was uncorked to seal it.

Her wedding arrangements had been quick in the end, because, after Maud's betrothal, a second marriage seemed the natural and correct course of action. By contrast, last summer's courtship had been a leisurely, rather thrilling period of shadowboxing. Jokes were written in the visitors' book about the two Fredericks sharing the long train journey from Dublin. Frederick Cunningham was first to come, ostensibly to court Maud, but distinctions grew blurred amidst that summer's gaiety, especially when Freddie Fitzgerald began to visit her and they all went for picnics together.

Freddie was a young mathematics teacher in a Protestant school in Dublin who talked constantly about transforming Glanmire House, his currently empty ancestral house in a small Mayo wood, into a shooting guesthouse that would sustain a family. He was one of the Turlough Fitzgeralds, though from a poorer branch than his uncle who owned the huge mansion called Turlough Park. Freddie came into his own when outdoors, with a humour that made both sisters laugh. Due to his club foot Freddie rarely swam, but Frederick

Cunningham was a superb swimmer. Eva would race him in the sea, enjoying his powerful, intelligent presence beside her, and emerge to spy Maud and Freddie on the sand, heads bent together laughing at some joke. Within weeks Eva had reached the dangerous conclusion that she loved Frederick Cunningham almost as much as she had loved the New Zealand officer, only now she was a woman who understood her feelings. Watching Maud and Freddie Fitzgerald clown about, she had concocted a fantasy where they both fell in love and she was left to console Frederick Cunningham.

Looking back, she realised that this was her problem, a tendency to retreat into fantasy and imagine that life should proceed in the way she wished it to. Even when Maud rushed into their bedroom to announce Frederick's proposal of marriage, for an instant Eva had convinced herself that Maud meant Freddie Fitzgerald. The realisation that Maud had merely been kind to Freddie all summer for Eva's sake had left Eva feeling deeply vulnerable. But her distracted attitude towards Freddie Fitzgerald had inflamed his desire. With Maud preoccupied by wedding plans, Freddie had courted her anew with such zeal that it had felt like she were only now looking beyond the disability of his bad leg to glimpse his soul. Slowly Eva grew to love Freddie's slightly lost-boyish nature, although his love for the outdoors was different from hers. Whereas Eva longed to sing the praises of every tiny scurrying creature, Freddie's desire was to blast them out of existence with an Eley Maximum snipe cartridge. But his opposite nature appealed to Eva, though she knew that Mother remained unconvinced. Here was a man who made her feel special and offered her a simple role to slip into. Her feelings for Freddie were different from those she had felt for Jack or Frederick. But perhaps this was what mature love felt like, instead of silly infatuation.

Freddie had shown her photographs of Glanmire House, and its winding woodland avenue looked beautiful. With her marriage settlement, they could live independently with a few servants to cater for the guests who would flock there for the best rough shooting in Ireland. Freddie had worked it out and as a mathematics teacher he understood figures. He made everything simple. During his visits Eva could cease wrestling to comprehend Mother's books on awakening the soul and discover the pleasure of wrestling with a man, one year her junior, who had never attempted to overstep unspoken limits until they were married.

The street outside was busy now, geese scattering everywhere as two civic guards cycled past in the direction of Bruckless. Most of Freddie's guests had already arrived. Eva's in-laws-to-be seemed very different from the Verschoyles. Their family scandal occurred over a century ago when Freddie's ancestor, mad George Robert Fitzgerald, had provoked duels with strangers, locked his father in a cave chained to a pet bear and formed his own Turlough militia. When they tried to hang him in Castlebar he had placed the noose around his own neck and leapt forward only for the rope to break. At the second attempt, his courage failed but the rope held firm. He had bequeathed to his descendants the appellation of *The Fighting Fitzgeralds*, but it was not signs of eccentricity which made Eva slightly uneasy in their company, but their narrow Anglo-Irish conformity.

The Fitzgeralds understood their social position and expected others to remember theirs. Therefore the practice of village children playing freely in the Manor House garden seemed to irritate poor Freddie. Still, Eva knew that his flash of temper yesterday had been to cloak his sensitivity. Thankfully Mother didn't see it but Eva had been watching from an upstairs window. Freddie had chosen to wear shorts

while reading the *Irish Times* in a deckchair, with a blanket
covering his legs. One village girl mis-hit a tennis ball, which
landed on Freddie's newspaper. Startled, he stood up, revealing
his club foot that the children had never previously seen. The
village girl's laughter had been a nervous reaction but it
enraged Freddie whose subsequent curses terrified the children. But this was just Freddie being nervous over the wedding
and acutely sensitive about his leg, imagining ridicule in any
casual reference to it. Eva was convinced he would lose this
trait with the confidence gained by having a wife, because
she could nurture his gentler side in Mayo.

The bedroom door opened suddenly and Mother stood there
smiling. 'Are you ready?' she asked and Eva nodded, not fully
sure what Mother was referring to. Ready to be dressed,
ready to leave home, ready for life as an adult. As a child
she had longed to know what sort of man she would marry,
imagining various gallant figures. None had possessed a club
foot, but it was the inner qualities that mattered, the love
people could radiate. Tomorrow she would finally be anchored
like the boat she had seen years ago out at sea.

She glanced at the cheap print of a child kneeling beside
a bed still hanging from the same nail. It had seemed too
childish an object to pack, yet she took it down to bring
with her to Mayo for courage.

'Let's get you started,' Mother said. 'We'll have you looking
beautiful. Maud is going to do your hair.'

Eva smiled and walked towards her, but Mother blocked
the doorway so that Eva had to halt. They did not embrace
because Mother never went in for embraces, but Eva could
feel her love and knew that Mother was reluctant to let her
cross the threshold to where a different life waited to claim
her.

'Father and I are always here for you, you know that?'

'Yes.'

'And even if you cannot come to me, you and I never needed words. If you think of me then I will know that you're in trouble and I'll pray for any problem which you cannot talk about.'

Eva smiled. 'Mother, Freddie and I love each other. We won't have problems.'

'I know. But mothers always worry. Strive to be a good wife and a good mother in time. But above all there is one thing you must never lose sight of. No matter what life deals you, promise me that you will strive tooth and nail for the right to be happy.'

'I will.'

Eva smiled again and Mother let her pass to where Maud waited on the landing with Agnes beside her. They beckoned, laughing and fussing about having so little time to get her ready, but saying that even in her nightgown she looked beautiful. Clutching the print, Eva glanced back at Mother who urged her on, then softly closed over the door of Eva's childhood room.

# TWELVE

## Eccles Street

### Dublin, March 1928

At eight o'clock the four Trinity students gathered opposite the Catholic Pro-Cathedral in Marlborough Street where the Men's Mission was taking place. Owen Sheehy-Skeffington had alerted Thomas to rumours of a march on Madame Despard's home in Eccles Street, which housed the Friends of Soviet Russia Society. Following last week's Mission, a Catholic mob had burnt out the Revolutionary Workers' Group's headquarters in Little Strand Street. Thomas was sick of public meetings being broken up by zealots from St Patrick's Anti-Communist League and the Catholic Young Men's Society. Within Trinity, most societies were dully conformist, with the Provost keen not to antagonise the Free State government who viewed the college as an enemy statelet. But a few radical minds still existed among the staunchly Unionist student body, chaps like Sheehy-Skeffington who argued for women's rights and risked blows by refusing to stand whenever the college band played *God Save the King*.

Grimes from the rowing club had come along as a lark, relishing any chance of a skirmish with the new Catholic state. He intended following his father into the British army and was unable to take anything outside the college walls seriously, convinced that at the first bad harvest the Free State would lapse into famine, with the London government forced to step back in. The fourth student, Foster, was more serious, aware of the danger of assault and expulsion, but determined to make a stand.

'Last week every policeman between here and Little Strand Street turned a blind eye,' Sheehy-Skeffington said. 'The mob knelt on the road saying the rosary to prevent the fire brigade saving the building whilst the Redemptorists were tucked up in their presbyteries disclaiming all knowledge of the attack.'

'Surely they won't actually attack Madame Despard,' Grimes said. 'I mean she stood shoulder to shoulder with Sinn Fein during their rebellion. Her own brother, as Viceroy, had to arrest her for treason.'

'She was a suffragette long before she became a Shinner,' Thomas reminded him. 'And a Protestant before she turned communist. Those are sins the priests won't forget.'

The mission ended and men began to descend the church steps, donning their hats. Most slipped away but the hard core who lingered glanced over at Thomas and his companions, sensing their foreignness. A priest emerged to address the men, with some bolder women in the shadows coming forward. A cheer arose and a bareheaded man shouted, *God Bless our Pope*. His words were taken up as a chant. A barefoot girl tugged at Thomas's sleeve, begging for a few coppers. When he looked up, the priest was gone and the men had suddenly organised themselves into ranks moving towards Eccles Street.

Even Grimes looked cowed by the size of the mob. But Thomas knew that Grimes would not turn back because – despite Madame Despard having renounced her class and squandered her wealth on the Dublin poor – for him she remained an elderly English aristocrat who needed protection from the lower orders she was trying to befriend.

Initially the students walked behind the mob but as it stopped outside tenements to exhort others to join, they managed to slip up North Great George's Street and reach the terrace of tall Georgian houses first. Eccles Street was crowded, with people anticipating trouble. Thomas spied James Connolly's son, Roddy, push through the throng to enter Madame Despard's home, protected from assault, at least for now, by his late father's aura as an executed 1916 Rising martyr. The door closed as Thomas led the way up the steps. The marchers were approaching Dorset Street, their chants growing louder. Thomas knocked and the door opened a fraction as a young man eyed them.

'Bloody students. Run away home to your mothers, this will turn nasty.'

'Let me in.' Sheehy-Skeffington stepped forward. 'My mother is secretary of the Friends of Soviet Russia.'

The young man extended a hand in welcome. 'Sure, I have you now and your poor murdered father. Liam Hennessy is the name. Get inside quick and maybe you can persuade the old dame to escape out the back way. This is too dicey a conflagration for an eighty-five-year-old to sit around in taking her ease.'

A shout arose as Sheehy-Skeffington entered the hall. 'Bastard! Enemy of Christ! Look at him step on the host!'

A stone caused Thomas to turn as the others entered amid outraged jeers. 'Decide, comrade,' Hennessy hissed. 'Do you want to come in or not?'

Thomas stepped inside. 'I want to come in, but I'm not your comrade. Why are they shouting?'

'A priest said that we had put a consecrated host under the doormat so that everybody entering must step on the body of Christ. As if anything under a mat here would last two seconds. When the slum shawlies are not screeching for the old dame's blood they're queuing up to wheedle every penny from her. Head upstairs. There's twenty of us now. She expected more support but cold feet is a contagious disease.'

A printing press occupied the front room, beside stacked copies of *The Hammer and Plough*. People at the windows surveyed the crowd. Outside, the chanting stopped as marchers knelt for the rosary. Sheehy-Skeffington leaned over Madame Despard, a tiny frail figure dressed in black who sat with ramrod-straight shoulders and milky half-blind eyes. 'Who's this?' she asked. 'Come closer, young man.'

'I'm Thomas Goold Verschoyle.'

She nodded. 'Donegal. Your mother and I used to correspond about Theosophy. Such an interesting woman.'

'Might it not be wise, Madame,' Thomas said, 'to slip away and let us guard your house?'

'It might be wiser for you to slip away, young man.' Her voice was so weak that it was hard to catch each word, but the resolve, which made her one of Britain's most famous suffragettes, remained evident. 'It's me those misguided souls want to burn as a witch. But I shall build this world for them, even if it means my having to leave it. I am not afraid of the last great adventure.'

Thomas joined Grimes and Hennessy at the window. Locals attracted from the nearby slums were swelling the crowd. The murmured prayers could not disguise an impending sense of trouble. The bareheaded man knelt on the pavement to face the mob, leading the rosary with beads entwined between his fingers. Thomas sensed that he was no natural leader. Without one, it was impossible to judge how far this mob would go. Then Thomas saw a black-clad figure push through the throng with purposeful strides. He lacked the aura of a priest, but seemed like some sort of Christian Brother. Hennessy watched the figure approach.

'It wouldn't be much of a circus without a ringmaster,' he remarked.

'Who is he?' Thomas asked.

'I can't see his collar, mate.' Hennessy called back, 'Roddy, who's this geezer coming to drown us in holy water?'

James Connolly's son joined them, staring down as the crowd parted respectfully to let the cleric through. However one man who examined the cleric more closely rose to place a hand on his shoulder that was angrily shrugged off. Connolly laughed.

'Mother of God,' he said, 'that's Goold.'

'Who?' Thomas asked, with sudden foreboding.

'He used to hang around some of our political meetings. My sister and I thought he was a tramp at first. I think he slept rough in Mountjoy Square. Only when he started to heckle the speakers did we spot his educated accent. He occasionally sold copies of *The Hammer and Plough* for us. He turned up at a meeting I addressed last week looking worse than ever. I told him if he wanted to join the party he'd have to clean himself up. But where did he buy that outfit? He's from Sligo, I think.'

'Donegal,' Thomas said.

Connolly looked surprised. 'You know him?'

'He's Thomas's brother.' Sheehy-Skeffington joined the company. 'And that mob will lynch him if you don't let him in.'

Several men were attempting to rip Art's jacket. Thomas realised that it was an old postman's uniform, too small for his brother. A combination of bad light and a black collarless shirt inadvertently lent him a religious appearance.

Hennessy ran down to open the front door and after a

scuffle, Art was pulled inside. The incensed mob started a new chant: *Burn the Communists!* while several authoritative figures stepped forward, judging the situation sufficiently inflamed for them to seize control.

Hennessy led Art upstairs. He stopped upon entering the room, more shaken by Thomas's presence than by the mob outside.

'What are you doing here?' he demanded.

'You don't get to inherit the franchise on civil rights too,' Thomas retorted. 'Some of us came to defend free speech. Can we not at least agree that freedom is being strangled in this city? I may not belong in here, but I will never belong out there.' He glanced out of the window, with sudden anxiety. 'Good grief! It couldn't be?'

'Who?'

Thomas pointed to a well-dressed figure pushing through the crowd. 'Our big sister.'

'Maud?' Art looked out, like a disappointed child whose party was being gatecrashed. 'Maud is a married woman.'

'She has as much right to enter my house as you have.' The voice was feeble, but when the brothers turned, the tiny figure confronting them looked resolute and fiery.

'Forgive me, Madame Despard,' Art apologised. 'I didn't mean it that way. It just feels like I will never be free of my family following me.'

Thomas glared at him. 'I assure you, if I'd suspected you were coming I'd have stayed in college.'

'I know you,' Madame Despard said. 'I've seen you surrounded by children in Mountjoy Square only for a priest to scatter them with a stick and threaten you.'

'I set up a hedge school,' Art explained. 'I'd sit on a park bench writing letters on behalf of people who can't write themselves. I was teaching the three Rs and history and politics to anyone who'd sit with me but the priests put a halt to that.'

Maud's manner was granting her a passage through the crowd, convinced that nobody so well dressed could be a subversive. She strode up the steps past the ringleaders to bang on the knocker, disconcerting the crowd who realised that she had not come to join them after all. Thomas shouted at Hennessy.

'For God's sake, man, let my sister in.'

When they opened the front door several black-clad shawlies were clawing at Maud who had lost her hat but stood her ground, hectoring them. Art and Thomas reeled her in. She spun around, defiant, a fleck of blood on her lip where a nail had scratched her.

'Well, here we all are,' she said, unflappable as ever. 'One big happy family.'

'You shouldn't have come,' Art complained. 'You're not a communist.'

'A walk through these slums would make anyone consider becoming one. I never saw such squalor. Nobody should be forced to live like this, let alone attack an old woman trying to educate them. The conductor on the Kingstown tram boasted about the fire being planned by the Catholic Young Men's Society. I gave him a piece of my mind, then got off and walked here.' She inspected Art. 'You look ridiculous. Still I steadfastly defend the right of people to make fools of themselves. If that mob have their way anyone different will be swept into the Irish Sea. Is Madame Despard still here?'

Several stones struck the front door, with one crashing through the fanlight overhead.

'We can't persuade her to leave.' Hennessy made for the sanctuary of the stairs.

Maud followed Hennessy upstairs. 'I'll talk to her provided Art doesn't introduce my husband to his tailor.'

Grimes and Foster were busy gathering buckets of sand with other volunteers. Connolly moved quietly about preparing for the onslaught, as commanding as his wounded father must have been when rallying Dublin workers amid flames in the GPO.

'Stay back from the windows when the stones start to really fly,' he said. 'The important thing is to get fires under control quickly to try and save the building.'

The chanting was more frenzied outside: *Bless the Pope!* One man screamed himself hoarse trying to be heard over the noise: 'Go back to Russia, you poxy atheist Protestant English bitch!'

Thomas joined his siblings around Madame Despard's chair, as Maud pleaded with her to leave.

'Leave?' The old lady laughed. 'Why, dear, I like being at the centre of things. Your brother is such a fine man. I've seen him in Mountjoy Square.' She addressed Art. 'Go to Russia while you have your youth. You will be appreciated there. I have seen it with my own eyes, factories run by elected committees, schools where punishment is taboo. It is not just the dream of Marx come true, but the words of Shelley's *Revolt of Islam*. Shaw went, but, being a man, never asked the hard questions. I made them show me the collective farms which the peasant proprietors are starting to embrace.' Stones crashed through the downstairs windows without making her lose her flow. 'And there is no crime nor punishment. Those unfit to be good citizens are briefly isolated on self-governing archipelagos. But no ideas are forced on them: they are gently encouraged to think for themselves. Go there and learn what it is like to live in a land ruled by love.'

There was a whooshing sound of flame. Volunteers with

buckets rushed down the stairs. Hennessy and Connolly each took one leg of her chair, telling Grimes and Foster to lift the others. 'We're bringing you out the back way, Charlotte, whether you like it or not,' Connolly said.

'But I wanted to address them. I assure you I've faced hostile crowds all my life.'

'I'll face them for you.' Maud turned to Connolly. 'I'll keep them focused on the front and give you time to get her out.' She patted the old lady's hand. 'I'll give them a song.'

'Would you, dear?' Madame Despard's chair was hoisted in the air. 'Isn't life exciting?' She grasped Art's hand. 'See Russia for yourself.'

Maud strode towards the window. Thomas gripped her shoulder.

'Are you crazy? You can't go out there.'

Ignoring him as she used to ignore everyone once she got a notion into her head in Donegal, Maud stepped out onto the small wrought-iron balcony. She got her balance, then began to sing:

> 'The Workers' Flag is deeply red,
> It covered oft our martyred dead,
> And ere their limbs grew stiff and cold
> Their hearts' blood dyed its every fold.'

The crowd could not hear the words but this did not stop some screaming that she was a whore while others chanted *Bless the Pope* more fervently. Smoke billowed from the smashed windows below in the rooms where fires were blazing. Art and Thomas tried to pull her back inside and she hissed fiercely, 'Don't you dare.'

Thomas looked down at the mob, hungry for blood and hungry for food. At the barefoot children staring up as if they were devils. At the ignorance and superstition and malnutrition and stunted growth and those protesters who were fervent and others swept up by the occasion who would just as easily join any other mob. He clambered out to be beside Maud and, with a laugh, she interlocked her fingers with his and took Art's fingers in her other hand. The three never arranged to meet in Dublin, knowing that they would each bring a baggage of grievance and accusation with them but this balcony was neutral ground, where they could briefly be united by their collective difference from the baying mob. Thomas raised his voice defiantly and Art joined in too, the three of them singing with the sweet harmony that had once been praised in Killaghtee church.

*'Then raise the scarlet banner high,*
*Beneath its folds we'll live or die,*
*Though cowards flinch*
*And traitors sneer,*
*We'll keep the red flag flying here.'*

# THIRTEEN

## *Deep in the Woods*

### Mayo, September 1928

It was not the fact that Art had left for Russia which hurt her, but that he never said goodbye to any of them. Even a noviciate entering a monastery rarely denied himself a last farewell to those he loved. Because Eva knew that Art loved his family although he had never returned to Donegal after her wedding. Mother only learnt that he was in Moscow when Mr Ffrench received a letter last week from a friend there who had met him.

Freddie gently prised Mother's letter from Eva's hand and read the news for himself whilst his heavily pregnant wife gazed out of the drawing room window of Glanmire House to where Mikey, Freddie's man, stood by the car, patiently waiting to accompany his master to the station. Eva knew that Freddie would wet his lips in the select lounge of the Imperial Hotel in Castlebar before boarding the Dublin train.

'It's for the best for all of you,' Freddie announced. 'At least now he won't be able to disgrace you, or if he does he'll be so far away that it will not be in front of anyone who counts. And, you know, with Art gone, the young chap may buck up. It's not too late for Brendan to get into some decent

177

college. Oxford will hardly take him now, but only a fool judges a man by the colour of his school tie.'

Eva had often heard her husband repeat this line, carefully watching the company for any perceived slight about how he had lacked the money to attend a top public school.

Freddie was relieved by this news about Art, though they had only met briefly at the wedding, an awkward encounter between two men whom Eva loved. It now felt like years since Thomas had played the bagpipes in his kilt as Eva's wedding party wound through Dunkineely. Locals had cheered as barefoot children raced after the Wolseley that bore her away to Mayo, with bonfires marking her arrival in Turlough where the Fitzgeralds had reigned for centuries. Her books were still stored in a trunk with her canvasses and easel. They were things she seemed unable to unpack, being too busy trying to appear like a young Protestant wife of social standing. She fretted over invitations to tennis parties and dinners at Turlough Park held by Freddie's uncle on one of his trips back home. He found it cheaper to maintain his family in a rented French villa rather than upkeep his Irish mansion. An avenging mob had ransacked the original house after 'Mad' George Robert Fitzgerald's public hanging in 1786, leading to the hasty erection of Glanmire House as a stopgap family home until the grandiose splendour of a new house at Turlough Park was completed. Glanmire House was as large as the Manor House in Dunkineely, but it was impossible to live so close to Turlough Park without feeling in every way the poor relation.

Freddie handed her back the letter, too much of a gentleman to read beyond Mother's news about Art. 'Let's see if he lasts longer in Moscow than the other lunatic.'

'Mr Ffrench is nice,' Eva protested.

Freddie laughed, downing the dregs of whiskey in his glass.

'Your brother may be mad,' he said, 'but at least he sticks to his beliefs. Ffrench has four times more servants than we could ever afford. Surely a good communist can fetch in his own logs.'

'He was an ordinary factory worker in Russia.'

'He was play-acting. At the first sign of trouble he ran home to his servants. What do you think they make of him? A man must set an example for servants to look up to. Your father should have taken a whip to him, like the Marquess of Queensberry did to that bugger boy. Ffrench is a laughing stock, even almost the madness infecting Donegal.'

Despite his imminent departure to Dublin, Freddie could not leave this festering sore alone. His conversation frequently returned to her family's perceived madness. It was a blame game he played whenever his monthly accounts refused to add up. Eva forgave him, knowing the financial stress he tried to shield her from. Besides, their life together was not all accusation and counter-accusation. Great tenderness had peppered the previous thirteen months, moments when Eva felt truly fulfilled. Glanmire House had been burgled several times during the years it lay unoccupied. The carpets were rotting with damp on the night they consummated their marriage here, with the house unnaturally cold despite Freddie having fires blazing in the front hall and their bedroom. Later he had taken her on a lamp-lit tour of the single-storey Georgian-style villa with its meandering basement, proudly detailing his plans to install a hand pump to harness the water collected from a huge tank suspended on two masonry piers outside.

Over the past year there had been the excitement of seeing each refurbished room take shape. She remembered her anxiety before presiding over their first dinner for paying guests and her exhilaration afterwards. The morning when their heads touched, leaning over the blank ledger as Freddie recorded their first ever income received. There had been the planting of four thousand new trees to mark their marriage, with them both covered in muck, delighted to find an outdoor task in which they took equal pleasure. There were her solitary walks in the woods at dusk when no more shots were fired and she was torn between a fraternising desire to befriend the shy rabbits and an impulse to throw stones and teach them to mistrust humans before the insatiable hunter came with his gun. In Freddie's favour, he never used traps and she was glad because she could not have borne them. He was humane in his own way, which was just not a way she understood. But the most tender sensation of all was his seed inside her, this child whom they could share and love, who would bind any slight fissures starting to appear as they began to see each other clearly.

Freddie checked his watch, resisting the temptation for another whiskey. 'I'd best be off. The train will hardly wait for me, though God knows it would be a first if it left on time. You'll be okay, won't you?'

'The baby isn't due for three weeks.'

'I know. Just don't do anything silly. My first port of call will be the nursing home. We'll ensure that their best bed is reserved for when you come up at the weekend.'

'Don't worry,' Eva smiled. 'Do your business and I'll join you on Friday.'

She could have travelled with him now but Eva knew that Freddie needed time alone in Dublin before the birth of his child. He would attend the Freemasons and go drinking with old chums, spending money they could ill afford. But even if his eyes were bloodshot on Friday he would be sober and solicitous when escorting her to their lodgings close to the nursing home which he had chosen for her to give birth in.

He eyed the whiskey again and restrained himself. 'Mind yourself, old thing, and I'll be waiting at Kingsbridge station on
Friday.' Taking the leatherbound *Book of Common Prayer*
from a bookshelf he tucked it under his arm. 'We mustn't
forget this!'

Freddie looked boyish as he smiled and Eva knew that his
proudest moment would come when recording his child's
birth among the family births listed there. The tradition had
started with his own father, born at sea in 1865, with the
latitude and longitude carefully recorded.

Eva accompanied him out onto the steps. Mikey nodded
and climbed into the passenger seat. He would drive the car
back and take any unexpected guests out shooting in his
master's absence.

Eva waved as the car disappeared down the long driveway.
She should have felt alone, but instead had an inexplicable
sense of relief. Descending the steps, she walked around by
the side of the house and up into the dense woods. The slope
was steep but it felt good to be alone. The maids would be
chatting among themselves with the master gone. The sole
guest at present, Mr Clements, was not the sort of man to
make demands on their time.

The only thing moving was smoke from the chimneys. Eva
began to climb, feeling like a child again. Running this guesthouse was proving harder than imagined. By now Freddie
had exhausted his contacts who might enjoy the local shooting
rights retained by his uncle after the Land Commission broke
up the Fitzgerald estates. Eva had brought few potential
customers to the business. She hardly knew anyone who shot.
Her few friends who had come to sample their hospitality
generally sketched by day and felt out of place amid the
constant shooting talk at night, with men priding themselves
on the quantity of tufted duck and woodcock slaughtered.

Being a good Fitzgerald was different from being a Goold Verschoyle. Familiarity was not encouraged. Her Protestant neighbours clubbed together, uncomfortable with – and, where possible, ignoring – the changing world beyond their gates. Ladies played tennis while the men drank whiskey and considered their options. Eva sometimes wondered if their best option as newlyweds might have been to live in Dublin on Freddie's teaching salary. Not that she minded any hardship during the early months when married life was dangerously exciting. Freddie had made her feel that here at last was reality, as shockingly new as his thrusts into her body at night. One thing she realised was that it wasn't just Freddie's quick temper that had made Mother wary of him. In Mayo, his name still carried allure, and the locals saluted his vehicle as respectfully as if he had emerged from the ornate gates of Turlough Park. But beyond his gruff exterior he was as much a dreamer as Eva, obsessed with starting a new life here where the only thing they were never short of was firewood. Still, he assured her that Mayo was a wildfowler's paradise and once their reputation spread people would flock from what he termed the 'mainland'.

As they could not afford a housekeeper, Eva's job was to supervise the menus with Mrs McGrory, the cook, and run the house, while Freddie took out the guests in search of woodcock, snipe and duck. Three months after their wedding Freddie had inserted the first small advertisement in the *Shooting Times* in England. Yet the first guest to walk up the avenue – lured by Eva's small hand-painted sign – was the retired English naval commander, Mr Clements, who abhorred shooting. Freddie and Eva had hidden like schoolchildren behind the drawing room curtains to study him – unsure if he would ring the bell or depart – as he stood on the daffodil lawn, gradually seduced by the vista of bog with Croagh Patrick rising in the distance. A man without roots – or anxious to escape them – the Commander had explained that he was on a walking tour of the West of Ireland. He booked in for one night, sent for his trunks a month later and ever since had not got around to leaving.

Despite Mr Clements's protestations, Freddie had insisted on taking him shooting on his first morning here. That evening after they returned Eva had excused herself and slipped into the woods to be sick out of sight of the cook and the kitchen maid. Returning to face the feathers soaked with congealed blood, the innards to be scraped out and the teethmarks made by Freddie's red setter, Eva had realised that her expectation of marriage was another illusion. But she had little time for conscientiousness about dead birds, because within weeks Eva felt nauseated for a different reason. This child was starting inside her. Neighbours had flocked in when the news spread, taking it as a portent that the Fitzgerald line was being carried on in these trying times. Elderly majors, whose accents betrayed a mixture of Connaught and Calcutta, sipped whiskey in the timber-panelled bow window. Their benign gratitude made her feel incidental, as if she was merely the vehicle through which another male Fitzgerald would be delivered to Mayo. They urged her to rest, then joked with Freddie about the madness of the voting age for women being lowered to twenty-one.

Beyond the baize door denoting the servants' territory, Mrs McGrory had grown comfortable enough with Eva's non-Fitzgerald ways to confide how she was saying a novena that the child would be a boy. Eva had retained her own counsel, but felt common ground with her visitors on only one issue – the child would definitely be a boy.

Climbing on now she reached three oak trees in a small clearing. It was while resting against the middle one that she felt the first stab of pain. The child wasn't due for three weeks, yet instinctively Eva knew that he was choosing his moment, waiting until the proud Fitzgerald was not here to take charge.

Where was the way back? Momentarily Eva lost her bearings, trapped in this wood owned by a family to which she felt she would never truly belong. But she would have to make herself belong, because she was bearing a Fitzgerald who was now trying to force his way out as if determined to be born amongst these trees. There was no point in calling because nobody could hear. All she could do was clutch her stomach and run, trusting that Mrs McGrory was still in the house. Why had she gone walking alone, after Freddie warned her to do nothing silly? He would be boarding the Dublin train now, glowing with affability after the Imperial Hotel. If she had gone with him she knew that the baby would have waited to be delivered by midwives in a warm room in Dublin. Freddie's best-laid plans were going the way of all their best-laid plans. It was not her fault, but Eva knew that in his heart Freddie would blame her again. Not that he was cruel, but his exasperation at her slow thought-processes was becoming more apparent. But a child would change that because here finally was something she could do right. However there was no more time to worry about Freddie, because this terror gripping her allowed for no other thought than that she must reach the house and find Mrs McGrory.

She stumbled on her swollen ankles and tried not to fall, then saw Mr Clements with his walking stick and a book strolling along the avenue below. He reminded her of Father and Eva remembered how Mother had said to think of her in times of trouble. A sound must have emerged when she tried to scream because Mr Clements peered up through the foliage. He clambered up to put his arm around her as she sat panting, then coaxing her on, calling out loudly as they neared the house. The pain was so great that she could not stop herself crying and suddenly Mrs McGrory was in the doorway, taking command.

Eva lay on her bed, with Mr Clements outside, pacing as anxiously as if it were his own child. The pains were intense now and so quick that there was almost no pause. When you became a wife you gave away so much – your name, your family, the sense of who you were. She was no longer Eva Goold Verschoyle. She was Mrs Freddie Fitzgerald. Eva no longer possessed anything that was truly hers, but suddenly she knew – though she tried to prevent the thought – that this child would belong to her and not to Freddie. The pain was overwhelming, but Eva pushed and prayed that whatever God looked over her would bring her through this ordeal. Her dreaming-time was over and there was just pain and a desperate love for the child torturing her. She and the child were one, united in this act where he hurt her for the sake of life and she willingly ached.

Eva thought of the Commander pacing the lawn and poor Freddie on the train with events bypassing him. But she couldn't wait for Freddie. She knew that her fingers hurt Mrs McGrory, digging into the woman's flesh, but the cook did not complain, just urged her to give one last push, one final desperate effort. When Eva looked up she could see nothing because her vision was blurred, but she heard the baby's first cry and did not want him cleaned because she wanted to hold him as he had emerged, coated in her blood and definitely a boy.

Mrs McGrory was in tears, saying, 'I said a novena for a boy and God never let me down,' and Eva's body ached as she pushed out the afterbirth. But she knew that her soul was rooted now. She was no longer a sycamore sepal blown about at will. She belonged in this wood, as the mother of this extraordinary gift. Everything else seemed distant. Her true life seemed to be only starting in the heartbeat of this boy whom Mrs McGrory coaxed back from her, anxious to attend to his needs.

'You'll give him back,' Eva pleaded, 'as soon as you can.'

'Let me wash the poor creature and wrap him up. Isn't he just the darling?'

'He is.' Eva smiled. 'Francis. My darling.'

# FOURTEEN

## *Chelsea*

### *London, 1930*

'Am I your first?' the baronet's daughter asked afterwards, as they lay between silk sheets in her Chelsea townhouse.

'Yes,' Brendan replied, because this was what older women liked to hear. To be made to feel special and young again by taking a man's virginity. Lillian was not far from the desert of middle age. She was approaching thirty at least. She reached over to insert a cigarette in her holder and lit it.

'My husband is progressive,' she said. 'He believes in free love. All the same I'd sooner say nothing to him. You see, he just doesn't believe in free love for women.'

Brendan was not sure whether to believe her. 'What would Gordon do if he walked in now?'

'What would you do?' She watched him closely.

'Reason with him. Confront him with his own speeches about overthrowing outdated nineteenth-century notions of what constitutes morality.'

Lillian laughed. 'How very rational. You think you can talk your way out of everything. But what happens when you reach the primitive bedrock within him? It's inside all men, buried in you too. It's one thing to surrender your property

187

in the name of revolution, but quite another to surrender your woman. Gordon would kill you if he knew.'

'Then why invite me back here after the party meeting?' Brendan reached over to kiss her shoulder. 'Why seduce me?'

'Because I enjoy risks. And so do you, dear boy.' She ran a finger lightly down his chest, the cigarette holder poised as if about to tip the hot ash on his naked flesh. Then she stubbed out the cigarette into a marble ashtray after just two puffs, unlike the people he generally mixed with who would drag on a cigarette until their fingers were scorched. 'Besides at this very moment the bastard is screwing that Cockney bitch from the Plebs League who kept raising her hand like a schoolgirl to ask questions.'

Brendan turned over, upset at hearing this. Ruth Davis was the first girl he had gone out with in London. He had seen her tonight at the party meeting and intended to go over afterwards until Lillian waylaid him, seeking help to pack away unsold copies of the *Daily Worker*. Lillian sensed his discomfort and leaned her breasts into his back.

'You think me a snob, don't you? I'm not. No doubt the little tart is a good comrade. I just think that you have to draw a distinction between those whom you fight side by side with and those whom you sleep side by side with. But Gordon was always intimidated by intelligent women. That's what I like about you. You're not scared of us. I wasn't your first. I can tell.'

'You were my most beautiful,' he replied.

'You're sweet.' She rolled over to stretch beneath the bed, with her buttocks and elegant white back on display, reminding him of Ruth on their first night together when Ruth had reached under her bed for a chamber pot. Lillian didn't look like she ever sat on a chamber pot, even in her father's country house which apparently had electricity and good plumbing long before any other house in Devon. 'A sweet boy who likes risks. Here's a little present.'

She wiggled her bum and looked back, knowing that he was hooked and already erect again. Settling back beside him, she laid a cheaply printed small volume on his pillow. 'Take it with you. Those mechanical parrots fresh from the Lenin School in Moscow ordered me to burn every copy. They're like Catholic peasants with a catechism, the way they trot out party doctrine by rote. It's funny how the Party insists that all recruits are taught to think for themselves, yet at the same time they must all reach the same conclusion.'

'Why are you still in the Party then?' Brendan fingered the now illicit copy of *Where is Britain Going?* by Leon Trotsky.

Lillian ran her hand slowly down his chest, pausing teasingly above his groin. 'Because it's rather thrilling or at least it used to be. And because I genuinely believe in it, in the same way that I believe in heaven without wishing to actually become a nun or a saint. Gordon however is an enthusiast who swallows everything. Not so long ago he could quote all of Trotsky's book and thunder about how the Communist Party needed to enter into an implacable conflict with the conservative bureaucracy of the trade unions and the Labour Party. Back then it was all about revolution in England. Then after Trotsky was expelled from Russia and the Party voted complete allegiance to Stalin it was like this book never existed. That's what I find frightening. I used to love honest arguments at party meetings. It was primitive and exciting, with people shouting and taking sides. It was about England and the here and now and I would join in and argue with the best. But now we're like a naive rabble kneeling before a foreign deity, awaiting the latest commandment from the Kremlin.' Lillian kissed his stomach. 'The Party will swallow anything now, whereas – being a well-brought-up girl – I'm highly selective about what I swallow.'

Her lips moved downward and Brendan closed his eyes because this really was a first time. Yet despite his pleasure he did not feel close to her because he knew that she would never have committed such an act if he was born among the working class. Like many who drifted into the Party, she was here on safari because communism seemed rather bohemian and she could briefly pretend not to belong among the oppressive reactionary class. Maybe the Ffrenches were contradictory too but they were sincere people about whom he could not think badly. They would never alter their beliefs, whereas on the day when Gordon came into his title and seat in the House of Lords, he and Lillian would shed their radicalism like a snakeskin.

Lillian surfaced for air and Brendan gripped her hips to position her on top of him. He knew that he was being used and there was callousness in the way that he entered her. This seemed to excite her.

'You're making love to a heretic,' she mocked. 'If you let them brainwash you, you'll want to burn me at a stake instead. But promise me you'll never become a mechanical parrot. Read Trotsky. No man can be a hero one day and a villain the next. You can give your allegiance to the workers without becoming Stalin's poodle. When the revolution comes I will gladly give away everything. But the one thing I refuse to surrender is my independence of mind.'

Lillian leant forward and gripped his shoulders so that her breasts hung down, swaying and trickling with sweat. He lay back to let her take control for now and knew that he would rather be with Ruth Davis who was giving herself to this woman's husband.

What would his life have been like if he had stayed on at

Marlborough, never meeting these people and tasting such freedom? Other lads studying electrical engineering at night sometimes teased him about his accent, but they accepted him as himself. They mocked his zeal for study, but Brendan could do nothing unless it was wholehearted. That was why Lillian fascinated him, in how she could both *be* and *seem to be*, how she could position herself half in and half out of things. From the look on her face she could easily be in love with him at this moment but she would just as easily forget him moments after he left, settling down on the sofa with a whisky and soda to dutifully await her husband. Brendan had to either believe completely or not at all. The party was correct to distance itself from the soft-Left enemies of the revolution and unite behind Stalin so that the spread of revolution was centrally guided. Lillian was too English at heart not to see the Home Counties as the centre of the universe. Being stateless, Brendan was not impeded by reactionary petty nationalism. Still he would read Trotsky's book because the moment you ran away from words like a coward you lost your soul. His body was lost inside her now and he did not want to come too soon. Closing his eyes, he tried to focus on whatever images arose. He could see Bruckless Pier, with Art and Thomas and Maud and Eva and him charging down it in bathing costumes, ready to jump together out into the waters of Donegal Bay. Their joined hands were spread wide as they jumped, but once in the air they had to let go of one another and focus on their own fall. Their bodies twisted as they hit the water with huge separate splashes, like pieces of Humpty Dumpty that could never be put back together. Brendan gasped as his body suddenly buckled and he came.

# FIFTEEN

# The Visit

## Moscow, 1932

An instinct told Art that something was wrong before he pushed open the front door into the building where he lived in the Sokolniki District. This sixth sense came from four years of living in Moscow. The hallway was silent with no children's voices or sounds of marital strife from behind closed doors. Officers from the United State Political Directorate, the OGPU, must be operating within this building. By now Art could recognise the special smell that the presence of this secret police force always managed to unearth among the other odours emanating from these crowded rooms: the stink of sabotage and treachery. After his long shift in the truck factory he had stopped at the *banya* as was his right as an *udarnik*. But now his body felt robbed of its cleanliness after that steam bath with the select band of other workers similarly rewarded for exceeding their quotas.

He had been naive to expect every foreigner who came to Russia to be a revolutionary. Some were cowardly simpletons like the American with the Russian surname who had arrived in Moscow on the same day as Art and offered to share a room in the Novo Varskaya Hotel until they could register at the Labour Commissariat. The man had then visited counter-revolutionary relations in Moscow, been swayed by their lies, sold his tools on the black market and skulked away on a train to Helsinki in Finland, urging Art to do likewise. Other foreigners were *agents provocateurs* sent to spy and disrupt industrial production by infiltrating factories and spreading discontent. These wreckers and saboteurs were trained by the Imperialist powers with the sole purpose of disrupting the Five-Year Plan launched by Comrade Stalin during the Great Turning Point.

The case of the Swedish saboteur arrested in work last week showed how insidious these counter-revolutionaries were. The man had frequently volunteered for thirty-hour work shifts in the factory and constantly suggested new methods to increase production and surpass the projected targets. Art had been deceived by the man's talk about the pride he felt when his children marched home from kindergarten chanting: *'Five years' work in four years, And not five years' work in five!'*

Still Art should have known that his constant suggestions to improve output were actually intended to deflate morale by insinuating that current production methods were wasteful. Last Thursday when the OGPU appeared at the end of a shift the bustling factory had grown so still that it reminded Art of playing statues as a boy in Donegal. Amidst the fear, he had experienced a sudden unaccountable homesickness. The OGPU did not arrest the Swede immediately. They had walked with casual strides among the motionless workers, pausing occasionally in front of a comrade before giving a half-smile and moving on. That was when Art noticed the special smell, a cocktail of fear and treachery. It sounded irrational but Art decided that the OGPU were trained like dogs to smell it, that when an officer stopped in front of him

193

the man was not just staring into Art's eyes but sniffing his sweat.

Eventually three officers encircled the Swede and asked him to accompany them. When the man sought permission to send a message to his family they explained that this was unnecessary because their chat would not take longer than an hour at most. That was when everyone present knew that they would never see the Swede again. After he was gone and the comrade workers filed away without comment, Art had noticed a cleaner smell about the factory.

That bad scent pervaded the building now and grew stronger with every step Art took up the stairs towards the apartment that he and his wife shared with three other couples. He expected his instincts to tell him which door the OGPU were behind. The smell outside would be overwhelming and he would pass on in relief to the sanctuary of his flat. But this did not occur. The stench increased as he approached his own door until Art realised that he was smelling his own sweat.

He pushed open the door and his wife looked up from a chair in the corner. Nobody else was in the room except for a tall man whom he did not recognise. Art knew that he was a secret policeman and the other occupants had been ordered to disappear for as long as the OGPU remained in the apartment. Therefore their visit could only concern him, his wife or his brother Brendan who was visiting them.

Irena looked too scared to speak and as the policeman remained silent, Art found himself examining his own conscience, in the way which Samuel Trench's daughter in Donegal once explained that Catholics did before confession. Secretly lying in the dark by the Bunlacky shore, she had once outlined the categories of Catholic sins of deed and thought and omission. His mind worked through these same categories now. Had he ever, even subconsciously, doubted the wisdom of the Five-Year Plan? Had he failed to meet any production quota and therefore held back his fellow workers? Had he unwittingly associated with closet Trotskyites who were agents of the forces of Imperialist reaction? Had the Swedish spy falsely denounced him? Could the fact that he had briefly shared a room with that American turncoat four years ago in the Novo Varskaya Hotel have placed a question mark over him? Had he cleansed himself from all traits of his previous class?

The OGPU officer indicated that Art was to sit on a chair opposite Irena.

'You are sweating, comrade. Have you been running?'

'No . . . I . . . the stairs are a steep climb.'

Irena discreetly glanced towards the door into the small kitchen and Art knew that other OGPU officers were present there. They had not been awaiting him. The only person they could be interrogating was Brendan for whom Art had managed to procure a brief visitor's visa. During his few hours free from the factory, Art had taken Brendan around Moscow to show him the workers' paradise at first hand, with Irena taking him to other places when Art needed to sleep. Neither had encouraged Brendan to venture out alone, but his brother possessed a stubborn happy-go-lucky independent streak that left him prone to foolishness. Art rose from the chair.

'Is it my brother? Is he in trouble?'

'Why should your brother be in trouble?' The OGPU officer spoke quietly. 'Has he done something wrong? Have you?'

'No.'

'Then why ask the question, comrade? Why are you interfering in state business?'

'I'm not . . . I . . .' The officer was right. His duty as a citizen outweighed his responsibilities as a brother. What had he been thinking of to question the OGPU in the course of their duty? Brendan was no traitor, unless he had committed some unwitting crime. True, he had glimpsed aspects of Soviet life which were usually filtered out from the carefully-choreographed tours laid on for foreign trade unionists and dignitaries. Art was sufficiently trusted to join the select band of workers allowed to meet such groups in the truck factory and play along with the illusion that white tablecloths and choice food in the canteen were everyday occurrences. With so much anti-Soviet sentiment in the Western papers, Art understood the necessity to counter-balance such propaganda. He never understood the cynical mutterings of some comrade workers at the notion of telling visitors how they all received one month's holiday per year and a pension at the age of fifty.

If Brendan knew that such privileges were still only aspi-rational, he had seen how they were integral to Stalin's vision for the future. At present the canteen might only serve fish soup with eyes and heads floating on the surface, but Brendan understood that this was the initial price of building a utopia. Surely the OGPU did not feel threatened by such disclosure, though Irena had scolded Art for taking Brendan to visit a comrade who lived with five hundred other Elektrozavod workers in vast unheated dormitories in the Cherkisovo Barracks. Art would only make matters worse now by asking the policeman more questions. He sat stiffly on the chair, trying to guess what was happening in the kitchen. He had never known the building to be so silent, with no feet on the stairs and no chatter of voices constantly queuing for the rickety toilet in the alcove on the first floor. As Art listened he realised that everybody else in the building was listening too. He could hear the sound of two hundred people collectively holding their breath. Then he heard a confident good-natured laugh from the kitchen. Another Russian voice joined in, louder as if enjoying a joke and then a third laugh came, carefree and familiar to Art from his childhood.

He glanced at Irena, who looked back equally baffled. Brendan's laugh lacked the slightest hint of fear. Was he so naive as to not realise who was interrogating him? Would he walk blindly into whatever trap they set? Irena had warned both brothers to be careful even when queuing outside a shop in case any remark might be misconstrued and reported to the OGPU by a zealous comrade. When addressing the OGPU, extreme vigilance was needed, but Brendan sounded so relaxed that he might let slip some seemingly innocuous detail that could lead to charges against half the comrades on this landing. The tall officer watched Art, scrutinising his discomfort.

'Your brother is a funny boy. His jokes make us all laugh. Georgi Polevoy is translating for him some of ours. Once the vodka flows Georgi can tell stories all night. We have no record of you telling jokes. Perhaps you are not a proper Irishman.'

'I am a loyal party member,' Art said. 'My wife too. Within three months of the Labour Commissariat sending me to the truck factory I had been graded an excellent worker.'

'*Udarniks* are to be valued,' the policeman said, 'but why can't you tell stories like your brother? Maybe you have not known the same number of women?' He glanced at Irena. 'The women all love your husband's brother, correct, comrade?'

Irena did not reply and Art felt angry because nothing in his political education had prepared him for being toyed with like this. He had given up everything to come to Russia, had shown his commitment by marrying a Russian wife and working every hour possible without the slightest complaint. Yet he sensed that this made him a figure of ridicule in the policeman's eyes. Angry was dangerous but suddenly Art didn't care. If Brendan was being arrested for some crime then he and his wife would be automatically sentenced as accessories. He rose to speak, despite his wife's terrified glance, but at that moment the kitchen door opened. An older officer, built like a weightlifter, stood in the doorway holding an empty bottle and addressed Art in English.

'Comrade Goold, you stock a very small cellar. Not like the racks of good wines in your family house in Ireland which your brother has been telling us about.'

Art drew a deep breath. It had been foolish to imagine that he could escape the curse of his birth. No matter how many double shifts he worked he was still a product of the class whom Stalin had termed the Former People, the *Byvshie Liudi* who once lived off the sweat of their workers? At heart he always knew that he would pay the price.

'My wife is a good comrade,' he said. 'She has not been contaminated by my character defects.'

The thickset man laughed. 'Comrade, you take life too seriously. Your main defect is a shortage of vodka. Still, such an oversight is easily forgiven between friends.'

He approached Art with Brendan following and a small, watchful man taking up the rear. Brendan looked slightly flushed, giddy with drink. He stared at his older brother.

'Are you okay? You look terrible.'

'I'm okay,' Art said. 'How are you?'

'Tiptop. Georgi here is bringing me to see *The Red Poppy* at the Bolshoi Theatre tonight. I was telling him you could not afford the tickets.'

'The Bolshoi first, then we party. We have a duty to show our visitor a good time.' The thickset officer raised his fists in a mock gesture to Brendan. 'Then we fight over whether Russian or Irish women are the more beautiful.' He turned to Art, his manner curt. 'This accommodation is not suitable for our guest. He will come with us for ten days.'

'You don't mind, Art, do you?' Brendan asked, more soberly. 'I don't want to just walk out on you, but they are very insistent and you're killing yourself trying to work in the factory and look after me.'

The three officers looked at Art, with no hostility in their gaze, just a curious indifference. If Brendan disappeared it would be impossible for Art to get word to Donegal. Not that he would have time to even try to post a letter. They would be back for him and Irena within the hour.

The thickset officer smiled. 'Don't look so worried, comrade. In ten days you will see your brother again. Meet him at noon at the October Station. It has been arranged that you will have that day and the next day off from the factory so you can spend time together before he returns to London. He is a good comrade. You must be proud of him.'

'If Art doesn't mind then I'll just pack my things,' Brendan said.

The small watchful officer spoke for the first time and Art knew that he was in charge. 'That is not necessary. All needs will be taken care of. You are our guest.' He looked at Art. 'Twelve noon at the October Station. You understand.'

'Yes,' Art said, although he could be certain of nothing. Brendan shook hands with him and kissed Irena while the OGPU men waited. Then they were gone, their descending footsteps breaking the silence. Eventually the front door slammed and doors opened on every landing as people tried to beat the queues for the water taps and the toilets.

Art sat opposite his wife. He did not know how long they would have together before the other couples returned to the flat. He did not know whether a knock would come for them in the night or if Brendan really would appear at the station in ten days' time. He knew nothing for certain, except that he would be held responsible in Donegal for whatever

199

happened to his brother. A small jealous part of him almost wanted Brendan arrested, because if they were telling the truth then Brendan was more important to them than he was. Art had never been afforded these privileges or treated with such respect, despite having given up so much – whereas Brendan was just a boy. It made no sense, but maybe this was a test. He looked up to find Irena watching him.

'He will be all right,' she said. 'We will be all right.' She repeated the words like a mantra to ward off evil, then whispered them fiercely for a third time, desperate to convince herself.

# SIXTEEN

# *The Letter*

*Donegal, August 1933*

The Manor House,
Dunkineely,
Donegal.
*28th August, 1933.*

My dearest son,
   *Writing to you feels like writing to the dead – though
naturally your mother would disagree, having long
entertained the belief that our dead loved ones avail of
every opportunity to address us, unlike the living whom we
love in Moscow. This, naturally, is your prerogative and I
do not criticise you for exercising it. I merely wish to
exercise my prerogative as your father to keep you abreast
of the condition of your estate-to-be.*
   *The house seems especially empty in this week of Eva's
birthday when I recall the excitement that her party used
to cause. Time is not just a thief but a conjurer.
Occasionally I look up from my desk and half expect to
see you all tramping down from the attic, clutching old
gowns and jackets as fancy dress costumes. You and
Thomas should be quarrelling over whose turn it is to be*

*Napoleon, with Brendan feeling slighted, Maud making the peace and Eva lost in her own world. Only mice occupy the attics now. I hear them scurry about and have not the heart to set traps. They have made their home there and are often the only company your mother and I have.*

*Not that we complain because we have each other and there is still enough love between us to keep out the sleet and rain of winter and those bleak January days when it seems that spring will never come. But come it did again this year and yielded a Donegal summer where the rain only reluctantly declared intermittent ceasefires. Dunkineely's happiest inhabitants are undoubtedly the ducks wandering between brimming potholes on the street. The new government seems as disinterested in filling them as their predecessor. Perhaps they are waiting to knock this house down and crumble up the stone to use as gravel. I have seen it done to many houses, compulsorily purchased or presented to this state. They gleefully demolish them, crushing up beautiful stone to use on the roads so that people can walk on us. But your inheritance still stands and the sweet peas lifting their heads to the evening sun beneath my window seem truly happy, radiating their wondrous scent of eternally renewed freshness after the rain. I wish you could smell them, Art, and taste the salty tang in the breeze coming in off the sea.*

*Have you window boxes packed with flowers in your apartment? Ffrench says that Moscow is awash with collective gardens. Indeed he says a great deal now that I am talking to him again. What was the point of holding a grudge? We are two educated men, lonely for company in this isolated place. I never thought I could be lonely,*

*especially in summer when this house was always filled
with visitors, but the rooms are so empty with my children
gone.*

*Thomas writes to say that he has found work as a town
planner in Cape Town. His health is much improved by
the sun. I blame his onset of consumption on the dampness
of this house, one of many legacies. His health would have
further deteriorated had he not followed his doctor's advice
and emigrated to a warm climate. In truth though, for all
his love of Donegal, he told me he was leaving for his own
sanity. He is bitter against you, I am afraid. Brendan
writes from London occasionally. What can I tell you of
him? Possibly you know more than I do. He remains so
light-hearted that it is hard to know what he thinks of
anything.*

*Maud is comfortable in Dublin. I fear that life is hard
for Eva in Mayo, although you would need to delve
deep behind the chatter of her letters to sense her pain.
It is no time to be a Protestant there. They must keep
their heads down since de Valera orchestrated a boycott
of the Mayo libraries because of the alleged danger to
people's souls when a Protestant was briefly appointed
as County Librarian. It helps to laugh at such things
because humour and resolve and a few ramshackle
houses are all our class have left. Even those grow fewer
every month. The IRA need not have bothered burning
out so many old families, they should have sat back and
waited for the stock market to do their work for them.
The last of the old money was lost in that crash. Houses
are just abandoned now, with local children using the
windows for target practice. Sometimes I take a pony
and cart into the hills to visit homes where your mother
and I once danced, with the great bedrooms and*

*libraries now left to the mercy of the rain and whatever few birds choose to build their nests there. You probably rejoice to see capitalism come crashing down so awesomely, but at what cost? There is hunger in Donegal like I never saw in my lifetime, caused by this depression which seems to affect everywhere except your beloved Russia, where, according to Ffrench, milk and honey still flows.*

*Civilised life did not end with Mr de Valera's ascent to power, despite predictions of doom from Mr Cosgrave's outgoing government. The mood in Ireland is sour and fractious though, with Donegal more divided into two camps than ever. In truth de Valera's former assassins in Fianna Fáil have proven no more radical a government than Mr Cosgrave's ex-gunmen. His old comrades in the IRA were cock-a-hoop at first when he released all political prisoners, but they soon found that he had little interest in letting them park their guns under his cabinet table. At the first sign of trouble he had the Civic Guards hound them back underground – though he could not resist a sly blow by sacking Cosgrave's Commissioner of the Civic Guards, General O'Duffy. O'Duffy is a buffoon but a vain and ambitious one. It is hard to credit the gentlemen in Mr Cosgrave's old cabinet placing themselves under his yoke. O'Duffy now parades across the land like an overfed cock, decking out his supporters in blue shirts and modelling himself on Mussolini.*

*I never thought to see fascism take hold in Ireland, but when a man sees his children go hungry it does terrible things to him. De Valera has declared economic war on Britain who are now refusing our cattle. I have seen strong farmers drive cows to market and stand there all day without an offer for a single beast. And I have seen them drive the cattle back at dusk with curses, and heard about the poor beasts being stampeded over cliffs and left to die because they were worthless. And I have seen those same proud farmers, led by your old friend, Mr Henderson, march in blue shirts to fascist parades demanding the overthrow of de Valera. But these farmers don't want a dictator like Mussolini: they want things the way they always were, with cheap wages and good prices for cattle. The poor support de Valera because if they are still starving, at least they see their rich neighbours starving too. So the IRA disrupt the Blueshirt Fine Gael meetings and the Blueshirts disrupt Fianna Fáil meetings, with fights and riots breaking out and at such times I thank God that you are abroad and cannot end up in an Irish jail.*

*The light is fading here in my study. Your mother is alone in her bed-sitting room with a paraffin lamp and arthritis for company. She will wonder what is keeping me, but I can't stop writing because once I put down this pen the spell will be broken. I will have to print the rough address that Ffrench gave me, knowing that I may never know if this ever reached you or if you could not rise above your contempt for us to deem it worthy of reply. Three times I have written to you and I might as well have thrown the letters over a cliff like the farmers do to their unfortunate cattle. I must accept that you have a new life. But I am still the guardian of your old one, caretaker of your inheritance. You are cursed with possessing this house after my death, whether you desire it or not. Neither of us can break that irrevocable indenture. Come home and I will give it to you before it is due. You can live here and I will take your mother away from this dampness to England. You love every stone and bush in Dunkineely, I know you do. You cannot run from who you are. I paint the windowframes every year, repair each cracked tile and broken pane. But even if I walk away so that the roof caves in and only rats and stray mongrels roam the cellars, this property will still be yours and one day you or your son will have to confront it. That is your curse, Art, you are a man of property. You can shed every other possession but this house is waiting for you and my curse is to be its keeper.*

*Often I dream about you. We walk along the beach at St John's Point together, not speaking or touching, but strolling in companionable silent understanding. I am no mystic like your mother, but I know in my heart that some nights you have this dream too. I know because you are part of me and I am part of you and I miss you and love you and forgive you and I want to feel that you forgive me too. Twenty minutes have passed since I wrote the last line. I have spent that time with my eyes closed, holding out my hand. If overwhelming desire could make a presence real then I would have felt your fingers brush against mine. I have lit a candle to finish this letter by. I am placing it in the window to light your way. Write to me. Just one page, one line, one word even.*

*I await your reply, even if I have to wait for all my remaining days.*

*Your loving father.*

# SEVENTEEN

# A Jaunt Abroad

## London, 1934

He knew it was them before the motor even stopped. It was
the old Daimler that Gordon's father gave him, which Gordon
and Lillian had kept locked in the stables behind their Chelsea
townhouse during their Communist Party days. Lillian had
once suggested making love in the back seat because she
loved the cool leather against her skin, but by then Brendan
had already tired of her novelty. She had been a brief diversion for him in the same way as communism had been one
for her. It took the stock market collapse, two months after
they first slept together, to unleash the reactionary in her.
Most of her class who were toying with communism had left
at that moment, suddenly aware of how tenuous their hold
was on wealth. 'We're not broke,' she had joked when Brendan
last accidentally met her. 'Gordon has accumulated a small
fortune by taking the simple precaution of starting out with
a big one.'

Gordon emerged from the Daimler and crossed the grass
in Hyde Park with such purposeful strides that Brendan was
convinced Lillian had confessed to her adultery. It would be
like her to save this revelation until Gordon was caught with

another mistress, then taunt him with it. Brendan rose uneasily from the bench to face the cuckolded husband, not knowing if he should prepare to defend himself. He didn't mind insults or even being punched once he managed to get the business over with quickly. In six minutes' time he was due to meet somebody and it would be disastrous if he were not alone. The chauffeur opened the door to let Lillian step out onto the Serpentine Road and savour the confrontation. She flashed an eager smile and waved, momentarily distracting Brendan so that Gordon was suddenly upon him and had gripped his hand.

'Goold Verschoyle, the very chap! We were only discussing you . . . oh, a week or so ago. Lillian was saying what damn good company you used to be and how we never see you now. You're not still . . . you know . . . involved in that stuff . . .'

'No,' Brendan reassured him.

'You saw sense, like ourselves. Excellent.' The man looked relieved. 'If it's any consolation we were not the only fools duped by that frightful Georgian peasant. It's amazing at dinner parties how when the brandy starts to loosen tongues you discover the number of good people who lost their reason and flirted with fire. You must come and dine with us. How about tonight? We're having some interesting people over.'

'Thanks anyway, but I couldn't.'

'Now listen . . .' The older man leaned closer and Brendan had to resist an urge to punch him, remembering how he had callously washed his hands of Ruth Davis after getting her pregnant. 'Our guests would not be concerned that you work in . . . whatever it is you do again.'

'I'm a qualified electrical engineer,' Brendan said.

'Excellent. Well done. People wouldn't mind that. It would be quite a novelty in fact. Once you're a guest at my table nobody present would dare to look down on you.'

'It's not that,' Brendan explained. 'Maybe another time. The thing is I'm actually meeting a woman.'

Brendan glanced past him at three office girls approaching arm in arm down the North Ride, laughing with their heads bent together.

'Well, bring her along.'

'Her husband wouldn't like that.'

The remark was a risk but Brendan suddenly didn't care. Gordon looked at him curiously, then laughed. 'You sly dog. I always knew you were a ladies' man.' He lowered his voice conspiratorially to avoid being overheard by an elderly gentleman who had just sat down to have his lunch on the bench behind them. 'Still, it takes one to know one, know what I mean, old chap? Catholics maintain that it's not a sin if you don't enjoy it. I take the Low Church view – it's not a sin if you don't get caught.' He glanced back at Lillian, standing beside the Daimler, with a smile fixed on her face. 'Not a word, of course, to you know who. So when are you meeting this damsel?'

The three office girls passed among the lunchtime throng in the park. 'It's rather embarrassing, Gordon, but I'm actually meeting her right here and now.'

'In Hyde Park in daylight?' Gordon laughed, no longer caring if the old gentleman could hear. 'You're a rogue, Goold Verschoyle, you ought to be shot.'

'Where could be a more natural place to meet someone by pure chance?' Brendan said. 'Encounters only look illicit when they take place down dark lanes.'

'Do you know the husband?'

'Intimately.' He knew that every word would be relayed to Lillian once Gordon returned to the motor.

'You're taking a risk, aren't you? I . . . I don't know what I'd do if I ever discovered . . .' Gordon scanned the passers-by.

'And she takes her lunch here? What is she, some sort of typist?'

'Hardly,' Brendan said. 'I always had class.'

'True. I often said that to Lillian. She'll be so relieved you're no longer mixed up in the other business. It was a dangerous ragtag of whingers and traitors.'

'I had a rude awakening,' Brendan explained. 'I saw Moscow. My brother lives there: he's an incurable fanatic.'

'My goodness, you actually went? What was it like?'

'The day I came back I cut all my ties with the Communist Party. Need I say more? Listen, if my lady friend sees me in company she's likely to run scared.'

'I understand, of course. You won't see me for dust in a moment.' Gordon placed a fatherly hand on Brendan's shoulder. 'Just one thing, would you be willing to talk in public about what you saw? The despotism in Russia and the conspiracy in England between the Bolsheviks and the Jews who have orchestrated this world depression. Both Lillian and I are now highly placed within the British Union of Fascists. Mosley himself has dined with us many times. Mosley would be sympathetic to you because he too started out as a misguided socialist. He has undergone the same journey as us. I respect you in trying to build bridges between the classes, and the British Union of Fascists does exactly that. Its great virtue as an organisation is that there is room for all classes – in their natural place, of course, but everyone has a role. You would be a brilliant speaker.'

'Follow your path, Gordon, but I'm through with politics.' Brendan politely but firmly removed the man's hand from his shoulder. 'I just want to enjoy my life, you understand, and unless you bugger off I shall miss out on considerable enjoyment today and will have made an unnecessary purchase at a barber's shop on my way here.'

'I hardly regard your tone as necessary,' Gordon replied curtly. 'I was about to depart. Still I'm not a man to bear grudges. Contact me when you see sense and I'll personally introduce you to Mosley.'

He turned and stalked off towards Lillian who ceased to smile and looked concerned. Brendan sat down on the bench with his heart beating. He took a deep breath and looked around at the throng. The old gentleman having lunch glanced up.

'Knows Mr Mosley in person, does he, your friend?' he enquired casually.

'He's no friend of mine.'

The old man took a bite of his sandwich. 'Just as well, seeing as you were sleeping with his wife.'

Brendan looked at him in surprise. 'How do you know that?'

'It's our job to know everything. Have nothing to do with that couple, it could be misconstrued.'

'I never wish to see them or traitors like them again. But I still find it unfair that I must stay away from good comrades within the Party.'

'The British Communist Party is riddled with police spies. We know who they are and they will be dealt with in time. But thanks to them, the police file on you is dormant. You are viewed as merely another renegade who fell away like your fascist friends. Scotland Yard sees nothing to fear from you any more. You are a respectable and presentable young man. Still you look pale. A foreign jaunt, some sea air would do you good. Don't leave from Hull this time. Go to Holland, then make your way to Finland. I wish I could get away myself. These few minutes sitting here listening to that anti-Semitic shitbag have left me quite nauseated.'

Brendan said nothing. One of the few things he knew

about his controller was that he was Jewish. Georgi Polevoy had almost apologised for this during the ten days of intensive instruction in how to become a courier. Georgi's vehement anti-Jewish jokes had shocked Brendan so much that when the OGPU officer noticed his reaction he stopped. This was not the only contradiction Brendan had encountered after agreeing in Art's kitchen to become a courier. But these contradictions had not disillusioned him because, unlike Art, he did not see the world in black and white. He had seen real starvation behind the propaganda of happy workers in the socialist paradise. But he had also witnessed hunger as a boy in Ireland and lived among it in England during these terrible years of soup kitchens and hunger marches. Capitalism was spent and the spectre of fascism sickened him. Communism offered real long-term hope – even in the hands of bigots like Georgi Polevoy who were the ignorant carthorses dragging the harvest forward. They had not coerced him in Moscow because, when approached, Brendan had given his services freely. But unlike Art he had not given them his mind.

The old gentleman raised his hat to a woman in a fur coat who rewarded him with a smile. He watched her pass. 'Our friend in the Home Office has been busy. You have a number of items to carry. Spend a day or two with your brother if you wish. Art is a good comrade: he won't ask questions about why you are back in Moscow. You know that far better accommodation can be made available to you?'

'If it's good enough for Art, it's good enough for me.'

The man nodded. 'Family is important. Take my wife. She makes the most wonderful sandwiches. Try one.'

He placed the brown paper bag containing his lunch on Brendan's knee. One sandwich remained. Brendan picked it up and took a bite. The sandwich was excellent. Brendan wanted to compliment him but the old man had got up and was walking away into the crowd. It was hard to tell how many envelopes were at the bottom of the bag. Enough to fill his usual hiding places and for him to need to create several more. He would buy presents for Art and Irena. The Soviet border guards would not dare to steal them once they saw his travel papers. Last time he had brought books after Art mentioned having little to read. This had changed since the authorities asked Art to work as a translator in a publishing house. As a mark of his increased status they now shared their room with only one couple. Georgi Polevoy had assured Brendan that Art would never know whose hand had guided his progress. Brendan would bring tobacco and a hand-carved chess set and contrive to let his big brother imagine that he could outwit him, as they companionably sat over the chess pieces late into the Moscow night.

# EIGHTEEN

# The Night Call

*Moscow, 1935*

The problem with the publishing house was that one could never work all the hours needed. When the huge clock struck six, the small army of translators ceased work like operatives in a factory rather than disseminators of great literature. It amazed Art how some colleagues could stop in mid-stanza and casually toss aside a poem until tomorrow, having mechanically ploughed though verse all day, producing faithful but leaden versions for which they got paid by the line. These were mainly the quango of Georgian, Armenian, Urkainian and Kazakh poets whose sole task was to simultaneously translate each other's work, or to 'take in one another's washing' as someone cynically called it. But not everyone worked like this. Some good comrades had not lost their reverence for literature, although careful never to promote the merit of poets over the endeavours of the workers they celebrated. Every evening Art watched these comrades reluctantly surface from the spell cast by the words they were translating and look around the vast room at the hack translators already reaching for coats and fur hats. Many came from abroad like him, although being unmarried they lived with other foreigners in

214

the Hotel Lux. Some mornings they made black jokes about the red seals marking the doors of guests taken away by the police at night. On such mornings they worked in grim silence, deliberately ignoring another empty desk in their midst. Some comrades followed his habit of taking work home to get it right without the pressure of supervisors with deadlines. Art treasured this period between midnight and two a.m., when Irena was asleep with their newborn son beside her. He loved to work by candlelight until the child woke, crying to be fed. Irena always gently scolded Art to bed then, and as the baby suckled on her breast Art would wash in cold water and reluctantly yield to rest.

Tonight he was correcting the proofs of his English translation of *Round Heads and Pointed Heads* by Bertolt Brecht. No British or American publisher had dared to translate this inflammatory text, so the responsibility fell on him though he worried if his German was good enough. Close colleagues helped with non-contentious linguistic problems and he had been pleased with his work. But now, glancing through the folios again, he wished for more time. It was invariably the case when he reread translations in this quietude where he could properly think. The publishing house was never silent, with translators constantly consulting rows of dictionaries or seeking advice to ensure that passages did not contravene the Soviet ethos.

Art rarely needed guidance in this area. He trusted his instincts and had never been called upon by Glavlit, the directorate for literature, to justify any translated passage. Indeed he noticed that the ones who made public displays of seeking guidance were generally those whom Glavlit, sometimes accompanied by the secret police, later questioned. Translators had come to resent advice being sought on anything other than strictly linguistic matters because you could never tell if the enquirer was an *agent provocateur* deliberately trying to concoct a reactionary context from your reply. At times Art missed factory work, though his present labours were stimulating and left him no longer dependent on the limited supplies and long queues in the Workers' Co-operative Store. Now he had access to the Government Stores where precious goods like tea were sold, although at six roubles for two ounces it was a luxury he could rarely afford. The downside of being a translator was that people avoided eye contact once they saw you leave the publishing house because they knew that foreigners worked there. Since the secret police had started the latest roundup of socially dangerous elements, neighbours had begun to avoid him. Some evenings when they hissed at their children to run into their rooms before he reached the landing, it felt like being back among the superstitious Dublin proletariat in Mountjoy Square.

Therefore when the faintest tap came on the door now, Art knew that it could not be a neighbour come to beg a quarter-loaf of black bread. As Irena sometimes joked, the only people still working at this hour were translators, prostitutes, thieves and the Secret Police. Art listened for a moment but no second knock came as if the visitor was confident that Art was merely stalling. The tap was gentle but Art knew that others in the building had heard it too. People slept as lightly as dogs, listening out for this sound they dreaded most. Last month a Finnish translator had joked about a woman answering a late-night knock only to be reassured by her neighbour: 'No need to panic, comrade, the building is merely on fire.' Two mornings later his colleagues discovered red seals across the door of the Finn's room in the Hotel Lux.

The knock had been too light to wake Irena or the child who were both exhausted. Art stared at them sleeping peaceably for a second longer, then deliberately placed the Brecht proofs down where Irena would find them. He opened the door a fraction. Georgi Polevoy – the thickset policeman now working for the NKVD into which the OGPU had been subordinated – stood there. The NKVD officer looked grave and Art wondered which former colleagues in Progress House had falsely denounced him. Perhaps it was the speed of events but Art felt no sense of terror. Instead there was a curious relief as if he had been long awaiting this moment when his loyalty was finally challenged. Nobody could have estimated the number of wreckers and saboteurs unleashed by Imperialist governments upon the Soviet Union in the guise of alleged volunteers but Art's conscience was clear and he knew he could logically refute any allegations about him. Georgi glanced past Art at the sleeping figures, then placed one finger to his lips, beckoning him out onto the bare landing.

'No point in waking them,' he whispered, 'Take a coat. You won't need anything else. This won't take long.'

Art reached for his coat behind the door. He did not look back because that would be to admit the possibility of never seeing his family again. Brendan had once been taken away and Brendan had come back. Maybe Brendan was in Moscow and Art was being taken to meet him.

He closed the door quietly and walked down onto the next landing where the NKVD officer waited.

'Best to let the child sleep,' Georgi said. 'They need their sleep. I know. I am a father three times over, though my wife thinks it is only twice.' He gave a self-deprecating shrug. 'Mistakes occur in life. You understand.'

'Yes.'

'Good. Follow me.'

The man gave no further explanation and Art knew not to seek one. The car parked outside had its lights off and another NKVD officer at the wheel. Georgi opened the door for Art to squeeze in beside a man and woman in the back seat, then got into the passenger seat and instructed his colleague to drive on. It was dark in the car but Art knew that he was seated beside two criminals. The woman in her fifties must have been snatched from bed because she wore only a nightgown. She was shaking but the man was utterly still. The blood on his forehead looked black in this light. The man's breath was unnaturally loud, as if running a marathon. Maybe it was being forced to sit beside them, but as they sped through the deserted streets Art found that he was shaking as if guilty too.

The car turned into Lubyanka Square, past the statue of Felix Dzerzhinsky who had established the first soviet secret police. The woman in the nightdress suddenly spoke as they drove through the gates of Lubyanka Prison which closed behind them. 'Comrades, I demand to know what I am charged with. Why are you arresting me?'

Neither officer bothered to reply as the car stopped and a group of warders emerged from a doorway to haul the two captives inside, ignoring the woman's increasingly hysterical protestations. Art expected to be told to join them but Georgi indicated to the remaining warders that he was to be left alone for now. The other officer followed the prisoners inside, leaving the two men sitting in the car alone in the floodlit quadrangle.

'Always the same question: *why, why, why*,' Georgi said, incredulously. 'If people did not know why they were being arrested then they would not be brought here.' From somewhere within the building an inhuman scream reminded Art of a badger in a snare. Georgi shook his head. 'Sometimes I am shocked by their depth of self-delusion. They must know that in the end they are bound to confess.'

'Why have you brought me here?' Art asked.

The NKVD officer sighed. 'It saddens me, Goold, to hear

even a man of your intelligence engage in this same pathetic *why* business as an ignorant *kulak*. You claim to be a loyal comrade, so think why. We have all night.'

Harsh light came on in a bare room. Through the window Art saw the woman being stripped of her nightgown and bent over to receive a crude gynaecological search. Ordering her to stand back up, the female warden forced open her mouth with the same hand, examining her teeth like a horse trader at a Donegal fair. Georgi Polevoy quietly observed his reaction.

'Even when the girls are attractive, comrade, this is not a pretty sight. You grow tired of the endless names and bodies and faces of the enemies of socialism. These are dangerous times, with so many saboteurs disrupting the Five-Year Plan. The trials you read about in *Pravda* are only the barest fraction of those we are forced to arrest.'

Art had followed each state trial carefully in *Pravda*, sickened by how traitors who had wormed their way into senior party posts kept publicly defying Stalin's authority by bleating about their innocence. Having been allowed to put her night-dress back on, the woman was taken out to be photographed. The man was brought into the room and Art watched the same procedure begin. It seemed a long way from cosy nights with Mr Ffrench discussing *The Communist Manifesto*. Still, this was the distance between vague theory and cold application. Only so much could be built with words alone. But equal pain would be involved in putting into practice the words that Jesus Christ was crucified for. Several times in the Soviet Union, Art's faith had been tested and this seemed like another test, with Georgi Polevoy playing Lucifer by tempting him into feeling pity for those who betrayed their fellow workers. Georgi was waiting for Art to speak.

'I stand with Brecht,' Art declared. 'The more innocent

they claim to be, the more they deserve to die.'

'How could they be innocent?' Georgi asked. 'Anyone arrested and brought into Lubyanka has to be guilty. To release someone whom we arrested would result in our judgement being queried. It would lower morale among the public who depend on us to protect them from traitors. Once people enter these gates then only those of them who seek to damage the prestige of the NKVD wish to leave and that in itself is a crime.'

'So what am I guilty of?'

'You tell me, comrade. You are the one who mentioned guilt. What do you confess to?'

'I have nothing to confess to. I've done nothing.'

'Is that in itself not a crime? To have done nothing? The Soviet Union is infested with spies, yet you have done nothing. In all your time here how many wreckers have you denounced? Your file shows, comrade, that you have not given up one person to the police. Surely you must have seen workers disrupt morale by arriving late or claiming that a production target is unobtainable? Have you deliberately closed your eyes against traitors, selfishly cocooned in your own world? Has your wife or neighbours never made an anti-Soviet remark? How can you claim to be a good citizen when the labour camps are crying out for people to be re-educated? It is every citizen's duty to root out this scum of parasites, yet you have done nothing. Do you still plead not guilty?'

Art lit a cigarette from the packet that Georgi proffered. His fingers shook and he tried not to think of Irena and the baby who would have woken by now. 'I came here to help build socialism in the Soviet Union. I came to serve. If I can serve socialism better by pleading guilty, then tell me my exact crimes and I will sign my confession.'

Georgi tut-tutted softly. 'Comrade, do you think I have

time to find crimes for every person who passes through here? Have people not got a responsibility for their own crimes? Sometimes it takes them just a few moments, other times it takes days, but people always find something to confess to once they leave this car and enter those doors.' He pulled on his cigarette. 'That is why you are still sitting out here. I can arrest you for a dozen things if you wish to step outside the car. However you still have a choice and so do I. But things change so quickly that soon the choice will be out of my hands. You were born into a despised class of parasites which left you with no useful skill. If you were an engineer or technician you would have been arrested long ago as the need arose. All you can offer as a prisoner is crude strength and we have sufficient *kulaks* for that. If you wish to serve the Soviet Union then I am willing to give you one last chance.'

'To do what?'

'Go home.'

'To my wife and . . .'

'To Ireland. You will be more useful there.'

'But my family . . . my whole life is here.'

'Do you love your wife?'

'Yes.'

'Then why continue to contaminate her with your foreignness? When you are arrested your wife will have to be charged too. Think of that. When the imperialists invaded America they killed the natives with smallpox brewing in the folds of blankets. The imperialists are trying to do likewise with us, only they are sending their viruses inside people. It was a mistake to let a single foreigner in. A few like you are good comrades but most are Jews whom the imperialists are keen to get rid of, knowing that they will work their mischief here. Within a year there won't be a foreigner left to spread discontent and counter-revolution in Moscow. Unless you leave now you will have to be arrested, along with your wife and all her family. I am giving you this chance, Goold, because I like your brother, although even he has repeatedly denounced you.'

'Brendan would never denounce me.' Art paused, suddenly unsure of everything as he watched the naked man through the window being casually beaten by warders. 'What did Brendan say about me?'

'All his life he has been jealous of you and all you stand to inherit. You must stay away from your brother in London, have no contact with him. Forget he ever existed and I will forget everything that he told me. You must think only of yourself. If you step outside the car into this prison yard there is nothing I can do to save you. Yet I am willing to give you this last chance, so why won't you give your wife one?'

'Can I take her with me? I love her. I can go nowhere without her and the child.'

'It's a funny kind of love to sign another person's death warrant. Are you denouncing her?'

'She has done nothing.'

'That is a start, the same crime you've admitted to. She also married a foreigner, for which under the new law she can serve ten years. Furthermore your brother has already denounced her too. However if you disappear then such things may be overlooked. If not . . . ?' Georgi shrugged. 'They may let her keep the child with her in prison. Then again, they may not.'

'Can I at least explain this to her?'

'She will understand. She understands reality far better than you.'

'What will happen to her?'

Georgi stubbed out his cigarette and glanced around as if

frightened of being overheard. He gave Art a disconcertingly honest look. 'Comrade, I no longer know what will happen to me or to any of us. Have you no idea of the great favour I am doing you? When you reach Ireland apply for her and the child to follow. Perhaps in time, based on your performance, you can apply to return here. Your file will remain open.'

'What does that mean?'

'It means that the NKVD will be watching to see how genuine your efforts are. I have studied Ireland and it puzzles me deeply, comrade. What was the point in having a revolution where absolutely nothing changes? Why did the proletariat not rise again when they saw how little was achieved? Petty bourgeois nationalism is a rust clogging the wheels of change. Our party in Ireland is small and fragmented. We have reports of renegade members attempting to find common cause with allegedly progressive elements of Republicanism, but such compromises can only lead to bastardised deviant thinking. It is important for us to have one man who will stand firm against any dilution of Comrade Stalin's right to control party policy and to ensure no deviation from the goal of a single clear voice speaking for communism and revolution worldwide. We depend on you to educate Irish comrades seduced by petty nationalism. You will be Stalin's rock.'

Any vulnerability was gone from Georgi's face. The prison gates opened and a van entered from Lubyanka Square. Warders emerged to seize hold of more prisoners and shove them forward, oblivious to their protests. These deviants were going to be re-educated, to work as heroically as the prisoners who carved the White Sea Canal out of rocks with their bare hands. If a few perished, at least they would do so under a Soviet sky. Art might have stepped from the car to join them if he was unmarried. But he had a family to consider, even if Irena or the boy might never know what happened to him. In Ireland he would be Stalin's rock. He would be a foot soldier, a missionary, John the Baptist paving the way among infidels and foreigners. He looked at Georgi who took an envelope from his pocket.

'I'll drive you to the station,' the NKVD officer said. 'In a day or two you will be in Finland. Along with your ticket here are four letters written by your father over the last year, describing the property in Ireland you still cling to. I have removed them from your file at great personal risk so they cannot be used against you.'

Art opened the envelope and removed the letters, which had been opened and officially stamped as evidence. It was hard to read Father's writing in the car, but on the back of one envelope was a quotation from Walt Whitman:

> *Of Life, immense in passion, pulse and power –*
> *Ocean of leaves of grass . . .*

He could hear Father's voice as he read the lines and saw his family gathered on the stone jetty that Eva had once christened Paradise Pier when he was a boy. He closed his eyes to let the image become drenched in the colours of Donegal Bay. Another scream came from within the prison. Art opened his eyes.

'Look happy,' Georgi said. 'You are going home.'

Art stared at him. 'Where are you from? Will you ever be able to go home?'

The NKVD officer started the engine, revving it angrily until the gates were opened. Ignoring Art, he drove recklessly, immersed in his private thoughts. Getting out at the train station Art asked if Brendan had really denounced him and why he could not seek out and confront his brother, but Georgi

Polevoy simply ignored him and drove off. Art knew that the next suspect Georgi picked up would pay the price for his careless remark. An hour's walk would bring Art back to the room where Irena would be pacing now, frantic with worry as she held the child. There might be time to say goodbye and catch a later train. But Art could not be sure if any of the figures outside the station had been posted there to watch him or if neighbours were primed to make charges against his wife and child if he reappeared on the landing. The ticket would get him as far as Finland. From there he would have to find the money. How could Brendan have done this to him? Taking a last glance back at the Moscow streets, Art walked into the station and turned his face towards Ireland.

# PART TWO

# 1936

# NINETEEN

# *Hunting and Shooting*

### *Mayo, 1936*

All her life Eva had loved nature – the billowing gales sweeping in to batter the Donegal coastline during her childhood, walking alone for hours feeling the exhilaration of winter storms where she had felt in danger of being washed away. So why did the wind oppress her now, whistling through the densely planted woodland which besieged her matrimonial home? Its inland whine increased her sense of being trapped on the cusp of her thirty-fifth birthday, running this sporting guesthouse with two small children and a husband from whom she seemed gradually more estranged.

Unable to sleep, Eva shifted in her makeshift bed in the damp basement of Glanmire House, a bed she had made for herself that was so different from any life imagined in childhood. Sometimes she recalled her dreams of art galleries clamouring for her paintings and hilltop retreats overgrown with scented verbena where she could sketch late into the evenings, content with the company of pets. It was years since she last held a pencil for any reason except to scribble down the lists perpetually running through her head. Provisions to order,

229

bills to try and pay, bookings to confirm by post for what few guests they could attract.

She slept naked tonight, an occasional childhood habit reverted to when Freddie was away. It was a bohemian impulse he would mistrust, another glimpse into the unorthodox character of her family. Freddie believed that only strumpets slept naked. Wives acquiesced to having their nightgowns rolled up for a surprisingly few brief thrusts, then lay awake while their husbands crumpled up asleep as though shot.

Two days ago Freddie had left for Dublin – ostensibly to attend the Freemasons and try to drum up business by letting any sporting types know about the excellent rough shooting on the nearby bogs. But Eva knew that it was also an excuse to drink more of the money they did not possess. His eyes would be bloodshot when he walked from Castlebar Station to the Imperial Hotel tomorrow afternoon for a last whiskey before retrieving his car parked on the Mall. But this was the price of married life and her lot was not bad compared to others she knew.

The two children had not drawn Freddie and her closer as she once imagined. Francis's softness confused Freddie and sometimes Eva wished that their daughter, Hazel, had been born a boy for his sake. Hazel was stubborn, even in her prolonged birth in a Dublin nursing home in 1929 with the world's stock markets collapsing. Looking into her daughter's face when the nurse held out Hazel, Eva had sensed that here was a true Fitzgerald.

The children's arrival had led her to suppress many of what Freddie described as her 'notions' as she focused on the role of being a good mother. It seemed that finally this was the person she was meant to be, not some mystic artist. Only the rich could afford to indulge such conceits and Glanmire

House had made them anything but rich. The Goold Verschoyles were soft compared to the Fitzgeralds because they were raised soft. Freddie had grown up without that cushion of money after his father died when he was seven, leaving him to survive by evolving a *hail-fellow-well-met* mask to hide any pain from the world and from himself. Eva should never have expected him to understand her abstract spiritual search. He understood the best cover for shooting woodcock, the relative merits of retrievers over red setters, the measure of good whiskey and how to deal firmly but fairly with servants – the attributes the Fitzgeralds were steeped in. Over the past eight years, as their guesthouse flagged, Eva had learnt that unfortunately he did not understand money.

Marriage taught Eva to understand camouflage, singing hymns each Sunday because she was expected to in the Fitzgerald pew in the small Protestant church beyond Glanmire Wood where Freddie always gave the reading. Back at the house her old books rested on high shelves that even the housemaid had stopped dusting. Some afternoons, lying down for her hour's rest, Eva tried to get lost within them, but more often turned to the American thrillers loaned to her by Mr Clements. It was hard to see herself as a questing child of the universe now: she was a Fitzgerald wife and mother – more mother than wife if honest. Since the children's birth she had thrown herself so utterly into their imaginative lives that Freddie was gradually being frozen from her emotions. She had little energy for anything but sleep by the time of night when guests could be left to nurse their whiskey and swap tales of poor shooting luck.

This emotional retreat caused intense guilt when she saw Freddie locked out from his children, unable to find a key to enter their fantasy world. He was growing old before his time, already acquiring the settled mannerisms of a middle-aged man. Behind his occasionally explosive anger she knew that he desperately needed love and, when she possessed energy, she tried to reach out. But her priorities were elsewhere and she could not help magnifying his faults when she grew exhausted. Unsurprisingly, he increasingly spent his time outdoors in baggy trousers with his Holland ejector 12-bore gun and the few guests they could muster. This was his domain. To Eva, he left the house and the hiring of maids who rarely stayed long before being lured away to England or the American cities glimpsed on celluloid in Castlebar on their evenings off.

Eva turned over in bed, with all thought of sleep banished. It wasn't just this sense of being confined that kept her awake. There was something unsettling beyond her window, an intruder in the wood. Eva thought she had heard a distant motor ten minutes ago. Perhaps Freddie had returned by the late train and gone drinking in the town. He could have driven into the ditch at the turn for their wood and be stumbling up the avenue trying not to waken her.

She glanced at the other single bed in this damp basement to which they decamped whenever a full complement of guests was staying. The lord and lady of the manor cooped up beside the ghost in the wine cellar. Its sole advantage was that serving girls were less likely to disturb her here over trivial matters, too scared of the presence they claimed to sense in the nearby doorway of the wine cellar. A curious melancholic foreboding did pervade that narrow crypt-like room, radiating onto the passageway step directly outside it. Initially Eva was not told how a former butler once hung himself from a hook there, after being wrongly accused of stealing a misplaced five pound note. Freddie's mother in Dublin had worried lest the tale frighten her, so at first Eva never understood the maids' apprehension on being asked to store provisions in the cellar or why she herself often shivered at that step. It was two years before their elderly neighbour, Miss MacManus of Killeaden House near Kiltimagh, told Eva how the butler had been unable to contemplate being dismissed when his honesty was challenged. '*Let him know you're there for him,*' old Miss MacManus urged. '*These Fitzgeralds are too practical to understand. Pray for his release because he can no longer pray for himself.*'

The butler had acquired a limp from three decades of breaking in his master's new shoes and Mary, the housemaid from Foxford, and the kitchen maid, Brigid, claimed to hear his distinctive squeak of leather at night. They locked the room they shared in the outhouse loft, maintaining that an unseen presence often tried the doorknob. Hurrying down the twilit avenue on evenings off, they used to scream when Francis followed them through the trees in a white sheet, until Eva discovered his tricks. The boy was more gallant now, an eight-and-a-half-year-old chaperone who escorted them through the darkening woods that he loved, utterly unafraid as he scampered back alone.

The young farm labourers who had accompanied various maids back up the avenue were always more fearful of encountering Fitzgeralds than ghosts. They gravitated towards the shadows when within sight of Glanmire House. From this basement window, Eva had sometimes observed their barely visible shapes among the trees. With a muted ache, she would envisage the brush of hands along thighs. The scrimmage over each button slowly undone, with outer fortifications surrendered between kisses until the girl knew it was time to break free and flit across the lawn, fleeing from ghosts and aroused young men.

Freddie dismissed talk of ghosts as superstition yet always suggested that Eva let Bess, their sheepdog, sleep in the basement when he was away. But Bess – though normally fearless – grew so unsettled on the only night when Eva tried this, pacing the room and whining, that she had merely increased Eva's unease. Still she wished she were here tonight as she sat up in bed now, because this sense of an intrusive presence made her apprehensive. Five minutes ago Bess and the two gun dogs had commenced a fierce barking from their kennels. She wondered could it be Mary, sneaking out to meet her Blueshirt boyfriend. Perhaps they lay breast to breast now on the overgrown slope beyond the lawn, with the maid's low cries smoothed by his kisses. Eva knew that she was allowing her views on Mary's morals to be swayed by Mrs McGrory's dislike of the maid's politics. Mary gave cheek unlike the local girls whom Eva generally employed. But surely the maid had more sense than to take such risks with a man?

The intruders could be robbers or IRA men from Leitrim – where rumours of communist unrest were rife – come to raid Freddie's gun cabinet. Last month the IRA had murdered Admiral Boyle Somerville in front of his wife in County Cork, accusing him of being a British recruiting agent because he gave a reference to a local man wishing to join the Royal Navy. In recent years, their conflict against General O'Duffy's Blueshirts had divided the locality. With the Blueshirts now in disarray, the IRA might feel free to attack whomever they wished. They could be hunting for Mr Clements to deliver their summary justice. Although anonymous threats were made to burn out the Fitzgeralds during the civil war, they had probably not emanated from Turlough where the family was respected. Still she discovered hidden fault lines when asking the local grocer and publican, Mr Durcan – the first local Catholic to own a car – where he had been born. '*On the side of the Bohola Road, mam,*' he'd replied tersely.

'*After my father died from apoplexy when your in-laws evicted us from our cottage.*'

Eva rose to peer up through the basement window, trying to convince herself that she was mistaken. With a house full of guests, she didn't need a phobia about intruders to add to her existing cocktail of worries. Becoming acutely conscious of her nakedness, she donned some underclothes and a night-gown. Goethe's poems lay open on the table under the window and she recalled the poem she had read before blowing out the candle, about an erl-king luring children to their death in the woods. Entering the passageway she passed the wine cellar, unable to prevent a trickle of cold sweat down her backbone from the irrational dread that a ghostly hand might seize her. She breathed a childish sigh of relief as she climbed the stairs and pushed open the baize door into the silent main house.

Francis and Hazel were sleeping quietly in the nursery where the fire's dying embers cast patterns on the ceiling. It was impossible to check the four guest bedrooms, though she doubted if the Dublin Roman Catholic, the Tyrone gentleman and the two Staffordshire guests who shared a room were wandering about at this hour. Mr Clements was in London on business, so his room was empty. She wondered could it be the elderly governess, Miss Crossan, whose proprietary way of sitting up at night drove Freddie to distraction. A low fire in the hall grate made her feel exposed to any prying eyes at the window as she unlocked the gun cabinet and chose the lightest gun. She did not bother loading it, hoping that the sight alone might scare off intruders.

At the front door Eva hesitated, suspecting that nobody would feel intimidated by her shaking with fear in a dressing gown. She only needed to cry out for guests to emerge from their bedrooms, pulling up braces and lighting candles as they gently ridiculed her fears. She dreaded them ribbing Freddie if no intruder was found almost as much as she dreaded a confrontation with one. But now she could discern definite sounds outside as several pairs of boots crossed the gravel. They passed the front steps and veered to the left. Eva opened the door and stood in the night air, clutching the gun. Traces of blood lingered on the steps where guests had displayed their bag of slaughtered game, after being taken out by Mikey in his master's absence.

Three men were ahead of her, crouching down to peer at her basement window. These were not IRA men or robbers but voyeurs. Perhaps they often spied on her, with the village aware of Freddie's absences. Had they seen her kneel in prayer with her back to the window or cry herself asleep with a pillow between her knees? She was about to confront them, when one man tossed a pebble against the glass. His action confused Eva. Perhaps they wished to make her wake up and walk sleepily towards the window, unsure if she had heard something? Yet they didn't back away from view. If she were down there Eva would be able to identify their faces. The man scooped up another pebble but his older companion put out a hand to restrain him, listening intently. Eva remained as still as if she were the voyeur. Still she must have made some noise because the older man rocked on his heels and sprang back to knock the gun from her hands, sending her sprawling on the grass with his hand covering her mouth. She bit into his palm and he winced and drew back his hand as if to slap her. A whisper stilled them both.

'Let her go, for God's sake. That's my sister!'

The older man rolled off, nursing his palm, and left Eva to stare up into her brother's face. Art's clothes were ragged but the branding iron of Marlborough College meant that he could never pass for a tramp. Even in a mud-streaked suit he looked handsome, with the stubble of several days' travel making him seem older than thirty-four. By comparison the youngest of the trio was an earnest baby-faced youth.

'We didn't mean to scare you.' Art reached down to help Eva up, then hissed at the older man: 'Never attack a woman, Gralton.'

'She startled me, Goold,' his companion protested in an accent that blended West of Ireland intonations with a pronounced American twang. 'Sensing a gun at your back is darn uncomfortable.'

The man's use of Art's abridged surname was more shocking than his previous lunge. '*Goold*' made Art sound like an amputee. Verschoyle was their true name. Grandpappy had merely assumed his wife's name of Goold when coming into her Limerick estates. Art shrugged, recognising her distress at another family connection severed. But Eva's heart thrilled at his unexpected appearance. He towered over her as they embraced and she felt safe no matter how bizarre the hour. Art was always her minder who made every day special. She remembered him bringing home schoolchums who played the balalaika, laughed a lot and let her win at tennis – boys utterly unlike his current companions who eyed her mistrustfully.

'Could we go inside?' Art whispered. 'It's not safe out here where we might be overheard.'

Eva didn't want to risk them making noise by trooping through the main hall. Indeed she didn't want his companions in her home at all. She longed to have Art to herself, to sit in the kitchen and feed him, talking openly to someone who understood her. The family only knew that he had returned from Russia because last year his name appeared in a Dublin court case concerning the banning of the Friends of Soviet Russia. Eva told them to slip around to the servants' door. She re-entered the hall, locked the door and quickly went downstairs with more than ghosts to fear now. Darting along the narrow passageway she unlocked the back door. The youngest man brushed past and when they reached the kitchens Eva heard him brusquely mutter, 'The first thing we ban, Goold, is the tradesman's entrance.'

'What do you want, Charlie?' Art snapped. 'To wake every imperialist tourist in Mayo?'

Yet when the youth sat at the table where she could see his face, he looked more hungry and exhausted than belligerent. She felt sorry for him, whatever he was doing with these men.

The range was almost out but she raked it up before adding turf and putting on the heavy kettle to boil. Art came over to place a hand apologetically on her shoulder. 'I'd never have come here had I somewhere else to go.'

'You know you're always welcome, Art.'

'I'm not the one who's staying.'

She glanced at the table. 'What do you mean?'

'That's Jim Gralton.' He saw her blank look. 'Do you never read newspapers?'

'I've two small children to raise.'

'What sort of country do you want to raise them in?'

'Don't lecture me,' Eva said. 'You're not on a platform now, *Mr Goold*.'

'You changed your name too.' Art sounded defensive.

'It's hardly the same thing. I got married.'

'So how is the old duffer?'

'Freddie and I are both fine.'

'Mother doesn't think so.'

'I haven't written to Mother for months.'

'That's why she doesn't think you're fine.'

Eva saw his companions hungrily eyeing the soda bread

wrapped in towels to cool for the morning. There was so much she wanted to tell Art and much that he might reveal if they were alone.

'I like the old duffer,' Art said. 'Freddie is solid, he earths you to reality.'

'Freddie thinks you're insane. My crazy Bolshevik brother that nobody here likes to mention . . .' Eva's fingers brushed against his stubble. 'Are you happy, Art?'

'Who could be happy back in this country?' Tiredly, he leaned against the wall. 'I see children die in Dublin every day from the most curable disease – poverty. Twenty-five thousand families packed into four thousand tenements where the landlords only spend money on thugs to evict those falling behind in their rent. In Russia I saw how life could be when a genius co-ordinates a blueprint. Here people are happiest being led like sheep by their priests.'

'Do they accept you?'

'Who?'

'The people you're with.'

'Why wouldn't they? I work as hard as any man on the docks.'

'You're still not one of them.'

'Every man is equal in this struggle,' Art said. 'You imagine me better educated than my comrades but I was a hundred times more ignorant. There were so many lies I had to unlearn. People look at me now and actually see me. They don't see you. They see a Fitzgerald and before that a Goold Verschoyle. In Dunkineely, villagers were trained like dogs to fawn at our name. It's not until you see yourself reflected in a policeman's polished baton that you realise who you really are.'

Eva remembered a summer's day and a sandy-haired farm boy with mottled bruises on his legs staring up at Art in

Grandpappy's trap. The slow process of losing her brother had commenced there. Art took her hand for a moment.

'I visited Dunkineely last week, the first time in years. I called to see Ffrench and tried to talk to Father but we only quarrelled again. Mother is worried for you. Did she ever climb to the top of this wood?'

'With her arthritis I doubt it.'

'She said that in a dream she watched you run in distress towards three oak trees in a clearing here. You put your arms around one which gave you comfort. It sounds nonsensical, but you were always on her wavelength.'

'I'll get your companions some food,' Eva said, agitatedly.

'Do the oaks exist?'

Eva shrugged and entered the pantry, where three recently slaughtered ducks hung. She wondered had she mentioned the oaks in a letter to Mother. They marked the wood's most inaccessible border, guarded by briars and hawthorn bushes. But the spot remained precious to her since Francis's birth. Eva turned to Art who had followed her into the narrow room.

'It isn't that I'm not on your wavelength too,' she said. 'But often I feel life here closing in on me. It's hard to keep my antennae open. Circumstances are difficult, Freddie and I are poor.'

Art examined the shelves. 'You're not. I've seen poverty.'

'There are different types of poverty, like different types of need. Your struggle is not the only one. Go in to your friends, I won't be long.'

There was whisky that Freddie didn't know she had hidden and cold meat for sandwiches during tomorrow's shoot. Eva brought in anything she could spare. Art's companions ate like they had not seen food for days, though she noticed how he held back. She made more tea, alert in case the maids stirred early.

Art introduced his youngest companion. 'This is Charlie Donnelly, student and poet. More poet than student these days, I'm afraid. His university studies have suffered since he fell into bad company.'

The older man laughed but Donnelly scowled.

'Activist,' he corrected. 'More party activist these days. Poetry is a luxury that must earn its keep.'

Despite his intensity Eva thought that he looked impossibly young to be involved in whatever they were doing.

'You'd like his poems,' Art said, then addressed his young companion, 'There's a touch of the poet in Eva, Charlie. Recite the poem you wrote when imprisoned in Mountjoy.'

Eva liked the bashful way the boy shook his head, having to be gruffly coaxed by the older man – whom she decided was an American who had acquired some local expressions – before beginning to recite. The American helped himself to more whiskey and half listened. Donnelly's poem lacked ornamentation, with images laid out as precisely as an architect's plans. Eva liked his Ulster accent and made him repeat the final verse.

'I'm sorry my boots made a mess of your floor,' Donnelly said when finished, as if anxious to avoid praise. 'I've been walking for days.'

'And sleeping rough before that,' Art added. 'Charlie's father kicked him out.'

'It's hard for him to understand.' The poet was keen to defend his father. 'He was a good cattle dealer who became a bad landlord. Something in him died with my mother's death. He married again, but unhappily. They're afraid I'll indoctrinate the others, start them thinking for themselves. But I've a new life now.'

'Like Art,' Eva said, the hurt visible in her tone.

'We have that in common,' Donnelly agreed. 'Some comrades

241

are suspicious of our background, as if only people born into the proletariat can be integral to the struggle. But that's a reactionary position. Art and I have shown how to push class boundaries aside to create a focused revolutionary movement.'

Eva wondered what exactly Donnelly felt they shared in common. Although Father treated all men as his equal and cautioned his children to give rather than take and not be beguiled by titles or Mammon, cattle dealers rarely dined at the Manor House.

'Charlie is moving to London,' Art said. 'Jim is why we're here.'

Eva examined the weary-looking older man whose name struck a chord now, not from newspapers which she rarely found time to read, but from overhearing the maids discuss some man of that name, with Mary blessing herself like he was the devil. But the Gralton mentioned by the maids had been an Irishman wanted by the police in connection with unrest in Leitrim. Eva thought of her children upstairs and how nothing must harm them.

'What have you done?' Eva asked Gralton.

'I came home after twenty years in New York.'

'That's hardly a crime.'

'It is to de Valera, the so-called republican who betrayed us all once he got his claws on power.'

Again Eva discerned the West of Ireland inflection within his American accent.

'You have something to do with the trouble in Leitrim.'

Gralton laughed. 'I *am* the trouble in Leitrim. The living incarnation of the Communist Plague.'

'Jim built a communal hall for his native parish,' Art explained. 'He let it be used for dances and set up classes to stop capitalist gombeen men robbing people blind. He lent out books and magazines to help them think for themselves. He wanted to bring people together and by Jove he did. He brought together people who were never on the same side before, with Blueshirt fascists stoning his hall and the IRA firing bullets into it.'

'Not all the IRA,' the young poet interjected.

'Sorry, Charlie,' Art retorted. 'Not your few pals in the Republican Congress. Just the rank and file rosary bead rattlers who tore down the anti-capitalist banner of the Belfast Protestant workers who were persuaded to join the march to Wolfe Tone's grave last year – the Neanderthals who will crush your Congress as a Red threat to Catholic Ireland. The IRA can't be reformed from within. Revolution can only come from a single internationalist communist movement owing complete allegiance to Stalin . . .'

'Will you pair give over your Jaysusing arguments,' Gralton protested wearily. 'You've my head done in these last two days.'

Art turned to Eva. 'The bottom line is that they're all determined to drive out Jim – the rancher farmers, the government and the church. This Free State has no room for those who won't conform. You must know this, Eva. Freddie thinks we have nothing in common, but there's no room in de Valera's kingdom for the likes of me or for Freddie either, despite his efforts to cling on.'

'Locals here respect us,' Eva protested.

'As what?' Art scoffed. 'Fossils? The further you fall the more they feel their status rising. They may still bend a servile knee but they won't be happy till this house is levelled.'

Eva now recalled Gralton being mentioned at a dinner-table conversation. Freddie's uncle from Turlough Park had mentioned saboteurs attempting to set up a communist canton among the Leitrim lakes, with Catholics warned from the pulpit under pain of excommunication not to give shelter to this dangerous Bolshevik on the run. From the state of Gralton's clothing it was obvious that people had heeded this episcopal warning.

'What do they wish to charge you with?' she asked.

'I've committed no crime,' Gralton replied. 'I spent two decades in the New York unions, staring down the gun barrels of cops bribed to break up strikes. The only reason I took out American citizenship in 1919 was so as not to travel on a British passport. I'm more Irish than de Valera, who used his American passport to save his neck from execution after the '16 Rising. But now he's using my American citizenship to brand me a foreigner, claiming it gives him the right to deport me as a subversive. Well, they'll have to find me first.'

He glanced at Art who cleared his throat. 'That's where I need your help, Eva,' her brother said quietly. 'Just two nights' shelter, long enough for Charlie and me to go ahead and organise a safe house in Munster.'

'I don't understand.' Eva tried not to betray her panic.

'Be honest, can you tell if Jim is a Yank or not? What's to stop him passing himself off as a tourist? Why should the hunted man not pose as a hunter?'

'We're fully booked, though it rarely happens.' Eva was relieved to have a valid excuse.

'You could find room somewhere.'

'I'm sorry.'

'I told you she wouldn't help,' Gralton said. 'Bourgeois people like her . . .'

'Whatever else my family were,' Art snapped, 'we never stooped to being mere bourgeoisie.'

Eva glanced at the poet to see if this distinction registered.

'Besides I thought we were creating an inclusive society,' Art continued, 'abolishing class, instead of rushing to easy

244

judgements. It's hard for any woman to have strangers land on her at night.' He looked at Eva. 'If you can't help I understand.'

'*You* won't be staying?' she asked, disappointed.

'Charlie and I must start walking for Castlebar soon to catch the first train. We'll send a coded telegram when we find a safe house. I've never sought your help before, Eva, and I'll never seek it again.'

Eva wavered. 'He'd have to sleep in the basement.'

'I've slept naked in stone cells,' Gralton interjected and Eva knew that, however grudgingly he accepted Art as a comrade, he harboured inbred suspicions about a house like this.

'Can you shoot?' she asked.

'Show me a peeler and you'll have your answer.'

'I'm talking about snipe and ducks.'

'That was the only way I ever tasted meat as a boy.'

The grandfather clock struck five. In an hour's time the morning routine would commence. Freddie was due home this afternoon, having promised Francis a surprise which the boy could not stop talking about. It was madness to contemplate shielding a fugitive, but suddenly it felt like a done deal.

'Freddie would kill me should he find out. You must never tell anyone, Art.'

Art clasped her hand across the table. 'You're a brick, Eva. One last thing, though. We haven't a penny beyond our train fares. You'll have to square Jim being a guest with Freddie and pay for his train ticket to join us. Can you do that?'

'Yes,' she lied. 'I'll put in my own cash when Freddie is doing his weekly accounts.'

In fact she hadn't money to pay the staff until the Tyrone man settled his bill in three days' time. Even with the Fitzgerald name most Protestant shops in Castlebar had already made noises about it being wiser to go elsewhere rather than be refused credit. Freddie wouldn't say how much they owed Mr Devlin, the Catholic grocer, whose shop on the Mall was one of many she always quickly passed in case the proprietors came out after her. But there was no time to worry about this. She rose and allotted tasks. The poet was instructed to make sandwiches for the train, while Gralton was dispatched to shave with one of Freddie's old razors in the basement bedroom. Art tiptoed with her up to Mr Clements's room, which was kept unlocked even in his absence.

Years ago – when it became apparent that the Commander intended to stay indefinitely – Mr Clements had sent to London for a large sea chest of clothes. Eva had never opened the chest, nor seen him touch it. Instead a tailor came from Castlebar twice a year to measure him for new outfits. The chest contained the remnants of a previous life put behind him after he chanced upon this hideaway. Over the years the Commander had become Eva's courteous confidant in times of crisis. Part of what people regarded as his idiosyncratic attachment to Glanmire House was the fact that since his first day out with Freddie he never again fired a gun. Eva didn't know what Mr Clements thought of Freddie and rarely allowed herself to speculate on his unspoken – though tacitly acknowledged – attachment to her. Yet, although she knew he would have readily assisted her if he was here, rifling through his possessions felt like a violation.

She opened the chest. An officer's white cap and dress uniform were neatly placed at the top, beside a photograph of him as a young officer, the inscription embossed in gold leaf as having been taken at *The Grand Studio, Malta*. The white civilian suits underneath were light and unsuitable for the Mayo climate, but had never been seen by Freddie or the maids. Gralton would have no option but to wear them. The shoes in the trunk were of little use over rough ground. Gralton would look comic and slightly vulgar in this non-Mediterranean setting but this was how Freddie saw Americans anyway.

Art fingered the Commander's portrait. 'So what does he do all day?'

'Walks and reads American thrillers and French books that cause the post office headaches for not knowing if they're banned. Most are eventually delivered with a frontispiece illustration cut out.'

'Is he in love with you?'

'He's forty years older than me, Art, and I'm married. Have you forgotten?'

'No.' Art carefully replaced the photograph. 'He has a nice face for an imperialist.'

Eva closed the chest and sat on it. 'You never wrote to me once from Moscow.'

'It was not easy to get letters out.'

'Or from Dublin since you returned. Have you seen Brendan? Thomas thinks you're leading him further astray.'

'I have no contact with Brendan.'

'He worships you.'

'He's no true Verschoyle so.'

'What do you mean?'

'They only worship money.'

'What do you mean, *they*?' Though fearful of waking the guests Eva could not keep her voice low. '*They* are you and me and Maud and Thomas and Brendan. Name one of us with any real interest in money?'

'Maybe because we're contaminated by Goold blood. Father was always a disappointment to our Dublin cousins. They felt his solid Dutch backbone had been corroded away. I wouldn't mind but for all the airs and graces our cousins give themselves we're not aristocrats at all. Only when I returned to Dublin did I discover where we really came from.'

'From Holland with William of Orange,' Eva said. 'Grandpappy said there was a General Verschoyle.'

'If so he was a general dogsbody,' Art snorted, keeping his voice low. 'We were foot soldiers, skivvies working our passage. We had no backside in our trousers when we landed in Dublin. The only job available was in the knacker's yard – the lowest, most horrible work imaginable. That's how our family started in Ireland, Eva. But being Dutch we were pragmatic. The yard owners were typical short-sighted Irish capitalists, only interested in a quick profit from animal skins. They virtually gave away the blubber and fat and bones. Well, we weren't long becoming grubby middlemen, finding new markets for the leavings: soap, candles and God knows what. We waded through offal and guts to maximise every last farthing of profit. And what do you think we did after we'd skinned enough old horses that our fingernails stank and no decent person would touch us? We bought a rat-infested slum going cheap after the tenants fled from cholera. We washed our hands, donned frock coats and spent money, not on sanitation but on the shiny plaque that's still there – Verschoyle Court.'

'That was over two centuries ago,' Eva argued, although shocked. She remembered how Grandpappy only spoke in vague terms about their family history, though Father – who loved genealogy – had traced the Goold side back to both the Saxon kings and Niall of the Nine Hostages.

'It continues,' Art replied fiercely. 'Since returning from Russia I've been unloading boats with men whose children are coughing themselves to death in Verschoyle Court.'

Art sat beside her, the passion gone from his voice. He sounded weary. 'I love you, Eva, but I want to build a country where we can hold up our heads again. How could I face the men I work with if I still bore a name that married into respectability on the back of animal guts and has grown fat on slum rents ever since?'

'I'm merely asking you to keep Brendan out of your private war,' she pleaded.

'The day Brendan walked out of Marlborough he became his own man. At one time I thought that he respected me but all along he seems to have been a viper in the nest. I have reason to believe that he betrayed me though I can't find out if this is true. But surely if he could look into my face he would make contact. Falling out with him is breaking my heart, but personal feelings cannot distract from the class war being fought on these islands and a bigger one stirring in Spain. A war for the soul of Europe.'

Art's hair was cut tight with the faint remnant of a bruise on his forehead. Eva took his hand. 'How could Brendan betray you? He loves you just like I do. If you two have had some quarrel then promise me you will make it up. You have given up too much already, you don't need to give up your brother. Remember Beatrice Hawkins?'

Art's smile returned. 'Every summer she grew lovelier until the Great War came. Ffrench and I often mention her. Those were happy days, Eva.'

'I wish you had someone.'

Art gently removed his hand. 'There is someone . . .'

'Who?'

'My wife.'

'What wife?'

'I had to leave her behind in Moscow when the authorities felt that I could be of more use by helping to build the Party here in Ireland.'

'How long are you married?'

249

Art fingered his stubble.

'We have a son. I write but my letters may not get through. I told Brendan never to mention them until I was able to bring them to Ireland one day.'

Footsteps on the gravel startled them. Eva opened the wooden shutter a fraction. One of the Staffordshire men whom Freddie regarded as poor shots had wandered out barefoot, with his braces down. Thinking himself unobserved, he began to urinate by the trees. Eva wondered had their voices woken him. His compatriot appeared and strode silently down to lay a hand on his shoulder. He then did something that Eva considered peculiar. He kissed his cheek. Eva closed the shutter.

'You'll have to leave,' she whispered, needing time to digest Art's news. He bundled up the clothes and they crept downstairs to where Donnelly and Gralton waited in the basement bedroom. Gralton sat on the bed, having shaved. She honestly didn't know if he could pass as a tourist. Art dumped the Commander's white outfit on his lap.

'You made your dosh in commodities and bailed out before the crash. You've been swanning around Europe as a capitalist parasite ever since.'

Gralton fingered the light suit. 'Well, you needn't think I'm going to swan around Mayo dressed like a gadfly in this!'

'Don't worry,' Donnelly commented from the window, 'if you're twigged, de Valera will trade you for some pyjamas with arrows down the front.'

'Buster Keaton must be quaking in his boots with you two comedians,' Gralton said sourly. 'Move over Laurel and Hardy.'

'Just get changed before the house wakes,' Art told him.

Gralton picked up the suit and glanced at Eva. Turning her back she approached Charlie Donnelly who sat on the window table, reading one of her small pile of books which Freddie never touched. They formed an emotional diary nobody else could decode. Wishing she was wearing more clothes, Eva drew closer, curious to see which one he had chosen. The sandwiches he had made were wrapped in newspaper beside him. He glanced up from the book.

'These poems are beautiful. I've never read them before.'

Eva recognised the slender volume – *Lyrics from the Ancient Chinese*, in versions by Helen Waddell, published by Constable and Company. She could still recall the bustling aisles of Foyle's Bookshop on Charing Cross Road after skimping on food for a week to buy it when she was an art student.

'I've had that for years.'

'The poems are delicate, yet strong,' he replied, 'like being inside a woman's head. Three thousand years old, yet those people had the same dreams and fears as us. It makes you wonder.'

'What do you wonder?'

He looked down. 'I wonder why you marked the poem, *Lyric XIX, Written 718 B.C.?*'

'I must have liked it.'

'In one sense I see why. She holds the lyric line well.' Holding open the roughly cut pages, Charlie Donnelly recited so quietly that only the pair of them could hear:

> *'Selling of silk you were, a lad*
> *Not of our kin;*
> *You passed at sunset on the road*
> *From far-off Ta'in.*

> *'The frogs were croaking in the dusk;*
> *The grass was wet.*
> *We talked together, and I laughed:*
> *I hear it yet.*

251

*'I thought that I would be your wife;*
*I had your word.*
*And so I took the road with you,*
*And crossed the ford.'*

'It's the last verse that confuses me.' Donnelly turned the page as Gralton softly bemoaned his tight shoes.

*'I do not know when first it was*
*Your eyes looked cold.*
*But all this was three years ago*
*And I am old.'*

He closed the book and handed it back. 'You'll never be old,' he said quietly, 'even should you live to be a hundred.'

Eva liked his honest gaze, with the belligerence gone. She smiled, closing her dressing gown tighter.

'God knows why I marked that poem,' she lied. 'Keep the book. Bring it back when you next pass this way.'

'It's yours. I couldn't.'

'I thought all property was a form of theft,' she teased.

'Books will be exempt from the revolution.'

Footsteps passed along the corridor. The room went silent till they faded away.

'That's the maid going to stoke the range,' Eva told Art. 'She'll be confused to find it blazing. You must be quick.'

There was no time for proper farewells or for the questions that Eva longed to ask Art. She glanced out of the back door to ensure the yard was deserted, then kissed Art. Charlie Donnelly held the book.

'Are you sure I can borrow it?' he asked shyly.

'Yes. Now mind yourself.'

'You'll get it back. I promise.'

Art hissed at him to hurry and suddenly both men had disappeared through the trees. The kitchen door opened at the end of the corridor and Mary stood there.

'Did I hear something, Mrs Fitzgerald?'

'Just me letting in the air.'

'The range is blazing like the fires of hell.'

'A guest arrived very late. A Yank. Must be still keeping American time.'

'That would be the Yanks for you, Mrs Fitzgerald.' The girl threw up her eyes knowingly, though Eva doubted if she had ever glimpsed an American except on a cinema screen. 'What brings him here at all?'

'The same as the others I suppose,' Eva replied. 'Hunting and shooting.'

'I've tea brewing, mam. Will I bring a cup to your room?'

'No thanks,' Eva said quickly. 'The new guest took my room. I made a bed for myself on the nursery floor. It's rather hard which is why I couldn't sleep.'

Eva didn't like the maid's sly look. In her six months here Mary had never fitted in. Perhaps it was because, as she kept boasting, her older sisters in New York almost had enough dollars saved for her fare. Her American wake had not yet occurred, but from her attitude Eva suspected that these final months before emigrating were like a posthumous existence where she need only pay lip service to normal behaviour. Even parading to Blueshirt meetings in her uniform seemed part of a charade.

Eva didn't trust Mary and waited until she closed the kitchen door before slipping into the basement bedroom. Jim Gralton examined himself in the small mirror.

'I'm not vain but I'm darned uncomfortable dickied up like a gander. I don't want to hide here any more than you want me, Missus. But your brother is persuasive and in truth

253

I couldn't take another night on the bogs. My arthritis is bad.'

'I know. My mother suffers from it.'

'It wasn't from damp cabins she got it.'

'Does it matter how she got it? She suffers the same.'

'I'm sorry,' Gralton replied. 'The nerves are making me snappy. What do your guests discuss?'

'Shooting, some barrack-room humour when they think I'm beyond earshot. Politics and religion are generally banned – a rule my husband says works well in the Masons. The suit fits you well. How are the shoes?'

'I'll survive.' Gralton shuffled forward in obvious discomfort, his gait reminding her of stories about the ghostly butler. 'I've not shown my gratitude well, Missus. I'll try to be no trouble. I could use some shut-eye though.'

'Take that bed.' Eva pointed towards Freddie's bunk. To avoid scandal it was vital to create signs of a makeshift bed in the nursery. Realising that it was too risky to chance a second trip for her clothes, Eva asked Gralton to turn his back and dressed hurriedly. She noticed how, in his interest in the poems, Donnelly had forgotten the sandwiches. She imagined him and Art keeping to the fields until beyond the village, probably aware by now of the journey ahead with no food. As she did up her buttons, more footsteps entered the passageway. Eva wondered what Freddie would think if he returned early and walked in. Aware that she looked a sight with her hair uncombed, she checked that the corridor was empty, then gathered up her blankets and ran. The kitchen door opened just as she reached the stairs. Eva raced up, praying that Mary hadn't seen the trailing bedclothes. Reaching the nursery, Eva threw the blankets onto the floor. Hazel looked up sleepily.

'What's happening, Mummy?'

'Nothing, darling,' Eva told her daughter. 'More guests arrived than we had room for.'

'Why is this house always cold, even in summer? My feet are like ice.'

'I'll rub them.' Eva sat on her daughter's bed to take Hazel's bare soles on her lap. Hazel got cross if Eva tickled her toes but always allowed them to be kissed.

'Francis says he'll build jumps on the avenue for my pony. Miss Crossan thinks I'm too young but Francis says he'll do it when her back is turned. Please let him.'

Eva glanced at her sleeping son who reminded her of Art at his age. Minding his sister, building things for her. She had not shown Art his sleeping nephew and niece in case he found it painful with a son growing up in Moscow without him. Francis had something of his features, yet she could not imagine him shouting at political meetings or living with dockers. Francis had a softness that she loved and worried about.

Eva stroked her daughter's feet until she heard the cart belonging to Mr Tyrrell, the farmer to whom Freddie had already sold land adjoining the wood. These days he hovered like a shadow, supplying milk and butter on credit and giving lifts to staff as he patiently waited for these final acres that he felt sure would soon be sold to him. Through the shutters Eva watched him survey the wood with a proprietary eye, then help Mrs McGrory down with bags of provisions – a sign, Eva saw with relief, that their credit had not stretched beyond breaking point in Mr Devlin's shop in Castlebar. The cook clutched her copy of the *Catholic Bulletin*, along with the *Capuchin Annual*, which Miss Crossan had made a show of splashing out 2s.3d for. On sufferance she would have also collected Mary's copy of *Tit-Bits* which Mr Devlin never displayed on the counter. Eva didn't wish to leave the nursery but knew that Mrs McGrory would be waiting with the news from town. She turned from the window to kiss Francis who was stirring.

'Miss Crossan will get you up in a few minutes,' she said.

'Will not. Cross Ears will let us lie on for hours yet.'

'Don't call her that name, Francis. It's not nice.'

'Cross Ears doesn't mind. She often lies on in bed until nine.'

'You know that you must be up, washed and dressed before breakfast,' Eva scolded.

'All week we've had breakfast here in our dressing gowns.'

Generally Eva was too involved with guests to check the children until much later, but she suspected that what Francis said was true. Miss Crossan was so concerned to establish her position as someone who lived in with the family, instead of being a mere servant, that the children were becoming neglected. The governess spent her afternoons off having her hair done in Castlebar so that she could try to blend in and converse with guests late into the night, finding little tasks as if to invent a role as a surrogate lady of the house. Not that Eva cared about social position, but there was something manic about the woman's efforts to belong to the drawing room. Learned manners would never suffice. Miss Crossan would have been happier downstairs had she not alienated the staff who secretly mocked her. Francis and Hazel were becoming undisciplined due to her inability to control them. But Eva had no time to worry about this now, with break-fast for the guests to supervise.

'I want you both up and dressed,' she said firmly. 'You can't dawdle for hours in your dressing gowns.'

'Miss Crossan does,' Hazel informed her primly. 'She never gets dressed before the maid brings her up tea at eleven.'

Francis never referred to Mary or Brigid as 'the maid'. But

Hazel had Fitzgerald eyes that expected to be waited on. 'I
hate her,' she added.

'That's not nice, Hazel.'

'I know, Mummy, but it's true. She lets Francis do anything
he wants.'

'Little fibber,' Francis shot back.

'Stop it, both of you. I shall speak to Miss Crossan myself.'

Eva tried to fix her hair at the mirror before going downstairs where Mrs McGrory and Brigid fussed over the breakfast. Mary leaned against the table, scoffing as she read aloud
from the pastoral letter in Mrs McGrory's magazine:
*'Company keeping under the stars has taken over from the
good Irish custom of visiting and storytelling from one house
to another, with the rosary to bring all home in due time.'*

'Better for you to be lending a hand than mocking the
bishops, you heathen,' Mrs McGrory snapped.

Mary laughed, savouring her ability to rouse the cook.

*'The evil one is forever setting snares for unwary feet in
the dance hall, the motion picture, the immodest fashion in
female dress ...'*

Sensing her employer's presence, Mary quickly lowered the
paper. Yet Eva wondered if the words were mockingly aimed
at her after being caught in her dressing gown at dawn. 'I'm
just fetching milk for the table, Mrs Fitzgerald.' Mary picked
up two silver jugs and brushed past an unfamiliar girl in a
faded frock with no stockings who could have been seventeen but her bare feet made her look younger. She returned
Eva's gaze.

'Mr Fitzgerald told my dada you wanted someone to scrub
the flagstones once a week, mam,' she said. 'Mr Tyrrell gave
me a lift on his cart, but I jumped off on the avenue. It was
so lovely I wanted to walk up through the woods.'

'The flagstones are backbreaking work,' Eva warned.

'Work never killed a body yet, mam.'

Eva liked her instantly and even more so when she noticed the small sack of good clothes beside her. This was how Eva liked to think that she herself would dress if going to work in a new house, unafraid to wear dirty clothes for dirty work, not trying to make an impression or pretend to be anything she was not. The girl saw Eva glance at her bare legs.

'I figured my stockings would only be ruined, mam.'

'You're right,' Eva replied. 'What's your name?'

'Maureen.'

'Mrs McGrory will give you breakfast and show you where everything is kept. Did my husband mention money?'

'My dada and him made some class of deal, mam. Mary showed me where the scrubbing brush is, so I'll make a start before breakfast if you don't mind.'

Male voices boomed from the dining room above, the hearty laughter of confident men.

'How was Mr Devlin?' she asked the cook when the girl had gone.

'You'll find out soon enough, Mrs Fitzgerald. Hasn't he only just gone and asked himself here for lunch.'

'What?'

'He says to me, "Mr Fitzgerald is killed asking would I like a day's shooting and I've a distinguished guest coming down that he would enjoy meeting."'

'He said that?' Eva was shocked at the shopkeeper's presumptuousness.

'Bellowed it loud enough for the whole shop to hear.'

'And what did you say?'

'What I always say to him, Mrs Fitzgerald – "Up de Valera" – when I'm safely out of his hearing.'

'Up de Valera on a rope,' Mary opined, re-entering the kitchen.

Both women ignored her as they mulled over the grocer's remark. Eva had grown used to indignity but the notion of a tradesman casually inviting himself to their house – even if they owed him a considerable sum – was humiliating. Mr Devlin hadn't just invited himself, he had flaunted the fact so all of Castlebar could discuss how the Fitzgeralds had fallen.

'Who is his guest?' she asked.

'Devlin muttered about "a dignitary from Dublin". Probably some carthorse sent down by the Blueshirts to crank up their oul' movement that is falling apart.'

'It's Mr Patrick Belton, TD,' Mary announced, delighted to know something they didn't. 'My boyfriend says he's addressing a meeting in Castlebar tonight. The Dublin big nobs may have sacked General O'Duffy, but he is starting a new movement called the National Corporate Party, which only decent fascists will be allowed to join. Il Duce showed the way in Abyssinia and it will be up de Valera . . . with a rope round his neck.'

'That will do, Mary.' Eva nodded for the girl to carry up the first two breakfast plates that Mrs McGrory had laid out. Mrs McGrory watched her go.

'That strumpet won't be happy till she's married Mussolini himself, strutting around in her blue blouse. Cardinal McRory wouldn't be so keen on O'Duffy's crew if he knew how half the unmarried girls of Ireland are trouser-chasing inside it.'

'We'd better set the lunch table for two more,' Eva said as casually as possible.

'Mr Devlin says he doesn't know the going rate but he'll fix up when he has a quiet word. He said you might be glad of the business.'

Eva nodded, knowing there was no question of payment. After all Devlin would be eating his own food. He was not a bad man, especially now that his exuberant young followers had started to drift away. For all the Blueshirts' talk of a new world order, she knew that the only way Devlin could think to impress his guest was by grafting himself onto life in this Big House.

Mary returned to take up two more breakfasts as Eva knocked at the basement bedroom. When she entered, Gralton was staring wishfully up through the window.

'I couldn't sleep a wink. Maybe it's something about this room or else I can't get warm after all my time on the bogs. Did your brother give me a name?'

Eva pondered the question, realising how little she knew about Americans. 'Fortune,' she said. 'Max Fortune.' She did not know where the name came from, just that it would impress the guests. 'Go up for breakfast, Mr Fortune.'

'In all my years there, mam, I never met a Yank called Fortune.' He glanced in the mirror and brushed back his hair. 'It's a goddamn funny place to meet one now.'

He walked upstairs in his uncomfortable shoes. Eva checked the kitchen before going up to take her place as hostess. Gralton sat beside Mr O'Sullivan, the Dublin Roman Catholic who was reciting a litany of American place names to which his relations had emigrated. Gralton's American accent was perfect. She noticed how the Englishmen and the Tyrone Protestant kept their distance.

'Did you come over on a Cunard liner?' Mr O'Sullivan asked, convinced that only someone rich would possess the audacity to dress so unconventionally. 'That *Queen Mary* is a ship I'd like to see around. They say the interior is based on the Dorchester Hotel . . .'

Staring out the window, Eva was startled to see Freddie's car appear and park at the front steps. In the midst of her panic at not having formulated a story to explain Gralton's presence, she was relieved to see that Freddie didn't look too bad with no outward symptoms of a hangover. He stepped out and addressed someone in the passenger seat. Her heart froze as Mr Clements emerged. He brushed down his clothes and stared at the vista beyond the daffodil lawn, reminding her of the first time they spied on him from this window. Mr Clements, the unobtrusive constant in their marriage. He must have cut short his business or simply fled London for the sanctuary of this wood with his routine and his books. Freddie laughed with him as they mounted the steps in the sunshine, two men with nothing in common who had learnt to accommodate each other's presence. Eva heard their footsteps echo down the hall, then both men entered the open doorway. Freddie took in the extra guest and walked hospitably over to welcome Gralton. She was relieved that he was too much of a gentleman to ask questions there and then. Mr Clements remained in the doorway, with eyes not on Gralton's suit but on her. Eva looked back, her smile unchanging, but her eyes pleading that he say nothing.

'Fortune, eh?' Freddie crackled. 'Let's hope your name carries over onto the bog, what. We'll have some capital shooting this afternoon. I had a spot of good fortune myself last night. Didn't fancy another night in Dublin so I walked down to Kingsbridge and slipped the guard a few shillings to get on the night mail train, with my old pal Major McCourt who jumped ship at Athlone. We thought we'd be the only hobos sitting on mail sacks, but who was there? Only Commander Clements to bless us with his excellent company and a full hip-flask.'

Eva rose, telling Freddie that she would organise more breakfast. She paused in the doorway beside Mr Clements. 'I was not expecting you back so soon,' she whispered.

'So I see.' His mild tone betrayed nothing. 'Mr Fortune has a unique dress sense.'

'Please . . .'

'My dear Mrs Fitzgerald, don't trouble yourself to say more.'

Eva went downstairs where the new girl, Maureen, looked up and smiled, vigorously scrubbing the basement flagstones. She gave Mrs McGrory instructions, then busied herself in the pantry, hoping that Freddie would not seek her there. She heard his step in the kitchen however, with Mrs McGrory addressing him differently from how she addressed Eva. Freddie stooped his head to enter the pantry.

'There you are, old girl, I was looking for you.' He kissed her cheek. 'You look tired. Who is our mystery guest?'

'He arrived very late. I was locking up, with the others in bed. I had to put him down in our room.'

'Where was he coming from at that hour?'

'I don't know,' Eva replied helplessly. 'People can arrive from nowhere. Remember the Commander.'

'Clements was on a walking tour and appeared at a respectable hour. Do you know anything about him?'

'I think he's rich.'

'With a name like that he should be. His clothes are vulgar enough.'

'He saw that small ad we put in *The Field* months ago but couldn't remember the address. He thought we were near Pontoon Bridge and had to walk from there. He's a keen shooter paying two guineas for two nights.'

'What does he hunt? Buffalo?'

The extra money would make Freddie pause, even though Eva knew that she could not produce it. He took her hand, with that awkwardness which characterised his efforts to be tender. 'I'm being mean, I'm sorry. He seems a decent chap. It's just that I worry for you when I'm away.'

'He won't be our only visitor.' She was keen to change the subject.

'What do you mean?'

'Mr Devlin has invited himself to lunch and the afternoon shoot. He appears to think he has a standing invitation.'

'The grocer? I may have made a remark about going shooting some time. All men are equal on the bog, or at least I feel they should be. But I'm stumped if I ever mentioned lunch . . . ?'

'He's bringing a guest . . . a politician called Belton.'

'Patrick Belton? That loudmouth jumped-up publican? Whatever is Devlin playing at?'

'We owe him money. You can't trade on the Fitzgerald name for ever.'

'I know, but still . . .' Freddie tried to see the bright side. 'I suppose our ads do say "all welcome". I just never envisaged the local tradesmen turning us into a curiosity shop. We must make it clear we're not running an eating house. Still we have nobody important coming to lunch, do we?'

'Just the guests.'

'That's what I mean. Nobody local need know. Thank God the MacManuses are not coming until tonight. Devlin may be content with his moment of glory and keep quiet about it.'

Eva spared Freddie the indignity of knowing how Mr Devlin had proclaimed his intentions aloud for all of Castlebar to hear. 'How was Dublin?'

'What?' He looked at her, still distracted. 'Fine. Met a man from Culpepers herbal shops in London. They're looking for people . . . intelligent couples.'

She saw him watch her reaction.

'I know nothing about herbs, Freddie.'

'That's what I told the blither, though he kept saying we could both learn.' Freddie gave a chuckle. 'Still, no matter how bad things are I hardly see us packing up for the mainland, do you?'

'This is our home, Freddie.'

'Aye, and we've the makings of a damn good business, as I told him. Things are rough at present, because, let's face it, all the Dublin crowd want to hightail it to Galway and learn that cursed Gaelic to get civil service promotions. All we have is word of mouth among our own sort and the odd ad in *Shooting Times*. But I could never sell this place.'

'I know, Freddie.'

'Tyrrell will start inviting himself to lunch next. But I'd sooner burn this house than see a non-Fitzgerald here. The man with no property to pass on is a nobody.'

Eva suspected that Freddie was musing on unspoken memories of his dead father. She could imagine him, younger than Francis, weighed down by the enormity of inheriting this house, with the staff muted in mourning as he poked about in this pantry as if expecting to find some trace of his father here.

'It's time I visited the young lad,' Freddie said heartily. 'I've a present, though it wasn't easy to find.'

Freddie was too impatient to wait for breakfast. He sent Mary up with Mr Clements's plate and fresh tea for the guests, then strode out to the car to retrieve a long package from the back seat. Eva watched him unwrap the brown paper. She stayed back, letting the moment belong to him as he entered the nursery, with the present concealed behind his back. Francis ran to embrace him with an openness that Freddie always found uncomfortable. Hazel was less demonstrative, yet there was a natural ease between them. Francis struggled not to mention the present, politely enquiring instead about the train journey. But his eyes kept trying to glance behind Freddie's back.

'Close your eyes and put out your hands,' Freddie said at last. The boy did so, shaking with excitement. Eva had never seen a rifle so small. It gleamed in the light. Francis's fingers closed around the cold steel. His eyes stayed closed. She knew he was afraid to betray his disappointment. Then he opened them to look up at Freddie who seemed incapable of decoding his son's expression.

'Thank you, Father.'

'Well you might,' Freddie laughed, pleased. 'I hunted half of Dublin for the perfect size. Remember how I measured your arm? You probably thought I was going to lumber you with a suit of clothes. There won't be a rabbit safe on the avenue from now on.' Freddie clapped Francis on the back, then leaned down seriously. 'Not that this is a toy. Care and discretion must be your watchwords. Never use it outside Glanmire Wood or the Civic Guards will come after your old father. Never aim in fun at another human because that is how accidents happen. Never shoot wildly or jealously. Never grouse about bad luck or boast about your prowess. Always praise the other chap's skill. Never try to wipe his eye, but if you take good and bad luck cheerily then you'll be counted as a good sport.'

Francis raised the gun to his shoulder and aimed towards the window, anxious to please his father. Freddie fussed over showing him how to wedge it into his shoulder, then squeeze the trigger gently. Eva marvelled at the ease with which Freddie could touch his son when there was a context. Mrs Crossan smiled indulgently in her dressing gown, then looked down as Hazel pulled at her sleeve.

'Can I go on my pony now?'

'Heavens above, child, you'll have that poor pony's legs worn to stumps.' Mrs Crossan smiled at Eva. 'They give us no peace, do they, Mrs Fitzgerald? Just give me time, child, to put my old body to rights.'

The governess disappeared towards her own room, from

which she would not emerge for another half-hour. The front door was open, with guests smoking and stretching their legs outside. Eva left Freddie with the children and returned to the basement. The passageway flagstones glistened, with Maureen waiting to start washing the kitchen floor once Brigid finished the dishes. Eva saw her peer towards the wine cellar.

'Do you want me to scrub in here, mam?'

'You must be tired, Maureen. Take a break. We don't use that cellar much.'

'I know, mam. They say in Turlough that the devil haunts it. Mary was telling me that the last girl to wash it saw the imprint of cloven hooves on the wet flags and her hair turned white.'

'Did you believe her?'

Maureen lowered her voice. 'I wouldn't believe that one, mam, if she said that saints went to heaven. God forgive me, but a curate himself wouldn't be safe from her clutches.'

Her voice was so conspiratorial that Eva laughed. It reminded her of Dunkineely when serving girls had wandered into her bedroom to gossip freely.

'Don't bother with the cellar,' she said. 'Your hair is too nice to risk it.'

'How about the Yank's bedroom, mam, whenever Mary gets finished inside it?'

'How long has Mary been in there?'

'Long enough to re-stuff a horsehair mattress.'

Nervously, Eva knocked on the door and entered without waiting for a response. Gralton sat on the bed, hands protectively around his knees as if anticipating an assault. Mary hastily snatched up her duster off the window ledge.

'Lord,' Mary said sourly to Gralton as she left, 'but you're a great one to keep a body talking.'

Gralton looked after her in amusement. 'If I opened my

mouth once it's news to me,' he told Eva. 'She was all over me at first, practising her Yankee-speak, talking about joining her sisters. She imagines it will all be strolls on Coney Island every evening. Then when she heard my name was Max Fortune it was like she was confronted by the devil.'

'Stay out of her way,' Eva cautioned.

'I'll stay out of everyone's way, including your husband's.'

'He'll be suspicious if you don't go shooting. I told him that's why you came.'

The clink of a bucket alerted them to Maureen's presence in the doorway. Gralton left and Maureen glanced after him as she got down on her knees.

'That fellow may be a posh Yank,' she remarked, 'but he has a face like a fish not long hauled out of the Shannon. He has a Roscommon man's nose – on the mother's side I bet.' She paused, remembering her place. 'Sorry, mam, I shouldn't be so familiar.'

'You're all right, child.'

'They didn't think so in Westport House.'

'You worked there?'

'We got a list of what they expected a maid to provide for herself: blue cotton dresses, white caps, black stockings. But we couldn't afford twelve white aprons with bibs, so my mother ripped up flour sacks, boiled them and made beautiful aprons.'

'What was the problem?'

'On my first day the lady admired my apron and I was so proud of how Mammy made it that I told her what it really was . . . thinking it would be all right as she liked it. But she let me go on the spot, saying they couldn't employ people wearing sacks. I shouldn't be saying this, mam, with you probably knowing her.'

'What will you do?'

'I was thinking of Birmingham. I've a class of an aunt there.'

'Would you like that?'

'I won't know till I go, mam, will I?'

Maureen splashed water on the flags and began to scrub. Eva heard a shot outside, then a scream from Hazel and angry voices. She ran out the back door and up onto the lawn. Freddie was gesticulating angrily on the avenue, while Hazel tried to remount her pony.

'Miss Crossan knew I was shooting with the boy. Why did the fool of a woman let you ride down the avenue alone?'

Eva saw Hazel's lip quiver as she reached them, but the girl was determined to stand her ground.

'I got tired waiting for Miss Crossan. She's too slow. I told her through her door I was going out myself.'

'You could have been killed.' Freddie paused to gesture for silence and steered Francis around to face the slope of trees. 'Under the small bush against the mossy wall,' he whispered. 'Aim carefully, take your time.'

A rabbit quivered there, too terrified by the first shot to bolt further. The wall meant that she had nowhere to run except straight towards them. Francis glanced at Eva, then up at his father who nodded encouragingly. The shivering creature reminded Eva of her pet rabbit as a child. She could almost feel the fur against her face again. It seemed to take an eternity for Francis to aim, though Eva suspected that he closed his eyes as he shot. The rabbit bounced back against the wall, then fell over, paws still twitching for a few seconds although dead. The pony bolted down the avenue with Hazel chasing after it. Freddie proudly pushed Francis forward.

'Pick it up,' he ordered. 'Your first bag with only your second shot. You're a Fitzgerald all right, my boy. We'll have many's the good day's sport on the bogs when you're older.'

Francis picked up the rabbit by the ears and held it out awkwardly. Eva remembered how Art's savagery shocked her in Donegal years ago when he partook in the mass slaughter of a shoal of mackerel. She wondered if this male instinct lurked within Francis. Freddie clapped him on the back, steering him towards the house.

'Mrs Crossan is a poor enough governess, you know,' Freddie remarked as they passed Eva. 'You might check that Hazel gets her pony. I want to show the men what a fine shot we're raising.'

Eva didn't worry about the pony fleeing too far. Her daughter had an instinctive way with animals and by the time Eva found them Hazel had softly called Molly and was stroking her head, calming her. 'We're fine, Mummy. Molly wasn't really scared of such a baby gun.' Hazel tried to sound disdainful. 'I'd be a better shot than Francis if I got the chance. Why didn't Daddy bring me a present?'

'Maybe he did and hasn't given it yet. I'll ask him later.'

'You mean you'll find something for him to give. Girls don't count for Daddy, do they?'

'You know Daddy loves you. He bought you Molly.'

'He really bought her for Francis who was too cowardy-custard to ride her.'

'That's not true,' Eva said, though it was. As a girl she had felt similar jealousy when Art was spoiled. But Mother had established such a close bond with her that she still seemed a presence in Eva's life. Eva remembered Art's remark about Mother's dream. She wondered if Hazel and she would ever feel so close. She loved her daughter absolutely, but even at this young age Eva sensed Hazel's impatience at her vagueness of thought when the child saw the world in stark colours. Hazel mounted the pony and Eva walked alongside, letting her daughter talk away, sharing jokes and childish secrets.

Yet amidst this excited chatter there seemed an invisible barrier which the girl was unaware of but Eva felt incapable of breaking down.

On the front steps Freddie had buttonholed Gralton and was insisting on helping him select a gun.

'You came via London, I take it, sir.'

'In a roundabout way,' Gralton replied, non-committally.

'At least you found us, even if only for a short stay. I wish more sportsmen could be persuaded across. You might tell your acquaintances about our small establishment. Many English sportsmen would be keen to share our sport if they knew of us. But they're cautious because sadly the old political order is gone. Recent upheavals have left a sorrow in my heart. But English sportsmen will meet with nothing but courtesy hereabouts. Oh, the Irish like their politics well spiced and blame "John Bull" for every imagined evil, but that's mainly hot air from pulpits and newspapers. In real life they enjoy the company of Englishmen and love seeing them at their sport. I differ in religion and politics from the majority of my neighbours, yet I receive nothing but kindliness and respect. I speak as I find them, you understand, sir.'

'Of course,' Gralton replied as Eva told Hazel to bring the pony around to the stable.

'In fact you will meet a good cross-section on our shoot. There's a local tradesman I've asked along, if you don't object, and a political chap called Belton.'

'Patrick Belton?' Gralton almost dropped his American accent.

'You've heard of him?' Freddie was surprised.

'I spotted his name in one of your newspapers,' Gralton said quickly. 'He's a bedfellow of that General fellow.'

'O'Duffy,' Freddie said helpfully. 'A rum braggart who's none too bright. But his Blueshirts enjoyed a lot of support in the recent past from big farmers whose livelihoods are destroyed by de Valera. I saw proud men beg me to shoot starving calves they have no markets for. But the politicians who united behind O'Duffy soon regretted doing so and ditched him. Not Mr Belton, who fought tooth and nail to keep him, but decent Catholics of good breeding. I hope you won't find our other visitors too bothersome.'

Eva understood Gralton's look of unease. She had begun to like her reluctant guest and knew that he hated the deception they had to foist on poor Freddie. She could not imagine Freddie keeping secrets from her, beyond the extent of his binges and scale of their debts, which he regarded as indelicate matters that a gentleman should hide from his wife. Gralton's presence reinforced how much of her life she hid from him. The abstract yearnings he would never comprehend. Her sense that another world existed, parallel to this physical one, perpetually beyond reach yet resplendent with levels of awareness if she could think clearly enough to unlock it, her dreams of previous lives that made it difficult to stay fully immersed in this one. Gralton steered the conversation away from politics by suggesting that Freddie recommend a good gun.

'You have applied for a licence to shoot?' Freddie enquired, stooping to examine the selection he had carried outside. Gralton glanced at Eva for guidance and she nodded.

'Of course. How about that gun there?'

'Too heavy, sir,' Freddie said, 'unless you are Samson's second cousin. Braggarts may boast about heavy weapons stopping a duck at eighty yards, but in truth they are invariably under every bird due to the weight on their shoulder. No, a light gun will do all the work you require of it . . .'

Eva went indoors, leaving Gralton to extract himself. She checked how lunch was progressing, then visited the nursery.

This was meant to be Francis's reading time, but he simply lolled on the floor with an unopened book while Miss Crossan read a copy of *Secrets* magazine. The *Capuchin Annual* was obviously for night-time display in the drawing room.

'How is Francis's reading?' she asked pointedly.

Miss Crossan beamed. 'He understands every word in my magazine. I made him read two articles aloud for me.'

Eva glanced at the unsuitable cover, emblazoned with *Denise Robins Replies to Readers' Problems*. The nursery was untidy, with cushions allowed to lie where they fell. Hazel entered the room and seemed immediately lulled into the prevailing lethargy. She sprawled on a chair, barely acknowledging her governess. A hint of Eva's disapproval permeated into the elderly woman's consciousness.

'Sorry if I seem hazy today,' she confided, woman-to-woman. 'But the men are inclined to sit up so late talking and, especially after you retired, it didn't seem right to have no woman of the house present in attendance if they needed anything.'

At least Freddie was not present to hear Mrs Crossan describe herself as a woman of the house. Excusing herself Eva went out into the hall, alerted by the noise of Mr Devlin's motor. Gralton must have slipped off because Freddie came into view alone. The Castlebar grocer got out in his best Sunday suit, though he knew they intended to go shooting. Eva suspected that Devlin lacked the confidence to dress casually. Their debt allowed him to flaunt an impression of social position, yet he would find this luncheon torture. He would stand out by trying too hard to blend in, just like Mrs Crossan stood out as an object of pity among the guests at night.

The politician emerged and Freddie greeted him cordially. But Belton's response was reminiscent of RC bishops who expected people to form a line and kiss their ring. He cast a dismissive eye over the house as Freddie led them up the steps where Mary waited to take their hats. The maid virtually genuflected before Belton. Only Freddie's presence prevented her from giving the Blueshirt salute. Before being spotted, Eva hurried down to the kitchen, where Mrs McGrory was agitated about the number of diners, not to mention the presence of a political opponent.

'I'll do my best to stretch our provisions, Mrs Fitzgerald,' she said. 'But I'd advise you to set up two tables. It wouldn't be like Mr Belton to wolf his way through an entire meal without causing a schism in whatever company he's latched onto. Will the Yank be joining you? He skulked past a moment ago looking in no fit mood for company.'

Gralton was deeply agitated when Eva knocked on his door. 'I'll not sit with Belton,' he hissed. 'I was better off on the bogs. Art was crazy to land me here.'

'I had no idea he was coming.'

'Aye, and no idea who he really is. That's how you Protestants survive, by keeping your heads down and pretending the rest of us don't exist.'

'You're not being fair.'

'I don't feel like being fair. I don't feel like being bundled handcuffed onto an ocean liner. But that's what will happen if Belton recognises me.'

'Maybe he won't.'

'You could be right. Stupidity is his sole virtue. Ask Art to show you his stitches after being hit with a baton during a protest over scab labour on a Belton site. Belton pays his men worse than any other builder. He's a vulture hopping between political parties, jumping ship when his new colleagues find him too stupid to trust with power. He has bayed for my blood in the Dail and for your brother to be shipped to

Russia. If he knew you were Art's sister he'd spit in your face.'

Eva believed him. Her home felt violated. 'We can't risk him seeing you. I'll say you have a stomach bug. I want no trouble for Freddie. He doesn't deserve it.'

In the kitchen Eva told Mary to serve Mr Fortune's lunch in his room. The girl wrinkled up her nose in a gesture Eva didn't understand.

'It's a peculiar class of a name, don't you think, mam? *Max Fortune.*'

'Why?'

'Oh, now.' The girl made a face and resumed her work. Eva waited until the gentlemen had enjoyed a pre-lunch drink and were seated at their soup before conveying apologies from their American guest. But Gralton's non-appearance only roused Mr Belton's interest.

'We can't have that from a Yank good enough to spend his dollars here.' The politician snapped his fingers at Mary. 'You, girl, take our guest down a brandy and port for me. Tell him it would settle an elephant's stomach and we'll await the pleasure of his company after lunch.'

Eva knew how the phrase '*our* guest' hurt Freddie. Everything about Belton's manner suggested that this luncheon was being held in his honour. Mary scurried off as Belton beamed at Freddie.

'I've never known a Yank to refuse a drink. They're still terrified Prohibition will return. He's probably hung over, but the hair of the dog always cures the man. You agree, Mr Fitzgerald?'

'Mr Fortune is somewhat a mystery,' Freddie replied. 'No one is quite sure where he came from.'

'You can't be too careful,' Belton warned. 'There are unsavoury types everywhere.'

274

'The chap seems a good egg,' the Commander interjected, politely but firmly.

'Maybe so.' Belton looked around, reluctant to yield the point. 'But you can never tell with foreigners.' He let the last word resonate before adding, 'With the exception of all present, of course, as I'm sure Mr O'Sullivan and Mr Devlin will both agree.'

'Of course,' the Dublin Roman Catholic and the Castlebar grocer rejoined, uncomfortable at being singled out. Eva watched Freddie sit stony-faced, labelled a foreigner at his own table.

'How exactly would you define a foreigner?' Mr Clements's mild tone betrayed a touch of steel on their behalf.

Belton shrugged as if addressing an imbecile. 'A foreigner is a foreigner and can never be anything else. Take de Valera, born a Yank and still a Yank. Only a foreigner would disgrace Ireland with his blather in the League of Nations, seeking sanctions against Signor Mussolini for liberating Abyssinia. Mussolini is Africa's Abraham Lincoln, the only man with the courage to end the slave trade carried on there by Jewmen. De Valera wants Ireland to sit on the fence, but we won't be silenced against Jewboys and Bolsheviks. Mussolini is a shining example to the world and if I were ten years younger I'd volunteer to stand with him in Abyssinia.'

'Thankfully he did not require your help,' Mr Clements murmured. The table had grown quiet. Mr Devlin caught Eva's eye, then looked away.

'Only a fool would think we may each not yet be called upon to fight,' Belton retorted. 'A festering plague is ready to sweep Europe if we allow it to take root.'

'We see it in our newsreels,' one of the Staffordshire guests said. 'Never more so than when the Reichstag was burnt to the ground.'

'And who makes *your* newsreels?' Belton inquired. 'Communists. If your writers were not communists we should not need to ban them. The plague I refer to broke out in Spain last month when the Bolsheviks seized power. It will spread unless stopped.'

'*Seized power*' seems an incorrect description for the results of a democratic election,' Mr Clements commented. 'Much as I disagree with their choice, you cannot deny that Spain's new coalition was freely voted in by the people.'

Belton snorted. 'Maybe it's time to stop paying lip service to the notion that an uneducated rabble will always get it right.'

'So you propose to abolish elections, sir?' Freddie asked.

'I said no such thing.' Mr Belton spread out his hands as Mary returned to serve lunch, starting, Eva noticed, with the politician. 'What I'm saying – and I only reiterate the teaching of Pope Pius XI – is that Spain shows the folly of unchecked democracy allowed to run wild. I see it in Dáil Éireann – a piebald assembly, chosen by defective means, forced to grapple with the complicated task of governing a great nation. Am I right, Mr Devlin?'

'What would you suggest?' Mr Clements demanded, not allowing Devlin to convey his token acquiescence. 'Dictatorship like in Italy?'

'Italy is no dictatorship,' Belton rejoined. 'Or one that will last only as briefly as is necessary to bang heads together. Already it is evolving into a more subtly organised democracy which Ireland should adopt – the Corporate State.'

'Indeed,' the Commander muttered dismissively. Eva wanted to speak up, but knew that the type of society she desired would seem nonsensical to these men, except perhaps to Mr Clements.

'Yes, indeed,' Belton barked. 'Don't you agree, Devlin?'

276

The shopkeeper lowered his fork. 'Well, I can't say I've rightly studied these matters.' Devlin faltered under Belton's gaze. 'Still the Pope strongly favours vocationalism in his encyclical *Quadragesimo Anno.*' He glanced hastily at Eva. 'Not that our gracious hosts will have read it, of course.'

'More's the pity,' Mr Belton stated emphatically. 'His Holiness says that the state's primary aim must be to foster harmony between classes by the establishment of vocational groups. Nobody is suggesting a dictator for Ireland. Right, Devlin?'

'Not among my old battalion anyway,' the shopkeeper replied nervously.

'Our Corporate State would be uniquely Irish, with every important trade granted a say based on its strength.'

Belton looked at Devlin for support, but the shopkeeper stared at his untouched lunch. The Tyrone man left the table, not bothering to excuse himself. Only Belton seemed oblivious to the strained atmosphere.

'Tonight I shall speak on how O'Duffy and I shall whittle away the dross and rebuild from scratch so that our new Greenshirts will be as victorious as Germany's Hitlershirts. No other option can save us from the Red Plague.' He looked at Freddie. 'You are a doubter, Mr Fitzgerald. I'll send you James Hogan's pamphlet, *Could Ireland Become Communist,* to show you how dark forces encircle this land.'

'I'll read it with interest,' Freddie replied grimly.

'Just as I read *Quadragesimo Anno,*' the Commander interjected. 'Indeed I have a copy in my room. Your Pope writes excellent Latin, far superior to my rusty grasp. But you appear so familiar with the text that perhaps if I fetch it after lunch you might translate some of the more salient passages.'

Belton glowered at him before his eyes darted around the table. One Englishman gave a short chuckle and lowered his knife and fork to disdainfully stare back.

'I came here to shoot,' Belton said sourly.

'And no better place.' Mr Devlin was anxious to hijack the conversation. 'I heard your lad enjoyed his first kill today, Mr Fitzgerald, with a gun especially sized for him. I wish I could find one for my boy.'

Freddie spoke with enforced cheeriness, determined to regain control of his own table. 'Only a bunny rabbit, Devlin, but a clean kill to the head. With a rabbit there is no point aiming for the body, as it will go clean through and allow the blither to crawl back into his burrow before you claim your supper.'

Relieved laughter came from everyone except Mr Belton, who sulked at attention being switched away from him.

'These woods are infested with rabbits,' the Commander added. 'Not that I hunt myself, but I'm always happy to eat them.'

'The bunny is the sportsman's standby when there's no better shooting,' Freddie said. 'If it wasn't for their penchant for diving into burrows they'd be welcome guests.'

One of the Staffordshire man joined in with an anecdote about a wounded rabbit and Devlin ventured a story about a day's shooting near Lough Mask. But the conversation spluttered and Eva could not recall a more awkward lunch at Glanmire House. They had safely reached pudding when Mr Devlin found the courage to risk using her husband's first name: 'Where do we shoot this afternoon, Freddie?'

'There's a flight line for plover over Toomore bog, Devlin. It's wet terrain but good shooting if you're patient.'

'Plover over a bog?' Belton snorted. 'That's too open. Any fool knows your best bet is to stalk them from behind a wall.'

'And any fool can kill them from there!' Gralton's American accent was pitched to ooze money and disdain. He had surprised them by coming quietly to the doorway. 'Plover are a sitting target in a field because they're so slow taking off. It's a sly man's shot. If you're any sort of sportsman you'll take your chances as they skim overhead on their evening flight.'

Despite her shock at Gralton's appearance, Eva felt pleased for Freddie who did not hide his pleasure at seeing the politician dressed down.

'I take it you're the Yank with the weak stomach,' Belton growled. 'What would you know about it?'

'He has a point.' A touch of mutiny crept into Devlin's voice.

'Has he now?' Belton's icy eyes scrutinised Gralton. 'You have recovered enough to join us, sir?'

'I came to thank the gentleman who sent down a drink,' Gralton replied. 'And to apologise to my host. Sadly I have not been fully honest.'

Eva held her breath, terrified that a revelation would shatter their tenuous hold on life here. She imagined the Civic Guards summoned, with Belton claiming credit for uncovering a nest of communist sympathisers. Every Mayo Protestant would be tarnished. Maybe Gralton had a gun behind his back, determined to take at least one enemy with him. Belton sensed her fear. He glanced at her, then back at Gralton.

'Well?' he demanded.

'The fact is that I cannot shoot,' Gralton said. 'I've not had time to apply for a gun licence from your authorities yet.'

'Gun licence be damned,' Belton snorted. 'Being with me is the only licence you'll need.'

'Still, I would not wish to compromise my host.'

'Who the hell will compromise him?' Belton retorted. 'You're a visitor in my state and it's my duty to show you a good time. Now I'll wager you the two pounds a licence would cost that I'll have the heavier bag at nightfall.'

The animosity between the men was obvious as Gralton turned to Freddie.

'What do you say, Mr Fitzgerald?'

'Ordinarily I'd say that a licence is a prerequisite. We try not to step outside the Irish law . . .' He looked at Belton. 'Still Mr Belton appears placed to know how things operate now. But I must warn you, the best shooting is over congested drains that are tricky to negotiate, often too wide to jump and too deep to wade through.'

'That's fine,' Gralton smiled. 'Surely, Mr Belton, as an Irishman you will agree that the wetter the better.'

'You do not strike me as dressed for the wet,' Belton sneered.

'Let's just see who falls first.' Gralton nodded curtly and withdrew.

Leaving the men to their whiskey Eva followed Gralton downstairs. She saw him shiver and glance around uneasily when passing the wine cellar. He hurried into his room which Eva entered without knocking.

'What are you doing?' she demanded.

'A spot of shooting as *you* people call it.'

'Stop being condescending. We did not invite him.'

'His like invite themselves. Into Abyssinia, into the Rhineland, wherever they choose to hoist their self-righteous swastika.'

'You promised to cause no trouble.'

'I couldn't sit here like a fox in a hole awaiting the hounds. I decided to meet the devil head on. The murderous clouds over Europe won't pass you Brits by as you sit buried away here, pretending that the world isn't changing.'

'I'm not British,' Eva countered fiercely. 'I'm as Irish as you.'

'I'm British,' Mr Clements interrupted from the doorway. 'The clothes you wear are English or at least were made by

an English exile in a tailor's shop in the back streets of
Valletta. And whatever else you are, sir, you're no American.
You may find this old hunting jacket, along with some plus
fours, more suited to an Irish bog. I also have boots upstairs
that might be pressed into service.'

The two men eyed each other, before Gralton nodded.

'I'm obliged.'

'I'm aware of the dark clouds you mention, sir. But I had
hoped they might avoid casting their shadow on this wood.
Last week in London I saw Oswald Mosley address his
Brownshirts. He looked impressive, articulate, quite chilling.
No doubt he had decamped to his gentleman's club by the
time windows were broken in Jewish shops in the West End.
I have always stayed outside clubs, and institutions. Likewise,
I am only familiar with the institution of marriage as an
outsider. What God has joined together let no man . . .'

'Now, wait here . . .' Gralton interrupted.

'. . . force one partner to keep secrets, come between their
trust.'

Eva felt that the Commander was using this opportunity
to speak indirectly about himself, setting out his stall as
someone who – no matter what attraction he felt – would
never stray from his own rules.

'I'm not here of my own choosing,' Gralton said.

'I don't wish to know the circumstances,' Mr Clements
replied, 'or what hold you exercise over our hostess. I do
know that she named you herself – Max Fortune being a
character in an American thriller I once loaned her.' The
Commander bowed slightly in parting. 'Mrs Fitzgerald is
assured of my silence. Still I suggest you do not overstay your
welcome.'

As the Englishman walked down the corridor Eva recalled
Mary's disdain at the name Fortune. Could the maid have

281

read the thriller while pretending to clean the Commander's room?

'Can you trust him?' Gralton asked.

'Can I trust you?' Eva replied angrily. 'What if Belton recognises you?'

'He won't, though we were born only twenty townlands apart.' Gralton uncocked the gun Freddie had chosen. 'For all his bluster the Longford peasant in him is so thrilled to lord it at the Ascendancy table that it would never occur to him he could be conned. I'm just an uppity Yank to be put in my place.' He snapped the gun shut. 'Trust me. Now I think your husband is calling you.'

Freddie's agitated voice came from upstairs. Eva didn't want to be found. Something in Gralton's manner made her unsure if she could trust him. It would be prudent to tell Freddie the truth before he unwittingly took this fugitive onto a bog with a target to aim at. But her deception since this morning would destroy Freddie's trust.

She felt unable to cope as she heard him descend the stairs. Darting out the back door, she skirted past the drawing room window with its babble of male voices and into the woods. Belton stood smoking on the front step. Mary hovered behind him, seeking the courage to approach. From behind a tree Eva watched the maid hesitantly touch his shoulder. Belton bent down to listen and Eva held her breath, terrified at what the maid might reveal. Belton straightened up and said something that caused Mary to step back as if slapped and retreat into the house. Eva skirted through the wood and emerged onto the avenue, spying Francis standing alone at the spot where he had shot the rabbit. She watched him stare at the blood-soaked moss.

'Are you okay, Francis?'

Surprised, the boy turned. 'Yes, Mummy.'

'Do you like your present?'

'Daddy says I'll be as good a shot as him one day.'

'I'm sure you will.'

The child hesitated. 'Do you think the rabbit was a mummy?'

'I don't know.'

'Won't the small rabbits be wondering where she is?'

Eva resisted the urge to put her arms around him. It didn't seem right to interfere. Francis was a Fitzgerald in name at least and Freddie kept insisting that he needed to toughen up.

'Young rabbits can mind themselves,' she lied. 'They don't have families like ours except in Beatrix Potter.'

The child nodded seriously, straining to derive comfort from her words. But his eyes strayed back to the moss as if only seeing blood properly for the first time, despite all the birds that Freddie had hauled out from the huge pockets specially sewn into his hunting jacket so as not to be burdened by carrying a bag. When Francis was three, Eva had seen him lift an unplucked pigeon from the kitchen table and hold it skyward in the doorway, saying, 'Go on, you silly, fly.' But he had grown so accustomed to dead birds that the actual killing may have been a blur until now.

'Where is Miss Crossan?' she asked.

'Lying down. The new girl, Maureen, played with us for a while. She tells great stories but had to leave to walk home to Ballavary. I brought her down the avenue.'

Miss Crossan was meant to be doing lessons with Francis, yet Eva was glad to find him here. Mr Devlin would be seeking a quiet word before the shooting party left, knowing that Freddie only made vague unkept promises, whereas guilt would force Eva to honour hers. This constant struggle to find money left her exhausted. Four guineas a week was not expensive for comfortable quarters and shooting, but if Gralton did anything crazy no amount of money would prevent their house of cards from tumbling down. What was Freddie hinting at by raising the notion of running a herbal shop in England? Why mention the idea if it was crazy? It wasn't only Mr Clements who was using Glanmire as a retreat from the world. At times Eva was relieved at how their poverty ensured that Francis did not yet have to attend a boarding school because she often wondered if he would cope with the bullying that Art had witnessed and frequently tried to halt.

'Let's walk in the woods.' She offered Francis her hand.

'Have you time?' The boy was surprised. 'What about your work?'

'To hell with the work,' she said conspiratorially. 'Let's see if we can find flowers for Hazel.'

Eva refused to look back towards the house where Mrs McGrory and Mary would soon also be seeking her. She should confront Devlin, have words with Miss Crossan, prevent Gralton bringing a loaded gun onto the same bog as Patrick Belton. Yet with every step into the woods her guilt lessened as if retreating back into being a child herself. As they climbed through the trees she remembered Goethe's poem about the erl-king. The terrified boy in the forest whose father refused to believe that it was not the wind calling but a bearded goblin luring children to the land of death. Eva could not shake the notion that an erl-king stalked them now. She didn't want to look back, but focused purely on walking with her beautiful son and seeing the shafts of light between the trees through his eyes as he invented stories for them both to believe in.

Francis halted and placed a finger to his lips, then crept forward with the instinctive Fitzgerald talent for stalking.

Two rabbits lifted their heads in a clearing, unsure if they had heard something. Francis did not move during the time they grazed there. His absorption was absolute, his features transfixed with delight until the rabbits finally sensed his presence and darted off. He led her on through the trees, the words babbling from him barely able to keep pace with the thoughts spilling out. As Eva climbed she remembered Mother's strange dream and several times tried to steer Francis towards the oaks. But the boy had his own destination in mind. He relished having Eva to himself and letting her share his secret places. He led her up an overgrown slope where she had to stoop at first, then crawl on her hands and knees. But she didn't care how dirty she got or what the maids might think when they saw her. In fact she never wanted this adventure to end. The sun emerged again with slats of dusty light through the trees, creating fantastical mosaics of colour and shade. Francis reached a small clearing and looked back to ensure she was still following. A rusty trowel lay beside three mounds of pebbles, with withered flowers arranged beside each one. The boy replaced some stones that had toppled from one mound.

'This is the birds' graveyard,' he said, imparting a great secret. 'Two blackbirds and a thrush. I found them dead and didn't want to leave them lying there for the foxes. Promise you won't tell Daddy.'

'Why?'

'He might think it sissy.'

'Daddy only wants what's best for you.'

'I know, but Mummy . . . I didn't want to kill the rabbit.' Suddenly his eyes were unable to contain the tears. 'I wanted to stroke it and keep it as a pet. I'm afraid I'll see it in my dreams. I don't want to be inside the house when it's hanging up and I don't want to eat it. I want to bury it here, but now that Daddy has bought me the gun I'll have to go out killing things every day.'

'You won't, darling.'

'You know it's what Daddy wants.'

'He'll understand if I tell him.'

'He won't. He'll think I'm a big baby.'

'Come here, darling.' Eva held out her arms. Normally Francis never refused a cuddle, but he hesitated as if firing that shot had changed everything, leaving him frightened to display weakness. Softly she urged him and reluctantly he moved forward to put his head on her lap. Eva let him cry for a long time while she stroked his hair and knew not to speak. Eventually Francis stopped and they both lay still like hunted creatures whose least movement might betray them to predators.

'Tell me a story,' Francis asked eventually and Eva started one of the imaginary tales that she never found time to write down, or which – if she attempted to do so – always died on the page. Being a writer was a dream that she never mentioned to anyone. But now in this forest clearing her story sounded so magical that they were both caught up within it. Gralton was right in one sense to claim that she was in hiding. But this did not mean that she was unaware of injustices in cities teeming with starvation. There were different ways to fight injustice, though her way would make no sense to Gralton as it barely made sense to her. But it was an equally vital struggle to try and remain true to your inner core, refusing in your heart to become other than yourself. In trying to be a perfect mother she had failed to do this, being too anxious to blend in and be what people expected her to be. Fleeing from her failure as an artist and her inability to unlock the truths which always eluded her. She wished that belief for her could be as simple as it was for Art. If there was only one reality, one sphere of experience, then perhaps mankind could be transformed by the rearrangement of wealth like he believed. She respected his belief despite the pain it caused her family, because Art was being true to himself, even if he seemed to have now quarrelled with Brendan too. But *Das Kapital* was too complex to be true. Just like the Bible and the Koran and every other sacred book, it was encumbered by rigid absolutes. Truth existed at the core of each, but only when stripped down and glimpsed at its most fragile. Truth was the radiance within every child that was quickly lost, the inner stillness that men of action were scared of, the intuition within the heartbeat of migrating birds who instinctively knew their path home.

Eva shivered, imagining the plovers' fate over Toomore bog, tumbling from the sky to be retrieved by dogs. She had lost her innocence through living off this slaughter and was unsure how to gain it back. But from tonight she swore that, although forced to pluck those birds, she would never eat their flesh again. She would never allow a fascist to sit again at their table and, for Francis's sake, she would persuade Freddie to sell that cursed gun. Her acts of rebellion might be small, but she would hold firm. She would learn to grow up, but not just yet. For another few moments she wanted to hide away and glimpse these woods through the innate sense of wonder in Francis's eyes.

'I'm never going to leave here, Mummy,' he whispered. 'I'll plant more trees and the animals will be safe with nobody allowed to shoot them.'

Several times Eva heard Mary anxiously calling. But she ignored everything until eventually the noise of a motor along the avenue forced her to confront the present. Her foreboding returned. Taking Francis's hand she crawled from the clearing, hoping to reach the house unnoticed in her muck-stained clothes. But the car stopped along the avenue, not far below them. Doors opened and she heard Freddie's voice.

'Drive on, Mikey. I'm sure our guests would enjoy a whiskey before dinner. Mr Fortune and I shall stroll the remainder.'

Freddie's barely suppressed anger made him sound pompous. The door slammed and the motor drove off. Through the trees she saw the two men confront each other, guns at their sides. A boy cycling down the avenue swerved around them and sped away. She prayed that he had delivered a telegram from Art.

'You're a damn fool, sir!' Freddie barked. 'I may be too much of a gentleman to dress you down in public, but by Jove I'll do it to your face now.'

'I filled four times the bag of your fascist guest,' Gralton replied in a surly voice.

'We are not discussing the bags!'

'You notice he didn't stay around to honour his debts.'

'Mr Belton owes you two pounds, I'll warrant you that.'

'He owes his unfortunate workers an awful lot more.'

Eva reached the avenue with Francis lagging behind. 'What's after happening?' she asked, alarmed and trying to catch her breath.

'Nothing,' Gralton replied.

'Thanks to the grace of God,' Freddie expanded. 'Our American visitor apparently has no notion about the etiquette of a shoot. We had a fair afternoon on Toomore, though not to Mr Belton's liking. Fortune seemed to delight in provoking him by jumping from tussock to tussock like a mountain goat while Mr Belton, determined not to be outdone, found himself twice up to his shoulders in mud and needing to be pulled out.'

'He wanted to be one of Mussolini's Blackshirts,' Gralton interrupted. 'At least he'll look the part tonight.'

'It's no laughing matter,' Freddie reproached him, then turned to Eva. 'Finally after Mr Belton fired enough shots to frighten off every bird between here and Clew Bay, we were returning to our motors when a man ran across from a cottage, looking highly agitated. *"Why the devil didn't yiz shoot over my patch of bog?"* he says. *"Shure there's always a few shnipe there."* Back we went to please him, with myself guiding Belton in from the right so he might have more than one bird in his bag. Next moment a snipe rises up low before us and Fortune lets loose from the left with both barrels, almost taking Mr Belton's head off. There's no excuse for a dangerous shot, sir. You could have killed him.'

Gralton aimed his gun towards a loose stone down the avenue. He fired and the stone bounced off into the undergrowth. 'If I'd wanted to hit him I would have.' He made little attempt to disguise his accent.

'What does that mean?' Freddie demanded. 'Who the hell are you? I have my doubts as to whether you're a Yank at all?'

'That is what my passport says. I take it yours is British.'

'I'm a Mayo man. I've never had need to apply for any passport.'

Gralton lowered his gun, wearily. 'Lucky you. I apologise for abusing your hospitality. Allow me to change and I'll be on my way.'

Freddie drew himself up to his full height. 'You're going nowhere. You took your dressing down and now you'll take your dinner like the rest of us. You're a damn fine shot and, by Jove, you gave me a laugh, even if I couldn't show it, watching our poor grocer trying to haul his fat friend out of bog holes with the pair of them black from head to foot like Zulu warriors. Walk on, Mr Fortune, and enjoy a drink before dinner.'

Gralton glanced at Eva. 'I hope you will not fall out with Mr Devlin.'

'Sixty years as esteemed customers of his family,' said Freddie. 'These things count for something in an Irish town – as perhaps you already know. Your gun, sir, the boy will carry it.'

Gralton handed his gun to Francis and walked on, leaving Eva alone with her husband and son.

'It is a terrible thing,' Freddie said, watching him go, 'for a man to be ashamed of his peasant roots. You're too taken in by people, Eva. That man is no more named Fortune than I am. He's a "*Mac*" or an "*O*" I'd wager. Made his money in the States and is now too proud to be associated with his impoverished relatives. I wasn't long fingering him and even Mikey spotted it once we reached the bog. It was the quick furtive way he fired. The telltale sign of a man who learned to shoot as a poacher.'

Freddie's smile was meant to convey man-of-the-world wisdom, but its boyish quality touched her. The vulnerability it revealed made her aware of how much she loved him still despite his flaws. She longed to end this terrible falsehood between them.

'Do you think Belton suspected him?' she asked.

'Of being a peasant? Oh no, Belton hasn't time to notice somebody else playing his own game.'

'How close were the shots?'

'Oh, well over the blither's head,' Freddie snorted dismissively. 'Though by Belton's theatrics you would swear his scalp had been scorched.'

'Was Mr Devlin annoyed?'

'Funnily enough I don't think so. Devlin will dutifully gather his men tonight but I don't see Belton recruiting many converts for his master's new movement. Devlin can't wait to be shut of him.' Freddie looked down at Francis holding Gralton's gun.

'How's my little hunter?'

'Fine, Daddy.'

'Come along and you can help bring the bag in from the car.'

Freddie patted the boy's shoulders, steering him towards the house. Mikey had parked on the gravel. As Freddie reached the motor Eva saw a tremor pass through Francis at the prospect of the dead birds. But no sooner did the boot lid open than a plover flew out. It did a low circle of the lawn before disappearing over the trees, leaving Freddie open-mouthed.

'Well, I'll be damned,' he said. 'I swear that's the only shot Belton got in all day and he must have just winded him.'

Francis excitedly stared after the plover, then looked down at the blood-soaked corpses as if praying for them to follow.

'Take these, son.' Freddie reached for a brace of birds. He looked up in amazement as Francis sobbed and ran off.

'What the dickens . . . ?'

'He's upset about the rabbit, Freddie.'

'But why?' Freddie seemed perplexed. 'He shot it clean through the head. The boy is a natural. He'll be a better shot than his old father.'

'It was a fluke; he had his eyes closed. Francis isn't like you. He loves you and wants to please you but shooting is not in his nature.'

'Nonsense. It's in his blood. He's a Fitzgerald. We're fighters.'

'Hazel is a Fitzgerald.'

'You cannot bring a girl out shooting.'

'You cannot bring him either. It will break Francis's heart.'

'I tramped half of Dublin for the perfect starter gun.' Freddie dropped the birds back into the boot and turned. 'What do I do, Eva? I never know what to do with that boy.'

'Sell the gun to Devlin. Buy him a small canoe instead. Francis is like a fish in the water. The streams aren't deep around here and he would love exploring them.'

'With the Crossan woman paddling alongside?' Freddie snorted. 'Do you honestly think she's up to any outing that doesn't involve getting her hair done?'

'Miss Crossan does her best,' Eva protested, though Freddie echoed her own thoughts.

'The guests find her presence odd. Men want to relax at night, have a whiskey and swap stories they can't tell with a woman about.' Freddie rooted in his long pockets as if searching for one last slaughtered bird. 'Maybe Francis will grow to like shooting. It's a noble sport, roaming the bogs with just a dog for company.'

'He won't, Freddie. But he won't stop being your son either.'

Freddie removed his hand and glanced at his fingers blackened from the bog. 'A canoe wouldn't be the worst present.' He tried to sound cheerful. 'Get him outdoors, build up his muscles and sense of responsibility. You might pretend it was my idea. Make him think that his father understands.'

'Of course.'

'I try to, you know. Understand him and you. I know you think me not very good at it. Still you can be slow too, old girl, in different ways. Infernally dreamy, in the ether. But we knock along together. I mean we're happy here and . . . what I'm trying to say . . . I've not disappointed you, have I?'

'No, Freddie.'

'The boy is too dreamy for his own good but he'll grow into a man, won't he?'

'Yes.'

'And things will pick up for us, eh? If we just keep our heads down through this rocky patch. We'll need money for a good school for Francis soon. But that doesn't mean we have to stick herbs into little bottles in England, eh?'

'No.'

Freddie smiled at the incredulity of the thought. 'Our Yank is in the way. I was looking forward to coming home . . . to . . .' He stopped. 'I guess it will have to be the barn for me. You'll take the nursery floor again?'

'Yes.'

'Makes sense. Though it might rather be nice if we were both outdoors. As a boy it was a great treat to be allowed to sleep in the loft above the horses. An owl nests there, swooping in and out, a deadly hunter. I'll not mind him and he'll not mind me. I'd swear his grandfather nested there when I was a boy. You'd like it . . . both of us in the straw . . .'

Eva knew how difficult he found these words and that she was being unfair in offering neither discouragement nor acquiescence, whereas at one time she would have grasped at any tiny chink of bohemianism within him.

'Still,' he said quickly, 'I suppose it would be broadcast the length of the county. The Fitzgeralds bedding down like a pair of tinkers in the stable.'

'The Yank is only staying another night.' Eva desperately hoped that this was true.

'Good.' Freddie turned to pick up the dead birds, awkward now, feeling he had revealed too much. 'I'd better bring in these blithers, what, before any more decide to fly off.'

He strode towards the kitchens and Eva saw Hazel in the doorway. 'Where were you all afternoon?' she demanded. 'Sneaking off with Francis. Why won't you spend time with me?'

Eva was exhausted but knew that Hazel was not in a forgiving mood. 'I want to spend time with you now. Once I check how things are with Mrs McGrory.'

'You never bothered checking with the cook before going off with Francis.'

Eva cajoled Hazel sufficiently for the girl to accompany her to the kitchen where Mrs McGrory's monosyllabic answers made plain her disapproval at Eva's absconding.

No telegram had come, Mrs McGrory said tersely. The cyclist had been Mary's brother with a message that left the maid even more contrary than usual.

A dozen tasks required her attention, but Eva decided to risk more opprobrium by sneaking out with Hazel to saddle the pony. She walked alongside the pony until her legs ached. Yet she knew it was still not enough, with Hazel convinced that Eva was holding back some secret she had shared with Francis.

They stayed out for so long that Eva barely had time to change for dinner. The MacManuses arrived from Kiltimagh in their pony and trap when she was still fixing her hair. Eva allowed Miss Crossan and Hazel to fuss over her appearance before she went out to greet Dermot MacManus, a fifty-year-old bachelor who had been gassed in the Great War and passionately believed in the countryside spirits. The children loved his gentleness and the bonfires he lit to appease the fairies on Midsummer's Eve. Freddie regarded his beliefs as tommyrot, but enjoyed Dermot's company as a fellow Mayo Protestant. Eva noticed that Dermot's maiden aunt, Lottie, looked frailer than usual, though her mind was still sharp. She made sure to sit beside her. Gralton was absent.

'Your Yank has a bad tummy,' Freddie explained. 'Sends his apologies. Mary will see to his needs.'

Eva tried not to show her unease. With Belton gone, Mary

was the person she still worried about. Miss MacManus leaned forward. 'How is your ghost?' she whispered loudly.

Freddie laughed. 'An old wives' tale, with respect, Miss MacManus.'

'Perhaps, Freddie,' the old lady replied. 'But I remember you running upstairs after wetting your trousers as a child when sent down to fetch something there.'

Freddie laughed dismissively. 'I disremember that.'

'Loneliness is the worst curse of all,' the old lady continued, 'as we discover in time. I don't know why you never had the cellar blessed. As I told your mother and grandmother his spirit needs someone to reach out and share his loneliness.'

'Bedad you're the man so, Mr Fitzgerald,' Mr O'Sullivan risked a joke. 'Seeing as you're well able to handle spirits.'

The Dublin RC faltered, his reference to Freddie's drinking prowess greeted by stony silence. But Miss MacManus seemed oblivious to the interruption.

'I know loneliness,' she continued. 'You might not think so in a big house like mine, but servants are no company and though Dermot does his best he can't be there all the time. That's why it's good to be out with such fine hosts.' She raised her glass. 'To Frederick and Eva and the wonderful go they have made of life here.'

Despite the stress of this day Eva flushed with pleasure at the toast. When Mary served the main course she managed to avoid eating the duck by saying that she had neglected to say goodnight to Hazel. Francis was asleep, but Hazel peeped out from under the blankets, her earlier crankiness forgotten.

'My feet are freezing, Mummy. Why are they always cold in this house?'

Used to the ritual – and drawing as much comfort from it as the child did – Eva lifted the girl's bare soles out from under the blankets to nestle them against her stomach. This posture reminded her of the story of a local couple during the famine. Sick of being separated in the workhouse, the husband had carried his dying wife eight miles across frozen tracks back to their cabin. When found dead he was still cradling her bare feet on his stomach to provide warmth. That hunger was etched in the memory of old Mayo people who never spoke of it. And etched in Art's guilt too because Grandpappy's father had cleared smallholders off his lands, profiting from other people's misery. Hunger brought out the extremes in people, which explained why desperate men locked into absolutist positions ruled so much of the world. Philosophy must seem a luxury if starving in a Dublin slum or South Dakota dustbowl. But there had to be room for dissenting thinkers, unnoticed and vital as plankton, who provided no answers but questioned reality.

Hazel wiggled her toes free. 'I love you, Mummy.' She put her feet sleepily under the blankets.

Eva remembered Mother sitting by her bed in Donegal, the scent of hand cream and the aura of being loved. Would Hazel recall such tender moments or just quarrels and imagined slights? Her absence from the table would become too pronounced if she stayed any longer. She kissed her daughter and promised that tomorrow, when the men were shooting, she would sit with her daughter and play the *Moonlight Sonata* – which Hazel loved – on the gramophone Mr Clements had purchased. Mrs McGrory would have left by now, walking to the village where she would talk to the Durcans in their shop while waiting for a passing cart headed for Castlebar. Eva checked the kitchens where Brigid was washing the pots. The girl looked uneasy when Eva enquired if Mary had served the pudding.

'She's in with the Yank, mam. She's been peculiar all evening . . . I don't rightly know what she's doing.'

The guests would wonder what was happening. Hurrying down the corridor Eva heard Mary's voice from Gralton's room.

'I want the truth from you just once!'

Eva possessed little to bribe the girl with. Not that bribery entered into it. The maid seemed too fanatical not to seize her chance to turn in a wanted communist.

'I've you told the truth,' Gralton's voice replied.

'Your sort never tell the truth.'

'You're mistaken about me,' Gralton said as Eva opened the door. The maid seemed near tears.

'I'm mistaken about nothing, *Mr Fortune*!' she snapped.

'You're mistaken about everything because you know nothing,' the man said gently. 'All your life you've been fed lies. I can't answer your question about what will become of you in New York, except to say that you'll cry yourself to sleep with homesickness at first, too scared to leave your sisters' room. But even though they have poverty over there as bad as here, there are opportunities, night classes, a chance to learn. I know you're afraid, but take this risk when you're young.'

Mary turned. 'My brother told me this afternoon that a registered envelope has come, crammed with dollars, Mrs Fitzgerald. I can go to America now whenever I like.'

'Isn't that what you want, Mary?'

The girl wiped her eyes, embarrassed. 'I thought so, but my sisters talked about sending the money for so long that I half thought it would never happen. You see . . . the boy I'm walking out with, he's sweet on me if he'd only say it.'

'Let him follow you if he's sweet,' Gralton said. 'Let him save up or let you send him the fare in time.'

'Michael save?' Mary laughed bitterly. 'That fellow couldn't save his life by passing a pub. Any dollars I'd send home would be drunk with every jackass hanging out of him.'

297

'Then forget him. Give yourself this chance because you know what will become of you if you stay.'

'What?' Mary snapped and Eva knew her pride was hurt.

'You know what,' Gralton replied quietly.

'I want to hear it from you. He'll stick me with a dozen squawling kids, is it? All of us starved in some cabin while he's out chasing tinkerwomen and drinking every penny? That's what you'd like, eh, so we'd fall into your hands? Because who'd be there to loan us the few bob, then come looking for it to be repaid a hundred times over? You know the answer, Mr Fortune, because I see through your fancy clothes. You might fool Mrs Fitzgerald who's away with the birds but not me.' Mary glared at Eva. 'Or maybe you knew all along, Mrs Fitzgerald, and still harboured him under your roof.'

'Knew what?'

'*Max Fortune* ... that's a Jewman's name. You're harbouring a crooked-nosed moneylender, with me skivvying to serve one of the race who crucified our Saviour.'

'Stop it, Mary.'

'I won't. You knew because you let him swank out shooting with Mr Devlin, but you have him stuck down here when your own sort, the gentry, came to dine. You'll burn in hell like all Protestants anyway, but I'll not risk my soul under the same roof as a Jewman.'

'I said *stop it*,' Eva repeated. 'Go upstairs and serve the pudding!'

'Don't address me like that! That's how Mr Belton talked when I tried to warn him he was consorting with a Jew. I thought he'd thank me and give me hope that O'Duffy will save Ireland from Jewboys and communists and I'd have no need to leave. But he just looked down his nose like you all do. Well, damn you and your precious pudding to hell, because

I'm taking myself away from this sanctuary for Jews and British spies. And I'll need no references from your sort where I'm going, mam.'

The girl threw down her apron before stomping off. Gralton looked at Eva who was shaking. 'I'm sorry I brought this on you,' he said.

'How can anyone carry around so much hatred?'

'She's scared. Scared people lash out.'

'I was convinced she recognised you. Is Fortune a Jewish name?'

'When you've only known the bog every new name is suspicious. I know this because no more ignorant gobdaw ever left Leitrim than me. I came home to show people that we could educate ourselves and make a fist of life here. Now here I am urging some girl to leave.'

'You're in no hurry to follow suit.'

'She'll come back to visit some day, dolled up with a brood of kids. When I'm put on that boat I'll never see home again. Art sent no word?'

'No.'

'It's time I stopped bringing trouble on your head. This room feels like a crypt anyway. I never knew anywhere so cold. I'll be gone in the morning after putting money in your husband's palm.'

'How?'

There was a cough from the doorway. Eva turned to find Brigid there.

'The pudding will be ruined, mam. Mrs McGrory was most particular about when it was to be served.'

Eva imagined the puzzled diners upstairs. 'Get a white apron, Brigid, and we'll serve it together.'

'I never served at table before, mam.'

'You'll be fine. Mary has left.'

299

'Good riddance, mam. She's only a blow-in from where they eat their young in Foxford.'

Eva helped the girl to carry the tray up to the dining room. 'It's help ourselves tonight.' She tried to sound light-hearted. 'I'm afraid that Mary has upped and decided to emigrate.'

'To somewhere cold I hope,' commented Mr Clements who never liked the maid.

'In the middle of a meal with no notice?' Freddie turned to the two Englishmen, needing to turn the incident into local colour. 'That's us Irish, you know, when the blood is up. She has by no chance eloped with Mr Fortune?'

'We have an American guest ill downstairs,' Eva explained to Miss MacManus as she served her.

'Not too ill I suspect,' Freddie ventured. 'I had to dress him down for dangerous shooting, but I thought he'd take it like a man instead of sulking.'

'I suspect he's tired,' Eva said.

'From leaping about like a mountain goat.' Freddie laughed. 'I never saw a man so at home on the bog. Irish blood in his genes, evolution and so forth.'

'I'd have no truck with evolution,' Mr O'Sullivan said testily.

'I don't think Mr Fitzgerald was referring to monkeys in trees,' the Commander pointed out. 'Though by the sound of it Mr Belton climbing from a bog hole did resemble a rather large angry black ape.'

Eva watched Freddie laugh, with his cares momentarily forgotten. The joke engaged the men's attention, severing any need for more explanations about Mary. Although Eva hated confrontations, the house felt cleansed with her gone. More changes were needed if she were not to simply drift with events.

Leaving the men to their brandies, she took the old lady into the drawing room where Miss Crossan had already staked a position by the fire. The governess greeted Miss

MacManus like a lost friend, enjoying fussing about and making her comfortable. Miss MacManus humoured her, glad of the company of someone closer to her own age to compare aches and pains with. Once Eva sat down she realised how exhausted she felt. Yet she could not rest easy until Gralton was gone. After a while the men came in to gather around the fire. The simile between the mud-caked Belton and an ape had obviously been much elaborated upon over the brandy, with even the Dublin RC laughing now. Dermot MacManus sat beside her, his jacket collar displaying flecks of dandruff.

'Aunt Lottie loves coming here,' he said. 'She gets lonely. I do my best but it can't be like the old days with parties and balls.'

'I'll call over soon,' Eva promised.

'I know you will.' Dermot squeezed her hand. 'You're a brick. On her wavelength as people say now.'

Eva moved around the room, fulfilling her last duties of the evening. Mr Clements sat apart, with his chair positioned under a gas jet. As usual he seemed content to be on the edge of things, half-listening to the conversation while reading a book in French. He looked up and smiled. 'It's good to be back,' he said quietly and Eva knew that he had stopped himself from adding the word *home*.

'The place doesn't feel like home without you,' Eva replied, deliberately using the word.

He acknowledged the gesture. 'You're kind, Mrs Fitzgerald, but the day I joined the navy I left home. I've only ever been billeted in quarters since then. One hopes that Mr Belton finds few recruits in Castlebar tonight.'

'I'm just glad to see the back of him.'

'Let's hope you have.' Mr Clements lowered his voice. 'And that your Yank doesn't become the talk of Mayo.'

'He's not my Yank,' Eva whispered. 'Taking him in was a favour I could not refuse somebody.'

'I wouldn't know . . . never having had a brother.' The Commander noticed Eva's tense expression. 'I hope I do not offend. Old sea dogs should mind our own business. But I didn't wish to see you compromised. That's why I paid him a visit. I just felt that when he leaves it might be best if he is in a position to pay Freddie.'

'I'm already too much in your debt.'

The Commander picked up his book. 'It's your home, Mrs Fitzgerald, not mine. But some nights this creaking house feels like a battered ship. I would happily go down with it, strapped to the wheel. Still I'd sooner keep it afloat a while longer. Good night.'

Mrs Crossan would be glad to see Eva gone so that she could swing into her role as fantasy hostess. Freddie followed Eva out into the hall.

'So Mary has left,' he said, rather intoxicated. 'Still, you're a marvel, you'll find someone else. The barn owl and I shall miss you. Still, one of these nights, eh, with no eyes watching.'

Naked breast against breast, straw stuck to her back with sweat. An owl flying noiselessly in from the dark with a dying mouse. The whinny of Hazel's pony below, nostrils arched, smelling their excitement. A scene from a different life, lived by the people they might have been. Would Freddie be excited or shocked if she ventured out to the stables to confront him with her demand for pleasure? She kissed his cheek lightly.

'One of these nights,' she half-promised.

In the nursery the children were asleep, with the fire low. Eva lay in her nightdress, listening to distant voices, then the sound of the front door opening and laughter outside as Dermot MacManus helped his aunt into their carriage. Time passed. The two Staffordshire men emerged, conferring in low voices before entering their room. Mr O'Sullivan left, chatting with the Tyrone man. Drink and the companionship of shooting had drawn them into a familiarity that would dissolve once they left Glanmire House. Soon afterwards Miss Crossan's quick footsteps tripped down the hall, intimidated by the remaining presence of the Commander and Freddie. Eva wondered what the two men were discussing, with so much time together and so little in common. But perhaps they felt no need to talk, the Commander absorbed in his book and Freddie staring into the dying fire. What shapes did he see there? Naked breasts and thighs? The wings of an unshootable bird? A boy coiled in distress, too scared to even cry at the death of his father? The taunts of other boys about his club foot? Her thoughts drifted and Eva felt she had been asleep for some time when she woke, convinced of soft footsteps in the hall. They seemed to stop at the nursery door. Eva was certain that whoever stood there had his fingers on the brass door handle. Was it Freddie, come to surprise her on this makeshift bed? Or the Commander, finally unable to face the loneliness of his room? She was wide awake now, but no other sound came.

Eventually she lay back, convinced that she had imagined the footsteps. Closing her eyes, she imagined her body as a ship sailing to sleep. She thought of the teachings of Meister Eckhart about how the warmth of prayer could become a light into an inner world normally bound in darkness. Eva tried to focus on this thought and imagine a tiny deserted skiff, with just one lantern in the bow, voyaging into the uncharted lagoon of her soul. But the worries of the outer world would not let her go. She looked over at Hazel, peacefully asleep, and could almost hear in her mind the opening chords of the *Moonlight Sonata*. A charred fragment of log collapsed in the fireplace, with more of a whisper than a thud. The brief spurt of flame lit up the ceiling's myriad cracks. This room needed painting, she thought. The whole house did, creaking in the wind. Eva turned over on the thin mattress, desperately needing rest but her mind refused to settle.

With a sigh she rose and stealthily undid the clasp on the wooden shutters. The night was steeped in moonlight beyond the glass. Foxes would be venturing out, with otters breaking cover by the river. A cat paused midway across the lawn, then darted out of sight. Eva was about to close the shutters when a movement near the forest's edge caught her eye. It looked like a raised arm. She watched with her heart racing and, just when Eva was convinced she had imagined it, a figure knelt up between the distant trees. Somebody was out there again. It wasn't paranoia. Mr Belton was sly enough to have known all along but gone along with the pretence as he bided his time. He could have led a detachment of Blueshirts to circle the house. They would dispense summary justice on Gralton before notifying the authorities, with disgrace engulfing the Fitzgeralds. Detectives would stomp about the house, taking statements that made her look like a collaborator or a fool. She and Freddie would have no option but to take the boat to England.

But perhaps it was Art returning for Gralton. Despite the risks Eva's heart thrilled at the possibility of seeing her brother again. She glanced back at her sleeping children: at Francis curled up with his face to the dying fire and Hazel who looked cold despite her warm blanket. Then, throwing a dressing gown over her shoulders, she crept into the hall. The latch was loud on the front door as she slipped out in her bare feet onto the cool stone steps. Loose stones bit into her soles as she flitted across the gravel to cautiously approach the woods. She paused behind the tree where she had spied movement. The silence was absolute, gnawing at her nerves until she heard a twig snap. A man cursed in a distressed tone with all the Americanism stripped away.

'Mr Gralton?' Eva asked. 'What are you doing here?'

Stepping forward she spied him huddled there. He sat up, his eyes manic.

'Help me,' he whispered. 'Don't leave me trapped eternally alone.'

She knelt, perturbed by his visible terror. 'How can I help you?'

'Not me. I didn't say it.'

'Who then?'

'You know who.'

There was no smell of alcohol. Eva wondered if the strain of being on the run had deranged him.

'Whisper please, my husband is in the stables. Who are you talking about?'

'You never warned me.' Gralton gripped her shoulder so tight that it hurt. His eyes disturbed her. 'I'd sooner face the cops than go back to that basement. I'd face batons and prison and any Johnny-come-lately Free State warder, but . . . Holy Mother of God . . . I've not prayed in twenty years, since I saw a baby-faced priest not six weeks docked from Dublin haranguing Boston strikers who wanted a few extra nickels to take the edge off their children's hunger. But I'll pray this night and every night to come never to see that sight again.'

Gralton became aware that his grip hurt. There was froth on his moustache and sweat glistened in his receding hair. 'I never liked that room from the moment I stepped into it. I woke and sensed something hover above the bed – not a shape, more a presence that I knew was a man. My body . . . too terrified to move . . . swamped by his despair like he was trying to suck my soul into the void of his own. "*Help me.*" His words weren't said aloud, but I heard them in a Mayo accent. "*Don't leave me trapped eternally alone.*"'

Gralton glanced towards the house as if expecting a figure to emerge.

'As a boy in Leitrim I was walking the road one night near a spot which old people said was a famine grave. From nowhere a family started walking towards me in the dark, the children starved-looking, bones poking through whatever flesh they had left. Half-skeletons. The man carried a tiny corpse, a bag of bones with matted hair. They came closer and closer without a sound and then they were gone, leaving the empty road that I was too afraid to pass. I scrambled through hawthorns into a field, scratched to pieces but didn't care. I kept running, miles out of my way before doubling back for home. I ate and ate and still the hunger wouldn't leave me. In the forty years since I was never so scared, but I'd face that road again rather than return to that basement of yours.'

'Did you see his face?' Eva asked.

'Have you?'

Eva sat back against the tree, uncomfortably close to Gralton.

'He hung himself in the wine cellar,' she said. 'His feet kicked out the glass in the little window as he swung there. They gave up trying to replace that glass: It would always be broken next morning.'

'Poor bastard.' Gralton looked up apologetically. 'Excuse the language, mam. I thought to shelter here long enough to recover my wits. Tell Art I went my own way. I left two guineas behind with the borrowed clothes. It's uncomfortable pretending to be somebody else. You haven't a cigarette?'

'Only back in the house.'

'It doesn't matter. Just now I'm thinking I might be as wise to walk a good way from this place, then hand myself up. They won't rest till they're shut of me. We drove out the English for what? To hand power to big farmers and shop-keepers with no room for the likes of me.'

'Or for Art?' Eva asked.

'Art has land and connections. A safety net to fall back on.'

'I don't think he will,' Eva said. 'He has left us behind.'

'I never needed to seek out injustice, I was born among the evicted, not the evictors. I never had anything to give up.' Gralton leaned closer. 'Say you'll do something for that poor bastard in your cellar.'

'What can I do?'

'How do I know?' He rose stiffly, using the tree for leverage.

'Have you food?' she asked. 'And your train fare? I promised Art . . .'

Gralton ignored her, walking off through the trees, shoulders stooped as if he had already journeyed for hours. Eva wanted to wish him luck but knew there could be no happy outcome. After twenty yards he looked back.

'Promise you'll pray for him.'

Eva nodded uncertainly and Gralton walked on into the dark. Her legs started to tremble. Previously she could always put the coldness in the cellar down to her imagination, fuelled by the superstition of servants. Now she could no longer escape the sense that some act was expected of her which she did not know how to undertake. She sat on for a time among the trees, reluctant to return to the house with its bills and crises. Back to this struggle to stay afloat for the children's sake. Back to the bed she had made for herself. New Zealand had never seemed so far away.

She had not bargained for also having to take on the

burden of a trapped soul, but sensed that the ghost was trying to reach her through Gralton. Perhaps he had been unable to approach her directly, knowing his place even in death. She recalled the sensation of footsteps at the nursery door earlier in the night. She did not know if a sense of kinship with Gralton had allowed him to make contact, blunt man to man. But perhaps if his spirit was appeased, this sense of melancholy within the house might lift. Hazel's feet might cease to be cold, no matter how many blankets on her bed; Francis might stop jumping up from chairs in the kitchen, unable to explain why he did so. And they might know peace here.

Yet she had no idea of what to do. The dew made her shiver. She crossed the lawn to the back door that Gralton had left unlocked. The passageway was dark and empty. She entered the kitchen, half expecting a ghostly presence to await her. Nothing stirred. She lit a candle and found her small Cambridge Bible on the shelf by the range beside Mrs McGrory's *Tailteann Cookery Book*. Eva took it down, unzipped it and read the inscription Father had written on her twentieth-first birthday: *Prayer is the soul's sincere desire, unuttered or unexpressed.*

All her journeys across London in search of revelation seemed like child's play now. Nothing had prepared her for this task. Miss MacManus's words returned. '*Let him know you're with him. Pray for him because he can no longer pray.*' What use would that do? Eva possessed no powers, and wasn't sure if she had the courage to face the claustrophobic wine cellar when a man as hardened as Gralton had run away. She longed to return to the nursery, climb into Francis's bed and lie with her arms around him. For ten minutes she stood in the kitchen doorway, too scared to move, until gradually she became conscious of the sense of another presence emanating from the doorway of the wine cellar at the end of the dark passageway.

It felt as if he were awaiting her. She forced herself to walk along the flagstones until she reached the step. The sense of his presence was overwhelming, though it had retreated into the darkest corner of the tiny cellar. There was no physical manifestation. Eva could not tell if he was staring at her or cowering. She just knew she had never felt so scared before. But the cold presence contained no menace, just an overwhelming sense of grief. Placing the candle on the flagstones she took one step into the cellar and then another. Barely enough light filtered in for her to distinguish the bible chapter headings as she helplessly scanned the pages of Exodus, Joshua, Samuel, Isaiah, Ezekiel and Matthew.

Eva's hands trembled as she took another step forward. Whatever was there seemed to press tighter into the corner. She wondered had his ghostly eyes witnessed everything that occurred in the nearby bedroom, her lovemaking with Freddie, her exhausted tears and frustrations.

She should not have been able to read the cramped print in this candlelight, but could just about discern the words that her hand finally stopped at, the story of Jonah inside the Whale. At first no words came when she opened her mouth, she had to swallow hard to find moisture for her throat.

*'I cried by reason of mine affliction unto the Lord, and he heard me; out of the belly of hell.'*

If Brigid rose early she would think her mistress crazy. Perhaps she was. Eva might have fled had her legs allowed her to.

*'For thou hadst cast me into the deep in the midst of the seas; and the floods compassed me about: all thy billows and thy waves passed over me. Then I said, I am cast out of thy sight; yet I will look again toward thy holy temple . . .'*

Eva paused to stare into the gloom and risked a step forward. Whatever was there did not draw back. It was only feet away, invisible, translucent, tentatively watching. Horrible images filled her mind: a skeleton or half-decomposed corpse.

'Please,' she said. 'Find peace.'

She took a step back, sensing the presence veer towards her, like a blown cloud. Face to face, she could hardly bear to look into the emptiness. She took another step back, then a third. But she was not retreating from what was there, rather it felt as if she was slowly drawing it forth, like a small tugboat guiding a liner through the mouth of a treacherous harbour. Trying to keep her voice steady, though barely above a whisper, she moved past the flickering candle on the flag-stones and read on.

*'I went down to the bottoms of the mountains; the earth with her bars was about me for ever: yet hast thou brought up my life from corruption, O Lord, my God. When my soul fainted within me I remembered the Lord: and my prayer came in unto thee, into thine holy temple.'*

Eva almost screamed but managed to remain still as the presence appeared to move through her out into the narrow passageway. During the seconds it took to pass she felt some-thing soar. She closed her eyes, hearing the book fall. The narrow stairs were only feet away. For a moment she thought he had gone up them. She imagined his soul gliding above Glanmire Wood, looking down at Turlough with its round tower and at the desolate bog beyond where Jim Gralton made his lonely way. But on opening her eyes, although she could see nothing, Eva knew that his ghost was still in the basement. Yet the presence felt different, like a weight was lifted from him, an edge shorn from his terrible loneliness. Eva held her hand out in the candlelight and kept it aloft, sensing something inside her lift also.

A path forward seemed clear. If she suggested to Dermot MacManus that Miss Crossan become his aunt's companion in Killeaden House, then Maureen, who had washed the flagstones, would not have to leave for some satanic English mill. With Eva supervising the children's lessons, Maureen would be perfect to mind them, practical and firm, yet brimming with fun. In the evening she could serve at table and that would be one wage saved.

Eva gazed into the bedroom where Gralton had slept. Tomorrow she would lie there with Freddie as man and wife. But before the morning's responsibilities claimed her, she had to be outside. She opened the back door and, breathing in the hint of oncoming dawn, began to run past the stables.

Twigs cut into her soles as she entered the forest's edge. Goethe's poem about the erl-king came into her head, but with no sense of terror this time. As long as she ran, nothing could touch her and she would be safe from sirens and harbingers of doom. The trees seemed to welcome her into their midst. Little girl lost. Little girl come home. Red Riding Hood with all the wolves asleep in bushes and barns. Her breath so was loud it drowned every other sound out. The overgrown slope was almost crested, the landscape shrouded in light mist. Eva stopped in front of the oaks Mother had dreamt about, at the spot where she had known that Francis was about to be born. It felt as if they awaited her. She closed her eyes and spun giddily like a child with her arms out, letting the world dissolve into a blur of motion. She imagined Mother's unconscious soul rising from her sleep in Donegal. A slender band of love radiating across St John's Point and the blue of Donegal Bay, passing over the isle of Inishmurray, the crags at Roskeeragh Point and the Ox mountains with their small lakes. It dipped down at Foxford where the Moy flowed into Lough Conn, drawing ever closer to the treetops of Glanmire Wood until it touched her when her arms encircled the tree. A scent of hand lotion filled her nostrils. Strength entered her as she was held within the clasp of Mother's love.

Eva grew so dizzy she had to grip the oak tight to prevent herself falling. Pressing her body against the trunk she could feel, beneath its gnarled bark, a warm heartbeat. Voices were calling from within the trunk if she only knew how to listen, voices of people who had died and others yet unborn. Her people. Her soulmates on journeys past and to come. Whose lives she would brush against and learn to recognise as having met in previous existences when encountered in this one. Their voices called to her from the core of this oak, though still inaudible to her ear. Her fellow children of the universe floating free of the nets of creeds. Whose thoughts appeared torturously slow to other people, whose perceptions made no sense in a purely rational world.

Slowly regaining her balance Eva lay against the trunk with her eyes closed, feeling the sun come up. Below her the house would be stirring, with tasks to be done. She could not truly be herself for as long as the children were young. This was the price of their security until she could be free. But she would strive to live in the real world until her time of liberation without starving her spirit, and she would journey within her soul without losing sight of those who needed her. She would strive to be happy, cutting away whatever obscured the simplicity of life, turning every task into an act of prayer to a God unowned by priests or ministers, to a vortex of love both infinite and indefinable. Eva stepped away from the oak and opened her eyes to acclaim the exaltation of dawn, before walking slowly back down the slope to face the tasks of this morning and all the other mornings to come.

# PART THREE
# 1937–1946

# TWENTY

## *The Volunteer*

*Barcelona, January 1937*

'You speak English, comrade? Where are you from?' The
young man with an unmistakably Dublin accent took a seat
at Brendan's table outside the café on the Ramblas. His
khaki beret was too big but otherwise he had scavenged well
in the scramble by new arrivals in the barracks storeroom.
His wafer-thin corduroy jacket buttoned up to the neck was
a different shade of brown to the equally inadequate trousers,
making it hard to regard his outfit as a uniform. But such
little sense of military precision existed among the volunteers from across the world who kept arriving in Barcelona
that their ill-fitting garb merely fitted into the euphoric
anarchy on the streets.

'I'm from Donegal,' Brendan replied carefully. The Dubliner
scrutinised him in that half-suspicious way of all working-
class people and Brendan lost the sense of freedom he had
known here amongst foreigners who could not distinguish
his caste.

'You sound like no bogman,' the Dubliner said.

'I'm a volunteer, the same as you.'

'Then why aren't you in with the rest of us Irish lads where you belong? I'll have a natter with Frank Ryan, our *responsable*, see if he can squeeze you into our column.'

'I don't think that would be possible.'

'Needless to say.'

Brendan resented the Dubliner's smirk. He had spent his lunchtime with Yuri, an elderly Soviet radio technician, discussing a problem with Yuri's ship's transmitter. Yuri had returned to the Soviet ship tied up in the harbour and now Brendan wanted simply to be left alone or at least as alone as a man could feel who knew that his movements were being watched. 'What's so funny?'

'Keep your hair on, comrade. It's just that you university intellectuals make me laugh. I see it when the new arrivals are being sorted out in the bullring. The ordinary English lads refuse to be separated while you toffs bugger off to join the Spaniards in POUM to avoid needing to mix with your own lower orders.'

'I'm not an English toff and I'm still among the volunteers I travelled with,' Brendan replied tersely. 'I'm with the Russian contingent.'

'Holy shit! Did they invade Killybegs?' He stopped laughing, seeing that Brendan did not intend to reply, and stuck out his hand. 'Liam Hennessy. From Dorset Street in Dublin.'

'Brendan.'

Hennessy managed to summon one of the waiters running the café which was now a collective enterprise since the owners fled. 'Two mud coffees with a dose of brandy, *entiende*?'

The waiter shrugged uncomprehendingly, dressed in a brown boilersuit with an anarchist neckerchief. This outfit was so common that it was hard to tell who were civilians and who were volunteers.

It had been part of Barcelona's exhilaration that initially touched Brendan, the sense of being in a true revolutionary city. But the free spirit evident here had made him realise how claustrophobic Moscow always felt. These Catalans had already withstood a major battle and knew that the untrained volunteers they greeted like heroes each day at the station were no match against the warplanes sent by Hitler. But this did not dent the genuine camaraderie infecting everybody except Georgi and the other NKVD officers in the Soviet contingent who viewed such relaxed kinship as a dangerous affront. Moscow and Barcelona abounded with revolutionary banners, but the ones here were not just constant shrines to Lenin and Stalin or to heroic factory workers who exceeded production quotas. The red and black anarchist colours flew freely, with slogans in Spanish composed by the locals instead of dutifully copied from textbooks. Brendan could not translate them all, but loved the way they often clashed in proclaiming different aims – Independence for Catatonia, Fidelity to the Popular Front of the Republic and Support for the Communist Comintern.

'*Café*,' Brendan told the waiter. '*Con coñac. Dos.*'

'Fair play to you.' Hennessy leaned closer, conspiratorially. 'Tell me this and tell me no more, as one Irish buck who may meet his death to another – are the brothels here as good as they say?'

Brendan laughed. It was a sound he had grown unfamiliar with. He glanced around the wide boulevard and wondered where was the minder who had tracked him since he left the radio centre. Laughter was viewed with suspicion by the NKVD unless in response to the political jokes they liked to tell the Russians in their charge who laughed with careful enthusiasm until they gauged it safe to stop.

'To tell the truth,' he admitted, 'I've never had to pay for it in my life.'

Hennessy laughed also. 'That's because you're a jammy

good-looking Horse Protestant bastard. Ordinarily my select repertoire of chat-up lines sees me over the winning post with the mots too, but it's not my bodily needs I'm thinking of. We've a Mayo lad with us called Bourke, a bit shy with the señoritas. We're being sent to Andujar tomorrow as part of the Marseillaise Battalion. It would be a tragedy if the first time he got laid it was in his grave. Could you point us in the right direction at least?'

Brendan downed the coffee and cognac brought by the waiter. He was taking a risk by not returning to the radio centre, but was sick of being corralled like a man in permanent quarantine. 'I'll do better than that,' he said. 'I'll show you.'

'A man after my own heart.' Hennessy downed his drink and insisted on paying. He rose and strode past a group of German POUM volunteers ponderously bellowing out a revolutionary song, and stopped at a table where four men sat drinking. Despite the berets Brendan knew that they were Irish and felt an inexplicable pang of homesickness. It was not merely to do with being in Spain and the two months before that being trained as a wireless operator in Moscow. But it suddenly felt as if a decade ago he had turned his back on part of his own identity, not realising what he had cut himself off from. At sixteen he had ceased to see himself as Irish, presuming that he could not belong there. Art and the others in his family had been emotionally wrapped up in Ireland's independence struggle, being old enough to understand what was occurring. He only began to understand life after that messy conflict ended and always viewed it as a revolution foiled by the bourgeois cancer of nationalism. But perhaps he'd only ever seen Ireland through Art's hurt, because these four drinkers did not look like superstitious peasants. They argued freely, not caring who overheard. It was dangerous for him to sit with them because one Irishman kept calling to the German POUM volunteers whom he could not risk being seen to associate with. But they gave him a sense that there might after all be a small band of Irish people – apart from his family – to whom he could belong. Then he listened more closely and knew that he was wrong, because these volunteers had not yet lost their political innocence.

'Lads, I bring you Brendan, a fellow Irish comrade.' Hennessy pointed around the table as men rose to shake Brendan's hand. 'This is Charlie Donnelly from Tyrone who will blind you with poetry if given a chance. Bob Hilliard, a good Protestant like yourself, unless I mistake the foot you dig with. Beside him Kit Conway and, last but by no means least, Mr Peadar Bourke from Westport, Co. Mayo. Brendan here is with the Russian volunteers.'

'I'm a radio technician,' Brendan explained.

'He's also a man with contacts,' Hennessy said. 'The only thing closed in Barcelona is the churches and Peadar can't go home and tell the mother he didn't light a candle for her in the Sagrada Familia Cathedral, seeing as her knees are worn out praying for his soul up on Croagh Patrick. Luckily Brendan has a key, so we have a personal tour lined up for you, Peadar.'

Brendan enjoyed Hennessy's soft Irish bullshit and the veiled sexual ribbing the men gave Bourke. Charlie Donnelly insisted on Brendan staying for a drink, while Bob Hilliard waved the Germans over to join their table.

It was three in the afternoon, two hours since Brendan left his post. All week the main transmitter had been faulty but Brendan was convinced that he had fixed the problem last night. He had slept in the radio centre to ensure that the equipment didn't malfunction, then told the Ukrainian in charge that he was slipping out for lunch with Yuri who had come in to try and scavenge spare parts. Yuri was the one Soviet comrade whom Brendan still trusted. The sailor from Archangel was fearless of authority. He was among the original Bolsheviks who repulsed Mr Fforde's imperialist navy in 1919 when they tried to shore up the White Russian forces who murdered Yuri's wife and children. Brendan suspected that Yuri had never recovered from this loss, as if willing a bullet to claim him in every battle since then. Yuri laughed at the young robots who learnt their communism in the Lenin School instead of on the streets and, while wary of directly confronting the NKVD, openly criticised their paranoia about foreigners when he was alone with Brendan.

Today Brendan hadn't needed Yuri's whisper to know that they were being followed from the radio centre. For the past fortnight his movements had been watched, ever since he realised that he had not been brought to Spain for his radio skills but so that he could be used to spy upon new arrivals to the International Brigade. While the Soviet-born volunteers were sequestered away, Brendan had been encouraged to stand most days among the cheering crowds as trains festooned with red flags arrived from Figueras with new recruits who had crossed the French frontier. He was even given money to drink with them, to discover their motives for enlisting and poison their minds against the Spanish government who were refusing to fully accept the wisdom of Soviet advice. Initially Brendan had befriended these new arrivals without grasping the implication of his actions. He had not understood that he was being debriefed in late-night drinking sessions with Georgi until he saw the NKVD officer take notes and realised that he had inadvertently set up a Welsh miner with Trotskyite tendencies to be shot. Since then he rarely approached foreign volunteers and tried to focus purely on his job as a radio operator, refusing to be drawn into Georgi's world, to his protector's increasing infuriation.

But still the nightly drinking sessions had continued, with Georgi obsessively demanding information about every casual remark made by visitors to the radio centre. It was one thing to smuggle British Foreign Office documents from London to Russia. The risks were high and during the past four years Brendan had varied his routes and sometimes his identity. But at least he had felt that his work as a courier was useful to the revolution. Spying on fellow technicians was not in his character. Brendan had come to hate drinking with Georgi, especially when André Marty – the Chief Political Commissar of the international Brigade – visited Barcelona. With froth on his moustache, Marty would harangue Georgi if the NKVD had not unearthed another anarcho-syndicalist spy to be executed during his stay. If allowed to choose between killing half of Franco's forces or being able to assassinate the POUM leadership which controlled Barcelona, Brendan knew that Georgi Polevoy and André Marty would far sooner wipe out those independent Spanish Marxists who refused to take orders from Moscow.

He noticed now the suspicious way the German POUM volunteers at the table were starting to regard him and knew that some Irish lad had mentioned where he was stationed. Bourke and Hennessy were asking him what action he had seen in Spain, mistaking his reticence as evidence of having witnessed battles that remained too raw to be described. In truth Brendan had not been allowed to leave Barcelona, though from radio messages he knew about the Seville fascists launching their offensive against the anarchist militias trying to hold Cordoba. But the only blood he had seen was when Yuri and he wandered by mistake into a cellar adjoining the Russian quarters and found congealed pools on the floor beside a wall pockmarked with bullet holes.

'Loan us a pillow case, Donnelly.' Hennessy reached for a cigarette paper and helped himself to some unrolled tobacco. 'It's fine for you lazy bastards, but we have a sacred duty to perform. That right, Brendan?'

Brendan nodded and the three young men rose amid much slagging aimed at Bourke. Hennessy shook the Germans' hands but Brendan did not attempt this dangerous charade, knowing that every detail would be reported to the NKVD. Georgi would be amused at him visiting a brothel, having failed to persuade the young Irishman to accompany him on his regular visits. Judging by the crowds at the whorehouse half the volunteers in Barcelona were due for the front. The older prostitutes were almost suffocatingly motherly to the younger clients waiting in the over-furnished parlour, making a special fuss about boys who confessed to having had to slip away to war without telling anyone.

Brendan's family had not known he was going to Spain. After the fascists launched their coup he had intended enlisting at the British Communist Party office located between two fruit wholesalers near Covent Garden. Then he would have had time to write letters. But Georgi always cautioned against contact with any communists – including Art – that might attract Scotland Yard's attention. So Brendan had travelled instead to Moscow to courier dispatches from his handler. While there he had discovered how Georgi was being made Political Commissar to a company of Soviet specialists sent by Stalin in response to a plea from the Popular Front government in Spain. Initially Georgi wasn't keen on Brendan joining the expedition, fearing the loss of a good courier on the London route. But perhaps Georgi sensed that these trips to Moscow were not the same for Brendan since the cloud of Art's unexplained deportation and the displacement of his wife and child. Perhaps Brendan had become over-used as a

322

courier and Georgi was afraid of his cover being blown, because finally he agreed to let Brendan travel with them to Spain, joking that they could check out the beauty of Spanish women together. In Barcelona, Brendan had sent a card to his parents and another to Eva, though he knew that Georgi disapproved of such communication. But he continued to follow instructions about having absolutely no contact with his disgraced brother. Brendan had never managed to get Georgi to tell him exactly what Art's crimes were that required his expulsion from Moscow, but Georgi sometimes intimated that only Brendan's importance had saved Art from being shot or sent to a re-education camp.

Bourke was quiet, seated between Hennessy and Brendan on the sofa in the brothel, still unable to decide which of the passing girls should take his virginity.

'Come on,' Hennessy urged, 'that tall one is a beauty. If you don't pick one soon they'll be shagged out. You don't want her falling asleep just before you work up to your big moment.'

'I don't want to be here at all,' the Mayo lad confessed. 'It's not natural.'

'Jaysus, are you a Jesuit or what?' Hennessy raised his eyes. 'What's more natural than wanting a girl? The priests got their claws deep into you.'

'I can't help being who I am.' Bourke turned to Brendan. 'My brother is also over here.'

'With the International Brigade?'

'No. With General O'Duffy's Irish fascist column. My father had us both tramping around Mayo in Blueshirt uniforms when I was too young to know better. On my twenty-first birthday I refused to attend any more rallies. He kicked me out. The last time I was back in Mayo was to heckle Paddy Belton at a National Corporate Party meeting in Castlebar where my father and brother were hanging onto his words like he was the Saviour himself. O'Duffy was on his last legs when this war broke out but they've a new platform now with the bishops cheering them on, claiming that nuns are being raped in Spain. O'Duffy is after dragging six hundred Irish lads over here, with women saying novenas like they were going to the crusades. My kid brother was never outside Mayo in his life. I had to come too, even though I'm on the other side. I still feel responsible for him. He's in Spain now, but God knows where.'

'Probably in a brothel,' Hennessy suggested helpfully.

'You don't know him,' Bourke said.

'I know O'Duffy. Your brother was never safer. Didn't his whole crew flog their uniforms for drink after arriving. Franco has them holed up in Caceres where they can harm nobody but themselves. At the first shot O'Duffy will run home like a headless chicken. Worry about yourself because we won't have that option.'

'It's hard when brothers fall out,' Brendan said.

Bourke glanced at him. 'Is your brother a fascist?'

'I've a brother I looked up to, the strongest swimmer I ever knew. I thought he was the strongest everything.'

'Where is he now?'

'I've not seen him in two years. One reason for coming here was that I was convinced he'd enlist too. I'd see him stepping off a train in Barcelona and we'd be equals on neutral ground.'

'My brother joined the British army,' Hennessy said. 'It means he can never come home.' He nudged Bourke. 'That girl on the stairs with the long hair, looking straight at us. Go on, lie back and think of Ireland.'

Bourke rose as the girl beckoned. 'I don't know what going into battle is like but it can't be more nerve-wracking than this.'

Hennessy patted his rump. 'If you're not down in two days we'll rescue you.'

They waited for Bourke to return, with Brendan ordering more black unsweetened coffee. Surveying the crowded parlour, Brendan wondered which man present was spying for Georgi. After ten minutes Bourke came down the stairs and his companions ordered brandy and let him sit in silence. Brendan wondered would Bourke feel as changed by his first encounter with death? Eventually the Mayo man managed a half-hearted joke and they walked back out to the street, past anarchist flags draped from the brothel windows. Every moment absent from the radio centre increased Brendan's risk of being charged with insubordination. He longed to never return to that claustrophobic atmosphere of fear, which always drained any sense of being part of the collective spirit on the street. But he knew he had no option but to go there. Georgi would never let him join the Irish column and, even if he could, he already knew too much concerning this war. Making an excuse, Brendan left Hennessy and Bourke at a small café near the harbour.

The radio station was operating smoothly when he entered. There were some messages to deal with, but none were urgent. Still he knew that he had been missed. If any other NKVD officer commanded the station he would be arrested, but his relationship with Georgi went beyond politics. At times the Georgian felt like another annoying older brother. Being cooped up in Barcelona suited neither of them. Of late they constantly argued but honest arguments between men instead of the ideological shadow-boxing that passed for debate between the others. Brendan saw Georgi's ruthless side when he screamed at the young Russians who were terrified of him. But Georgi revealed a different side when drinking with old Bolsheviks like Yuri who refused to be intimidated by someone they regarded as a Georgian upstart. Georgi would let his mask slip in their company as he bemoaned his fate as a man constantly ensnared by young women.

Brendan seemed to have been adopted like a lucky mascot by these older men for their occasional marathon drinking sessions. But on most nights, with demands for updates from Moscow, and André Marty baying from Albacete for death warrants, Georgi would drink in his office with Brendan forced to keep him company alone.

Only four staff remained in the radio station now. Brendan liked when it was this quiet with the operators reminding him of one of his earliest memories – his siblings on a van listening in to a travelling showman's radio headphones. Brendan had been too young to understand their silent awe, but never forgot it. In some ways it was the first step on his journey here.

Yuri was back in the office and Brendan watched the old sailor curse silently as he examined a dismantled transmitter in the corner. Whoever did the inventory of spare radio parts for this expedition was the only true saboteur Brendan had come across. Yet he was probably a party stalwart whose unthinking loyalty mattered more than his incompetence. Most of the parts sent were incompatible with the transmitters and only by guile and improvisation could the technicians keep the station working. Brendan took pity on the old sailor trying to scavenge yet another part for the ship's radio that he had obviously still not managed to get working. If the sailor had been properly trained then the valve he stole this morning should have worked. Pilfering was illegal, but with no young zealots around Brendan tried to help Yuri locate a new part. After a few moments Yuri nudged Brendan, warning him that Georgi had entered the office.

'That bastard's in a shit mood,' the sailor whispered. 'Maybe his whore gave him the pox or he couldn't get it up for her. Watch yourself and remember these Georgians are never as drunk as they seem.'

Brendan stood up and walked quickly towards Georgi so that the NKVD officer did not spot Yuri kneeling behind the bench. Georgi indicated with a shrug for Brendan to follow him into his office. He kicked the door shut after they entered and took out vodka and two glasses. 'Your afternoon's whoring must have been thirsty work, comrade. Still, another drink won't kill you.'

'Why insist on having me followed?'

'You deserted your post. Marty could have you shot for less.'

'I was here all night and only left when I knew the equipment was working. I had no further duties.'

'I've asked you to keep an eye on people here.'

Brendan downed the vodka. Spanish wine and brandy had their place, but Georgi always retreated to the safety of Russian vodka at night.

'You have sufficient lackeys spying on each other to know everything.'

Sourly, Georgi refilled the glasses. 'And what would you do, Irishman? Let the whole world wander through? Why not simply hand out our secrets to every fascist and Trotskyite spy in Barcelona? But perhaps that's what you've been doing with your loose tongue.'

'I say nothing to nobody.'

'Today you said an awful lot of nothings to an awful lot of nobodies. Report to me.'

Brendan downed his vodka again, feeling the alcohol burn his throat. 'Nothing to report, sir, except ¡*no pasaran!* The Republic still holds.'

Georgi slammed down his glass. 'Don't *sir* me like you

327

were still in your English public school. You spent your day whoring and associating with Trotskyite scum, yet have nothing to report. We are besieged by enemies, yet you see nothing that might endanger our interests.'

'I saw passion and enough real idealism to make me realise how little of it I see in this station. I saw the difference between conviction and indoctrination.'

'You were seen drinking with German members of the *Partido Obrero de Unificacíon Marxista*.'

'Is that a crime? POUM are on our side.'

'Are they? How can they be a communist party when they refuse to accept orders from Moscow? They are known Trokskyites.'

'Everybody must know it except them because I never heard a single one mention Trotsky.'

'So you admit to fraternising with them!' Georgi almost danced back, like a boxer after landing a punch.

'They never stopped singing in German,' Brendan said. 'All I can tell you is that whatever they kept singing about it wasn't Leon Trotsky.'

The Georgian spread his hands on the desk as if addressing an imbecile. 'Trotskyism would not be a conspiracy if he was mentioned out loud. Trotskyites suck in good comrades and spit them out like olive stones. I'm tired of always having to protect you.'

'And I'm tired of always being watched. We spend more time spying on our own side than fighting the fascists.'

Georgi leaned across the desk, speaking with deliberate softness. 'Watch yourself, Goold, before you go too far. Watch yourself and watch those you mix with.'

'I mixed with good communists today. The fascists don't need spies. They control the air. When they want to locate our troops they simply fly up and look. If Stalin really wants to eliminate spying let him send warplanes to provide cover.'

Brendan became suddenly sober as if he had dived off Bruckless Pier into icy water. Georgi sat back.

'I could have you shot for questioning Stalin's wisdom. And I could be shot for not having you shot. You presume too much on our friendship. I remember when you were a good comrade who asked no questions. Now I wonder why you came to Spain.'

Georgi's voice held no anger, merely mild enquiry. This was what frightened Brendan. 'I came to fight fascism. I came because Spain is a battleground for the soul of Europe. I came to stand alongside a nation armed with just a few rifles and their courage against Hitler's warplanes.'

'Maybe you came to be a saboteur like your brother?'

'Whatever Art did he was no saboteur.'

'A typical baby brother. Would you still be defending your hero if you knew that he denounced you?'

'Art would never denounce me.'

'Really?' Georgi's smile was patronising. 'Two years ago he walked into my office in Lubyanka, begging like a dog for an exit permit from the Soviet Union. He offered me names – fellow translators who were spies, his wife's family who belonged to an anarchist cell, neighbours who deliberately tried to deflate morale. He spewed out his treasonous guts, pleading to be allowed to return to Donegal like that renegade fool, Fforde, who fled before we could shoot him.'

'Art loved Moscow.'

'Art loved property. It was in his diseased blood. He never stopped belonging to your despised class. Your father wrote to say that he had found a clause in your grandfather's will which allowed him to leave his property to your brother Thomas once a doctor testified that Art was insane.'

329

'Nobody told me this,' Brendan insisted.

'Why would they? The last born counts for nothing. Art came to me with your father's letter. His tone had changed once there was a chance of losing the property he used to boast about renouncing. He offered bribes. The fool didn't realise that the Soviet Union has no use for scum like him. If he wanted to leave we would just give him a visa and get rid of him. But he was not happy until he got every denunciation off his chest, until he denounced you too.'

'For what?'

The Georgian smiled. 'You tell me.'

Brendan was angry and confused. 'There's nothing to tell. I don't believe a word you say any more.'

'I have never lied to you. I've always looked after you like a son. I refused to write down the hatred your brother spat out. About how *he* had been the real revolutionary and you were forever trying to climb onto his back. How your cock was the only principle you were ever led by. How you fucked a fascist Lord's wife and plotted with her to distribute illicit copies of Trotsky's *Where is Britain Going?* How you met her husband in Hyde Park and agreed to spy for Oswald Mosley if you could continue to fuck his wife. How you got a good comrade, Ruth Davis, pregnant but blamed it on the fascist lord when the girl was left half-paralysed during a backstreet abortion. If I had written down your brother's accusations you would never have been allowed to come to Spain. But I wanted to give you a chance. This war is a farce with infiltrators pouring in from everywhere. Can't you see that we will never form a proper government here unless we purge the Trotskyites and anarcho-syndicalists with the same ruthlessness as in the Soviet Union?'

'Spain already has a democratically-elected government that the fascists won't accept. That's why we're here.'

Georgi sighed, exasperated. 'We're here to save the Spanish

people from their own leaders' incompetence. Thankfully we are gradually putting this war on a proper ideological footing but we are being hindered by infiltration. That is why you must pull your weight. Tell me about the Irish drunkards you were with. What did they want?'

'One wanted to lose his virginity.'

'Don't toy with me.'

'They're honest volunteers who came to help the Spanish people.'

'Fuck the Spanish people.' Georgi rose. 'I've enough problems without you moaning about the Spanish people. Have you learnt nothing, Goold? This war is about weeding out the chaff so we are left with loyal comrades who will return home and organise in a structured way so that we can grow strong with one voice and one vision.'

'And what about Spain?'

Georgi took a deep breath. 'I am not indifferent to Spanish suffering. I like it here.' He looked at Brendan with a piercing honesty he only occasionally allowed to surface. 'I feel safer here. I don't always like the things I have to do. Your Irish friends think that a revolution can be won by love. Love stirs people but only fear makes them move. That's human nature. Sadly we're all too human. Was she beautiful, your fascist lover in London?'

'She was no fascist when I knew her. She was a dilettante and, yes, she was beautiful. She possessed a disarming air of vulnerability.'

'That is a trick all women learn, yet men never learn to defend against.' Georgi laughed softly. 'It's funny how you have that same trick of vulnerability which makes me want to protect you.' Georgi's expression changed, making Brendan suddenly wonder could the NKVD officer be homosexual. 'What do you really want?'

'I want to go home.' Brendan was so rattled that the words came out before he could weigh their implications. He continued, seeing no alternative. 'When I volunteered in Moscow you said I would be free to come or go. If I return to London I can still be of use to you like before, but this is not the war I thought I was joining.'

Georgi studied him closely. 'But you did join this war, even though I warned you not to. Try to leave and you become a deserter. André Marty can have you shot.' The NKVD officer opened a drawer to remove a sheet of paper. He studied it, then signed. 'Do you know what I am holding?'

It could be a death warrant or a confession to be signed before they shot him. It could be a report of his movements or a list of Russian volunteers who had denounced him. Brendan's throat was dry. He closed his eyes and saw himself as a small child standing on the return of the stairs in Bruckless House in Donegal. It was a summer's morning with light filling the hall below, but for some reason his family had gone on a picnic and left him behind. He was too scared to stay up there alone, yet convinced that a terrible presence waited if he descended the staircase. It was years since he last had this childhood dream, but it was vividly clear.

'You're going to shoot me, aren't you?'

'Why would I shoot you?'

'You don't need a reason to shoot people.'

'You think I enjoy shooting people? I enjoy fucking. You and I should have gone whoring together just once. Two beds in one room, a contest to see who would be the last man standing. Line up the girls, see how many we could plough our way through. You'd have youth and I would have oysters. That would have been the way to finish it. It's too late now, your health will not allow it.' Georgi's hand reached into the drawer and came out holding a revolver. 'Unbutton your shirt.'

The NKVD officer rose and Brendan did what he was told. His skin looked so white against the brown corduroy, with a trickle of sweat over his nipple. Georgi placed the revolver's steel butt against his breast like a stethoscope.

'Cough,' he ordered.

Brendan obeyed, puzzled at being toyed with.

'Just what I thought, you have your brother's complaint.' He paused. 'Your sickly brother Thomas.'

'What do you know about Thomas?'

'I make it my business to know your business. I know that he contracted tuberculosis and had to leave Ireland for South Africa. I know that tuberculosis is contagious and it would be dangerous to have a volunteer suffering from it. I know that you were my protégé. You have disappointed me but I'm still responsible for you. I read you like a woman and with women you need to guess their next hysterical demand in advance.'

Georgi removed the cold steel from Brendan's breast and dropped the paper onto his lap. It was a certificate of discharge signed by a doctor. The NKVD officer walked over to open the door. 'I've arranged a ticket for you on the morning train to Figueras. You're on your own after that. I don't want to see or hear from you again. War is men's work and all you're good for is taking it up the arse. Get out of my sight.'

Brendan rose, his legs shaky. 'Thank you.'

'Just go,' Georgi said. 'Tell nobody or I'll have signed my own death warrant. You could have been a good communist.'

'Did Art really denounce me? I need to know.'

'Have I ever lied to you?'

Brendan paused in the doorway. Despite his disillusionment in recent weeks he wanted to embrace this man or make some gesture of appreciation. His body trembled from relief and he desperately needed to use the filthy urinal at the end of the corridor. For a moment it seemed there might be some last words between them, but then a movement in the radio centre caught the Georgian's eye.

'What the hell are you doing there?' he shouted.

Yuri rose, hastily shoving a valve into his pocket. 'Just looking . . . I was comparing . . .'

'You were trying to steal. I am being asked to fight a war surrounded by invalids and thieves. Get the fuck out!'

'I'm going, comrade.' The old sailor shuffled towards the door. 'Don't take it out on me because you woke to find a scum mark around your prick. If it's red it's probably just lipstick. Though if it's green it's gangrene.'

'Out! Both of you!'

Georgi slammed his door and Brendan faced Yuri who shrugged wryly. 'He caught the clap last year, hates being reminded. Are you okay, comrade?'

'I could use a drink,' Brendan replied. 'Otherwise I'm fine.'

He was more than fine. Folding the discharge certificate carefully in his pocket, he laughed. He was going home. He wasn't quite sure where home was – Donegal or Dublin or London, but in twenty-four hours he would be in France. He would be on his own, but he could restart his life properly out of Art's shadow. His brother had denounced him. When the possibility arose of losing his precious inheritance Art had turned his back on every principle. That was why Art left Moscow so secretively and never made contact. However Brendan did not feel betrayed, but liberated. He walked out onto the packed streets with the old sailor and stopped at the first café they reached. Brendan studied the Catalan faces and the men from across Europe who had come to stand alongside them and felt an echo of the euphoria he had known during his first week here. A group of men sang in

English at a nearby table: '*Fascist bullets, fascist bombs make our land a smoking mass. Hurrah for courage, hurrah for bravery. At Madrid they did not pass.*'

Brendan joined in with the shout: '*¡No pasaran!*' Only Yuri remained oblivious to the gaiety, obsessed by his inability to repair the ship's radio. The sailor's frustration was souring Brendan's mood. Brendan asked to examine the valve the sailor had stolen and Yuri produced it surreptitiously, anxious not to be caught. The ship was five minutes' walk away, the repair job no more than two minutes' work. Yuri protested when Brendan suggested they both go and fix it now. Their waitress had just brought more wine and Yuri promised to try and remember Brendan's instructions properly in the morning. But Brendan knew that the old sailor could not relax until the task was done, so he asked the waitress to hold onto their wine until they returned. Singing was starting at all the tables, with different nationalities trying to outdo each other. The waitress teased them that she would drink the wine herself if they were not back in ten minutes. Brendan saw Hennessy with Charlie Donnelly and Bourke at the café on the quay. He went to call their names then stopped because the discharge certificate set him apart. However, as he was passing, Hennessy saw him and rose. Yuri urged him on, anxious to return to his wine. But Brendan broke free to tell Hennessy he was going home and to ask if he wanted any messages delivered. The Dubliner shook his head and Brendan saw how his eyes ceased to regard Brendan as a comrade. Hennessy turned away as Yuri hissed at Brendan from the gangplank.

The ship was quiet, the radio in a small room below deck. The puzzling thing was that Brendan could find nothing wrong with the transmitter. It seemed in perfect order, more powerful and better maintained than the ones in the radio centre. Only when he turned to tell Yuri this did he notice Georgi and two younger NKVD officers blocking the doorway alongside the old sailor. Brendan charged towards them, desperate to escape to the safety of the quayside crowds. But he knew there was no chance, he knew that he had been tricked, with Georgi wanting to ensure no struggle on the quay with foreign volunteers intervening. The young NKVD officers pinned back his arms, forcing him onto his knees as they put on the handcuffs. One placed a sack over his head.

'Now we can hold a proper conversation, Goold.' Georgi's calm voice was close to his head before the Georgian stepped back. 'You did well, Yuri.'

Yuri's laugh was wistful – the sound of a man who had survived every upheaval. Brendan felt no anger towards the old man, but only at himself and his hapless naivety.

'It was easy, comrade, like reeling in a little fish. So little you'd almost wish to throw it back overboard. I have some wine waiting if you care to join me.'

'Don't let us detain you, comrades.' This voice belonged to one of the young officers, a product of the Lenin school. 'We know how to deal with Trotskyite spies.'

Brendan instinctively curled up just before the boot smashed into his stomach. He lost count of how often they kicked him or how long it went on. He just knew that Georgi and Yuri were back at the café, drinking in the midst of the singing throng. And he knew that his ribs were broken and three or four more kicks would hopefully edge him towards the mercy of oblivion.

# TWENTY-ONE

## *Night*

### *Donegal, January 1937*

Mrs Ffrench did not know what time it was when she woke, but the cold sensation inside her was so intense that she had to slip out of bed and onto the freezing landing so as not to disturb her sleeping husband. Crouching beside the banisters she shivered in her nightdress. The only sounds were the grandfather clock in the dark hallway below and a desolate wind howling in from St John's Point. Stones on the driveway would be whitened by hoarfrost, with dew transforming the lawn into a brittle glistening sheet. Yet although the house was perishing, the chill within her was deeper as if she had witnessed a hideous deed in her sleep. If she could explain this sensation she might have woken her husband and sought comfort. But the feeling was so illogical that she could confess it to no one. It felt similar to the guilt she experienced last month after the kitchen cat gave birth to more kittens and she discovered a covered bucket of water in the yard. From the desperate cries emanating from the bucket she realised that the newborn kittens were drowning inside it. The mother cat had frantically tried to claw at the bucket and kept glancing at Mrs Ffrench, like one mother pleading to another. Mrs

Ffrench had not helped but returned indoors to where the cries could not be heard. Yet for nights afterwards she heard the kittens in her sleep and woke convinced that she had sinned by doing nothing and not questioning her husband's perceived wisdom about what was best.

Crouching on the landing Mrs Ffrench knew that she had spent too much of her life like this. Things were simpler before the Great War when they were newly wed and her husband allowed himself to be consumed by her Baha'i faith. It had felt like she was guiding him, opening up his mind to Prophet Baha'ullah's predictions of a new era for mankind devoid of prejudice and extremes of poverty and wealth. Was this the first step in his embrace of communism? Back then Mrs Ffrench had imagined them equally mixing the colours on the palette of their lives. But at some stage she fell into step, dutifully letting his beliefs and passions become hers. Not all his passions though. Rumours of one passion had been whispered in this lonely place for years. She knew it from the pitying way that other wives looked at her.

The religion she was born into and the one she adopted both made her used to feeling an outsider in Ireland. The godlessness of Marxism merely reinforced her sense of difference. She could cope with these badges of isolation, but what she could not bear was having to compete against the fragile beauty of the sole remaining neighbour with whom she shared anything in common. Now in the past week even that neighbour had abandoned Donegal.

Not that anything untoward ever occurred between her husband and Mrs Goold Verschoyle, who was ill at ease with Mr Ffrench's unspoken infatuation. But the entire district knew of his puppy eyes since the day when Mr Goold Verschoyle, in a rare lapse of manners, dressed down her husband before a police sergeant on the mountainside. Mrs Ffrench should

338

have been glad to see the back of this woman who had always possessed some indefinable ailment, yet still managed to hold the admiration of every man in the district. But all week she had mourned her departure like a sister with the Manor House now empty and the Goold Verschoyles gone to Oxford.

There had been a sale of wine and old port from their cellars with local farmers gawping mistrustfully at the dusty bottles as if they contained a dubious fairground elixir. Her husband, along with the few other remaining Protestants, had purchased the wine. Catholic interest only arose when the sale of spirits came up. Watching this auction had saddened her, with most onlookers present to merely gawk at the possessions of the departing gentry, and Mr and Mrs Goold Verschoyle mutely observing proceedings from an upstairs window. They had not emptied their cellar for financial reasons, which was just as well because the auction raised precious little, but Mr Goold Verschoyle considered it prudent not to leave alcohol or valuables in the boarded-up house. Most items of real value had been transported to Oxford, though the family silver was missing – presumably having been purloined by Art and donated to some communist cause. Only the curtains and heavy furniture remained, like a baited trap to try and lure back their eldest son.

Art had only visited Donegal once since his return from Russia, possessing such a haunted look that Mrs Ffrench had wanted to take his hand and confess how she too hated Moscow. But his stiff shoulders hinted that he would brook no criticism of the state that expelled him.

Little remained of the intense wide-eyed boy she first knew. He had been replaced by a cipher whose only language was rhetoric. For him to utter a single criticism of Stalin would be to shatter the foundation on which he'd built his adult life.

339

On that visit she heard that Mr Goold Verschoyle had again pleaded with him to take an interest in the Manor House, but Art declared his intention to let the house rot rather than allow himself to be contaminated by the evil of inherited wealth in having any dealings with the cursed business, now or after his father's death.

Yet during that short visit Mrs Ffrench had also seen Art strip to the waist to spend an entire day lovingly repairing a section of roof where the tiles had come loose. It was plain that the boy still loved the house and this irrational love tormented him. Mr Goold Verschoyle's final act in Dunkineely had been to write to Art, saying that he was leaving the key with Mr Barnes, their old bank manager in Donegal town. He had left for Oxford because the Irish winters were too wet for his wife's acute arthritis and they would have more company in an hour's walk in Oxford than in a day's drive in Donegal. But she also knew that Mr Goold Verschoyle was departing because he no longer had the heart for the struggle to maintain a house with nobody to pass it on to. She knew this weariness herself because in time Bruckless House would pass, if not to strangers, then to distant relations. This made it harder for her to care about the gardens or rooms filled with unread Soviet magazines that her husband had imported in bulk until the post office refused to deliver them. On some nights this home felt like a mausoleum, but even the grave surely felt warmer than the way she was feeling now.

She should fetch a robe for her shoulders or venture into the kitchen to make hot milk and honey. But it felt like her legs would not move. She sat on the top step to stare down into the dark hall and then, for some irrational reason, sensed that a child stood behind her. She did not know who the child was and knew there was no point in turning because she would not be able to see him, just as he could not see

340

her. But she could feel his lonely terror and knew that he was staring down at an unseen menace lurking at the bottom of the stairs. She also sensed this evil and wondered if she might now still be dreaming. Because the evil had a calm inaudible adult voice – almost like her husband's – coaxing the child down. She wanted to say, '*Wait here with me, I won't let you come to harm like those kittens in the bucket. Trust me, I'll mind you.*' But she was no mother and this was why the child could not sense her presence, why he stepped forward, one step, two step, slowly descending the stairs. She wanted to follow. But all she could do was sit shivering in her thin nightdress and rock herself back and forth, like a mother whose child had drowned while she failed to hear him cry out in great distress.

# TWENTY-TWO

## *The Bailiffs*

### *Mayo, Autumn 1937*

Carts passed along the Turlough Road and occasionally even a motor car but Eva did not want a lift, especially off any local men. They all knew of her shame. Most of them probably knew more about her circumstances than she had known before her visit to Castlebar this afternoon. Today she had finally decided that she had no alternative but to make this inventory herself, because it was impossible to distinguish between truth and alcohol-induced fantasy when Freddie discussed their problems any more. She was unsure if his reticence to discuss money arose from chivalry or pigheadedness. However after visiting every shopkeeper in Castlebar she could now finally assess the crippling extent of their debts.

Only two shopowners had refused to divulge the figures, reluctant to discuss indelicate matters with a lady. They had felt ashamed of her shame. The others were eager to total up the Fitzgerald account to the last farthing, although no one had made her stand in the shop to discuss the matter. She had been escorted into their offices or parlours and offered tea or sherry. Most were more respectful than annoyed, but all stressed the necessity of being paid. Her final call had been to Mr Devlin who was solicitous to the verge of being over-familiar. He even offered to drive her back to Glanmire Wood, but she had thanked him and lied about having sufficient money in her purse to hire a hackney.

Crossing the Mall afterwards, Eva could sense eyes watching behind curtains as she passed the Imperial Hotel – where she feared that Freddie (who had disappeared on a drinking spree yesterday) was holed up in the select lounge, intimidating the young manager into extending his credit. In the two months since the last shooting guest left Freddie had nobody to take onto the bogs. He still ventured out most days, returning with a brace of duck or rabbits that he silently placed on the kitchen table. But Eva knew that much of his time was spent in remote *shebeens* or alone with his dog, drinking cheap Skylark whiskey and brooding. They could not afford another advertisement in the *Shooting Times* and Eva was almost relieved to have no bookings because the silver and table linen had been pawned.

A cart slowed now on the road a mile from Turlough and the farmer enquired if she would like a lift. Eva shook her head, managing to smile as she claimed to be simply out on a walk to take the air. The farmer asked after Mr Fitzgerald and the children, then wished her well and shooed his horse on. She felt selfish in not taking the lift because, with only Maureen left, she was needed at home. In the past year the eighteen-year-old girl had become the friend to whom Eva and the children each confided their secrets. At first Maureen had been simply employed to mind the children but will-ingly accepted more duties when Eva had to let go of Brigid the kitchen maid and finally Mrs McGrory. The cook had worked without pay for the final two months and cried when leaving, not for herself but for Eva and the children. They could not even afford the houseboy who used to come and chop logs but the steadfast Mr Clements, who remained their solitary permanent guest – undertook this task with surprising relish. Maureen and Eva did everything else between them, with Maureen refusing to abandon Eva despite the rarity of wages. Maureen's father had surprised them once with a gift of potatoes, with Freddie awkwardly greeting him and her young sister Cait jumping down from the donkey cart to race into the kitchen and hug Maureen.

Looking up now, Eva was surprised to see her ten-year-old son ahead of her on the dusty road. Spying her, Francis began to run. Eva thought he was alone until she noticed Mr Clements some distance behind. Francis flung himself into his mother's arms.

'Hazel has been bold,' he announced. 'She ran away.'

'Where to?' Eva felt too exhausted to cope with this latest crisis.

'We don't know. She's been missing for hours. Maureen is searching the Breaffy Road.'

Although tougher than Francis, Hazel was more conscious of their circumstances. As Freddie's drinking grew in tandem with the welter of bills, the girl had taken to living outdoors on her pony, although not allowed to leave the wood alone. This morning she had questioned Eva about where she was going and asked to be taken into Castlebar as well. Eva's last memory of leaving the wood was of Hazel staring from the last bend on the avenue, a hurt, silent figure mounted on her small pony.

Taking Francis's hand, she greeted Mr Clements, the old man slightly breathless as he outlined the route they had already searched. They hurried on past the old trees shading the road at Pigeon Hill and down the slope towards the village.

Her entire family seemed to be disappearing. At the start

of the year she had felt extraordinarily lonely when her parents moved to Oxford, leaving the Manor House empty. She had not heard from Art since the night he brought Jim Gralton to her house. Thomas regularly corresponded from South Africa and Maud dispatched sensible letters from Dublin, but Eva found it impossible to convey her sense of entrapment in her replies. She had no idea where Brendan was. The only card she'd received from Spain had been nine months ago. Brendan could now be a Republican general or be back in London or in one of Franco's jails. At least his name never appeared among the Irish casualties listed in the papers so he was still alive. O'Duffy's fascist Wild Irish Geese had quickly returned home as national heroes without appearing to ever fire a shot and the General's biggest battle seemed to be with Patrick Belton's Irish Christian Front over the disappearance of funds collected for their Catholic crusade in church gate collections.

Brendan's current silence left Mother paralysed with fear. He was never extreme like Art in disavowing contact with his family: the boy was always too sociable, loving life. But he hero-worshipped his brother and could be aping him in refusing to contact anyone. Art had hinted at some quarrel when Eva last saw him, but the hope remained that Brendan was at least in touch with his oldest brother. Maud suspected Art of knowing something because when she last saw him selling the *Daily Worker* on a Dublin street he had stalked off when she tried to mention Brendan.

Reaching the village school, they decided to try the small road that wound down towards the bridge. Mr Clements did not ask about her trip to Castlebar. He rarely asked questions, but kept out of the way as he waited, like them all, for their world to collapse. Hearing shouts from a tinker encampment beside the bridge, they saw that Hazel must have ridden into the field because tinker children surrounded her, mocking her pony. Older boys were challenging each other to jump the ditch bareback on their piebald horses, but each horse refused, sometimes violently throwing them off. Eva stopped in terror, seeing an older girl help Hazel up onto a horse. Her daughter had no saddle or helmet but no fear either. The ditch seemed impossible to clear, yet the horse tried with all his strength for Hazel. They almost made it before he skidded and fell onto his side.

Convinced that Hazel was crushed, Eva raced towards the bridge with Mr Clements and Francis. But Hazel rose unaided and managed to scramble back up onto the horse. She made a long circuit of the field while a woman emerged from a wattle tent to scream that she would kill the beast. Eva reached the gate as Hazel jumped. Horse and child disappeared into the steep dip beyond the ditch, with even the tinker children shocked into silence until Hazel reappeared, having waded back across twenty yards upstream. Resentful of being beaten by such a small girl, they seized the reins to drag her down while chanting, *Proddy, Proddy, go to hell – ringing out the Devil's bell.*

Defiant and haughty, Hazel was taunting them back: *Cathy, Cathy, go to Mass – riding on the Devil's ass*, when Eva and the Commander reached her. They managed to escort her to where Francis waited at the gate while tinker women cursed and sods of turf rained after them. Eva knew she should scold Hazel but no longer had the heart to do so. She simply wanted to reach home and lie down with the shutters drawn as if to block out the endless figures circling around in her head. Reaching the village they saw a crowd outside Durcan's pub-cum-grocery. People fell silent as Eva approached. Mr Durcan emerged in his white apron.

'That's a fine day now, mam.'

'It is indeed, Mr Durcan.'

'Could I offer you all a lift up home, mam?'

'Thank you, Mr Durcan, but it's a nice walk.'

'It is that to be sure, but all the same I think you'd be wise to send young Missy on by pony and step into the car with me now.'

People were watching closely. Many of the same faces she remembered welcoming her as a bride over a decade ago. She could not decode their expressions.

'Is it Mr Fitzgerald?' she asked, alarmed.

'Oh, he's right as rain, a true gentleman. He called in some hours back for a dram to keep out the cold before heading home.' The publican gently steered her towards the car proudly parked outside his premises. His wife and daughter watched anxiously from the pub's deep-set window. 'It's the callers we had half an hour ago who are a wee concern. A misunderstanding, I'm sure, but it's a class of occurrence we've not seen here for a power of Sundays.'

Eva urged Hazel to canter on, then got into the car with Mr Clements and Francis. Once she closed the car door the huddle of people began talking. The engine started with a splutter, startling nearby hens on the road.

'It might be wise to tell Mrs Fitzgerald what has happened,' Mr Clements said.

'Aye.' The publican nodded. 'I was coming to that in the privacy of the vehicle. There were three of them, having a whiskey before seeking directions to Glanmire. Dutch courage. Decent enough men but I'd sooner starve than do their job. If their business was in the village they would not have stopped for fear of a mob blocking them. But it wouldn't be our place to interfere in the gentry's affairs.' He looked at Mrs Fitzgerald. 'Bailiffs, mam, clasping a possession order signed by the Bank of Ireland.'

They turned onto the small road by the Protestant church, passing Hazel on her pony. Mr Durcan was quiet, letting Eva digest the news. She glanced back at Francis's scared face, knowing how the boy loved those woods. She had been so focused on their local debts that she never questioned Freddie about the Dublin bank to which he had mortgaged the house and lands.

'What's a bailiff, Mummy?' Desmond asked.

'Generations of them are burning in hell.' Mr Durcan's bitterness was all the more striking for his quiet tone. Eva recognised the irony that he had been born on the roadside after the Fitzgeralds evicted his parents.

'Bailiffs are like fleas,' the retired Commander told Francis. 'We all encounter them at some time and we get over them. I think we've become a bit too cosy here. Maybe it's time you saw the world, lad.'

Halfway up the drive they met Maureen returning from searching for Hazel. She got in, scared by the funereal silence. A car was parked on the gravel, though the bailiffs had retreated so that Mr Durcan had to steer around them as he reached the lawn. Eva got out and the oldest bailiff approached. 'Are you Mrs Fitzgerald? Your husband has gone inside, mam, with a loaded shotgun and I think it would be wise of someone to take it off him before he does himself or the rest of us harm.'

'What right have you to be here?' Eva asked.

'The bank were insistent that we take possession of the house, ma'm. There's a wad of correspondence between your husband and them.'

'I've not seen any letters.'

'Obviously, mam, they'd be addressed to the owner of the property. He'd be well advised to do nothing silly to bring more scandal down on his head.'

The Commander touched her arm lightly and crossed the lawn to enter the open front door. She thought that he was attempting to talk sense to her husband, but just then Freddie appeared. The two men passed in the doorway and Mr Clements nodded like it were a normal encounter. The Commander entered his room and closed the door as Freddie emerged onto the front steps with a five-gallon drum of paraffin oil.

'Keep back!' Freddie unscrewed the lid. 'Take the damn woods but you'll never have this house. I'll burn it to the ground rather than see a non-Fitzgerald live under its roof.'

'There'll be no fear of that, sir.' The bailiff stepped forward, trying to be reassuring. 'I'm sure the land will fetch a good price when the trees are felled, but our instruction is to sell the house for salvage and clear the site. A builder might want the stone, but you can rest assured that nobody will want to live in a place that's falling down. Now put away the paraffin like a good man before there's an accident.'

'I am not your good man and I will do what I like on my own property.' Behind his fury Eva knew that Freddie was humiliated. A sound of hooves came up the driveway and she wished that the children did not have to witness this. At least the servants were gone apart from Maureen. Mr Durcan was saying nothing.

'I'm afraid, sir, that unless you can pay what's overdue this is no longer your property. We'll not stop you removing personal items but there will have to be an auction of furniture and contents at which you'll have the same right to bid as anyone present.'

Freddie went to reply, then blinked as if trying to wake from a nightmare. He wearily sat down on the drum, his shotgun on his lap, reminding her of a sheriff, standing guard over a prisoner with a lynch mob outside. He stared at the bailiff as if trying to place him within the strict social hierarchy of Mayo. Eva suspected that the bailiff was probably the second son of a big farmer with sufficient clout to swing the job with the local politicians who awarded such positions as their gift. At one time her father could have organised good jobs for Thomas and Brendan, back in the different country where they were born. She knew that Freddie was contemplating these changes too. For him all history was directly personal. At this moment it would appear as if the IRA had fought their war with the sole intention of one day allowing a Catholic farmer's son to order a Fitzgerald off his land. Hazel broke the silence.

'If you took my pony would that pay off what we owe?' she asked. 'He's frightfully clever and a great jumper.'

The bailiff turned and spoke softly. 'Take your pony for a ride in the woods, Missy. If I don't see him I can't put him down on my inventory.'

Instead of retreating into the woods Hazel nudged the pony forward to where her father sat. She dismounted to stand beside him and stared defiantly at the bailiff. Freddie seemed unsure whether to scold her or be proud. He rose and took his daughter's hand.

'Do you know how long my family have lived here?' he demanded. 'Do you think that I would let every half-wit in Mayo bid for my possessions?' He released Hazel's hand. 'Go back to your mother, child.' He repeated the command with sudden fury when the girl refused to move. She stepped back, frightened, and he lowered his voice. 'Be a good girl, Hazel. We don't want the pony hurt.'

This convinced Hazel to lead the pony back towards the small watching group. Francis trembled, not knowing if he should join his father. Eva took his hand, then placed it in Maureen's palm and walked forward to stare into Freddie's bloodshot eyes.

'It's over, Freddie,' she urged softly. 'I know how much we owe in Castlebar. Come inside. The men will let us pack some suitcases. You'll be surprised how little we actually need. Maybe all this is for the best and we'll only be free when we walk away from here.'

Freddie stared at her so coldly that Eva knew he considered her insane.

'It's just a house,' she continued. 'What's important is that we have each other and the children.'

'You're your mad brother's sister,' he said bitterly.

'I am your wife.'

'Then you should know that what's important for a man is to have something to pass on to his son. Otherwise he is nothing.'

A door opened down the hallway, startling them both. She had forgotten that Mr Clements would be anxious to remove his possessions before the house was seized. The elderly man walked towards them, holding an envelope.

'Think it's time I gave you my notice, Freddie, if it's all the same with you. I never meant to stay half as long. Silly really. A man gets too comfortable, starts to hate change. Shall we say two weeks? That should allow me to find somewhere on the mainland. I expect it would be for the best if you went across the water yourself. You pair could make a wonderful fist of life there. I've been selfish expecting you to keep this place going just so that I'd have somewhere to lay my head.' He lowered his voice, placing the envelope in Freddie's hand. 'See off that blither, will you. His sort give me the creeps.'

Freddie examined the crisp English banknotes inside the envelope. He swallowed hard.

'Are you sure? It's a small fortune.'

'Pay me back at your leisure.'

'I will.' Freddie rose. 'Every penny.'

Freddie put down the shotgun and crossed the lawn to the bailiff.

'Look here, what's your name?'

'Mr Flaherty, sir.'

'Remind me of the sum outstanding, Flaherty.'

Freddie carefully counted out that figure, then reached into his own pocket to produce an Irish ten-shilling note. 'That's for you three men to have a drink with in the village. You're doing your job and I respect that. However I must ask you to get the hell off my land.'

'I'll make sure they do, Daddy.' Hazel mounted her pony.

'They can find their own way.' Freddie turned to Mr Durcan. 'A financial oversight, Mr Durcan. I would not want this misconstrued in the village.'

'Sure people have more to be talking about, Mr Fitzgerald,' the publican lied smoothly. 'Good day to you now, sir.'

Freddie stood on the grass to watch the two cars drive off with Hazel silent on her pony and Francis still grasping Maureen's hand. The Commander opened his cigarette case and offered Eva a cigarette. Eva said nothing because she knew that just now he wished to be left in silence. He was saying goodbye to the vista that had seduced him a decade ago, this day of shame marked the end of their struggle to life here. Mr Clements would need to find a new niche out in the real world and could ill afford the money he had just thrown away. But she knew that he had made his gesture out of love, so that even if he was cast into exile she and the children could have the possibility of returning here one day. Maybe in his mind he would harbour that dream too. Dying in a boarding house in Brighton or Bath he might close his eyes to imagine that he could still hear the wind in the trees at night and the creaking timbers that had become the sounds of home for a lonely man. She touched his arm lightly like a daughter. He nodded, then lit his cigarette and retreated to his room, leaving her to confront Freddie with their search for a future.

# TWENTY-THREE

## The Crumlin Kremlin

### *Dublin, Autumn 1938*

Locals had christened this rubbish dump 'Siberia', yet salt was possibly the only thing that the children of Crumlin didn't forage for in the makeshift tunnels they dug under the weight of rubbish dumped from Corporation bin trucks. The dump was a long distance from the sea, hewn out of an old quarry on the up-slope of the Dublin Mountains, but this did not stop seagulls from wheeling overhead and swooping to pluck at the displaced earth. The gulls barely stopped short of snatching the diseased fruit and mouldy potatoes from the hands of boys who emerged triumphant after scavenging underground.

Last week a tunnel had collapsed with a nine-year-old boy inside it. Art was among the first adults alerted by the shouts, careering down into the quarry to start digging with his bare hands. Within minutes a dozen men were digging alongside him, too focused on their work to curse or pray, while children cried or stood still with shock displacing their usual feeling of hunger. Art wasn't sure how long they had dug before reaching the boy – but long enough to convince Art that he would have stopped breathing. However the child was lucky because a corrugated iron sheet had created a small dust-filled air pocket. Although his face was blue when Art pulled him out and gave him the kiss of life, within seconds the boy had retched up bile and started to breathe unaided. The circle of men had kept a respectful distance while Art administered first aid, and their faces when he lifted up the boy had radiated gratitude and a bond of comradeship which made Art feel accepted within their midst. All the same, two unemployed fathers had instinctively stepped forward to claim the crying boy and bear him back to his mother.

From the changed reaction of local women since then, Art knew that he was recognised as having saved the boy's life. This afternoon he had promised his friend Kathleen Behan – in whose Corporation house he was lodging – to watch over two of her sons at the dump. Her oldest boy, Brendan, had already left school and was serving his time to become a housepainter like his father, Stephen. But the younger brothers, Brian and Dominic, were experienced dump scavengers at eleven and nine who recognised that most of the discarded food was inedible and the real treasure came from finding cinders and half-burnt coals thrown out from bourgeois households back in the city. Already they had filled a quarter-sack with Brian having found a perfectly good shoe that fitted him if he could only find the other.

Art had a secondary motive for spending time at this dump. Since last week's accident more adults were coming to watch over their children. When they questioned Art about the incident and complained of unfinished roads and the difficulty of getting back into the city, he would mention his plan to establish a Tenants' Rights Committee. Tenement dwellers were being banished to these new estates, miles away from jobs or the labour exchange, without schools or doctors and at the mercy of a few gombeen shopkeepers.

Stephen Behan had resisted previous attempts by his wife to move the family from their tenement in Russell Street. Indeed Mrs Behan had only effected this move to Crumlin by signing the papers herself and borrowing a neighbour's horse and cart while Stephen was conversing over his evening pint. The housepainter had first discovered that his family was emigrating to the suburbs when he saw the cart, piled with children and furniture, pass the pub door and was forced to either starve or follow them into exile later that night. Stephen Behan still resented being cast into this wilderness where he claimed the locals ate their young. Crumlin was desolate but Art was excited by this raw world in which people must surely start to think for themselves. The next uprising would not start in the General Post Office like in 1916. It would be fermented in these new suburbs with uprooted people refusing to be exploited, rising to demand not just better conditions but a new communist order.

Mrs Behan thought so too. Every evening after her family finished reciting the Angelus, she opened the front parlour window to play the Soviet National Anthem at full volume on the gramophone that Art had purchased for them. Art had never met anyone who possessed an equal devotion to the Blessed Virgin and Joseph Stalin. But the Behans' tiny parlour was a cradle of revolution, with her sons doing their schoolwork amidst a nightly plethora of visiting communists, socialists and republicans who made the pilgrimage out to the house which the locals termed the Crumlin Kremlin. Art argued his stance fiercely in these nightly debates, stressing how the prime consideration of any political act was to mirror the line propagated by Stalin, so that Irish comrades did not strive in isolation but remained part of one broad international struggle. In this he possessed two motives – an absolute belief in the supremacy of the Communist Comintern and a fear that someone could be reporting these meetings back to Moscow. One attempt had already been made to denounce him. Now when his file was finally reviewed in light of his plea to be allowed to rejoin his wife and child, it was vital that no single word of evidence existed which might be misconstrued as being counter-revolutionary.

A shout came from the rubbish dump and Brian and Dominic Behan emerged with blackened faces, having located the second shoe. They jumped about triumphantly, waving at him to come down. Art extinguished his one cigarette of the day, saving the butt to savour before he fell asleep on the parlour floor tonight. He insisted on carrying the sack of cinders as they set off through the maze of streets, with the boys' exuberant happiness unlocking such memories that Art had to strive against this loneliness perpetually waiting to ambush him. Reaching into his jacket he sought comfort in the petition folded there. His dream of a Tenants' Committee was taking hold. The first meeting tonight in a disused barn near the estate would hopefully be attended by the many locals who had visited the Behan house to affix their signatures to the list of demands which he and Mrs Behan had drawn up.

Mrs Behan had the table set for tea when they reached the terraced house. Her husband read a Charles Dickens book by the fire while their five-year-old daughter played on the floor. Brendan was not home. Art suspected that he was drilling with *Na Fianna* because the boy had boasted about wanting to join the IRA on his sixteenth birthday. The gramophone was gone from under the window. Mrs Behan followed his gaze.

'You can't eat records, Art. Isn't our own singing good enough? Still the pawnbroker thought we were coming up in the world. Did you play records as a boy?'

Art smiled. 'We played musical chairs for forfeits.'

'That's the difference, *comrade*,' Stephen remarked from behind his book. 'You had bloody chairs.' The man's tone was more sardonic than bitter.

Stephen was rarely present in the house after tea. Only after the pubs closed would he join in whatever argument or singsong was ongoing upon his return. Still, he had served time for the causes he believed in – having first glimpsed his eldest son from a cell window when Kathleen stood outside Kilmainham Jail to hold up Brendan as a baby during the Civil War. More recently as a union leader, Stephen had spent last year's building strike picketing outside sites owned by whoremasters like Patrick Belton – being the first man out and the last man back in – while his family endured starvation in their new house.

Brian answered a knock at the door, proud of the noise of his new shoes. He returned with a baby-faced priest who surveyed the triptych of pictures on the wall, with the Sacred Heart framed by photographs of James Connolly and Lenin. This array of family icons briefly rendered him dumb until he drew a deep breath and demanded information about tonight's meeting, warning the Behans about the danger to their souls in sheltering Art. Mrs Behan hushed Art who went to reply. Being a Catholic, this fell into her ambit. It was an unfair confrontation. The Behan children ate their meagre supper and watched the young priest being torn apart like it was a floor show. They looked disappointed when he fled after ten minutes. With his supper finished, Stephen rose to follow him out the door.

'You may have me barred from heaven but at least I'm not barred from my local.'

His wife admonished him. 'Stephen Behan, you promised to attend the Tenants' Rights meeting.'

'Be fair, Kathleen, how can I? You're the tenant, you signed the papers. If the cart hadn't passed the pub I'd still be searching for yous in Russell Street.' He wilted under her look. 'All right, I'll look in later, once you make sure the barn is cleared of dangerous farmyard animals.'

Stephen departed and half an hour later Mrs Behan accompanied Art across the fields where white crosses marked out the sites of the next houses to be built. The barn would be demolished soon but until then it was the only local space where a crowd might gather. Art had brought a paraffin lamp and hoped that other people might do likewise. Mrs Behan was unusually quiet.

'Are you upset about the priest?' he asked.

'Not at all. Didn't they try to excommunicate us during the Civil War? That clawthumper wouldn't know Jesus if Our Saviour bit him. Something else has me troubled. Brendan got a letter.' She took a ripped-open envelope from her bag. 'For some reason I got a chill when the postman delivered it this morning. I've never opened another person's letter in my life and please God I'll never do it again.'

'Is it from a girl?' Art asked.

Despite her anxiety, Mrs Behan smiled. 'What chance has he of discovering girls out here? If we'd stayed in Russell Street he'd know everything about women by now just from being on the landings at dusk. I'd not mind him losing his heart, it's losing his life I'm afeared of. It's from the Communist Party. The child is after volunteering to fight the fascists in Spain. He's only fifteen. It will break my heart if he goes and break his heart if I lie to him. Should I show it to him?'

'It's not for me to say.' Art was uncomfortable, as always when people discussed Spain.

'Why not? Somebody said you have a brother in Spain but you never mention him.'

'You know how families are,' Art said. 'One day you are all playing games together, then before you know it the game is over and you're not even speaking to each other.'

'Did yous fall out?'

Art could not remember a cross word during Brendan's stays in Moscow. Maybe he had not always treated Brendan as an equal, but it was hard to see him as more than a boy. Certainly not as the viper who denounced him to Georgi. The fact that Brendan had never contacted Art suggested that he was guilty. Art still could not understand what had possessed Brendan to utter such lies. The jealousy of the last born? Art recalled Brendan as a baby desperate to get Mother's attention. At heart he could not believe that Brendan was a Trotskyite counter-revolutionary. Only by chance had Art discovered that Brendan went to Spain. Liam Hennessy who had been wounded out seemed to have briefly met him, but he always clammed up when Art was in his company. Art heard that Georgi Polevoy was there too, so at least Brendan was enjoying his protection. But Art suspected that going to Spain was just another way for Brendan to steal Art's thunder, with Art stuck in Ireland, having been ordered to build the revolution here.

'We grew apart,' Art told Mrs Behan. 'I don't honestly know how it happened. He never writes. It's his way of punishing me.'

'For what?'

'For being the heir.'

There was a gap in the bushes leading into the field. Mrs Behan tore up the letter and scattered the pieces down into the ditch filled with hawthorns and brambles.

'God forgive me and God help the poor people of Spain, but their race is run and they can't have the body of my son.' She looked at Art. 'And God help your poor mother with the worry she must have waiting for news. Light that lamp and let's hope we're not sitting alone in this barn telling each other ghost stories.'

They were not alone, but the crowd was small compared to what Art had hoped for. This was no mass rally. They could have all squeezed into Mrs Behan's kitchen like she had suggested. Still, there was an old loading bay to stand on and at least tonight's meagre attendance was a start. Stephen Behan arrived as Art began to speak amid the weak lantern light. He had a detailed agenda, a list of basic human demands, a campaign of protests, a blueprint to ensure that no Crumlin child foraged in a rubbish dump again. But he had barely begun when a car entered the field, blinding the small crowd who turned to stare into the headlights. The car stopped but the headlights remained on. Four figures emerged through the dazzling glare. The first was the baby-faced curate being pushed forward by an older wiry man whom Art recognised as the parish priest. He raised a walking stick and, shaking with fury, pointed it at Art.

'There he is! The Antichrist! Don't just stand there, men, do your duty, arrest him.'

The words were addressed to two young Civic Guards whom the parish priest had collared en route to the meeting. One garda swallowed. 'For what?'

The priest turned. 'Suffering heart of Jesus, are you making fun of me? *For what? For what?*' he screeched, impersonating the garda's accent. 'Is it that you want me to be doing your job as well as my own? You're supposed to be a guardian of the law or do you live in a communist country now? Use your initiative, for God's sake. Can you not see the disturbance of the peace here?' He thumped his stick against the corrugated iron and advanced menacingly on the crowd. Only

Stephen Behan held his ground, leaning against a girder. The priest eyeballed him.

'I should have known you'd be here, you old gunman. You were a failed clerical student and you've failed at everything else.'

'I didn't fail, Father. They threw me out of the seminary for adultery around the same time as they kept you in for stupidity.'

'Why don't you go off to Russia?'

'To tell the truth, Father, the Corporation built this kip so far from Dublin that I thought I was there.'

Local people were trying to surreptitiously slip away. The priest turned. 'Where do you Reds think you're going? Stay still till I get your names to read out at Mass.' Summoning the Civic Guards he pointed to Art. 'Get his name into your book. We drove out Jim Gralton and in the spirit of St Patrick we'll drive this communist snake back into the sea.'

One garda advanced on Art. 'What's your name?'

'I don't need to give you my name.'

'Listen here, Goold. I said, what's your name?'

'You know my name already.'

'You needn't come the smart boy with me just because you're a swanky Protestant. That doesn't work around here any more.'

'I'm not a Protestant.'

'He's a saint,' Mrs Behan said, 'if you all only had eyes to see it.'

'What is your address?' the garda demanded, ignoring this interruption.

'I live in the Sokolniki District.'

'Where's that?'

'Moscow.'

'Art Goold, I'm arresting you with refusing to give your

name to a member of the Garda Síochána, with breach of the peace, trespass onto private property and provoking a riot. I'll ask you to come quietly now, like a good man.'

'I'm not your good man!' The words exploded with venom. 'These trumped-up charges are a mockery of free speech. You are the fascist hireling of this priest who is the most reactionary unit of the class enemy in the camp of the proletariat, sanctifying the abominations of this capitalist regime with holy water and terrorising his flock with the spectre of eternal punishment.'

'I'm what?' the garda asked, baffled.

'If you want a show trial you'll need to work harder. If you want a scapegoat at least charge me with something you can stand over in court. I come here to fight for a Workers' Communist Republic and if this is the first blow struck for it then it won't be the last. Long live Comrade Stalin!'

The punch caught the policeman off guard, sending him to the ground. Art had taken care to hold back, lest he broke the man's jaw. But he knew that the garda would feel no such compassion as the man rose and his companion pulled a truncheon. Art would have been able for the two of them, but the car's headlights had attracted more locals and, at the prompting of the priest, several pushed forward to drag Art to the ground where the Civic Guards kicked him in the ribs and stomach. Art felt a sudden *déjà vu* about this beating, an uneasy familiarity which so perplexed him that he almost didn't feel the kicks. Mrs Behan screamed, with Stephen trying to intervene, shouting at them to 'Go easy, lads.'

'There's the communist bitch and her Protestant fancy man,' he heard a woman shout. 'As if two husbands wasn't already enough for her.' Art was lifted up roughly and handcuffed, with a policeman pushing Stephen Behan away.

'It's my one consolation in life, Goold –' Stephen declared,

'– at least my boys can never become coppers – their parents were married.'

As the policemen pushed Art towards the car where newcomers were starting to spit and jeer at him, Mrs Behan raised her voice in defiant song:

> *'Come workers sing a rebel song,*
> *A song of love and hate,*
> *Of love unto the lowly*
> *And of hatred of the great,*
> *The great who trod our fathers down,*
> *Who steal our children's bread,*
> *Whose greedy hands are outstretched*
> *To rob the living and the dead.'*

Art knew that there was no chance of a Tenants' Rights Committee being formed. The city had cast its poor out to the edge of the mountains. It wasn't even a fodder farm for capitalist factories because there was no work to be had. This was just a breeding ground for the emigrant boat. But at least he had tried. He had sat in small kitchens to explain how society was organised in Moscow and seen genuine interest in the hungry faces gathered there.

Punching the policeman would ensure that he had his day in court. If he made a strong speech from the dock, the *Daily Worker* in London might pick up the story. The *Daily Worker* was scrutinised carefully in Moscow, and surely the NKVD officers in charge of his appeal would notice, with the press cutting filed away as an affirmation of his fidelity, proof that he remained a loyal servant. Such actions had to be recognised. Letters to his wife might still go unanswered, pleas to the Soviet embassy in London to rejoin his family were ignored because the time was not right. But when conditions were right for his case to be reviewed, Art would have the scars and prison terms to show his unceasing work for the cause. They would know that he remained steadfast, working for a future where his son would grow up with Irish cheekbones and a Russian accent, the citizen of a new world, cleansed of the sins of his ancestors.

# TWENTY-FOUR

# The Journey

*16–17 November 1939*

At dawn Freddie accompanied Eva from their small flat above the Culpeper Herbal Shop on Jewry Street in Winchester, past the Buttercross and the great cathedral and down to the bus station opposite the Guildhall. The station was as dark as the streets outside. It felt eerie, with intending passengers being mere shadows in the gloom and the sole light coming from a two-inch hole in the cardboard covering a single lit headlight of the bus. After purchasing her ticket they went back outside to be alone, walking down to King Alfred's statue on the corner. The fringes of thickly curtained windowpanes along Broadway were coated in black paint in case the faintest chink of light escaped, though Eva suspected that for now householders were more fearful of bullying wardens than of bombers in the sky. The immediate blitzkrieg that Chamberlain warned of had not yet occurred, but panic still ensued whenever the town tested its recently installed air raid sirens.

'What will you do?' Eva asked, already knowing the answer.

'Naturally, I shall work out my notice in full,' Freddie replied. 'Thereafter I shall be unavailable to pack herbs into little boxes because I will enlist in the Royal Artillery Territorial Army.'

Three days ago Eva had decided to return to Mayo, after hearing two customers discuss Chamberlain's prediction of a hundred thousand deaths before Christmas. Factories were working through the night to stockpile cardboard coffins, with lime pits already dug in expectation of stacked corpses. The only deaths so far were from collisions between blacked-out vehicles with drivers unable to see each other approach. But the scent of war pervaded everything in England, from the gas masks people carried to the stirrup pump and long-handled shovel to deal with incendiary bombs delivered to the herbal shop which Eva and Freddie had run for the past eighteen months.

It seemed impossible to Eva that any pilot could bomb Wolvesey Castle, visible from their window, but Freddie got angry when she made such remarks and lectured her about coming out of the ether to live in the real world. In the real world children were being evacuated from the cities and, as a mother, Eva was determined that her children's safety came first, even though their boarding schools seemed remote and unlikely targets. In her heart however she knew that this war was the perfect cover to rescue Francis whom she sensed was suffering terrible homesickness. Freddie was stoic when she announced her intention, but the general manager of Culpepers proved less sympathetic – possibly because the woman came from Coventry, where a bomb had recently killed five people, planted not by Germans but by Irish Republicans. When Freddie phoned to say that his wife was leaving and he would need to employ a girl part-time, he refused afterwards to discuss what the general manager said. But her voice grew so shrill that Eva had overheard her declare how no English public school man would permit his wife to flee dishonourably in time of war. She had hired them as a responsible couple. If Freddie was the kind of man who allowed his wife wear the trousers, then he could have a month's notice and also flee to his cowardly isle while she found a true married couple to manage her shop. Next morning when the weekly sales figures reached head office and the general manager discovered that Freddie had sold most of shop's stock to a party of visiting Americans, she hastily phoned back to say that he was welcome to stay. But Eva knew that the proud Fitzgerald had been hurt by her inference of cowardice and the reference to not having attended a good school. It was a cut Freddie could neither forget nor forgive.

The bus from Winchester was slow and it was noon before Eva reached Hazel's boarding school. School life was changing Hazel. Her headmistress remarked upon it during the brief conversation in which she made plain her disapproval at Eva running away to Ireland.

'You must be careful with the child, Mrs Fitzgerald. She takes on the local colour. Allow her to consort with Billingsgate fishwives and she will become one. Allow her to consort with the worst sort of snobs and she will become one of those.'

They were standing in the corridor watching Hazel emerge from class amid a pack of chattering girls. Seeing her like this, for a perturbing moment Eva felt that she did not know her daughter. Hazel seemed not to recognise Eva either, until her features softened and she ran past the headmistress to embrace her mother. Eva had feared that Hazel might not want to leave school, because she disliked holidays in the Winchester flat. But once Glanmire Wood was mentioned the girl had only one question before her classmates were forgotten: 'Will I be able to keep a horse?'

Eva nodded, with no idea how to keep her promise, and

they travelled together to Oxford to meet up with Francis who was being collected by his grandfather from his school. They spent the afternoon with Eva's parents, whom she tried to persuade to return to the safety of Donegal. But since boarding up the Manor House, Ireland was like a closed book to them, especially with the news that Maud and her children were now stranded in South Africa after being trapped by the war's outbreak while visiting Thomas.

Brendan's continuing disappearance left a raw wound cutting into their hearts. Father was unable to mention his youngest son, while, when alone with Eva in her bedroom, Mother could talk of nothing else. Brendan's silence since his solitary card from Barcelona left Eva's parents paralysed. The hope remained that he might still be in touch with his eldest brother, but Art refused to have contact with any of them. Eva did not even know his whereabouts until Mother produced a recent press cutting received from Dublin.

*Mr Art Goold, of Mountjoy Square in Dublin, was yesterday brought before the Special Criminal Court pursuant to the Offences against the State Act, 1939, after being arrested during a public disturbance. Goold was only released from jail seven weeks ago, having served a sentence for public order offences. When the date of his latest trial was being fixed, he insisted upon interrupting and insulting the court by shouting in a violent and unseemly fashion. Although called upon to stop he continued shouting in such a manner that no member of the court was able to speak. Goold was sentenced to suffer imprisonment for three calendar months for contempt of court, with the original charges to follow upon completion of this sentence.*

Eva sat in silence with Mother after reading this, while Father took Hazel to see some horses in a nearby paddock. It was Francis who tried to cheer them up by donning silk scarves from Mother's wardrobe and dancing about. The boy loved his grandmother and seemed punch-drunk at his unexpected release from school. Mother appeared to momentarily forget the ache of Brendan's absence while laughing at Francis's madcap agility in waltzing around. But after a time Eva noticed Mother's smile being replaced by a wary look and suspected that her grandson brought back too many memories of her own lost boy.

Father took them to the station for the evening train to Liverpool, insisting on giving Eva money to obtain a cabin for the night crossing on the MV *Munster*. When they boarded, the noise of singing from the bars still reached them and each time she closed her eyes Eva kept visualising the empty pens on the lower deck from which she had seen cattle unloaded on the dockside before they were allowed to board. Terrified beasts shoving against each other and slipping on the wet cobbles while a white-bearded man calmly waited with a gun to summarily execute any beast injured in the crossing from Dublin. The cattle became juxtaposed in her mind with the Irish faces she had also seen disembarking – the more experienced emigrants encouraging the unbearably young-looking ones, all seeking jobs offered by the war that she was fleeing.

The children only slept fretfully and were cranky when they docked at dawn in Dublin, urging her to get the first train to Mayo. Eva was exhausted, but determined to confront Art. For her parents' sake she needed to discover if he knew anything about Brendan's whereabouts. If Brendan had died then surely some comrade would have contacted the family. If he managed to flee Spain, he would have made contact himself, unless his wounds left him suffering from amnesia in an overcrowded ward with nobody to watch over him. If he had been held in one of Franco's jails, the victorious General had nothing to gain by keeping him when newspapers reported that almost all foreign prisoners were now released. Father's appeals to the Foreign Office had yielded no record of Brendan being captured by fascists, unless they had simply shot him and dumped his body. Another alternative was that Brendan could be staying with Art's wife in Russia or, even better, had gone to live in Dublin with Art. This idea was so alluring that Eva had made herself half believe it.

Her arrival in Mountjoy Square caused a stir along the row of Georgian houses now subdivided into tenement dwellings. Francis and Hazel shied away from the dirty children gawking at them while Eva asked a shawled woman if she knew where Art Goold lived. Hearing his name, the woman blessed herself and hurried on. Several others claimed not to have heard of him until a man detached himself from a pitch and toss school to direct her past a door off its hinges and up a long flight of stairs. Shouting children raced down past her, one almost shoving Francis through a gap where the banisters were missing.

A woman half opened her door on the first landing and eyed Eva suspiciously. 'What are yiz after?'

'I'm looking for Art Goold's flat?'

'And why would that be, Missus?'

'I'm his sister.'

'So you say.' She impersonated a snooty voice. 'Well, he's not currently residing in his residence.'

'He's in jail. I wondered if anyone was sharing his flat?'

'You mean a trollop? Goold wasn't like that, so go to hell. You're not the first interfering biddy sent by the Legion of Mary to save us.'

371

The women went to slam her door. Eva pleaded with her. 'Please. I really am his sister.'

'How do I know that?'

'For goodness' sake, the Legion of Mary is Catholic!' Hazel interjected, her exasperated voice, which had picked up a tinge of an English accent, further antagonising the woman. 'If he wasn't my brother why else would we visit a place like this?'

It was Francis who prevented the woman from closing her door. 'Please, we've travelled a long way and have a long journey ahead. Mr Goold Verschoyle is my uncle.'

The woman relented, opening her door fully. 'Come in,' she said gruffly. 'If you're Goold's kin you're welcome. Since he last got out of jail we've had a hundred clawthumpers sprinkling the stairs with holy water.'

Eva gazed around the immaculately clean but cramped room. Two small children watched from the bed and she sensed another child hiding beneath it.

'Art asked me to mind the back attic for him, but the landlord will burn everything and rent it out again,' the woman said. 'He's lived in different rooms here on and off for years. I thought he was a tramp till I heard his accent. Never knew a lonelier man or one so badly dressed. Any few pence he had seemed to go on books. For a while he taught a sort of hedge-school in the park, but the priests put a halt to it. You'd see him selling the *Daily Worker* outside the GPO with people spitting as they passed. His own kind don't really want him and he'll never be one of us. But he was good to me when my husband was out of work and loan sharks were trying to get their claws on my few sticks of furniture. Will you take tea and some bread for your chislers?'

Eva noticed a half-finished loaf on the square of wood that served as a table when put on top of the bathtub. From the bed, hungry eyes followed her gaze. 'We've just eaten,' she lied. 'Did Art ever mention his brother?'

The woman shook her head. 'Not to me. He turned up some weeks back after hearing the back attic was free. He'd been in jail and before that was staying in Crumlin with Mrs Behan who used to live in Russell Street – though that poor woman has her own sorrows with the Liverpool police after catching her eldest lad with an IRA bomb. You'd think Art would have had his fill of jail but he was barely settled in upstairs before the cops got him for creating a nuisance on the bogs of Kildare. Trying to unionise turf workers.' She snorted. 'You might as well unionise donkeys. Still you couldn't talk to Art with the weight of the world on him. Is your other brother cracked too?'

Eva did not want to discuss Brendan. She had been stupid to yield to the hope that he could be lying low here. Her old mistake of wanting reality to fall into step with how she wished the world to be.

'Can I see his room?'

'Are you sure you want to? The police left a queer mess.'

Eva and the children followed the woman up flights of stairs that grew steeper as they neared the attic. The door was smashed open, with papers and books scattered on the floor.

'Rowdies from the Catholic Young Men's Society did most of the damage.'

Eva knelt among the debris to salvage any personal items. But nothing here reminded her of the brother she loved. It was like Art's life was now only lived through slogans. Unsold copies of *Moscow News* and crudely printed pamphlets had been torn apart in a frenzy.

'This one is for children.' Francis gathered up some pages from a magazine called *Sovietland*. The cover showed five boys playing violins, standing behind another boy at a piano. Eva read the headline: '*The Bolsheov Corrective Labour Commune for Juvenile Delinquents attracts worldwide interest from educationalists.*'

'Take anything you want,' the woman said. 'If you need more copies they're hanging from a nail in the toilet in the yard.'

Eva searched around, feeling she should take something. A few books had survived the onslaught, including a play entitled *Round Heads and Pointed Heads* by someone called Bertolt Brecht. Published by International Literature in Moscow it was in English. Eva would have returned it to the heap of papers had she not spotted the translator's name in small type: *Art Goold Verschoyle*. Another secret he never mentioned, denying Father the chance to feel proud. She saw Francis pocket a copy of *Sovietland*.

'Do you think they might let me visit him in jail?' she asked the woman.

'Ask for a warder named McCarthy. He's a good skin or at least as good as a screw can be. Say Mrs Fleming sent you.'

'Thank you.'

'And tell Art his neighbours say hello. It's a lie but it might make him happy. He cares too much for people nobody else gives a toss about.'

Eva and the children trudged along the North Circular Road, avoiding the mess left by beasts being walked from the cattle market down to the Liverpool boat.

She caught the vague impression of a face behind a grille in the huge iron gates of Mountjoy Jail when it was pulled back in response to her knock. It slammed again after she asked for Mr McCarthy and nothing occurred for so long that she thought they had forgotten her. Francis and Hazel felt intimidated by the high walls and foreboding atmosphere. But eventually a small door opened and an elderly man stepped through. Mr McCarthy listened to her story, then shook his head.

'Visiting is not till the afternoon,' he said, 'and Goold will be gone by then.'

'Set free?'

'Far from it, mam. I follow the rules but that doesn't mean I always agree with them. De Valera has introduced internment for subversives. Goold is being transported to the Curragh camp today along with a young Murray Bolger, an IRA bowsie from Wexford. But your brother is no gunman, he's just a public nuisance. There's no reason to intern him, unless de Valera wants to stir things up by throwing a few jokers in among the IRA.'

'How long will he serve?'

'For as long as there's trouble in Europe. Dev is taking no risks of any lunatic dragging us into it.' He lowered his voice. 'The army will be here at eleven to collect them. Hang about and you might sneak a word or two.'

The day had turned bitter, with squalls of rain. Eva was afraid to move away in case the soldiers came early but it was half-eleven before the truck reversed up to the gate. Four soldiers entered the prison, while two more kept watch from the back of the lorry. One winked at Francis. Another soldier got out of the cab to survey the narrow road, his rifle cocked. Children from a row of warders' cottages came to watch. Hazel stared back at them, feeling humiliated. Finally the door opened and two soldiers led out a handcuffed young man. He laughed, turning back to jeer at a warder.

'You have your mother's looks, McCormick. She must have been a Kildare man.'

'You'll be wasted in the Curragh, Murray,' the warder

replied. 'You should be on stage in the Gaiety . . . with some fecker sawing you in half.' He stepped aside to let the other soldiers through. 'Here, don't forget your *comrade.*'

The young prisoner threw his eyes to heaven as he climbed onto the truck. Mr McCarthy must have forewarned Art, because Eva's brother stopped after stepping through the door. Mr McCarthy nudged the soldier Art was handcuffed to. The soldier halted nervously, concerned lest his colleagues object.

Art had been allowed to wear his own clothes. His great-coat was open over a black suit which – were it not for his high-laced old army boots – would have given him the appearance of a pietistic, down-at-heel cleric. He held himself erect, but had a haunted look as he stared at Eva.

'Are they treating you okay?' she asked.

'Yes.'

'Have you heard from Brendan?'

'No.'

'Do you know where he is? Is he alive or dead?'

'I . . .' He hesitated, with the soldiers growing impatient. 'I know nothing . . . for certain.'

He glanced towards the truck as if it were not a vehicle to bear him into incarceration, but one that would allow him to evade her questions.

'What do you mean, Art? Could he be with your family in Moscow?'

He shook his head, his distress obviously to everyone. The soldiers stood on either side of him, reminding Eva of the crucified robbers. 'I don't even know where my wife and child are.'

Eva grew frantic, knowing he was about to be taken away. 'Write to me in Mayo? Why are they locking you up?'

'I don't know. My country is not at war.'

'And we intend to keep it that way,' one soldier said, indicating that it was time to board.

Art turned. 'I don't refer to Ireland. I'm a citizen of the Union of Soviet Socialist Republics.'

'It could be worse,' the soldier scoffed. 'Your mother could be a Kildare man, like McCormick.'

The soldiers laughed and Eva couldn't bring herself to ask anything else. No good answer could be forthcoming in such a desolate place. She went to embrace Art, and Mr McCarthy intervened, embarrassed.

'He's been searched, mam. They don't want to have to search him again.'

She stepped back, abashed.

'I will try my best,' Art muttered, leaving Eva unclear as to what he meant.

She pushed Hazel and Francis forward and they were allowed to shake their uncle's hand before the soldiers helped Art up to join the IRA prisoner. Art sat upright with a more militaristic bearing than his guards as the truck drove off.

The children waved. When Eva turned to thank Mr McCarthy, the iron door was already closed behind her.

# TWENTY-FIVE

## *The Camp*

### *The Curragh, 17 November 1939*

The irony was that Art had passed along this same winding Kildare road three weeks ago, handcuffed and being driven towards Dublin by the Civic Guards on the day after his return from visiting London. Now, Free State soldiers were bringing him back, past the same stooped figures harvesting turf on the bog who had leaned on their long-handled loys back then to regard him like an escaped lunatic. In truth, Art knew that he must have appeared insane, both out on the bog when he preached until the Civic Guards came and the next morning in court when it took four Civic Guards to carry him from the dock. One garda knew about the colleague Art had punched in Crumlin last year because he mentioned him by name, swinging a boot at Art as they hurled him into the cell below the court.

The prison warders in Mountjoy had cleaned the blood off his face in a kindly fashion. They were mainly the offspring of peasants, fond of regulations, wary of the city and not overly intelligent. Art had caused them no trouble during previous incarcerations because he recognised that they were merely doing their job in the same way as he was doing his.

They might not have understood that his duty was to ferment revolution, but they recognised him as no ordinary criminal. Life in Mountjoy Jail had a structure that he had liked and the food was better than in Moscow. He knew little about the Curragh except that it was an army base which, until recently, had been served by a tribe of wrens – prostitutes living in makeshift holes on the bog, their hard lives shortened by the odium of local people and diseases carried by the troops.

De Valera's Diehard Republican followers had been interned here during the Civil War. And now – fattened by power – de Valera was repeating the medicine. Art was unsure how this new camp was run, but at least it would contain a body of politically active men whom he might convert. Ordinarily he would have felt a surge of excitement at this challenge, similar to that which Cousin George had described in letters from Africa when, finding himself with a dwindling Irish congregation, he emigrated there as a missionary. But Art had been rattled this morning by Eva's appearance outside Mountjoy. He knew that his family was seeking answers. Eva and Maud and Thomas held him responsible and had him condemned. He could cope with this if only Brendan would stop staring at him in dreams. Art asked nobody to follow him, but even when he walked into the desert his family had still insisted on walking behind him.

Yet if he was not his brother's keeper, why had he visited London last month? Uncertainty had gnawed at him as he watched the Spanish Republic fall and the Trotskyite POUM scum attack the good communists in Barcelona so that the fascists could storm the city. Rumours about Brendan were circulating and last month Art had travelled to London convinced that somebody in the British Communist Party must know about his brother. He had not recognised the sour-faced woman with cropped hair whom he was eventually allowed to see in party headquarters, until something about her features recalled the General Strike and he said her name aloud – Ruth Davis. Agitated, the woman had walked to the window, dragging one foot behind her, when he mentioned Brendan.

'Volunteers keep returning from Spain,' she said. 'Some seem to think we owe them something instead of recognising that we did them a favour in allowing them the privilege of fighting against fascism. They come looking for handouts like we were a relief agency. Your brother did not enlist through this office, so he is not our administrative problem.'

Thirteen years had altered her character, though Art knew that she could recall bandaging Art's head while Brendan stood in her kitchen as a runaway schoolboy. Had thirteen years utterly changed him too or was his problem an inability to change? At that moment there had been so many memories that Art wanted to talk to her about. But when Ruth turned, he realised that he could say nothing, because she was aware of how Art knew that she had left Brendan for a renegade aristocratic comrade who abandoned her to suffer at the hands of a quack abortionist.

Ruth had promised to make enquiries and arrange for a letter from Art to be delivered to Georgi Polevoy in Moscow. Art had spent the next week sleeping in a shelter for the homeless and attending political gatherings. The bitter talk of many Spanish veterans angered him, with their inability to grasp the larger picture. But Spain was being forgotten as London prepared for war, with air raid sirens and the giddiness of people caught between terror and excitement.

A week later he had returned to party headquarters. At first Ruth would not see him, but six hours later when he still refused to leave, she relented and summoned him in. Her manner was curt. Their encounter lasted a few seconds. She had torn up his letter to Polevoy and although Art should be reported to Moscow for trying to communicate with a counter-revolutionary, on this one occasion she would not do so. Thankfully she had discovered in time that Georgi Polevoy was arrested as a fascist spy after his return from Spain. His trial was reported in *Pravda*, along with the names of large numbers of fellow traitors whom he also named as involved in a spy ring in Spain. Ruth had refused to answer any more questions and harried Art from her office as if he were contaminated.

With a jolt, the army truck reached the gates of the Curragh camp. Art looked up at a line of tin huts behind two rows of barbed wire. Men stood about, watching the new arrivals. The young IRA man from Wexford had spent the entire journey discussing horse racing with the solders, ignoring Art. To be incarcerated was lonely and to be imprisoned among reactionary monolithic nationalists was to be doubly alone. But just now Art welcomed the lines of barbed wire because he felt like a penitent, needing to atone. That was why he had provoked the court after his latest arrest, why he had screamed his allegiance loudly despite there being nobody left to hear. Because if Georgi Polevoy was a traitor then Art was lost for having trusted him and Brendan had probably been betrayed by him too. Everything Georgi had said about his brother denouncing him was untrue. A wedge had been deliberately driven between the brothers, when Art should have trusted his instincts. Despite all his labours here for the Party and his reports sent back to Moscow, perhaps nobody in the NKVD cared or remembered him. His name might be removed from all records, his wife declared unmarried. The only hope was that with Georgi arrested, the Party might realise its past mistakes. Art could be sure of nothing, except that he must keep faith with the Party because the fate of no individual could stand in the way of the great push forward.

The truck passed through the cordon of barbed wire and the first two soldiers jumped down as an orderly appeared from a hut with a list of names. Murray Bolger sprang onto the ground, stomping his feet with the cold. The orderly looked at his list and then at him.

'What are you?'

'IRA.'

'Are you?' He looked at Art who had dismounted and was staring at the barbed wire, resisting an irrational urge to run his fingers over the knotted strands as if, at a human touch, they might blossom into flower.

'Guilty,' Art replied. 'I'm guilty.'

## TWENTY-SIX

# The Man from Spain

*Mayo, 17 November 1939*

Francis's hand-painted sign remained in place above the front door where he had nailed it up two years previously, with the boy refusing to climb into the dicky seat of his father's motor until certain that any intruder into Glanmire Wood would spot it. He had grown tall in the intervening period – as Delia O'Donnell from the small shop and the Durcan women had exclaimed, clucking around in delight when the Castlebar bus deposited Eva and her children in Turlough an hour ago. Yet as Eva watched him stand on the twilit over-grown lawn, she knew he was still the same child who had painted in white letters: *Please keep out. This is my home.*

All three of them were finally home. Twelve-year-old boys were not meant to cry but Eva knew that tears were not far from Francis's eyes. Hazel looked sullen, though Eva suspected that the girl was simply exhausted after their journey from England. Two full days of travelling had left Eva worn out as well.

A noise made Eva turn. Mr Durcan was unloading their cases. His headlights casually illuminating the lawn seemed extravagant after the blackout darkness of England. She knew he would be insulted if she offered him money: he was no hackney man. He picked up a heavy case with an ease that belied his years and carried it up the steps to the door. 'Stand yourself up on that yoke,' he told Francis, his gruffness belying an instinctive understanding of the boy's emotions. 'You won't be needing that old sign to frighten the crows away now.'

Straining on his tiptoes, Francis stretched high enough to prise the wooden sign from the wall. He stared at it in silent triumph, then stepped down, nodding to Mr Durcan. The nod was a perfect replica of the almost imperceptible gestures through which local men communicated. Hazel plucked at Eva's sleeve.

'When is the man leaving?' she whispered.

Mr Durcan looked back, though Eva felt certain he could not have heard.

'You'll be wanting to get warm inside, Miss Hazel. If you'll unlock the door, mam, Francis and myself will shift these cases into the hall.'

Eva knew Mr Durcan was not being sly in the different way he referred to each child. Hazel was instinctively a Fitzgerald, fitting in more at Turlough Park than here. She was recognised as such locally, whereas Francis was allowed to belong, in so far as a Protestant could, to the closed fist of village life. It meant a great deal to the Durcan women that Francis had written to them each Christmas from England.

The house – although freezing – did not smell as musty as Eva had feared. But when she pulled back the shutters the last vestige of twilight outside took on a green tinge because of ivy colonising the windowpanes. The icy drawing room – with its few remaining pieces of furniture draped in dust-sheets – had a curious echo. She knew that the children would find everything smaller than they remembered.

Mr Durcan carried in the last case and joked with Francis

while Hazel sat, holding her rag doll, beside the cold fireplace. Eva thanked him and the two adults walked outside.

'You'll be grand entirely here, mam, but be careful in the times they are in it. Some class of a tramp was mooching about over the weekend.'

'Up here?'

'Aye. My wife ran him from the shop on Saturday evening. She felt he was a young blackguard on the lookout for anything to rob, but from the window he looked harmless enough to me. Still he wouldn't be the best paying guest if you were thinking of opening the guesthouse again.'

Perhaps there was no tramp and this was the man's subtle attempt to extract the gossip that his wife and daughter would plague him for.

'I've no plans,' she replied. 'Just for now we'll live in one or two rooms and see.'

'Still you got away home in time, judging by the news from Scapa Flow.'

'What news?' Eva asked. 'I've been travelling all day.'

'Herr Hitler has just sank the *Royal Oak* at anchor. Hundreds of young sailors are dead without ever seeing the ocean. This could be a short war.'

'My husband is enlisting,' she said quietly. 'The Territorials.'

'Aye.' Mr Durcan's tone was neutral, his opinion kept to himself, though all of Turlough would know the news by morning.

'Who do you think will win?' she asked quietly.

'There's a question, mam.' Mr Durcan shrugged. When the IRA Diehards raided his shop during the civil war he had refused them supplies, even when they stood him against his gable to stage a mock execution. Eva could imagine him staring down the barrels of British or German guns with equal stubbornness. He got into his car and the children waved with her as he edged down the overgrown avenue. They kept waving until he was gone from sight, dreading the moment when they had to confront this desolate and rapidly darkening house.

Hazel lowered her hand first. 'I'm cold,' she complained. 'Why is this place always so cold?'

'We'll get it warm,' Eva promised. 'And maybe Maureen got my letter and will cycle over to visit soon.'

While Eva lit a candle, Hazel entered the drawing room and gazed at the empty grate. Eva remembered how she used to rub Hazel's bare soles here to get them warm and wondered would her daughter still allow her to do so. 'Are you glad to be home?' Eva asked and Hazel placed her rag doll on the dustsheet covering the sofa.

'The flat in Winchester never seemed like a home, did it, Mummy?'

'No.'

'Not when you're used to space. I always loved the silence here at night and the stars are brighter in Mayo. The other girls bored me anyway, droning on about how much money their fathers have. We don't have any, do we?'

'Daddy will send some every week.'

'Will Hitler come here?'

'Ireland's not at war with Germany.'

'Why not?'

'It just isn't. Not yet anyway.'

'Can I go out to the stables? I want to check they're okay. I have this silly fear that the roof will have caved in and we won't be able to keep a horse there.'

The girl glanced sharply at Eva as she spoke. Hazel knew in her heart that Eva barely had money to feed a horse let alone buy one. Their only hope lay in begging Freddie's uncle for the loan of a mare, but relations with Turlough Park had been strained by the disgrace of the bailiffs two years ago.

Freddie entering trade as a shopkeeper hardly helped. His nephew would redeem himself by enlisting, but Eva's pride meant that she dreaded making the trip to Turlough Park.

'Come on,' she told Hazel, picking up the candle. 'Let's ensure we have a roof to keep the poor horse dry.'

Hazel took her hand as they entered the dark hall. A light shone from Mr Clements's old room. Eva pushed the door open. Having found a paraffin lamp, Francis knelt on a rug beside an open trunk of books. A horsehair mattress was neatly folded on the bed. On top of an empty chest of drawers lined with dusty newspaper the Commander had left his gramophone and two records, The *Moonlight Sonata* and Handel's *Water Music*. Francis looked up.

'Mr Clements left these behind, Mummy. Do you think he's coming back?'

Eva shook her head. That old sailor was probably back in uniform somewhere. Maybe he had trained some of the young sailors who lost their lives on the *Royal Oak*. Mr Clements had remained here for some days after the family left in 1937, awaiting the men due to ferry his possessions to London. Perhaps there had been no room for this last trunk, but she suspected that he deliberately left part of himself behind, to remind her of him when she returned. She wondered if he sometimes lay awake, in whatever quiet hotel he had secreted himself away, to imagine this moonlit room with the door ajar for mice and his silent gramophone like a faithful dog patiently anticipating its dead master's return?

'Perhaps he left the books for you to read one day.' Eva longed to escape from the unbearable sadness of his absence. 'We're going to the stables. Will you light the way?'

The hall had grown pitch-dark in the few moments they were in the Commander's room. Hearing a branch knock against a window they stopped and moved closer together.

Then Hazel laughed slightly, unable to bear the unspoken anxiety. 'I wonder what the girls in school are doing now?'

'Writing French essays on how to be little pests,' Francis replied.

'I should write one this weekend,' Hazel sniped. 'Called "My cowardly brother, the weakling who cried at school".'

'Stop bickering,' Eva ordered, anxious for Francis not to be reminded of the unhappy letters he had sent them all. They went quiet as she opened the door because the basement stairs looked forbidding. Francis shone the lantern down and hesitated. Then, mindful of Hazel's taunt, he walked ahead with Eva following and her daughter close behind.

They had grown up hearing stories about the ghost in the cellar and Eva suspected that they had embroidered them into elaborate sightings when whispering after lights out in school. She did not know what she expected to encounter after two years away but if any presence emanated from the wine cellar it almost seemed to be welcoming them. She stopped to stare into that cramped vault as Francis moved on and Hazel anxiously brushed past her to join him. The atmosphere in Glanmire House had never seemed as cold after the night she stood here to pray with the trapped spirit. Eva raised a hand to the empty cellar as if in greeting, then saw her children back away from the kitchen.

'What's wrong?' she asked.

'Someone's been in there,' Francis replied. 'The range is lit.'

Eva took the lamp from him and entered the kitchen. The range was low but had obviously been stoked up earlier. On the table a loaf of soda bread was wrapped in a towel beside some homemade butter in a twist of newspaper.

'Has anyone been living here?' Hazel asked anxiously.

Eva realised how isolated she was with two children and

not a soul for a mile. Previously there were always dogs and people. She missed the dogs more than servants or guests. The house seemed soulless without them padding about. She remembered Mr Durcan's warning. It was important not to betray fear. 'Maybe Maureen called in,' she said.

Mr Devlin had arranged a shop job for Maureen as a last favour to Eva, but, as the girl never replied to letters, Eva didn't know if she remained in Castlebar or had emigrated like her older siblings. Eva had written to Maureen last week, not because she could offer the girl work but because she longed to confide in somebody. When she told Freddie she was leaving, he had understood her to refer to England and not to him. But Eva wasn't merely fleeing the war, she was fleeing the strictures of an unwise marriage. Truly she had been *'in the ether'* when imagining that their polar opposites could live in harmony. She still loved Freddie and respected him for pulling himself together after his dream of a life in Glanmire died. His drinking had moderated since moving to England, never affecting his work in Culpepers. He had created a new life for them, knuckling down to learn the herbal trade – even if he believed that many products, based on Nicholas Culpeper's seventeenth-century remedies, were poppycock. He often joked that they only stopped short of recommending customers to cover their bodies with leeches. Life in Winchester had been peaceable, without the terror of being confronted by final demands each time the postman arrived. But it was dangerous for the soul to slip into the routine of thinking that a day had been good simply because it wasn't bad. Only when Mr Durcan's car bumped its way up the tree-lined avenue this evening did Eva realise how free her spirit felt at being alone.

Except that it seemed they were not alone. At any moment a tramp might intrude upon them. Perhaps the stranger had heard them arrive and left the untouched bread as a parting gift. Eva unwrapped it, knowing the children were hungry. 'It wasn't baked by a ghost anyway,' she joked. 'I'm sure it's safe to eat.'

The old cutlery remained in the drawer. Eva deliberately used the sharpest carving knife to cut the bread and kept it beside her while Francis and Hazel ate slice after slice. She should have checked the rooms upstairs for signs of inhabitation. Her courage failed her now as she kept imagining noises in the creaking house. She didn't know what she wanted to find. A vague flicker of hope was gnawing at the edge of her consciousness since Mr Durcan mentioned a tramp. Eva didn't want to extinguish that hope just yet. Instead she watched Hazel take the torn copy of *Sovietland* from Francis's coat. The girl glanced through it incredulously.

'Russia has the world's stupidest children,' she said. 'In this questionnaire the average French girl's ambition is to own a bicycle, but for a Russian girl it's to . . .' Hazel glanced down. '. . . *overthrow capitalist oppression and build communism.* French girls hate doing homework and Russians hate the bourgeoisie.'

'Are we the bourgeoisie, Mummy?' Francis asked.

'Don't be ridiculous,' Hazel snorted, sounding old beyond her years. 'We're Fitzgeralds. I'm going out to the stables. Who's coming?'

They all went in the end, having only one lamp. The bolt on the stable door opened smoothly for one that should have been untouched for two years. Hazel held the lantern high. The roof beams were solid and the ladder still in place up to the loft where Freddie had sometimes slept. But Eva was gazing at a heap of straw in the stall nearest the wall. Blackened stones were arranged in a ring where a fire had been lit. Francis went to investigate.

'Somebody has slept here,' he said. 'This ash is cold but fresh.' He looked up, fearful that an intruder could be lurking in the loft. Eva realised that if anyone outside pushed the door shut and bolted it, they could be locked in the stable for days until villagers came to investigate. Trying not to show panic she hurried the children out and dragged the door shut.

'Let's go inside,' she said.

It was only twenty yards to the house, but the overgrown path never seemed so dark. Francis stumbled and cried out, unnerving them further. They pushed in through the open back door, which Eva quickly bolted. She leaned back, breathing a sigh of relief, while the children hugged her for comfort. Then the sound of footsteps crossed the kitchen flagstones. Eva tightened her grip on the children, but Hazel broke free to call: 'Who's there? Show yourself!'

The kitchen door opened and a voice spoke. 'I would if I could find a light.'

'Maureen!'

The children ran towards their former maid, while Eva raised the lantern to make out the young woman's features.

'The back door was open ... I didn't know where yous had gone. My goodness, how you've grown.' Maureen released the children and smiled at Eva. 'I called earlier, Mrs Fitzgerald. I've a key these years back. You got the soda bread?'

'We didn't know who brought it.'

'I was never one for writing notes. I lit the stove. If I'd had more time I could have done more.'

'You have your own life, Maureen. Are you still working for Mr Devlin?'

'God save us from harm, mam, but if I slice another rasher for that skinflint I'll go crazy. I wasn't cut out for shop work.'

'I haven't the money to employ anyone, Maureen.'

391

'Don't I know it, mam. Still I thought I'd spend the night here if you wanted and get you settled in. I can cycle into work in the morning.'

'And come back tomorrow evening,' Francis urged. 'I mean it's not half the cycle from here to Castlebar as it would be from Ballavary.'

'I'm sure Maureen wants to be with her own family,' Eva said, attempting to cushion his expectation.

'She wants to be with us,' Hazel insisted. 'Don't you, Maureen? It will be like old times, only you could be the guest and have the Commander's old room. Say she can stay, Mummy, say it!'

Eva watched Maureen laugh at the children's enthusiasm. The young woman glanced at her.

'Well, my sister Cait would welcome a bit of space in the bed for a night or two.'

'You'd be more welcome than you could ever know,' Eva said. 'But you'll freeze here in winter.'

'Sure we can all freeze together so.'

Thrilled, the children sat Maureen down at the table, competing to tell her about England. Eva's pleasure was tempered by knowing that someone had slept in the stables. A tramp might have thought the house deserted, but Mr Durcan's warning made her uneasy. Maureen was suggesting that they sleep on mattresses in the kitchen for tonight, as it was the only warm room. The children loved the sense of anarchy and adventure in this idea. Eva unpacked more candles and arranged them around the room. She gave the children the lantern, ostensibly for them to check if the mattresses in the nursery were damp, but really so that she could speak to Maureen alone.

'Was there anyone around here when you cycled over earlier?'

'There was and he gave me a fright,' the girl replied. 'I didn't see him until he stepped out from the woods as I was leaving. A stranger. I think he'd been sleeping rough.'

'A tramp?'

'I don't rightly know, mam. A quiet-spoken class of man. Something odd about him, like maybe he'd been in jail. It was his half-starved face and his skin burnt like he'd been somewhere foreign. I didn't think him Irish until he spoke.'

'What age was he?' Eva couldn't prevent a desperate hope from overwhelming her.

'Not old, mam, but he looked old.'

'And his accent?'

Eva's agitation made the girl nervous. 'He spoke like a man not much used to speaking English any more. Hoarse like he'd been ill. He asked for you by name and when I said you were across the water but due home he said nothing but went on his way. I felt desperately sorry for him, mam. Did I do right to say you were coming back?'

'I need you to look at a photograph, Maureen,' Eva said. 'This is very important.'

Francis barged in and was surprised by the brusque manner in which Eva sent him away. But she had no time for her son now. She was remembering another boy his age in a funny hat holding her hand on the Bunlacky road at night. A boy everyone adored who had vanished off this earth. How often in Winchester had she sat up in bed, convinced that a knock had woken her, with Brendan outside, having found his way to her? But he would not have known her English address. With the Dunkineely house lying empty like a cursed palace, if Brendan had reached Ireland then Mayo was the only place where he could come for help.

Eva led Maureen to the basement bedroom where she had stored any personal possessions they could not take to

England. There were pictures of Brendan as a boy in an album here. But pressed between the pages of Goethe's poems she had kept the last photograph received from him, taken by a London street photographer in 1936. She showed it to Maureen.

'Take a good look.' She tried to stay calm and not scare the girl. 'Take as long as you want. Then tell me if this could be the man you saw in the woods.'

The girl held the candle so close to the photograph that Eva was afraid it would become stained with wax. She seemed to take an eternity to make up her mind.

'He's good-looking in this photograph,' she said, 'but he's gaunt in real life now – if it was him. Mam, I can't tell. He's lost so much weight and his hair . . . there was grey in it despite him being so young. And his teeth were like an old man's whereas in this photo he's a picture of health. I can't say if this is him or not. It's your brother's picture, isn't it?'

Eva did not reply, as if any articulation of her hope would see it wither. The children were calling from the kitchen. Their anxiety had vanished with Maureen's appearance and they were giddy, the best of friends. Maureen knew better than to question Eva further. The girl returned to the kitchen and Eva heard her scold them playfully, sending them to fetch pots as she prepared supper with the provisions Eva had purchased in Mr Durcan's shop. Eva was glad that Maureen could distract them and give her time alone to think and pray.

There were more candles in her bag upstairs in the hall. Eva collected an assortment of empty bottles from the cellar and, using them as holders, set a lighted candle in every window. This was how she remembered Dunkineely at Christmas, with candles in windows and doors ajar to offer shelter if Mary and Joseph should pass. Bruckless House was also once festooned with candles, but – although Eva loved the Ffrenches – to recall those lit windows reminded her of the false beacons with which shipwreckers lured unwary sailors onto the rocks. But perhaps Brendan had survived this voyage that Mr Ffrench had inspired. She opened the front door to stand out in the freezing night with three candles spluttering on the hall floor behind her as she scanned the dark trees.

Her mind was strangely calm. She had placed herself at God's mercy and was waiting for his pattern to be revealed. Prayer would be superfluous in the rich silence. She would wait until dawn if necessary. She was no Thomas needing to put her hands into the wounds. Perhaps this was the reason why she had chosen to return home tonight.

Making no effort to stay warm, she waited, so lost in meditation that she did not hear Maureen and the children calling until they came upstairs to find her.

'Whatever are you doing, Mummy?' Hazel asked, exasperated.

'I'm waiting, dear.'

'For what?'

'Whoever is out there.'

Both children peered anxiously into the dark, unnerved by her behaviour.

'There's nobody out there,' Hazel said decidedly.

'You'd best come in, Mrs Fitzgerald,' Maureen urged. 'You'll catch your death on such a night.'

'You know who's sleeping in the stable, don't you?' Francis said. 'Why are you just standing here, Mummy?'

'Because I'm scared to move.'

'What do you mean?' The boy was near tears, finding her behaviour unsettling, but she could not reply because she herself didn't know what she meant. As long as she stood here in silence, Eva had felt that she could keep alive the dream but the children's presence allowed reality to intrude. A candle went out behind her. She turned to blow out the others so that there was just the distant candlelight from the drawing room window and the lantern Maureen was carrying. Eva became aware of how cold she was. Maureen saw her shiver.

'We'd best be having some supper downstairs, Mrs Fitzgerald.'

Eva allowed herself to be led away and Maureen beckoned for Francis to close the door. When they reached the stairs to the cellar Maureen told him to hurry on, but the boy remained in the spot where Eva had stood.

'There *is* somebody out there,' he said quietly. 'By the chestnut tree at the start of the avenue.'

Eva started forward and Francis stepped back, looking like he wished to bolt the door and keep whoever was out there at bay. But he let his mother run down the steps onto the gravel that was choked with weeds. A lank figure stood beneath the tree, a hand raised to his eyes as if the distant candles were blinding him. He began to approach, like a ghost arisen from a battlefield. He was Brendan's height, with Brendan's gait. Only his gaunt face seemed older, his hair prematurely grey. Eva ran towards him in the moonlight, afraid that if she averted her eyes the apparition would disappear. He seemed surprised by her eagerness, unsure of how to respond. He stopped to let her approach. Her baby brother, the laughing boy she had pushed in his pram, carried on her shoulders, lain beside in hayricks at night to teach him the names of stars.

For several seconds she surrendered to a feeling of bliss, as if willpower and longing could transform his features into those she yearned for. Then she stopped running and her hands gripped her stomach to block out the surge of grief. Silently she cursed her naivety and cursed this stranger. Because wherever Brendan was, he was not standing before her.

'I thought you were someone else,' she said feebly.

'I'm sorry.' The voice was hoarse, the words hard to make out.

'Somebody who went to Spain.'

'That's where I've come from.'

The tiniest flicker of hope stirred.

'Which side?'

Scornfully he looked down to emphasise the state of his clothing. 'I was among the Irish who actually fought. I wasn't led by a cowardly buffoon who ran away at the first shot. When I was released from the hellhole of Franco's jail, where warders would half-hang men for amusement, my father shut the door in my face. You tell me which side.'

'What brought you here?'

'You are Eva Fitzgerald?'

'Yes.'

'My name is Peadar Bourke. I've something for you. From a comrade.'

Eva stepped forward, desperate hope fanning up again inside her. 'When did you see him last? Please God, tell me he's all right.'

The stranger shook his head. 'I wish I could. We tried to stop the fascists capturing the Madrid road at Jarama. But our only training was firing a few shots at rocks to get the feel of our guns. Frank Ryan was wounded there and poor Kit Conway killed. There was no shelter except a few scraggly olive trees in the valley. The firing stopped for a second and I saw him pick some fallen fruit from the dirt. He said, *"Even the olives are bleeding."* Then the fascists advanced and Charlie tried to cover our retreat. He copped three bullets, one in the head. Poor bastard, it took us ten days to retrieve his body.'

'Charlie who?' Eva said, caught between conflicting emotions.

'Charlie Donnelly,' Bourke replied angrily. 'Who do you think we're discussing?'

Eva recalled the young poet whom Art had brought here once. Impassioned, dogmatic, barely out of his teens. A cattle dealer's son whose voice mellowed when he recited his terse verses. His young face scarred by a bullet hole, baked for ten days under a merciless Spanish sun. Eva should have felt grief for him, but instead was overcome with guilt-ridden relief because it was not Brendan mown down by machine-gun fire. Her hope could live on.

'I found this in his kit bag.' The gaunt stranger reached into his coat pocket. 'Several times Charlie mentioned his promise to give it back to a woman. I thought it must be important, but you don't even remember him.'

Eva stared at the book, *Lyrics from the Ancient Chinese*, with her name and address inside it. She accepted it back, wondering at what journeys this slender volume had undergone in the three years since the poet slipped away from here at dawn.

'I do remember him,' she said. 'It's just that somebody else I love is missing in Spain.' She paused, afraid to mention Brendan's name in case all hope was extinguished. 'Have you eaten?'

'I bought bread in the village. You'd swear I was a black man from the way the women in the shop looked at me.'

'Not many people pass through here,' she said apologetically.

'That's all I'm doing, mam. Passing through from Westport. Charlie made this sound like a place where a man might seek shelter. This past week I've slept in your outhouse. I hope you don't mind.'

'We can offer you a blanket on the floor.'

'I'd sooner be on my way. I just wanted to return your book so I could feel I'd done something on my visit home.'

'Did your father really turn you away?'

'I think he would have taken me back in only he claimed that the peelers have their eyes skinned for me. De Valera is locking up anyone he dislikes while Hitler and Chamberlain fight it out.'

'I know. My brother, Art Goold, has been interned in the Curragh camp.'

'That lunatic? I'm sorry ... no offence. Charlie never mentioned the connection. I knew Art in Dublin, on the fringe of everything. You couldn't hold a conversation without Art deciding it was a public meeting and shouting "Long Live Comrade Stalin." They put him in the Curragh, you say?'

'Yes.'

'That's where they'll put me unless I get a boat to Liverpool.' He paused. 'If your Art's sister that makes you ...'

'What?'

He went silent.

'Did you know my younger brother in Spain?'

'Sweet Christ, that's who you thought I was.'

'Is he alive? Please tell me. Does Franco have him?'

'You know that Franco doesn't have him.'

'We know nothing.'

'Surely Art told you? I heard he was crazy with worry. He almost doubted his God.'

'Art doesn't have a God,' she said.

'He has. A cobbler's son with a peasant moustache and a smile that would turn your blood to ice.' He looked past her towards Hazel and Francis in the doorway with Maureen watching over them. 'Are they your children?'

'Yes.'

'In Dublin they say that Art has no chance of ever seeing his wife and son again.'

'What do you mean?'

'In Spain there was an invisible line between the Russians and the rest of us. In theory we were each fighting Franco but really it was two separate wars. Stalin didn't give a toss for the Spanish people. If Franco is Hitler's puppet, then Stalin wanted to install his own. Pretty soon we all knew where we stood but your brother's problem was trying to have a foot in both camps.'

'What happened?' Eva asked in dread.

'It shouldn't be me telling you this. I don't know what's true or false. Brendan wasn't really one of us. I was only in his company once, on a long afternoon in Barcelona. He accompanied me on a journey I might never have taken alone. I can't be sure what happened. With the Russians you never know.'

'What do people say?'

'That he was tricked on board a Soviet ship. He told a friend of mine that the Russians were letting him go home, he just had to fix a radio as a favour. He seemed to genuinely trust them. Typical Protestant – not knowing when it was wiser to make a sly run for it. Once he stepped on board, the gangplank was raised and the Russians in the radio station shrugged their shoulders at any mention of him like he had never existed.'

'But he was on their side?'

'That makes it worse. It means he's no prisoner of war, he's a traitor. Some said that Goold wasn't taken prisoner at all but had been spying on us for the Russians who stage-managed his mock disappearance. Others said they saw him later in the war under a different name. But mostly people said nothing, afraid of suffering a similar fate. It was hard enough being target practice for Hitler's pilots, without having to worry about being shot in the back. After a while I was only interested in saving my own skin.'

Eva shivered, with coldness pervading every vein in her body. Images rushed through her mind so forcefully that she had to struggle to remain standing. Brendan as a boy in a comical hat. Brendan smiling in that last photo from London. Shaven-headed boys gathered around the piano on the cover of *Sovietland* and how it was obvious that none had ever held a violin before. '*On the basis of new principles of education, thousands of former criminals are rehabilitated in the Bolsheov Corrective Labour Commune for Juvenile Delinquents, in conditions of absolute freedom, to a new life of labour as fully-fledged members of the socialist society.*' Lies and more lies. If Brendan's body had not been thrown overboard with ropes binding his wrists, he was probably caged in some Soviet camp, as desperate to return to Ireland as Art – in an Irish camp – was desperate to reach Russia.

'Are you all right?' Bourke put out a hand to steady her.

'I'm not all right. I want my brother.'

'Don't give up hope. The Russians have nothing to gain by holding him. No volunteer I've met since my return wants to talk about him. They're building their own legends and have no room for messy loose ends. If he's alive he needs someone to speak out. But just don't expect help. With one Goold under lock and key, de Valera won't exert himself to get his hands on another.'

'You're cold,' Eva said. 'Come inside. Have some supper. We can give you a bed.'

'No.'

401

'Please.' Eva was desperate to do the things for this man that she could not do for Brendan, as if he could somehow be a proxy. He was the last person she knew who had seen him, the only link. She looked at the book. 'You have nothing belonging to Brendan?'

'I barely knew him. But Charlie Donnelly was my pal. He wanted you to have your book back. I have to go now.'

'Where?'

'I've thought things through in the woods here. I never imagined that England's fight could be my own. The IRA think that if we help defeat the British, Hitler will benignly hand over the Six Counties. But I saw his planes above Spain and knew that I was looking at evil.'

'My husband has enlisted.'

'He's a Protestant so people will expect no less, but when I don a British uniform it won't be just my father's door that will close on my face. Still, maybe between the pair of us your husband and I will keep Mayo out of this war. Go back to your kids, mam, they're worried for you.'

He turned to walk down the avenue without looking back. Eva wanted to return to the house, but her limbs were so cold that she couldn't move. It was the children who came to wrap their arms around her, besieging her with questions.

'Who was he, Mummy? What did he give you?'

She allowed them to escort her back to the kitchen. Maureen asked no questions as she sat Eva down by the range and placed another log inside it. But Eva felt that she would never be warm again. Maureen began organising the children, arranging makeshift beds on the flagstones until the mattresses were aired. Francis and Hazel kissed their mother before climbing into bed but Eva barely registered their presence. Maureen went upstairs and soon the exhausted children fell asleep, leaving Eva alone. More alone than she had ever felt.

The copy of *Sovietland* lay on a chair. She picked it up, opened the range and watched the flames consume the picture of the shaven-headed boys. She closed over the range. Her untouched supper was on the table but Eva could not bear to eat it when Brendan – if alive – was probably starving at this moment.

Maureen came back downstairs to quietly get undressed, knowing that Eva would confide in her in time. The girl began to wash at the sink and Eva walked out along the haunted corridor and up the stairs to enter every room and blow out the candles. She paused in the drawing room and thought of poor Freddie alone on Winchester's blacked-out streets. The skies were dark across Europe, waiting for the drone of planes. War seemed so remote from this Mayo wood, yet she knew there was no guarantee of sanctuary here. She would try to make for her children an ark in this old house but some force of evil, which she could not name, held the world balanced on his palm. It was raised to his lips so that all he had to do was blow and their lives and hopes and dreams would scatter like cigarette ash.

She had so much to pray for. Her frail parents in Oxford, her brothers, her husband too crippled to fight, Peadar Bourke trudging through the Mayo night, her two precious children downstairs. What prayer could be powerful enough to protect them all, what incantation or spell? Eva stared out into the darkness and offered God the only gift she could proffer, her silence like an empty vessel aching to be filled.

# TWENTY-SEVEN

## *In the Hold*

### *Off Magadan, Soviet Union, October 1940*

Tomorrow they would reach the port of Magadan. The dead would be unloaded from the ship first and stacked in batches with their ice-cold carcasses carefully counted. Then the sick would be laid out on canvas stretchers on the cold sand and finally the remaining *zeks*, squinting against whatever grey half-light existed. Only then would the full count be taken, with the *zeks* being shouted at by the sailors and NKVD officers anxious to off-load their cargo and return to Vladivostok. Tomorrow this nine-day sea nightmare would end, even if a new nightmare beckoned in a march to the Kolyma gold fields across the frozen landscape which Brendan could glimpse now as he ascended from the ship's hold.

The sailors refused to ever risk descending into this pit of vomit and shit and terror. But every evening they would briefly allow small bands of prisoners up on deck to use the latrine which smelt no worse than the hold they had left. These few minutes were precious because you could suck freezing air into your lungs and you were safe from the *urkas* who controlled life below deck. Brendan's bladder had been aching all day, but he'd learnt to nurture that pain because of the blissful sense of relief he could savour now in finally being able to piss. An old Pole squatted to his left, frantically trying to move his bowels in the short time available. He was so emaciated that Brendan knew he would not survive tomorrow's march to the gold fields. But Brendan could not afford to feel sympathy at present. He was focused on the warm flow of piss, which momentarily allowed him to forget everything else. Rising steam froze immediately in the air.

Sailors screamed at them to hurry on, but these *zeks* had waited all day for their moment above deck and nobody wanted to be the first to turn because once one man left the latrine they would all have to follow. A guard shouted again and this time they emerged from the latrine in unison, their instincts honed to recognise the exact second when you risked receiving a blow or a bullet. Brendan helped the Pole beside him to rise, but the old man stared ahead, too ensnared in the failure to move his bowels to acknowledge the gesture. The next group of prisoners cursed Brendan's slowness in walking back, breaking into a trot as they struggled to control their bladders while being beckoned forward.

Time was running out for the desperate men at the back, mainly because the *urkas*, who were always allowed up first, had taken so long to stroll back to the hold where their rule was the only law. Some nights the sailors grew tired of standing in the cold and closed over the hatches before all the *zeks* had a chance to relieve themselves. Brendan's companions had already climbed back into the hold but he risked standing on deck for an extra second to stare at the barbed wire surrounding the steps. An irrational desire possessed him to touch those knotted strands as if a human hand might transform them by magic into hedgerow flowers. A sailor shoved him forward with his rifle butt and Brendan passed down through the queuing men. The hold seemed utterly dark after the weak light on deck, but he managed to seek out Yasili and squat next to him.

Yasili was a former portrait painter who received an eight-year sentence on suspicion of espionage for an unknown foreign power after it was discovered that he had once been taken prisoner of war in Austria in 1915 and had therefore once consorted with foreigners. He always loitered near the base of the steps, even at the risk of receiving blows from the *urkas*, because you needed every chance mouthful of clean air to survive this voyage which carried the risk of typhoid. Yasili was unique among the *zeks* in having been sent to the gold fields once before. However he had been transferred to a camp at Siblag when the commandant there wanted portraits done of his children. His talent had saved his life because outdoor work was compulsory in Kolyma unless the temperature fell below minus fifty degrees. Yasili expected that few of the men with whom he first made the trip would still be alive.

Brendan closed his eyes, hoping – after his glimpse of the sea – to conjure up the blueness of Donegal Bay in his mind. But these days he rarely dreamt of Donegal and could barely visualise Dunkineely. Three years in gulags had stripped away most memories. Now when he dreamed of water it involved his first glimpse of the Black Sea at twilight after being brought up on deck to glimpse the port of Sevastopol in 1937.

Brendan had shared that journey from Barcelona through the straits past Gallipoli and Constantinople with two young Russians from the Communist Youth League who were accused of spying after having been seen fraternising with British volunteers. The boys had been too scared to talk to him, in sufficient trouble already without associating with another foreigner. Brendan would have welcomed any interrogation on his voyage from Spain, when he was still furious about being tricked on board. He had craved the chance to defend himself or at least know the charges against him but his only dealings had been with brutish sailors who were not intentionally cruel but regarded the three prisoners with the same indifference as if transporting cattle. Occasionally the two Russian youths were dragged from the small room where they were kept chained beside Brendan. From their screams Brendan knew that they were being tortured, but the NKVD officers on board did not seem interested in extracting confessions. They were merely going through the motions of their handiwork to remind the sailors of their power.

Brendan opened his eyes as a groan of protest arose from the men who had not yet made it up onto deck. The sailors were starting to close over the hatches. Desperate pleas were made for the right to piss, but once the crew embarked on a course of action Brendan knew that they never changed their minds. There was no possibility of food tonight either. From tomorrow the *zeks* would be somebody else's responsibility and therefore somebody else could feed them. The *urkas* had been fed earlier because even the sailors were wary of these common criminals who banded together in a fraternity of thieves that lived by their own code.

After years of hearing *zeks* attempt to puzzle out exactly what alleged conspiracy they were arrested for, Brendan suspected the *urkas* to be the only genuine alliance in the Soviet Union not under the Kremlin's heel. Yet, ironically, the gulag authorities encouraged these common criminals because, being merely a socially harmful element, they ranked above the *zeks* accused of sabotage or treason, and the brutality of the *urkas* helped to keep the political prisoners in their place.

In truth, few *zeks* knew what they were charged with. After being taken by train from Sevastopol to Moscow in

1937 Brendan had indignantly demanded the right to contact the British Consulate and for his first interrogators in Lubyanka prison to produce proof of the unspecified charges against him. Expecting them to have inherited a file from Georgi Polevoy, he had reviewed each detail of his life like a Catholic before confession. But his interrogators merely sat with a sheet of blank paper, outraged by his attempt to defend himself and his refusal to supply them with a list of crimes to try him for. They maintained that he only wanted proof so as to twist and distort it. The case against him was water-tight precisely because there was no proof. Therefore his guilt was indisputable, because Brendan could produce no defence against it. Impatient with his non-cooperation when they had so many cases to get through, the interrogators had bound his feet and hands behind his back, using a hoist to lift him high into the air, then dropped him onto the stone floor. With his face such a mass of blood that he could not have managed to mumble a confession even if he had still been able to think clearly enough to formulate one, they brought him to a standing cell like an upturned stone coffin. Brendan had no idea how long he remained standing in it, without space to even lift his hands to the congealed blood on his face. But after hours or days they lifted him out and dumped him in a small cell where a hundred men fought for space. Nobody befriended him, but by trying to follow the conversation with his limited Russian, Brendan had learnt the importance of self-denunciation if you wished to have any chance of surviving.

His second interview had occurred at night when he was led down stairs ringed with nets to prevent suicide attempts. Screams came from each room in the long corridor set aside for night interrogations. Brendan felt that this was a place which Art obviously don't know about, because his brother's sense of justice would never have let him pledge his soul to a state which tortured and butchered its own people. Every survival instinct told him to invent a conspiracy. He should confess to having plotted with POUM members to smuggle Trotsky into Spain to create a fifth column to collaborate with the fascists. But even in the torture cell with the huge thug whom the prisoners called 'the Boxer' lurking behind him, Brendan's character had not allowed him to engage in such ludicrous falsehoods. He had not seen the eyes of the interrogator enquiring if he had formulated a hypothesis for the reason for his arrest. Instead, he had visualised Martin Luther's eyes in the portrait in his father's study. The interrogator had looked pained by Brendan's silence, insisting again that Brendan must know the reason why he was brought here. When Brendan still refused to reply he had nodded to the Boxer and stepped from the room.

The bones of Brendan's left hand had never set back into their proper shape and he blacked out twice while being throttled. He was hallucinating by the time the interrogator returned and so could not even remember the charges to which he must have confessed. His trial had occurred without notice two days later. The chairman of the troika read out the charges so quickly that Brendan barely heard them. He was sentenced to eight years. It was over before he had time to speak, with the next case already called. Even allowing for how everything appeared to happen in slow motion, he knew that at most his trial had lasted ninety seconds.

Looking back now, Brendan knew how illogical it had been to put himself through such unnecessary suffering. Nothing was gained. His crippled hand had hindered him in the years since, making his work rate suffer so that he was often punished with starvation rations. But, despite that, he still sometimes had a feeling of pride in his defiance on that night. It was the one moment that still gave him a sense of himself.

Life before his kidnapping in Barcelona was lived by a naive stranger. Since his trial he had no real life or self-worth. At first he was shocked by how the camp guards treated people as if they had forfeited the right to exist. Now he understood that such brutality was easy, because *zeks* were not people, but enemies of the people. However, balanced between his old life and this non-life there hung the moment in that interrogation cell when he thought of Martin Luther and refused to yield. Just before he lost consciousness for the first time, he had felt an extraordinary surge of foolish triumph at the realisation that he was actually stronger than Art. Because if Art found himself there he would have bent the knee for the sake of the Party, confessing to any lie like a dog doing tricks to please its master.

The squash of men in the hold was getting worse as *zeks* tried to retreat a safe distance from a group of *urkas* playing cards nearby. The old Pole whom Brendan had helped in the latrine managed to squeeze onto the floor beside Brendan, who silently cursed him for disturbing his thoughts. Even memories of torture were preferable to sitting here unable to focus on anything except his incessant hunger. He tried not to think of food, knowing that once he did he would start a vain search through every fold of his rags in case a crumb of bread had somehow lodged there. Still, maybe rations were not as bad in Kolyma as Yasili claimed. Maybe his family knew where he was. Maybe he could escape and join the hunter tribes who somehow survived in this wilderness. But he knew that the tribes would be indifferent to his plight, hunting him down like a bear, interested only in the eleven pounds of wheat that the NKVD offered for an escaped *zek*.

A rough shout from the card game disturbed his thoughts again.

'You. Give me your shoes.'

Brendan looked up, realising that an *urka* was addressing him.

'You heard, foreign bastard. Fascist spy. Give me your fucking shoes. It's your tough shit I'm after losing them. You think I like losing to this bastard?'

Brendan knew that no *zek* would support him against the *urkas*. They had such a network in the camps that no *zek* they targeted could escape retribution. This card game was one of several going on since the voyage started. At first, the *urkas* had gambled their own possessions, but when these ran out they simply gambled the possessions of the *zeks* around them. Brendan knew that he had been fortunate. It could just as easily have been his clothes, the use of his body or even his life that was forfeited. But without shoes, he stood no chance of surviving tomorrow's march.

'Don't do this, comrade. You have no use for his shoes.' The old Pole spoke up. Silence greeted his intervention, not just because he risked his own life by interfering, but because it was a crime for prisoners to use the term *comrade*.

'What's it to you, grandfather?' the *urka* said. 'Be careful or I'll gamble your teeth and pull out the last stumps in your stinking mouth.'

'The foreigner will die in the cold.'

'He's a spy, it will save the waste of a good Soviet bullet.' The *urka* looked around, sensing that his authority was being defied. 'On the next hand of cards I'm staking your throat. Don't run away, *dokhodyaga*, with my luck you'll soon be grinning from ear to ear.' He glared at Brendan. 'Now give me those fucking shoes.'

Brendan handed over the rubber shoes made from strips

of old tractor tyres. So far the nearby *zeks* had shown little interest in this altercation with the *urka*, being too preoccupied with their own misery. However the threat to the Pole's life ignited interest in the card game. The old man said nothing, watching the homemade cards being dealt. From his expression Brendan could not tell if the Pole wanted the *urka* to win or lose. Truly he was a *dokhodyaga*, one of the walking dead barely clinging to life. Perhaps a slit throat was preferable to a slow death from frostbite and exhaustion in the snow tomorrow. It would end the perpetual hunger which haunted every second of a *zek's* day. Brendan wondered would the Pole try to scramble his way into another part of the hold if the *urka* lost, hoping to hide among the thousands of prisoners? Or would he remain seated, summoning a final surge of human defiance? Nobody belonging to him probably knew where he was or would know of his death. Though with rumours of people being executed for simply having a Polish surname maybe nobody belonging to him remained alive.

Brendan felt an irrational need to carry the Pole's name in his memory until his own turn came to die. He had seen this desire to be remembered in condemned prisoners in Lubyanka. They had invariably scrawled their names on the wall of the holding cell prior to execution, even though they knew that when the cleaning lady finished wiping their blood off the tarpaulin in the cellar where they were shot, she was always sent up to whitewash the cell walls.

'Who are you?' Brendan whispered.

'A member of the family of a Traitor to the Fatherland. They arrested my brother for counter-revolutionary activity. I hadn't seen him for twenty years but they still tracked me down. For his sake I hope you have no brother.'

The Pole went silent as the dealer dealt out the last cards.

He gripped Brendan's wrist with sudden vice-like strength. Brendan was unsure if this was for human support or because the old man wanted to offer him as a victim instead. But as the *urka* slapped down his cards with a triumphant shout, curses from the other player told Brendan that he had won. The Pole released his grip, only now starting to breathe heavily as if he had previously been too scared to show fear. The *urka* turned.

'Your luck held, grandfather, I don't have to kill you. I am a butcher, very clumsy. The man who lost is much better with a knife. It's he who has to cut your throat.'

The Pole was surprisingly quick in rising to push his way through the mass of bodies. But the *urkas* would have easily caught him had Brendan not deliberately tripped as he rose to get out of their way. They stumbled against him and one kicked out but with men so tightly squashed together there was little force in his kick. The Pole might conceal himself for a short time but he could not get far in this crowd. The *urkas* would search all night because under their code no forfeit could be unpaid. If the *urka* who lost at cards failed to kill the Pole, he himself would be killed so as to restore the thieves' honour.

With a survivor's instincts Yasili had absented himself from Brendan's side at the moment when the *urka* demanded his shoes. Now the painter was back, urging Brendan to disappear from this part of the hold until the prisoners were led up onto deck tomorrow. With luck by then, the *urkas* would have forgotten his existence. Their power would be lessened in the gold fields, though they would still do less work than political prisoners and secure all the indoor jobs. But casual killings there would be infrequent because camp commandants hated to see a unit of labour wasted. Brendan would survive, but only if he found warm shoes.

Men cursed as he stumbled against them in the hold. Here and there a stub of candle burned and it amazed him how much you could actually see with a flicker of distant flame to give you bearings. Yasili said that the ability to create a flame was the most vital skill in the gold fields. Striking sparks from a flint was the only way to start a bonfire out there on the frozen wastes. Without a bonfire you could not melt ice-blocks cut from the river and without boiling this water over the fire you could not soften the frozen sand to sieve it for gold. If you could not sieve like this for twelve hours a day you did not receive the meagre ration of bread needed to keep you alive.

In the transit camp in Vladivostok, the gold fields had sounded more terrible than any gulag he had been in so far, but now in the belly of this dark ship they sounded like freedom.

Brendan pushed further on into parts of the hold he had never previously entered. Occasionally he trod on bodies lying amid pools of urine and vomit. Some cursed while others lay as if dead. It would be easy to steal shoes from any of these figures. But Brendan's character refused to allow him to do so unless certain that they were dead. Most of the dead were already stripped of every possession. No *zek* knew how many men had been crammed onto this ship at Vladivostok. Some said four thousand and others said ten. It was impossible to imagine such a cargo. All Brendan knew was that his holding cell in Vladivostok, with bunks for a dozen prisoners, had contained a hundred and sixty-eight men.

Another group of *urkas* played cards by candlelight to his left. Behind them he could see the ship's steel wall, the first time he had seen it in days. The dull sheen reminded him of the time last year when, passing a shaving mirror in an orderly's hut, he had glimpsed the face of a man whom he could not recognise as himself.

Ordinary *zeks* were trying to stay clear of this other card game, crowding into the shadows, desperate not to be caught up in the bets. One man had not been so fortunate however because his body lay on the floor in a pool of blood close to the *urkas*, gagged and stripped with his hands and ankles neatly tied together. The strands of rope left Brendan confused as to why the man had died. If it had been a fight he would merely be stabbed. But this was a deliberate execution. Perhaps he was an *urka* who betrayed their code of honour or a *zek* publicly murdered as a warning. Or maybe he had been chosen at random, with each stage of his being bound, gagged and stripped representing a separate hand lost in the card game. Maybe the victim had been forced to lie there and watch each card being dealt, until the eventual loser was handed the knife and ordered to slit him open like a pig. The corpse's back was to Brendan so he could not see if the throat or stomach had been cut, but Brendan had never witnessed such a sight before. He sensed the silent terror of the *zeks* nearby.

The corpse's feet were bare, with his shoes having obviously been among the first possessions gambled away. The body was thin, with protruding bones trying to push their way through the skin. But something about the hunched shoulders seemed disturbingly familiar. Brendan recalled the Pole's story of being sentenced because he was related to his brother. But Art was in Ireland or somewhere safe. Surely he had not been mad enough to try and return to Moscow? Art could not know where Brendan was. But perhaps word had leaked out, with Art arriving in Russia to try and save him because that was what older brothers did. Dunkineely was suddenly clear to him again, being carried on Art's

415

shoulders along the Bunlacky shore. These couldn't be the same shoulders, yet Brendan was unable to prevent himself from stepping forward, surprising the *urkas* who halted their card game to observe him.

Brendan knelt by the body, resisting an urge to cradle it. He did know these features, this chin, the nose, even if starvation and beatings had altered them. He pushed the body over. The neck was untouched, as was the breast. It was the testicles that had been cut off with the man left to bleed to death. How long had it taken to die? Brendan wanted to shake the body and ask. Brendan wanted to scream into his face. He wanted answers, wanted to unravel the previous ten years. He wanted to remove the gag and hear his own name being spoken. But an instinct for self-preservation prevented any such rashness. He let Georgi Polevoy's head drop back onto the floor and stood up, knowing that the *urkas* were scrutinising him. He had no idea what Georgi had been arrested for or if the *urkas* who killed him knew that he was a former NKVD man. Perhaps his death was random, with Georgi not knowing his place as a mere *zek*. Or perhaps back in his glory days when he reigned in Lubyanka prison Georgi had made the mistake of torturing one of these *urkas*. If Brendan appeared to recognise Georgi now they might think that he too had once been a policeman. Therefore he gave the *urkas* a practised imbecilic glance, shrugged his shoulders indifferently and slunk off. He waited until he was a distance from the card game before starting to run, not caring what blows he received when he pushed past men or how often he fell over bodies huddled on the floor.

It was pitch dark in this part of the hold but he knew where he was heading. The steps up to the deck were packed tight with men perched there. It was colder with night air coming through the air vents in the shutters. Men cursed at him as he invaded their space, but he didn't care or even feel their kicks at his bare feet. All he could see was Georgi Polevoy's defiant stare in death.

He felt no sense of revenge. Yuri was also probably dead or in a gulag. Brendan had met many Russian volunteers arrested as spies once they returned from Spain. But Georgi had always seemed too ruthless and clever to be ensnared, one step ahead of everyone. Perhaps cleverness was treasonable now too. Maybe Stalin really was like God and came for all men in the end.

A hand reached out to grab him from the mass of men.

'Sit down.' Yasili had cat's eyes in the gloom. Brendan sank down, forcing the cluster of men to reluctantly yield space. 'Are you okay?'

The Irishman did not reply because this was one lesson Georgi had taught him. You must know nothing and be nobody to survive. Brendan savoured a strange emotion. It was not anger or pity for Georgi, or revenge. What he felt in the depth of his soul was triumph. He was still living while that bastard was dead. He had outwitted the fox. He could still piss and shit and eat while his puppet master would be stacked tomorrow with the other corpses to be subtracted from the cargo list. Yasili nudged him, producing something from inside the rags that constituted his clothes.

'These belonged to the Pole,' he whispered. 'In all the excitement I slipped them off. He would have wanted you to have them. The gold fields aren't so bad really. Winter only lasts twelve months – the rest of the year is a blaze of summer.'

Brendan took the shoes. They were worn thin but it didn't matter. Even hunger did not trouble him just now, as he considered how more horrific Lubyanka must have been for Georgi who would have known in advance the details of every torture to be inflicted on him. In Barcelona, Georgi had wanted them

417

to go whoring together – a test to see who would last the longest, but Brendan had always known that he would win. Tomorrow in Magadan, when Georgi's body was being doused with petrol and burnt, he would still be standing, shuffling towards the Kolyma gold fields in the shoes of a dead man.

# TWENTY-EIGHT

# *An Encounter*

*London, October 1940*

Eva caught the two-thirty train from Oxford, hoping to meet Freddie at Paddington Station at four o'clock for drinks before going to dine with two fellow officers and their wives. She knew how difficult it was to organise such a meal in London at present. In all likelihood it would end with diners and waiters uneasily sharing the nearest air raid shelter, because London had been bombed without a break for the past fifty-six nights.

Two nights ago, after she arrived from Ireland, Freddie had introduced her to the two other wives and Eva instantly hated their piercing laughter and how they had called another wife 'common' for referring to writing paper as notepaper. She dreaded having to endure their company again, but knew how important it was for Freddie to show her off. Tomorrow she could escape back to Ireland but this evening she would play the dutiful wife and make him at least seem proud of her.

However, as the train neared London an inspector announced the presence of an unexploded bomb on the track near Ladbroke Grove. Passengers would have to disembark at White City, if and when the train reached there. No passengers complained, even when the driver reduced his speed to five miles an hour. Refusing to smile at setbacks was considered as unpatriotic as loose talk. People must make do and mend, as Mother had said last night in Oxford, using her time in the air raid shelter to patch up an old jacket of Father's and join women from the Royal Air Force Comforts Committee in knitting socks for young pilots at the nearby airfields. Last night there had been none of the impromptu air raid shelter singsongs that Eva had heard about. People were too preoccupied by the latest rumours of a planned German invasion, which was only being delayed by the last-ditch courage of the Spitfire pilots who were buying Churchill time. Nobody mentioned the rumour aloud, just like nobody would discuss it now on this train, because loose talk in public cost lives. But Eva knew that behind their exhausted smiles people were anticipating the worst. This nightly blitzkrieg was to soften them up before the attack. For weeks, people had been snatching whatever sleep they could, never knowing the moment when they would have to dig or be dug out by their neighbours. When visiting old haunts from her art student days, Eva had been shocked to find the church of Austin Friars and the High Altar of St Paul's destroyed. But London was also alive in a way she never experienced before. If she was not a mother she would happily stay here to share this suffering, spending her nights not with officers' wives but with the ordinary population in underground stations and digging with them in the rubble of each dawn.

But two children in Ireland were dependent on her and she had to get back. Maureen was minding them in Glanmire House, having taken a week's holidays from Mr Devlin's shop. Eva felt guilty at taking the risk of leaving them, just like she felt guilty in Ireland when imagining Freddie alone here. Her sense of duty as a wife was partly responsible for this present visit. But there was also her duty as a daughter. Last night in Oxford she had once again tried to persuade her parents to return to Donegal. Father would not hear of it. He might be old but by volunteering as an air raid warden he wanted to play some role in the fight against fascism. His quiet resoluteness had reminded her of Brendan. Mother also refused to leave, feeling that she had more chance of getting information about Brendan by writing to the Foreign Office from an English address. Last night she showed Eva the curt non-committal replies. The Foreign Office neither knew nor appeared to wish to know about Brendan. Mother had also written to Walter Krivitsky, the Russian intelligence officer who defected to Britain. But there was no hope of a reply now, following his suspicious death in a hotel bedroom. Occurring so soon after Trotsky's murder, it left Eva feeling that nobody was safe from Stalin.

It was four o'clock by the time the train reached Ealing Broadway. It halted for a time with blinds ordered to be drawn, as there were reports of German planes in the skies. Eventually it was given permission to limp as far as White City. By now Eva was fifty minutes late. Train and bus schedules were chaotic, with many streets barely passable, yet Eva knew that Freddie would still inwardly blame her for not reaching Paddington on time. He would make excuses to the other couples, claiming that Eva spent her whole life in the ether. The woman he should have married would navigate her way through any Blitz to arrive on time with perfect hair, orthodox beliefs and a carnivorous appetite for red meat. Eva found her efforts to be this perfect wife more exhausting than the constant German bombardment. Tonight she would again do everything that a wife should do to please him and afterwards feel guilty at her pretence of pleasure.

The passengers left White City station and crowded onto gas-powered buses. A huge *Dig for Victory* sign had been erected across a ruined terrace of houses. The front walls were gone, but she could still see fireplaces suspended in mid-air in the back rooms.

It was impossible to follow the route with so many detours to avoid damaged streets but eventually the bus halted near Marble Arch with the conductor apologising that they could get no further due to rubble and craters on the road. She was not too far from Paddington. If she ran, there was a chance that Freddie might still be there and their evening could be salvaged. Instead she began to walk in a different direction, past teams of men trying to clear the debris. Children watched while one old woman stood in bewilderment beside the rubble that was once her home. People tried to coax her away, but she ignored every kind voice. The Pavilion Theatre was destroyed. Many buildings along Baker Street and Marylebone Road were in ruins though others still miraculously stood. The bombers had tried to destroy Baker Street station, aware of the recent carnage when Balham tube station received a direct hit, with scores of people drowned in a flood from the shattered sewage pipes. The nearby cinema was flattened but workers had got a truck down the street to remove the rubble. The work stopped and she suspected that a body had been unearthed. Not wanting to be a voyeur, she walked on past Queen Charlotte's Hospital with only its walls still standing. Every step made her later for Freddie's dinner but suddenly she couldn't face those officers' wives with their snobbery and condescension.

It was dusk as she entered Regent's Park, where the gates had been taken away to be smelted down. Much of the park was transformed into allotments, but other parts were as she remembered them. Rounding a bend she stopped, shocked at the sight of a grass bank crowded with girls and soldiers who barely bothered to use their greatcoats to conceal their desperate couplings. She could sense a shameless frantic passion, with these couples sensing that they might never see each other again. Any German spy could guess troop movements by the tangible sexual libido in the air. Eva wanted to move on but something about the way that one girl – blatantly having intercourse beneath a bundle of coats – threw back her hair and stretched out a hand to clasp the damp grass, stirred Eva. She was witnessing a passion that she had never personally experienced.

She walked quickly on then, annoyed that she had strayed this far. Freddie's party would have gone on to the restaurant by now. She would have to go there and apologise for her lateness and slowness and her personality. She would have to bite her tongue and not talk about admiring the Quaker ambulancemen who refused to hold a gun or discuss Bernard Shaw or mysticism or any of her troublesome family. She would make herself be a good wife until she could flee back to her children in Ireland.

'Eva?'

The shout startled her. It came from one of four officers standing at a jeep parked near the boating lake. The man called her name again, leaving the others to their cigarettes as he walked towards her. His accent was not English or Irish, but familiar. She knew his features too. His face had aged but differently from how she imagined. The way he had filled out only made him more handsome.

'My word, it is Eva, isn't it?'

Eva didn't know what she felt or wanted to say or do. How often had she longed to see him just once again? She had imagined him settled on a ranch in New Zealand but perhaps he had never gone home? If she had searched London for him as an art student perhaps her life might have been different. She made herself stop thinking like this. If she had not married Freddie she would never have given birth to Francis and Hazel. Her children were worth any unhappiness. She tried to focus on them and not blush like a silly girl. She tried to stay calm and shook his hand.

'Jack, how marvellous to see you. I thought you went home years ago.'

'I did.' He smiled. 'There must be a serious shortage of officers though because they called me up again and made me a brigadier. I'm just passing through London. I'm away in a few days, obviously can't say where.'

'I know.' Eva saw that he had taken in her wedding ring, just as she had spotted the one on his finger. 'My husband is in the services too.'

'Excellent. Maybe I'll run into him.'

She felt his eyes examining her and wondered who had he married and if she looked like her. Perhaps Eva had only been a brief infatuation whom he had not thought about for the past twenty years.

'Well, I can't say where he is posted.'

'Very wise.'

She felt guilty concealing the fact that Freddie was in the Territorial Army. It was not his fault to be born with a club foot. He would gladly have been among the soldiers evacuated from Dunkirk. His duties were unglamorous but essential and if the German invasion came he was ready to take to the streets and die. But she didn't want to talk about Freddie or her life during the past two decades. She wanted to remember what it had felt like to be young and to feel loved. Jack's smile hinted that he was sharing those memories.

'How are all the mad Goold Verschoyles?' he asked.

'Fine.'

'Are your brothers in the war?'

'In their own way.'

Jack laughed. 'Sounds like them. The Goold Verschoyles never quite did things like anyone else. Will you remember me to Art?'

'Of course.'

'And to your father. Is he in Donegal still?'

'Yes.'

'And is the Manor House as madcap as ever? A new generation arguing and singing into the night?'

'Yes.'

Something in her voice told him that she was lying. He glanced back at his watching companions.

'Look here, would you like a cup of tea and a bun? I have an hour to spare. It's rather dark or I could hire a boat for old time's sake. You don't by any chance have Brendan hiding around the corner as a chaperone, do you?'

He stopped, disturbed by the way she looked away and fearful that he might have offended her. 'That was clumsy. Nerves. I didn't expect to run into you again.'

'I was very young, Jack.'

'I know. I'm sorry. I shouldn't have pushed you for an answer.'

'Too young to really know my feelings.'

He produced a packet of cigarettes and she saw how his hand shook slightly. He offered her one. 'Funny how life pans out, isn't it? We only know how to live every moment when that moment is over. It makes us look darn foolish.'

'We live our lives forward but only understand them backward, that's what Father says.'

'Is he really in Donegal?'

'The house has been boarded up for years. Art is interned

425

in Ireland and Brendan has disappeared. Thomas lives in South Africa and Maud is stranded over there with him.'

'Golly, you've all been busy.'

Eva looked over at Jack's companions and wondered what they were making of this encounter. Their gaze made her feel like an adulterous woman.

'Do something for me, Jack.'

'Anything.'

'Remember us the way we were, as the family on Paradise Pier. We didn't know it but we did live in a kind of paradise.'

Jack lowered his voice. 'You haven't changed, Eva, you're still beautiful . . .'

'Please stop.'

'It's the truth. You were always so free.'

'Back then I didn't know what freedom was. It's a commodity, like on the black market. Something you trade.'

'For what?'

'To make other people happy. People who depend on you.'

He stubbed out his cigarette. 'You have children?'

'Two.'

'They are what's important. I've a son in New Zealand. His mother died. My sister looks after him.'

'Is he like you?'

'I wouldn't know. What am I like?'

'You haven't changed either.'

Have I really not changed? she longed to ask. Could he see anything of that young girl in her now? If he sat at her shoulder would she be able to paint again?

'This war is about freedom,' Jack said, 'though I suppose they say that about every war. Freedom is the right to be ourselves.'

Eva wanted him. Her desire was so sudden and fierce that it shocked her very core. She wanted him to wrap his greatcoat around her and take her to the grass bank with the other couples. She wanted to be occupied by him and not by some foreign force. But another part of her would be horrified if he reached out one finger to touch her shoulder. Her desire was perfect because it could never be realised. What she really craved was the knowledge that he still desired her, not just in his memory but in the present, beneath all her layers of responsibilities.

'Do you still paint?'

'I didn't possess enough talent.'

'You did. I remember.'

The other officers climbed into the jeep and the engine started. Jack looked back at them again.

'I hope your husband knows he's a lucky man. I was lucky too. Eleven good years until cancer got her.'

'You keep safe, Jack.' Eva held out her hand.

'Can we give you a lift?'

'I'd sooner walk. I haven't far to go.'

He shook her hand. 'Good luck, Eva.'

She turned and walked quickly into the gloom. She didn't want to see the tiny pinpricks of light from the covered headlights as the jeep drove across the grass to pick up Jack. She didn't want to remember the sight of a small boat rounding the moonlit bend on the Bunlacky shore, his shoulders stooped, rowing away from her.

Eva did not look up at the couples on the grass bank as she hurried past. She was late for dinner. At any moment the air raid sirens could go off and she would be forced to shelter. It was hard to see on the blacked-out streets, with perilous craters and broken pavements, but she began to run, not caring about the danger of falling. When she reached the restaurant they would laugh at her tossed hair and how her skirt was covered in ash and dust off the streets. But she didn't care because it was her duty to be at her husband's side. She had to focus on that stark fact as if nothing else mattered.

## TWENTY-NINE

# The Great Betrayal

### Ireland, July 1941

Two German army officers pushed their way onto the train and glanced down as if sensing his hostility. Walking through the carriage they stopped beside him with a militaristic click of their heels. The tallest leaned towards Art.

'Are these seats taken?'

Art stared up into the face of the enemy. He imagined their jackbooted advance towards Moscow and Leningrad, their tanks heading south to encircle the oilfields, his own wife and child possibly starving in some city under siege, the worthless Nazi signatures on the Non-Aggression Pact. No party manual had equipped him for this eventuality. The German officer surveyed him with mild bemusement, as if wondering if Art was a local imbecile.

'I asked are these seats taken?'

'What difference would it make? You would just take them anyway.'

The officer looked at his companion who shrugged. They pushed past Art to occupy the seats as country people crowded onto the afternoon train to Dublin. Art stood up to let an old woman sit down and, soon after, as if mocking him the

429

two Germans did likewise. They stood behind Art in the packed corridor as the train eventually pulled out of the station and, fuelled by damp turf, began to slowly chug towards Dublin.

He wanted to ask if they had crash-landed in Ireland before dropping their bombs on an English city or was it afterwards, damaged by flak and trying to limp back to Germany. But he refused to address these two fascist internees out on day parole. They would drink coffee in Dublin, stroll freely through the streets and honour their agreement to return to the Curragh internment camp on the evening train because indiscipline was unheard of in the German section. The Germans were segregated from the IRA internees who enjoyed no parole rights, but Art knew that regular communication existed between the two camps. Many Germans captured after parachuting into Ireland were spies attempting to reorganise the IRA and help it launch bombing missions in England like the one that Mrs Behan's young son Brendan had embarked on in 1939. This alliance with the Nazis caused division among the IRA volunteers whom Art had been interned with until today. Some were so consumed by hatred of England that they gleefully hailed Hitler's progress on crude maps in their huts, as if his sole intention in invading Poland was to force England to hand over control of Northern Ireland to them. Others – veterans of Spain or the Republican Congress – recognised the true dangers of Nazism. However not even these men had been willing to support Art's recent assertion that the IRA – in the light of Germany's invasion of Russia – should now cut all links with the Nazis and actively support Stalin's call for an internationalist popular front against fascism.

He should still be interned in the Curragh now, preparing his speech for this evening's political discussion forum where he had planned to demolish their misguided petty nationalist shibboleths and once again argue for this change of direction. It should not be viewed as collaboration with Britain, but as using the Allies as a vehicle to crush fascism under Stalin's leadership.

The discipline of camp life had suited him over the past two years. It was the sole advantage gleaned from having attended public school. The difference was that in the Curragh every internee was equal. There were no prefects or fags, no casual bullying or ritualised beatings. In Marlborough you were force-fed lies, but until this morning Art had felt that a forum existed in the Curragh for genuine discourse. Few IRA men possessed open minds but most had grown relaxed with him, especially after he began to kneel alongside them at night while they recited the rosary. Art did not pray, but he considered it essential to morale to show respect for their beliefs. At heart they were *kulaks* who would need to be prised from their few boggy acres when the time came. But the Curragh was an ideal environment to recruit and educate them. However the camp leadership had grown afraid of him since Hitler's recent treacherous invasion of the Soviet Union. He saw this in a reduced attendance at his Russian language class.

He had been going to give a language class this morning when two men pinned his arms and bundled him between the huts where a deputation awaited. The IRA camp commander held a knife to Art's throat, announcing that he had been court-martialled for subversion and sentenced *in absentia*. He said they had informed the governor that unless Art was gone from the camp by today he was a dead man. Art had been forced to walk towards the gates, where the Irish soldiers had orders to shoot anyone encroaching too close. If he turned back he was told that he would be found with a hundred knife wounds in the morning. The sentries had shouted at him as he neared their watchtower, but knowing that the IRA were watching he had refused to betray fear. Then for some unknown reason, as the sentries cocked their rifles, he remembered Brendan swimming alongside him in a dream and had stopped, not through fear but because he was overcome by *déjà vu*. A sense of foreboding had made him shake as he closed his eyes, trying desperately to grasp what was occurring. It felt like the sort of experience that used to happen to Mother when playing planchette. Art did not know how long he had remained trembling in no-man's-land until arms grasped him and he knew that the soldiers had descended from the watchtower. They bore him, not roughly but like a sick man, up two flights of stairs and into the governor's office overlooking the gates.

Art had sat, trying to recover his composure, as the governor turned from the window where he had been watching proceedings. He examined Art's file on his deck. 'The funny thing with extremists like the IRA,' he said eventually, 'is that they always keep their word. I am exercising my discretion in releasing you in light of the changed circumstances.'

'What changed circumstances?'

'You may huff and puff, Goold, but you'll not do much harm by yourself. I would return your possessions but you appeared to have none when taken into custody two years ago. I will give you the train fare to Dublin, but you must make your own way to London.'

'Why would I go to London?'

'You have this camp in uproar demanding that the IRA throw in their lot with the RAF. If you are so keen to fight England's war then go and fight in it.'

'I've been fighting a war for twenty years,' Art replied. 'You just couldn't see it.'

'Well, you'll be fighting it on your own now.' He leaned forward. 'You're not a bad man, Goold. You never gave me trouble. I feel responsible for you. The Curragh is a grand billet to sit out this mess. Three meals a day, good company. Sometimes I envy you lot. But if I keep you here you will be found dead. Could you not just have kept your head down and your mouth shut?'

'Who runs this camp?' Art had asked. 'The IRA or you?'

'I run it and handle all sorts. When English pilots crash we tell them they're interned, then release them on day parole on their word of honour that they won't escape across the border, handing them a train ticket to do just that. If they break their bond what can we do? To show our neutrality we also give the Germans similar day parole and if they want to start swimming towards France that's their business. The IRA is a genuine threat to security, which is why we've hung several members since the Emergency started. You're no threat, Goold, and certainly not since last week. But if I keep you here we'll need to hang another IRA man when we already have enough martyrs. If you want this war so badly then get a boat to England.'

With those words the governor had pushed Art's release papers across the table. Money was pressed into his hands and he was driven to the station with two soldiers to ensure that he boarded this train.

He should feel liberated now after two years of incarceration, he should be savouring every mile of this slow journey. But he could not shake off a feeling of unease. What had happened last week to change the situation? The important thing was to re-establish contact with his comrades in the Communist Party of Ireland and develop a position to galvanise public support in favour of Stalin's rallying call to fight fascism.

Eventually the train entered Kingsbridge station, with people pushing towards the doors. The German officers politely stood back to allow him to climb down first. He ignored them, with no time for minor confrontations. A party discussion group met every Tuesday at seven. If he walked quickly he could make it. Irish public opinion would be hard to change but proposals must be well advanced to counter these monolithic prejudices. Art strode along the Dublin quays, so intent on making the meeting that he barely had time to look around. Contact with the Party was difficult while interned but Art had managed to get letters out to their broadsheet, the *Irish Worker's Weekly*, on any issue where he suspected deviation from the official line.

It was ten past seven when he climbed the stairs up to the room used as party headquarters. At first Art was unsure if he had entered the wrong building. The room was empty apart from an old desk on which a workman stood, removing shelving. Art only recognised him when he turned.

'Hennessy, isn't it?'

'Jaysus, Art Goold, when did they let you out?'

'Today.'

He laughed and raised his eyes. 'Word spreads fast.'

'What do you mean, Hennessy?' Art looked around. 'Where is everybody? What happened to the Tuesday meetings? Are they finished?'

Hennessy gave the shelf a last blow with his hammer and it came loose. 'The Tuesday meetings aren't finished, the Party is.'

'What do you mean?'

'There no longer is a Communist Party of Ireland. We dissolved ourselves last week.'

'Under whose orders?' Art gripped the desk in his fury. 'Who instructed you to do so?'

'Under nobody's orders, for God's sake, Goold. The few of us left did so ourselves. We discussed the impossible position we were in, then voted to break up as a unit and integrate ourselves as individuals within the trade union movement to guide them to embrace socialist principles. This way we can help to fend off the attacks being launched on the conditions of Irish workers. It's the first time we ever passed a practical resolution. It makes sense, Goold, even to you. We were a lost tribe baying in the wilderness. From now on we can work as individuals on the inside, bringing people around to our way of thinking instead of always being on the outside hectoring them.'

'But nobody asked me? I never voted.'

'What did you want us to do? Dig a tunnel into the Curragh and consult you?' Hennessy attacked the next shelf with his hammer. 'You're not Moses. You didn't part the sea from Russia with two stone tablets. Maybe nobody thought to contact you because nobody considered you to be one of us.'

Art banged his fist on the desk. 'I'm the only true believer among you. You people are an opportunist faction of traitors, sham communists and Trotskyite renegades.'

Hennessy aimed another blow at the shelf. 'Save me the shite, will you? You're not in Russia now.'

'I know what this is about. You are petty nationalist cowards. The Soviet Union is being attacked and you haven't the courage to align yourselves with Stalin and fight in his hour of need.'

Hennessy ripped down the shelf and turned, holding aloft the hammer. 'Don't talk to me about fighting, pal. I was dodging bullets in Spain – half of them Russian – when you were running around the Irish bogs frightening donkeys and screaming at turf workers.'

'I couldn't go to Spain. My orders were to build communism here.'

'Maybe there's more to life than taking orders. Do you ever think for yourself? I met your brother in Spain and saw what your precious Russia did for him. Do you know where he is or have you simply passed a resolution to wipe him out of history?'

'That's not fair.'

'What happened to him wasn't fair either. I became a communist because I believed in James Connolly, not Joseph Stalin. You couldn't build a fucking sandcastle, Goold. Do you honestly want us to stand on the streets and urge the Irish people to throw in our lot with Britain because Stalin clicks his fingers? Go ahead and see how popular you become by suggesting that the Dublin slums get blitzed too.'

'I have a wife and child in Russia.'

'Then get on a boat to London and fight for them.'

Art gathered himself up with quiet fury. 'That's what you want. You wish me gone so you can poison Irish communism with your counter-revolutionary plot. Maybe it was you who falsely denounced my brother in Spain and arranged for me to be locked away in the Curragh so you could spread your lies.'

Hennessy turned back to the shelves. 'Yeah, me and de Valera take tea and scones regularly. You're cracked, Goold, with one foot in and one foot out of everything. If you're too chicken to fight then bugger off to the colonies and find a few misfortunate heathens to take soup in a Protestant church. We Irish natives like to do our own thinking. Now, fuck off.'

Art walked back down to the street where hawkers screamed the price of apples and urchins shouted the names of evening papers. Flocks of office girls passed on bicycles.

Art felt cold and sick. All day this sense of catastrophe and betrayal had been looming. He had been sent back to Ireland on a mission and failed. He should have known that Trotskyite saboteurs were everywhere. Never had he felt so alone. Whoever held his file in Moscow would blame him for the liquidation of the Irish branch of the Party.

He began to walk through the drizzle, unsure where he was going. For a moment he longed to be in Eva's wood in Mayo where he could reflect and know that someone still cared for him. But he could not go there because Eva would want to talk about Brendan. Over the past two years he had fought with his guilt about Brendan and won. Still Hennessy's words hurt. The strange thing was that Brendan's spirit had never felt closer than during these last few hours. Art had not eaten all day but the hunger he felt went deeper than anything he had previously known. It reminded him of stories in Donegal about the hungry grass growing over unmarked famine graves. Art tried to focus on the crowded streets, but could not shake off a feeling of being watched, as if he had only to turn his head to see Brendan behind him, dogging his footsteps. The feeling grew so strong that he began to walk quicker, pretending that it was to savour the sense of not being trapped by barbed wire. Eventually he stopped in Mountjoy Square and, breathing heavily, turned to confront the emptiness behind him.

Hennessy's reference to Brendan was a typical counter-revolutionary smear tactic. Stalin had never imprisoned any man unjustly. After Georgi Polevoy's arrest Brendan's case would have been re-opened and scrutinised. The slightest doubt would lead to Brendan's release. Brendan might be living in Moscow now as a free man, maybe serving in the Red Army. Even if Brendan was still imprisoned, Soviet camps were places of re-education with higher living standards than many Western countries. It was Art who had suffered false imprisonment for the past two years but Hennessy had only sneered at him, hatching plots with other traitors to destroy every last trace of communism here. But communism would never be dead as long as there was one righteous man still standing. If Art had to restart the movement from scratch then he would be Stalin's rock on which truth was built.

But just now a cold dread returned as if unseen eyes were watching. He leaned back against the railings of Mountjoy Square, exhausted by twenty years of constant struggle. He would have slept on a park bench but the summer drizzle was turning into heavy rain. Art wondered who lived in his old attic and what had happened to his few possessions there. Crossing the street he entered his former doorway and climbed up the bare staircase. Mrs Fleming answered the knock on her door.

'The dead arose.' She surveyed him. 'There isn't even a shoebox for rent here now. Besides, I doubt if the landlord would want you back causing trouble.'

'What happened to my stuff?'

'Burnt years ago by the Catholic Young Men's Society. I tried to save a few books but sure we couldn't even pawn them.' She sighed. 'Have you a bed for the night?'

'No.'

'A lady showed up here some years back claiming to be your sister. Said you had a lovely big house going empty in Donegal.'

'It's not empty, it's full of ghosts.'

Mrs Fleming opened her door fully. 'We've barely room for the living never mind the dead. There's space on the floor for a night or two at most. Just mind that himself doesn't fall over you staggering in from the pub.'

The children were asleep, six of them in the one bed, three

at each end. Art took the blanket Mrs Fleming offered and lay on the floorboards near the window. It was so long since he had heard traffic at night or girls' voices calling. He tried to savour every sound in this city that refused to accept him, but found himself shivering beneath the blanket as if he would never feel warm again.

THIRTY

# The Plane

## The Soviet Union, July 1941

A parched twilight began to close around the unlit prisoner train. For over a week the *zeks* in Brendan's wagon had jolted across an arid landscape they rarely glimpsed, crushed together in putrid darkness. Only those crammed against the wooden slats ever saw the small worms of daylight flicker in through the slight cracks there. Little sound penetrated into the wagon either, just the ceaseless rumble of the tracks. Sometimes the train stopped and prisoners shifted eagerly, yearning for guards to untangle the barbed wire around each carriage and eventually wedge open the doors. In the stampede to relieve themselves, dignity would be forgotten as men and women squatted together under the gaze of the guards and their dogs. But often those stops occurred for no obvious reason. There would be no sound after the wheels came to a rusty halt, no footsteps, no safety catches unleashed, no orders screamed for *zeks* to get onto their knees and be counted. Instead the train would remain motionless for an indeterminable period until eventually the wheels slowly jolted forward again and each *zek* felt a stir of relief amidst their disappointment because no decision had yet been made to liquidate them.

Three weeks ago Brendan had known that his position had become perilous when the music on the camp Tannoy was abruptly replaced by a voice from the radio denouncing Germany's treacherous attack on the Soviet Union. Even the guards stopped their morning count and during those few seconds guards and *zeks* were suddenly equal, stunned that anyone – even Hitler – could dare to defy Stalin's confident declaration that there would be no conflict in Russia. But the crackling voice spoke of German troops on Russian soil and German planes destroying the Soviet Air Force. The voice had carried defiance, exhorting comrades everywhere to give their last breath for the Motherland. But the voice also betrayed panic and indecision until it was suddenly replaced by static, with guards starting to yell at the *zeks* as if even this invasion was their fault.

Kolyma barely had enough food in times of peace. But, being no longer people, the *zeks* knew that they would suffer in this war, even though the invasion was on the other side of the USSR. That day had been like no other on the gold fields. The *zeks* had worked in silence and for once did not want their labours to end. June was milder and as nobody could recall *zeks* being shot while out on the actual gold fields, they had felt safe sieving there. That evening the guards had needed to shout at them to march quicker back to camp.

Nobody knew if they would live through the coming night. During the long count the guards had gone through lists of prisoners, weeding out those with German surnames. Brendan had been unable to stop shivering because his nationality confused the guards. Most considered him English, but some who had heard him deny this might think him German. Few guards admitted to having heard of Ireland because expressing a knowledge of countries outside the Soviet Union could be misconstrued as treason. Brendan had not known if his file still contained details of having been seen drinking with German members of POUM in Barcelona. Such information might have been enough to have him rounded up with the German prisoners that evening who were told that they were being marched to catch a boat with no time to collect their personal belongings. Few had believed it but Brendan saw them cling to this desperate hope as they were counted and then led away from the Kolyma camp.

That night the soup ration had been cut with barely a fish head or a few small bones in the bowl. But nobody had any appetite. People were waiting for the distant sound of machine-gun fire, knowing that when they returned to the huts the *urkas* would share out whatever few possessions were hidden in the mattresses of the German prisoners now in a mass grave.

During the next week in Kolyma there had been no other mass executions, but every *zek* knew that his file was being reopened. Access to radios was forbidden, letters and parcels stopped arriving. Most political prisoners had made token confessions of spying for the very forces that were now invading the USSR. This made them enemy soldiers, especially foreigners like Brendan. Every morning he had yearned for the gold fields where he could toil in safety. No slacking was allowed there, with defeatism viewed as sabotage of the war effort and punishable by death. Even after the prolonged evening counts Brendan had never felt safe because of the midnight searches, with guards stabbing open mattresses as if a fifth column of Nazis might lurk inside them. Finally, Brendan's name had been called out, along with every foreign national in the camp. They were told that they were leaving for a new camp. They had marched out beneath a banner painted by Yasili before his death, which proclaimed the glory of working for the USSR. Dogs had hurried them along, with some *zeks* openly crying and others too numbed to care. But after several days' march all had gasped in relief at the sight of a waiting boat, knowing that they were not going to be shot, for now at least. They had been crammed into the hold, with guards screaming at them until every inch of space was used. Brendan had no idea what port they finally reached, but once there they were herded towards these waiting carriages with planks nailed across the doors and this long journey had begun.

Brendan was starving now but his hunger would be worse later. He would wait until the apex of this agony before starting to slowly chew his small hunk of black bread. Nobody had yet soiled themselves so there was no stream of urine and no stink of shit. Nobody had died in the wagon today or, if they did, they had done so without attracting attention. The wagon was so quiet that for a few moments, despite a phobia that his bread might be stolen, Brendan blacked out into sleep and dreamed of Donegal. They were bathing off Bruckless Pier with Art racing hand in hand with Eva along the stone pier to tumble laughingly into the waves. Brendan saw himself, sleek as a silvery fish, flitting through the green water. Art surfaced to ruffle Brendan's hair and asked if he liked the kite that he had made for him. Brendan plunged his head into the water to glide behind his beloved big brother.

The train's unexpected jolt woke him as he crested the waves. The *zeks* began to talk, wondering if they would be allowed out into the air. Others shouted for quiet so they could listen for the click of the guards' rifles. Brendan discreetly checked that his bread was still there. No *zek* spoke but he sensed a new terror. There was just the gusting wind and the drone of an aeroplane leisurely approaching. Then the silence was broken by indistinct sounds, the bark of released dogs, guards shouting in panic, a scramble of boots scattering across the barren ground.

'The bastards,' an older *zek* muttered. 'The guards are more concerned with saving the dogs than saving us. Come back, you cowards, unlock these doors.'

The entire wagon was on its feet now, banging at the roof and wooden walls. Bursts of machine-gun fire came from above, interspersed with cries and the noise of frantic hammering from inside every wagon. Brendan heard the crush of timber and knew that one set of prisoners had succeeded in breaking free. Their shouts turned to screams amid a heavy burst of gunfire, but he could not tell if it came from the plane or if guards might have set up a machine-gun post in the undergrowth. Two men beside him kept hammering on the roof, being lifted up by other prisoners. They broke away a wooden slat, yielding a glimpse of blue sky. Everyone was screaming, but Brendan was utterly still, mesmerised by the sky above him. It was the deepening blue of an Irish summer twilight and crossing that blue patch was a small aircraft, either departing or wheeling around for another assault. The gleam made him catch his breath as it turned in a slow loop. Others saw it too and began to scream louder. But Brendan said nothing because he had become a boy again, standing on Bruckless Pier, drawing in the bright kite that his big brother had made for him.

Then a bomb burst, bringing him to his senses as it struck a carriage further down the train. The impact rocked Brendan's wagon so violently that the walls almost buckled before it toppled sideways down the siding. The wagon was filled with screams but Brendan barely heard them because the explosion left him disorientated and partially deafened. He closed his eyes and the sensation felt like being underwater amid a shoal of tumbling bodies. He knew that his face was bleeding and he could feel a wrenching pain where his right arm got wedged between falling bodies. People trapped near the roof had surely died while breaking his fall and those of the *zeks* around him.

Wooden slats burst open at the side of the wagon, wide enough for a person to crawl through. He joined in the scramble, climbing over *zeks* who were dead or dying. It was impossible to save anyone trapped there, because the German plane was swooping low, anxious to destroy the locomotive. The second explosion was blinding. Now there were flames all along the track as carriages ignited. The smell of burning flesh reminded him of Georgi's corpse being burnt in a pyre at Magadan.

Brendan's hands were covered in blood and the explosion had damaged his retinas, so he could see little beyond after-images of light. He rose to run amid the flock of *zeks*, all wheeling and turning in panic as if they possessed a single mind. They were swallows in search of Africa. They were children seeking their mothers. They were humans stripped of everything except this last impulse to live. Behind them the German plane wheeled around, the machine gunners on board spraying bullets along the tracks, delighting in their power to mow down the stragglers trying to flee. A further crackle of machine-gun fire came from the bushes where the Soviet guards were arrayed to prevent *zeks* from escaping, even though they themselves would be shot for letting the precious rolling stock be destroyed.

Brendan stopped running but the momentum of people fleeing the burning train carried him on, until he was halted by the crush of bodies at the front trying to push their way back. All that was saving him from death was the mass of bodies caught between the two hails of bullets. But, judging by the shrieks of the dying, this wall of flesh was growing

445

thinner. A man directly in front of him turned around to face Brendan, desperately trying to push deeper into the bodies. Brendan's sight was clearer now and by the light of the flames he recognised him as a vicious *urka* who had been put on the train after it was discovered that he had a foreign grandmother. Managing to free his arms amid the crowd, Brendan pinned them around the *urka*'s neck. *You're going nowhere, comrade, except to hell.* He didn't say the words aloud, but the *urka* understood them. The man had twice his strength and should have been able to fight back but seemed momentarily paralysed by fear. Then he roared into Brendan's face and lifted his hands to break the grip. He would have succeeded had a bullet not entered him. He jerked forward, eyes fixed on Brendan. His arms kept moving but only managed to drape themselves around Brendan for support. Brendan swayed with him, using the dead body as a shield, even though he knew that a direct hit would slice through them both.

Enough space was clearing for bodies to fall. Many *zeks* were dead or playing dead or so terrified that they had lost the use of their legs. Among them a small child sat on a dead woman's body, banging on the chest with her fists as if demanding that her mother rise. A lull came in the firing as if the Germans were bored, and the Soviet guards had decided to flee. But Brendan knew that this would not last. He had more chance on his own because the child would only weigh him down and even if he managed to flee he had no way of feeding her in this wilderness. But it was not in his character to leave her there. At first she screamed when he picked her up, reaching out to claw at his bloodied face. But then the firing resumed and she pressed her face against his chest, shivering in shock and with the cold. Yet her body felt warm, her face reminding him of a child he once saw in London during the General Strike. He cradled her like he knew that he would never have a chance to cradle a child of his own. Crouching down, he pushed blindly through the screaming *zeks*. He had a purpose now, a mission. All his life he had simply wanted to know that he was helping humanity in a small way, that his presence on earth would make some slight difference. This desire had led him to leave Marlborough College, had led him to Spain, had eventually led him here to run across this blood-soaked soil. Because maybe in the end it boiled down to this, to hold one child in a crowd and fight to give her an extra few seconds of life. If he succeeded he might finally have done something that earned him the right to stare back into Martin Luther's eyes.

The child pressed tightly against him, whispering words that he could not hear. He wanted to share so many things with her, wanted to describe the feel of his mother's hand stroking his hair in bed at night, the attics in the Manor House where he had played at her age, his sister Eva sketching in her studio. He wanted her to have heard a church bell instead of a siren, to wake up without the stench of mildewed clothes, to see a dog not snarling at the end of a chain. Just once in her life he wanted her to have known what it was like not to be hungry, to have lice-free hair, to picnic on a beach and have a big brother to look up to. Brendan wanted her to know these things, yet he couldn't speak because he needed to save his breath for running. A gap appeared ahead, a space through the dying *zeks*, though he was so dizzy that he no longer knew in what direction he was running. But now they were out in the open with fewer bodies here and for a second he thought they were free. Then he saw the Soviet guards with their machine guns and knew that the German plane had gone and he was running directly towards the bullets with no time to turn. He knew that the same bullet which passed through the child would enter him. They would die at the same moment, with him bearing her to her death. More than anything he wanted to tell her about Bruckless Pier. About the great dread he had always felt when running down it to fling himself out into the mercy of the waves. Because tumbling down through the depths there was always this moment when he felt truly done for, before his body instinctively turned amid the green water and he knew in the core of his being that he would rise again into the light.

# THIRTY-ONE

# The Knock

## January 1942

It was nearly midnight when the knock came. Art had just finished stapling a batch of his latest pamphlet: *Trotskyism: Its Roots and Its Fruits*, which he had self-published under the banner of Proletarian Publications. Priced at 3d, he needed to sell four hundred to recover his printing costs. After that he would give the remaining stock away free. Today it took him five hours to sell two copies, but at least it was two minds saved from the cancerous treachery that had liquidated the Communist Party of Ireland. Trotsky's paid agents in Dublin must feel threatened by his defiance as they sensed the keen edge of truth homing in on their lies. This was why their knock did not surprise him now. The opportunist traitors would want to seize every copy so as to suppress the one small voice of dissent. Art took the one knife he possessed and, clenching it in his right fist, kept it concealed behind his back as a second knock came.

He flung the door open, making himself as big as possible. Only one figure stood there, an old man with a raincoat folded under his arm. Art glanced past to see if others lurked on the stairwell, but the man seemed alone. He was no

449

policeman or cleric – Art had developed a second sense for these. But there was something familiar about his quiet gentility, recalling memories of childhood. It was hard to distinguish his features in the unlit hallway of this, the coldest tenement Art had ever lived in. The only light came from two candles stuck in old ale bottles in his room. The man removed his hat. He seemed breathless and slightly disorientated. Perhaps he was lost. Art stepped back to pick up a candle so that they would see each other clearly.

'Hello, Art.'

'Mr Barnes?'

Art could not remember when he last saw the retired manager of the Royal Bank in Donegal town. Mr Barnes whose son used to play duets with Eva on the piano. Art reserved a special contempt for bankers as lackeys of international capitalism, but found it hard to feel hostility towards this quiet figure.

'You'd better come in.'

Mr Barnes took the single chair beside the small table where the pamphlets were stacked. Art sat on the bed, watching the old man examine his spartan room. The walls were bare except for a portrait of Stalin hung from the nail where a previous tenant had erected a Sacred Heart candleholder. Noise came from the pavement below, with men congregating around the now closed pubs of Wexford Street. Somebody had started singing *The Foggy Dew*. Mr Barnes produced a white handkerchief and scrupulously cleaned his hands, although Art knew they were not dirty.

'I'm afraid I can't offer you tea,' Art said, 'or anything else for that matter, unless you would like some dry bread. There is a tap on the ground floor if you would like me to fetch you some water.'

'That's not necessary,' Mr Barnes replied. 'The stairs just

left me winded, I have been up and down so many of them. Two days I have been looking for you. I didn't want to stop and have to start again tomorrow. There's so little time, you see.' His gaze was neither kind nor aggressive, but contained a hurt bemusement. 'Prepare yourself, lad, the news I bring is bad.'

'Brendan?'

Mr Barnes shook his head. 'It's your father. He died in London three nights ago. Your mother wanted him to deliver a letter in person to the Soviet Embassy, hoping they might be more co-operative now that they're our allies. He was on his way back for the late train when an oil bomb fell close by. Having his warden's armband with him, he helped people leaving the local cinemas to reach the nearest shelter. By that time there was no chance of a train back to Oxford. An old lady was refusing to leave her kitchen because she had two cats and animals aren't allowed in bomb shelters. But your father persuaded them to let her bring one cat, then he went back out to help direct the fire crews. Afterwards people thought that he was asleep in a corner of the shelter. Only after the All Clear was given did anyone realise that he was dead, with the second cat curled up inside his coat.' Mr Barnes paused. 'Nobody knew how to contact you. I am executor of your father's will. I know a man in the Dublin constabulary who was able to say that you are frequently seen around this area.'

'So they're still keeping files on me?'

The banker leaned forward. 'Just for once in your selfish life forget about yourself. Your father is dead. Did you not hear what I said?'

'My life has not been selfish. I have kept nothing for myself.'

'Your father . . .' Mr Barnes sounded exasperated.

451

'Yes, I heard you.' Art rose. 'Do you think I am not grieving? All my life I've grieved in advance for this moment.' Walking to the window Art looked down at the men below whose casual camaraderie could turn as easily to blows. These were the people for whom he had left his family, people who jeered him when he tried to sell his pamphlet in the pubs.

One of his earliest memories was of his nurse saying that one day he would be master of the house when Father died. He had been five years of age and previously never understood why people treated him differently from his big sisters. Nurse's words had promised riches but also filled him with dread because he had never previously contemplated the fact that his beloved father could die. Her remark had set a clock ticking in his mind, a clock he had spent his life trying to hold back. Perhaps his hatred of inherited wealth sprang from the fact that what he most wanted was for Father not to die. Now that clock had finally struck. He turned to Mr Barnes.

'You think me a bad son.'

'What do you think?'

'I loved him more than any of you realised.'

'All I know is that you hurt him more than you may realise.'

Art saw that Mr Barnes was uneasy with this conversation. He was a practical man, here for practical reasons to do one final duty for a friend.

'I also know, whether you wish it or not, that you are now head of the Goold Verschoyle family, with the responsibilities that entails. You have your Travel Identity Card, don't you? I can advance funds for your trip to Oxford for the funeral. Your sister Eva has already travelled over. It will just be the pair of you and your mother. Afterwards I can explain the details of the estate to you. There is a considerable volume of papers . . .'

'Can I sell the Manor House?'

Mr Barnes sighed. 'This is hardly the time. Come and see me in Donegal.'

'It's a valid question.'

'You know the answer. The Manor House is yours for your lifetime only. After that it must be passed to your eldest son.' Mr Barnes looked up. 'You possess a son, I believe.'

Art looked down at the secondhand army boots that had seen him through the past six years. Did his son have boots for the Russian winter? Judging by reports, conditions in Russia were atrocious. Stalin's genius had made the Germans walk into his trap, imagining that the Soviet people were fleeing as they retreated towards Moscow, leaving not one grain of flour or can of gasoline behind to aid the fascists through the winter. This retreat had caused riots among traitors in Moscow, imagining that Stalin had fled to safety. But Stalin had publicly stood on the roof of the Lenin Mausoleum to steady the population. He refused to leave his people and had suffered with them as they dug machine-gun nests on every street corner. His brilliance had twice repelled the Germans who tried to storm the city, and then in the ice of December, he counter-attacked. The Germans had not taken Moscow and never would while Stalin lived to inspire liberty. The people were united in this Great Patriotic War, along with their neighbours in the newly-liberated Baltic States. But they were also starving and being butchered by enemy fire. To be stuck in Dublin was worse than manning an artillery position in minus forty degrees outside Moscow, because Art was helpless here, unable to discover if his wife and child had died in the desperate slaughter and unable to protect them if they had survived. Stalin would ensure that nobody needlessly suffered, but not even Stalin could be everywhere to watch over his people at every moment.

'What else is in the will?' Art asked.

'Can you not wait until your father is buried?'

'You're the one placing responsibilities on my shoulders. Surely you're pleased that I am not shirking them?'

'I don't have the will with me,' Mr Barnes replied. 'There is a settlement naturally on your mother – the house in Oxford goes to her. There are bequests to your siblings – you will hardly begrudge them that. Brendan's share will be put in trust, I made sure that you would not get your hands on it. There is cash and some shares and finally a property on Raglan Road in Dublin that your father inherited from his cousin. He left it to you, against my advice I may add. Still that was your father, to the last he refused to judge you.'

'What's that house worth?'

'It's a handsome property. Worth more than enough to get you out of this squalor, more than I would leave you if you were my son. I can arrange its sale, have the cash paid to you. After that I will have done my duty to your father and can wash my hands of you and the whole affair.'

Art touched one of the damp stains like obscure maps on the wall. His fingertips were black when he showed them to the retired banker. 'This squalor is how thousands of Irish people live. I possess a room to myself, therefore I am rich compared to some of my neighbours. I am sorry if the sight of reality offends you.'

Mr Barnes rose. 'I have lived longer than you. I was born ten years after a famine. People don't recover from famine, their faces never fill out again. Squalor offends my sense of justice, but a man unnecessarily wallowing in it offends my sense of decency. People here would sell their souls for a fraction of what you will receive after probate. You mock your neighbours by pretending to be like them. They are here through lack of opportunity while you are here by choice.

You cannot earn their respect like that. I imagine they think you a fool. Remember Madame Despard. Half of Dublin fleeced her until her money ran out, then they burnt the roof over her head. A fool and their cash are easily parted.'

'Have you the deeds of Raglan Road?' Art asked.

'It cannot be sold until after probate.'

'I wish to give it away.'

'At least bury your father before starting to mock him.'

'I always respected my father.'

'What sort of respect is it to scatter his possessions to the four winds?'

'I will use each possession wisely. I know people who need them.'

'Your sister in Mayo is one,' Mr Barnes insisted. 'Your brother in South Africa . . .'

'Do you understand nothing?' Art asked. 'Where would be the justice in that? I begrudge them nothing but in all conscience how can I give them what they have not earned?'

'That was their father's money, their grandfather's and great-grandfather's.' Mr Barnes was animated, consumed by a passion Art had not seen in him before – the naked self-preserving instincts of the bourgeoisie.

'It was stolen from ordinary people in rack rents and cheap wages,' Art replied. 'I will honour my father by returning it to its rightful owners. Naturally I shall pay you the standard commission for administering this.'

'You go too far in insulting me!' The old man donned his hat. 'Your father was my friend. I want no fee. I came here for his sake and because I remember you as a compassionate boy. Something terrible happened to you.'

'I grew up.'

Mr Barnes produced an envelope. 'I am advancing you enough money to get some decent clothes en route to Oxford.

You will go, won't you?' He looked anxiously at Art. 'At least do this one kindness for your mother.'

Art counted the money in the envelope and tried to return half of it. 'I will go, but in the clothes of the common man. I cannot change who I am. Father understood that.'

Mr Barnes ignored the money Art held out. One candle on the table was so low that its flame flickered wildly, slowly being snuffed out by molten wax. It cast distorting shadows on the ceiling.

'I have done my duty to an old friend. I can do no more.' He reached into his pocket again. 'The key of the Manor House.'

He placed it on the table and left. Art did not follow him out onto the dark stairwell, but stood at the window to watch the old man emerge and walk slowly away. Art kept staring down at the street because he did not want to turn and face the key on the table. He felt small and lost, a father-less son. It was good that Eva was with Mother. They shared much in common. He would be the outsider when he took the boat in the morning.

Art wanted to pray but did not believe in any God. Even atheists could believe in ghosts however. He knew why he was afraid to turn. Father's ghost was standing beside the table, watching Art not with his own eyes but with the eyes of Martin Luther. Grandpappy's ghost was there too and others in the list of ancestors which Father had traced for him as a boy. All of them gazed at him, all waiting. Art trembled. This room had never felt so cold. He was not sure how long it took him, but eventually he turned to survey the emptiness lit by a single candle flame.

'I refuse,' he said, repeatedly. 'I refuse my place in your line.'

# THIRTY-TWO

## *The Grave*

### *Donegal, May 1943*

She was always fond of tea. This was one fact that the four
men digging her grave all agreed on. The war ration of just
half an ounce a week hurt her badly, but it would have been
against Mrs Ffrench's principles to buy extra supplies from
the smugglers who plied their trade across the border. She
had been a great woman for principles, but in hard times
ordinary people needed to survive by any means possible.
So when they first set to work, the diggers – who were all
once employed by Mr Ffrench – kept up a lively conversation about the growing list of commodities that could be
smuggled across the nearby border. Potatoes and meat were
being secreted out from the Free State, while precious white
bread, petrol, bicycle tyres and black market tea were
brought in from the North. Ironically the original owners
of Bruckless House had made their fortune through smug-
gling. But, when found dead in the kitchen three days ago
Mrs Ffrench had been trying to concoct a tea substitute by
boiling up a potion of common ash and hawthorn leaves,
exactly like the poorest farm labourers used to do. The pot
had boiled dry on the range, leaving an overpowering stench

of burning. But thankfully the fire in the range had gone out or Bruckless House might have burnt down.

The young fish-seller who found her body had not really known Mrs Ffrench. That was another fact the workmen agreed upon as they walked slowly up towards Bruckless House after the grave was dug. Mrs Ffrench had lived amongst them for decades, yet nobody really knew her as anything except the communist's wife. Before the Ffrenches became communists there were rumours of some queer class of religion she was supposed to belong to. If Mr Goold Verschoyle was still walking the boreens with his hawthorn stick and a book in his pocket he would have been able to explain what it was called. Anyway, it was the sort of queer Protestant sect that a foreigner might belong to. Not that Mrs Ffrench had wanted the Protestant minister at her burial. Entering the library now where her unadorned coffin rested, the workmen fervently wished that she had. Obviously, as Catholics they could not have risked their souls by setting foot in Killaghtee Protestant church to attend such a service, but it would have felt less desolate than this.

There again, when they thought of her as anything except the master's wife, she had always cut a lonely figure even when throwing curious tea parties for local children in her young days. Seamus, the eldest workman, remembered talk about a short-lived fascination with lamps. At one time nothing would do Mrs Ffrench but to set lamps burning in every window of the house. She had made a skivvy out of herself by insisting on personally attending to each one, to the mortification of the serving girls who felt that she did not trust them with this simple task. Her lamps were the talk of the parish but then she stopped lighting them or people stopped noticing them because the gentry often got up to strange antics to pass the time. Still, for all their peculiarities, the

Ffrenches treated people fair, unlike some local farmers like Henderson who were terrors to work under. Bruckless had been a good house to work in where the master never shouted, but instead called you comrade. The one thing to be wary of was that he had always been dying for a chance to make a speech. Indeed, as the youngest man present joked, he had died trying to make one, cycling into Killybegs on a stormy night determined to confront de Valera.

The three others lifting up Mrs Ffrench's coffin had been among those left with the queer task of burying him on unconsecrated ground at the end of the garden two years ago, like a suicide or an unbaptised child condemned to limbo. But Mrs Ffrench had been insistent that his last wish be carried out. It had seemed the queerest funeral any man there ever attended. But now, as they carefully manoeuvred her coffin through the door, each realised that today was worse because there was nobody present to be a mourner. Not that the whole district didn't wish to pay their respects, but it would be a mortal sin for any Christian to attend such a pagan act. Indeed the four men had only felt able to dig her grave after the priest gave his permission, saying that the poor creature could not be left lying alone in the house.

Since the master died she had been alone in the house, heartbroken, with people seeing her walk abroad some evenings as far as the empty Manor House in Dunkineely. Sometimes she stood outside it, staring up at the unlit windows. It was said that she had loved the Goold Verschoyle children like she would have loved her own had she been blessed by any. Nobody had known who to contact when she was found with the back door wide open to the wind and rain. Likewise the four men didn't quite know what to do now as they crossed the sloping lawn and came to the open grave beside the small pier.

Very gently they placed the coffin on the grass. The three older men were silent because it didn't seem right to speak. But the youngest man started to blabber on about the first funeral he ever attended. His hands shook and the others knew how he had downed two whiskeys for courage. It was the queerest loneliest feeling to pass two ropes underneath the coffin and lower it down until it rested with a bump on the exposed wood of the master's coffin. There was not a word from the youngest man now and none of them looked at the others as they let the ropes fall. But every man was praying for the soul of this lonely woman and that God would forgive her heresy.

With uneasy haste they begin to fill in the grave and, when that job was done, turned to go. But it didn't seem proper to leave without some words being spoken. The others looked towards the oldest man who broke the silence.

'This is what the master would have wanted,' he declared softly. ''Tis the least we could do for him. It would be better if she was buried with her own kind if any of her own were left.' Glancing furtively over his shoulder, he knelt on one knee. 'But seeing as there isn't, she'd not take offence if we recited the sorrowful mysteries, would she now?'

The others didn't reply, but one by one they slowly knelt to pray for this stranger's soul.

# THIRTY-THREE

# A Tutor Comes

## Mayo, April 1944

Francis and his twenty-one-year-old tutor were walking in the woods with the dog – ostensibly to give Eva time alone with her husband before he commenced the trek back to London, but more so because she knew that Freddie made them both uncomfortable in different ways. Even Maureen had contrived to disappear after breakfast so that – with Hazel in boarding school – only Eva and Freddie remained in the crumbling house they still officially called their home. But during Freddie's four-day furlough it had not felt like a shared home. It certainly radiated a sense of belonging for Eva when Freddie was absent, and she suspected that Freddie would experience the same sensation if he returned to find all trace of her gone. But it had taken these four nights together for Eva to realise how far apart they had grown.

She could not tell what Freddie thought beneath his brusque exterior. His British army uniform – defiantly donned, against instructions, for the long train journey across Ireland – made him look like a stranger, with its various braids and insignia denoting his elevation to the rank of lieutenant colonel. But even yesterday when he entered the kitchen in his old corduroy trousers after going shooting on the bogs, he had resembled the ghost of someone she once knew rather than the person she was now familiar with. Eva heard the whiskey decanter clink against his glass as she stared out the window.

'I'm worried about the boy,' Freddie repeated, unable to drop the subject.

'Francis is fine again,' Eva replied.

'Fine when hiding in this blasted wood. But he can't hide here for ever.'

'He's studying hard.'

'Dreaming, you mean, while supposedly being taught by someone who transpires to be dreamier than he is. They could both use a haircut. When I engaged Harry Bennett I thought he would whip Francis into shape. But the reverse is true. Francis has reduced him to his own marshmallow level. I can't imagine how Harry served as a officer.'

'Harry was a classics student before donning a uniform.' Eva turned. 'You hired him as a tutor, not a drill instructor.'

'Still, I hoped he might put some backbone into Francis.' Freddie fingered his whiskey glass. 'Where the hell have they gone anyway?'

'Walking.'

'And is this how he teaches Francis his lessons?'

'It's their routine. They converse in Latin on the way out and French on the way back. It's better to be out of doors rather than stuck in some damp room that's caving in. This house is collapsing around us, Freddie, even you can see that.'

'It needs work. But nothing that can't be fixed after we give Jerry his beating.' He placed his glass on the table, steeling himself to speak with his fingers drumming softly on the surface. This was the moment he had been building towards, the question they could no longer avoid. This house had shrunk since he entered it, with Eva forced to share her bed for the first time in six months. Husband and wife and yet strangers. The alien feel of his body or any body against hers after so long. Eva was glad that Freddie had not been able to see her panicked face in the dark when he touched her on his first night home. It was his right and her duty, yet Eva had not known how she would get through it. The price of being married, the price of a crumbling sanctuary for her son. But then as Freddie's lips touched hers, the most shockingly unimaginable thing occurred. She might have cried out had his tongue not entered her mouth. Before then it had been a secret, even unto herself, and she had refused to allow the fantasy to enter her mind in their dutiful lovemaking since then. But the confusion caused by this unexpected image would not abate until Freddie returned to England.

'Do you propose returning to take your place beside me this September?' Freddie asked quietly. 'I know you hated London last year because of the difficulties surrounding the boy, but that is where our new home will be when the war is won. I could never sell Glanmire, but with my salary this could be our summer house. There's no company for you here anyhow, with half the houses gone. De Valera is using high rates to drive the rest of us out. Soon there'll only be peasant cabins and roofless Big Houses. My future lies in the army and we should plan ahead.'

Eva stared back out the window, knowing that Freddie was too proud to suspect her secret. He was right about the lack of neighbours. This current conflict had not caused the same devastating cull as the Great War, but that was only because so few Protestants remained anyway. Some had followed a path of assimilation, marrying Catholics in muted ceremonies behind closed sacristy doors with the disapproving priest's sermon consisting of a reiteration of the *Ne Temere* decree. But most had packed up for the colonies or for England. Last month she had seen Hazelwood Castle advertised for sale by the Land Commission on the stipulation that the new owners level the site. The advertisement had ignored its beautiful rooms, stressing instead the quantity of reusable lead to be scavenged off the roof. Glanmire House barely had a roof, so what excuse could she use to cling on here?

'Another English boarding school would destroy Francis,' she said.

'I have said that you can let him board in the soft Quaker place you picked in Waterford. So stop hiding behind the boy.'

'He needs me to be close for him.'

'What if I need you?' This expression of need was so unlike Freddie that Eva didn't know which of them was more shocked. She felt guilty, as if her unexpected passion on their first night had led him on.

'*Do* you need me?' She faced him.

Freddie sipped his whiskey uneasily. 'All I'm saying is that Francis must toughen up. Your Waterford Quakers won't do that for him. How do you expect him to cope with university?'

'University will be different. There'll be no bullying.' Eva didn't mean to sound so accusatory.

'There was not bullying in the last school,' Freddie snapped. 'Just some character-building ragging. I drill boys barely older than Francis to sail across the Empire on ships that could be torpedoed at any moment. Do you expect me to tell them that my own son cannot cope with some harmless traditions?'

'Those pranks were not harmless,' Eva protested. 'They were carried out by ruthless bullies. But the moment you became a lieutenant colonel nothing would stop you from packing him off to an upper-class school just so that you could feel as good as your fellow officers.'

'That's unfair.' Freddie downed the remaining whiskey. 'I wanted what was best for my son. If Castlebridge College was so terrible a decision why didn't you stop me?'

It was a valid question. One freezing winter of trying to educate the children in Glanmire Wood had been enough to endure. In the autumn of 1940 Eva had rented a house in Bray to allow Francis and Hazel to attend progressive Dublin day schools. But last spring when Freddie received his promotion and announced that he had secured Francis a place in a Hertfordshire boarding school Eva instinctively knew that such a move would be disastrous. Still she let it happen for Freddie's sake, hoping that the school might forge a bond between father and son. Although settled in Bray, Francis had been prepared to go to please his father and so Eva had dismissed her foreboding as a selfish desire to keep Francis to herself. But nothing had prepared the boy for Castlebridge College. The headmaster – with a steel plate in his skull from the Great War – flew into furies that even terrified his staff. Eva had gone to live with Freddie, to be near Francis, with Hazel happy to become a boarder in her Dublin school. Eva still felt sick at the memory of awful London cocktail parties with the other officers' wives. Battling to see who could conjure the smartest frock amidst the austerity. She had rarely heard Freddie talk at such gatherings without mentioning Francis's boarding school.

'At least I removed him from Castlebridge before too much damage was done.' Eva broke the terse silence.

'Before he found his feet, you mean,' Freddie sniped. 'Six weeks into the autumn term hardly gave the boy time to settle back in.'

'All last summer he was terrified to return. The child was losing his mind in that school and so was I with worry.'

'Don't be ridiculous!' Freddie poured another whiskey. 'He's not a child any more for a start. He merely had some problems adjusting after your mollycoddling. There may be mental illness on your side but Francis is a Fitzgerald.'

'None of my family ever locked their father in a cave with a bear,' Eva snapped.

'My ancestor might have been a lunatic but he was no coward,' Freddie said. 'He would not have been reduced to a shrivelling sissy by a few schoolboys.'

Voices came from outside as Francis and his tutor returned.

'Don't let him hear you say that,' Eva pleaded. 'He's still your son.'

'I hardly recognise him,' Freddie said wearily. 'Every time I come home he's more of a stranger. And you have changed too.'

'I haven't.'

'Life wasn't that bad in London, was it? The other wives often ask about you.'

'I'd nothing in common with them.'

'You're not being fair on yourself. You're a good-looking woman still, you could compete with the best of them.'

'Can't you understand? I don't want to compete.'

'I understand less and less. You're stuck here in the ether and I don't know how to make you think in a sensible fashion. Even your brother has started to make more sense than you. Where is your brother these days?'

'Which one?' Eva replied unfairly.

Freddie spread his hands. 'What do you expect from me? I've badgered the War Office to ask their Soviet counterparts for some record of Brendan, but do you know how many Russians are dying in this war? They haven't time to locate one misguided Irish adventurer.'

'You've done your best,' Eva admitted. She deliberately

consulted the wristwatch Freddie had bought her, to emphasise her appreciation of the gift. 'At what time is Mikey taking you to the station?'

'Any moment now. I intended to bring Francis a watch on my next trip, but he seems to have already acquired one.'

'Harry bought him one for his sixteenth birthday.'

'That's rather forward.' Freddie sounded annoyed as if the tutor had usurped his role.

'He's just showing his affection. They're like brothers at times.'

'Really?' Freddie's voice soured. 'I'm not sure I didn't make a poor choice of tutor.'

War had been the making of Freddie, giving him a chance to show leadership in a world he understood. He could be tough with those who needed toughening, fresh-faced boys with no notion of how quickly death could come in Burma and Sicily. But last October he had shown himself capable of kindness when he arranged for a young Scottish lieutenant – being invalided out of the army because of injuries received when routing the Germans in Cap Bon in North Africa – to come here and recuperate as Francis's tutor. Freddie must have felt that he was solving various problems at once. Harry Bennett was handsome and likeable but not the type of man whose company Freddie enjoyed. Perhaps he had chosen sensitively, recalling Francis's distraught condition on the night when Eva removed him from Castlebridge. But Eva suspected that Freddie hadn't really looked beyond the rank of Harry's uniform. Perhaps he was only seeing the tutor properly on this trip home.

Freddie finished his whiskey and stood up. Their conversation was over. Eva had kept him at bay, cautiously playing for a stalemate. Poor Freddie. She wondered what he said about Francis now at cocktail parties, surrounded by officers whose sons had witnessed the boy's breakdown.

'Naturally I shall stop off in Dublin to see Hazel,' Freddie said.

'Boarding school suits her,' Eva replied.

'Quite.'

Hazel was enjoying boarding school, standing out for her good looks and tomboy behaviour. Francis had been equally popular as a dayboy in Dublin. But his confidence was so shattered after Castlebridge that Eva had brought him back to Mayo to let him slowly regain his self-belief. Since Harry Bennett's arrival his old high spirits had returned. But symptoms of nervous tension, evident throughout his father's stay, were visible now as Francis opened the drawing room door, aware that they had been discussing him.

'I hope Harry and I were not too long,' Francis said. 'We hurried back for fear of missing you.'

'There's little enough chance of Mikey being on time.' Freddie's joviality was forced. 'And no chance of the train.'

'The train would wait if they knew you were coming,' Francis replied.

'Probably hoping I'll bring a few logs along to burn, eh?'

The laughter sounded hollow on both sides. During this trip they had skirted around each other, equally at a loss about what to say next.

'I'd better pop downstairs and bid adieu to Maureen if she's back, what?'

Freddie disappeared into the hallway. Francis stared at Eva anxiously.

'He's not sending me back to England, is he?'

'He has agreed for you to stay here until September and then go to the Quakers.'

'And he won't send Harry away until then either? I mean we work hard together.'

'Your father is not proposing to send either of you anywhere.'

'That's okay then.' The boy was relieved. 'I knew you'd put in a good word. I know how . . .' Francis glanced at her as if they shared a secret, then listened. 'There's the cart.'

Eva heard a creak of wheels and both she and Francis gave a sigh of relief, then shifted guiltily for allowing the other to see it.

'I'd better tell Father. He has a long journey.'

'Yes,' Eva said. 'Tell him.' Her son's conspiratorial glance worried her. Francis knew her better than herself. Had he already guessed that Eva couldn't wait for Freddie to be gone so she could be alone with her two young men? She had not faced this shocking truth until she found herself returning Freddie's kisses in the dark and imagining the feel of Harry Bennett's lips. Over the past six months she had grown close to Harry, with the tutor reading her poetry late at night when Francis was in bed. Their souls shared much in common, yet Eva had previously not allowed her mind to dwell on him in a physical way. It was impossible. She was married and Harry far younger. So four nights ago Eva had been shocked to find herself committing mental adultery. In her mind it had been Harry Bennett's body moving inside her, making her respond in ways that excited Freddie. For the last three nights she had carefully blocked out all such thoughts. But by day she felt confused and guilty. She could never be unfaithful and certainly not with someone closer to Francis in age. Yet she yearned for tonight when the house would belong to her again, with Francis asleep and Harry sitting up with her, their heads bent close over some book.

She heard Freddie ascend the kitchen stairs with Francis and Maureen following. Harry Bennett came to the doorway of the bedroom he shared with Francis – the only one upstairs still inhabitable apart from her own. Freddie glanced around, sensing them all secretly waiting for him to go.

'Better not keep Mikey waiting, eh?' He picked up his single case. For every trip home he seemed to pack less. Francis accompanied him to the doorway. Eva suspected that this awkwardness between father and son could only grow worse with time. The tragedy was that it would not take much to make Freddie proud. He was not a father who needed to produce a genius. Freddie just wanted his son to be an able-bodied version of himself. A good shot and sport, a man's man who could hold his drink and talk as an equal to anyone. But Francis made friends in a different way. Freddie's fellow officers would think him frightfully wet, someone who left himself open to the possibility of ridicule, a spirit too free for his own good. She watched them shake hands warily. Harry Bennett kept his distance until Freddie turned.

'Keep up the good work, Bennett. His Latin sounds capital to me.'

'Thank you, sir.'

'We have a gold medal prospect for Trinity, eh?'

'Francis should certainly be able to hold his own when he resumes his schooling.'

'And no doubt the time is coming for you to rejoin the war effort. You look a new man after your rest here.'

'Late summer should see me back in London if they can find use for a cripple. I'll look you up, sir.'

'Excellent.' Freddie peered down the hallway. 'Meanwhile you keep them all shipshape, Maureen.'

'I'll do my best, sir.'

Freddie shouldered his case and limped towards the cart, with the dog at his heels wagging her tail. Eva followed, aware of a collective release of tension behind her. He hoisted the case onto the cart and turned, while she fed the horse the apple she had been saving.

'London isn't that far away,' he said, quietly so that Mikey couldn't hear. 'The Irish Sea is the safest for shipping in Europe. They never shifted me from those married quarters after you left. I rather rattle around in them alone.'

'Let's see how Francis does in Waterford.' Eva removed an imaginary thread from his uniform to emphasise his smartness.

The petrol crisis meant that it was months since Eva had seen a motor car on the roads in Mayo. But she knew that Freddie would enjoy sitting up on Mikey's cart as it passed through Turlough village. It would help erase the shame of his penniless retreat six years ago, with bailiffs at his door. He would nod to the Durcan women and Delia when they came to their shop doorways, accept good wishes from men waiting with their horses at the forge and women chatting outside McQuaid's post office, store up nods of respect against any bad times ahead. Finally he was the poor relation who made good.

He kissed Eva and climbed up, his greatcoat and officer's cap folded on his lap. Mikey made a noise in his throat and the horse started off, bearing him back into the army world in which she had been lost when trying to live as his wife. When would they meet again? She felt a familiar foreboding for him as he returned to the constant bombardments of London. Freddie looked down with an echo of the smile that once charmed her in Donegal. Momentarily he seemed younger and there was much she wanted to say.

She put her hand on the slowly moving cart as if to stop it. He said something, softly so that Mikey couldn't hear, but the creak of the cart prevented his words from reaching her. He touched her hand before the cart slipped beyond her grasp as the horse strained forward. Freddie called cheerily to the others as he was borne away beneath the overhang of chestnut branches.

Eva walked back up to the steps. Nobody said anything, their looks conspiratorial, unwilling to admit their relief at his departure. Freddie had sensed this too. Throughout his stay he must have known that he was an outsider in this sanctuary paid for by his wages.

'Will you be eating upstairs or down?' Maureen asked, despite already knowing the answer.

'The kitchen will do fine, like before. It will save the carrying.'

Eva felt a sudden stab of jealousy at the way Maureen glanced at Harry and smiled as she went back inside. Harry and Francis went off to resume their lessons, her son touching her shoulder as he passed. Eva was tired and confused. She wanted to change the sheets on her bed. She wanted to bathe. Just for a moment she wanted to be in a good house with electric light and bath taps. She lit a cigarette, held the smoke deep inside her, then breathed out. Spitefully, she thought of eating upstairs with the boys. Even farmers with meagre holdings rarely ate with their servants. Then she stubbed out the cigarette, ashamed. When had she ever considered Maureen a servant? They lived as equals, confiding secrets. But the girl's smile at Harry had infuriated her. Though why shouldn't Maureen smile? She was Harry's age, he was a good-looking man and even the slight limp left by shrapnel added to his attractiveness. Eva doubted if Harry would marry a girl like Maureen, but romance blossomed in unexpected circumstances. She should know this, but in truth Eva knew nothing. Over the past few days she had found herself analysing every comment the young Scotsman ever made, unsure if she was conjuring meanings that were not there.

She recalled the night when he first came. In Italy the Allies were breaching the German lines on the River Volturno and in Mayo there was sufficient snowfall to make the avenue impassable except on foot. Francis had been sent down to the gate lodge to await him, still nervous of meeting people after Castlebridge. An hour had passed, with Eva anxious about her son freezing in that roofless lodge. She had been unsure if the tutor would object to sharing a room with Francis. His journey would have been difficult. When boarding a train in Dublin there was no guarantee of how long it would take to reach Castlebar. Freddie's letter had been short on specifics: '*The chap was a classics student in Edinburgh University before enlisting. From a good Scottish family. I met him by chance, visiting one of my boys in hospital. He seems more your type than mine. I sold him the idea of getting some peace, a bit of shooting, a chance to recover his strength. The poor blither definitely needs country air. He will be good for Francis in the short term, though I suspect he'll soon be raring to get back into the swing of things . . .*'

Another wounded soldier seeking refuge. Eva had half expected that, if and when he appeared, Francis would need to support him, head bandaged, wincing in pain. The way she sometimes imagined Brendan reappearing. But when she finally spied them beneath the chestnut tree, Francis and the tutor had been walking steadily, his limp barely perceptive, their heads close together, both clasping a handle of his cardboard suitcase. They were laughing and something about their faces that night was beautiful. She knew at once they would be friends. But only now did she realise how important Harry had become to all of them living here.

Eva went inside to change the sheets on her bed in the Commander's old room, which by now was almost as damp as the basement bedroom where Maureen slept. Through the wall she heard Francis and Harry discuss something in low voices. She locked her door, undressed and washed fully with cool water, then chose a frock that made her younger, something Maureen occasionally asked to borrow. Freddie's train would leave Castlebar soon, crammed with emigrants bound for England. The Free State government was so concerned about this exodus that they were trying to ban farm labourers from emigrating, while actively encouraging a clear-out from the Dublin slums. The Liverpool boat would be packed by the time Freddie got on board. She should have persuaded him not to wear his British uniform. It was one thing in Mayo where his name was a shield, but she worried for him among the dockside crowds.

Maureen looked up when Eva entered the kitchen to help her.

'Mr Fitzgerald gave me a bigger present than he needed to. He's a generous man.'

'Freddie was never good with money.'

'It's lucky he doesn't need to be any more. Dinner won't be long.'

'Is there anything I can do?'

Maureen eyed her summer frock and freshly washed hair. 'Sure I'm right as rain, Mrs Fitzgerald.'

Convinced that she was about to blush, Eva walked out into the sunshine. The air was still. Even the squabbling songbirds were silent in the trees. A scent of wild garlic came from a bank of woodrush and bilberry. Normally Eva hated to see wild flowers indoors but just for tonight she allowed herself to pick a whole armful. Filling a vase with water she left them on the kitchen table before setting it for four. Francis and Harry clattered down the stairs in a cacophony of clowning and laughter. They washed their hands at the basin, flicking water at each other as Maureen half-teased and half-scolded them. Eva picked up the book that Freddie had smuggled home for her, *Put Out More Flags* by Evelyn Waugh. Another writer banned from Castlebar Library. She would finish it quickly and loan it to Harry.

Because she was so looking forward to sitting by the fire with him, she felt that dinner would never end, with the small talk afterwards and the nightly stroll by all four of them through the woods. But eventually it came time when she could suggest that Francis think of bed. Maureen finished moving about and the house was dark except for three candles in the candelabrum above the hall fire where half-burnt logs yielded a marvellous scent of ash. Just Harry and she were left in two fireside chairs. Shadows stirred around them, an odd spark spat from the logs and they could discuss things which Freddie would never understand. Harry made the war distant, rarely mentioning his experiences in France. He made the poverty and rationing of wartime Ireland distant too. His manner reminded her of the classmates Art once brought home to Donegal whose youthful idealism had made poetry seem as vital as bread. Both of them were tired, yet neither seemed keen to stop talking.

An hour passed before Harry excused himself for a moment and opened the door out into the night air to cross the gravel. She could imagine him in shirtsleeves and braces, relieving himself at the forest's edge. A noise made her turn. Francis had opened his bedroom door and stood there, his face pale in the candlelight.

'Did our voices wake you, darling? I'm sorry.'

'I haven't been asleep, Mummy. But I'm exhausted.'

'What's stopping you going asleep?'

The boy swallowed, choosing his words carefully.

'Waiting for Harry.' He paused. 'I don't think Harry will ever marry, Mummy. He told me he never intends to.' Eva sensed that he was trying to convey something she had not yet grasped. Francis glanced towards the open door. 'The thing is, Harry is not really interested in women.'

'I'm already married,' Eva sounded like a guilty schoolgirl. 'You don't think I . . . ?'

'I think . . .' Francis searched for the right words. 'He would sooner not have me lying awake so long for him.'

His gaze was patient, knowing how her brain was slow to grasp things. But she was piecing together clues she had never understood. Mother's unease on the night Francis dressed up to dance in her room. Freddie's discomfiture at the length of Harry's stay, a displeasure she had interpreted as relating to herself. Francis telling her how the boys in Castlebridge mocked him because he didn't want to swap picture cards of women in suspenders. But girls flocked to Francis and he loved their company, so he couldn't be . . . Eva didn't even know the correct term, just vulgar expressions overheard from men swapping jokes when they thought she wasn't listening.

Harry's footsteps began to cross the gravel. Eva stared at her son who had never kept secrets from her. The fear on his face showed that he knew she now understood.

'You won't tell Father?'

'Of course not.' Her voice was barely a whisper as Harry's footsteps drew near. 'Go back to bed, son.'

Francis closed his door. Harry entered and went to sit down, but something about Eva made him stop.

'What is it?' he asked.

'It's late.'

'Are you tired?'

'I think . . .' She paused. What did she think? Eva thought of asking him to fetch her a brandy from the bottle Freddie hadn't finished. She considered ordering him to leave the house immediately. She thought of her own innocence and all the missed signs during these months. Did Maureen know? She doubted if Maureen knew that such men existed. What attracted her to Harry was the exact gentle quality that existed in Francis, the sensibility that made Freddie bristle. There was something deeply alike in them. They had been lovers, perhaps from the night he arrived. Eva didn't know how such men recognised this quality in each other, who made the first move or who did what. She had never needed to consider such things before. She had thought to create an ark here for Francis, a safe miniature universe. But at night in their room they had created a smaller world within her world, a galaxy of male love where she knew instinctively that Francis felt happy and secure.

Harry looked concerned, his face betraying an anxiety she sometimes glimpsed when Freddie addressed him. The terror of being exposed, dragged into the dock or down a lane for a beating. *Bugger boy* – that was the phrase Freddie once used to refer to a young soldier drummed out of the army and into prison. Would he use it about her darling son, his son? Did he suspect or simply not want to know? How long had it taken Francis to find the courage to tell her? He had done so partly to protect her, sensing her growing interest in Harry, just like she sensed Maureen's similar interest. Subconsciously, all three of them had been competing for the same man. The notion of Francis and her as rivals was too bizarre. Besides Francis was only a child. But he wasn't any more. Eva thought of how mature he had looked in that doorway, how he lay awake now. Children did not belong to you. They grew beyond you and could not be caged by your expectations. Her hands shook as she stared up at Harry's concerned face.

'I think I'll sit here for a while.' She struggled to keep her voice steady. 'But maybe it's time you went to bed.'

She held his gaze, knowing how he could sense a change between them. Eva picked up the Evelyn Waugh novel and pretended to read. Harry watched her for a moment longer.

'Good night then,' he said.

'Good night, Harry.'

Eva waited until his door was closed before lowering the book. She blew the candles out and stood in the dying firelight listening to the silence from the other room. She knew that she should go to bed but seemed unable to move. It had been such a long day and there would be other long days ahead. Her perpetual fear for Francis. The secret she could never share. Art's communism would seem a minor scandal compared to this. Despite the fire she felt cold and desperately alone. But another sensation was growing within her. A curious relief amidst her fear, a faint inkling of joy. Her son had been lost, cast adrift in boarding school with his secret burden, terrified and imagining himself to be one of a kind. Yet here in the midst of this wood, he had found happiness with a lover who made him sane again.

Eva ran her fingers down the blistered paintwork of the bedroom door behind which her two young men lay entwined, then took away her hand, knowing she could not intrude into that world where he was safe. Bolting the front door against the world, she went alone to her bed.

# THIRTY-FOUR

# Make Room

*Russia, 1944*

The original rail track here had been destroyed during the initial retreat under Stalin's scorched earth policy. The advancing Germans had repaired it when they imagined themselves rulers from the Baltic to the Black Sea. But the remnants of the occupying German armies were now fragmented, no longer connected by this railroad since the Red Army's advances at Nevel and Ovruch. For months the fascists had been on the run, surrendering Zhmerinka and Vinnitsa and Kamenets Podolskiy in disarray. Odessa had been taken without a fight and soon the Crimea would be fully in Soviet hands again. The fascists were retreating so fast that this small company of fascist soldiers had become isolated here or else had been left behind on a suicide mission to try and briefly slow the Red Army. If so they were unfortunate in encountering Savinkov's unit. The generals in Moscow could focus on the overall battle, but Savinkov's expertise – built on three years of slaughter – was to attack, regroup and attack again in a succession of constant local actions that hounded the Germans. Therefore his unit was well blooded for this short combat during which they encircled and then annihilated the German soldiers who refused to surrender. Savinkov lost five men before the final fascist was killed. He was used to the smell of death and the wide-eyed stares of the slain. Even so, something shocked him now as he stalked through the corpses searching for telltale signs of men faking death. This war had aged him. Last winter his hair turned grey, not as a result of the wounds he received but upon hearing of the deaths of both his sons.

It was their faces he kept expecting to glimpse as he turned over each body with his boot, because almost every boy here was the same age as them. Their faces were young, yet each had the eyes of a wizened man. His own baby-faced soldiers who were now starting to dig a mass grave had the air of veterans, though few were out of their teens. Their hands were hard. At times their hearts terrified him.

No movement came from the young German whose body he turned over but even without kneeling Savinkov knew that he was alive. The boy's eyes were tightly closed, his uniform soaked in blood. It was impossible to tell if he was conscious. Savinkov knelt and touched his smooth unmarked face. He wondered if either of his sons had ever learnt to shave, or kiss a woman. They were sixteen and seventeen when they died but, as it was three years since he was last home, he found it hard to envisage them being that old. This German boy had never shaved. Savinkov now knew that he was conscious, terrified to open his eyes. Even if he were a Russian, Savinkov could not save him with those wounds. The least he could do was ensure that he was not buried alive because that was the fear which haunted Savinkov's dreams, that his sons had been tossed in a grave while still breathing, unable to speak but forced to mutely watch the clay being shovelled in as they lay among the corpses. A shout from one of his men made him look up.

'Comrade Savinkov, we can't dig any deeper. There's a mass grave here from before.'

'Who is in it?'

'Impossible to say. *Zeks* maybe, by the look of the uniforms. There are dozens of adults and children or what's left of them.'

The German boy gave an involuntary twitch as the pistol gently touched his forehead. Savinkov hoped that the eyes would not open because he knew that he would recognise them. 'Keep digging, comrades,' he ordered. 'We haven't time to start again. Why should only the living suffer? We've endured enough.' Looking away, he pulled the trigger once. 'The dead will simply have to make room.'

# THIRTY-FIVE

# *Home*

*January 1945*

The stationmaster in Donegal town was unsure if any service could be provided this evening, because, as he phrased it, an engine that had chugged out into the blue this afternoon had stayed out in the blue, unable to scavenge sufficient fuel to complete its return journey. When Art was finally summoned from the freezing waiting room an ancient carriage had been rigged up so that a single horse could pull it along the track. The only other passengers were an old couple travelling to Killybegs, the man bereft of teeth and with such a thick mumble that Art could not decide if he was addressing his wife in Irish or English until he finally made out a few words about the state funeral for the fascist leader, O'Duffy, in Dublin. The carriage was unlit, with the driver, wrapped in a greatcoat, sucking on an empty pipe on the open platform at the front. On their slow journey out from Donegal town Art convinced himself that the key in his wallet would not fit. He had been carrying it on him since that night in 1942 when Mr Barnes sought out his Wexford Street flat. On a dozen occasions he came close to flinging it away, but at other times found himself waking in an irrational panic and needing to check his wallet to ensure that it remained safely there. The key to the Manor House was like a curse he could not escape from and finally, after years of prevarication, it was leading him back to face the ghosts.

It appeared as if all that was left to face *was* ghosts because when they eventually reached Dunkineely, nobody was present in the station, lit by a single oil lamp suspended from a hook above the deserted platform. Art wondered if news of his arrival in Donegal had reached the village in advance.

The driver looked back, expecting Art to leave the freezing carriage. But although he opened the door for a moment, a foreboding prevented him from stepping down. He shouted out that he would continue on to Bruckless. The driver shrugged and made a soft clicking noise to the horse before the carriage lurched forward again.

The smell of the sea in Donegal was different from anywhere he had ever visited. Art remembered trying to describe that special aroma of seaweed, salt, heather and poverty to his wife in their Moscow flat. As the horse lumbered on he realised how much he loved this coastline. The memory of every outcrop of rock and crooked ditch was implanted in his brain. Such irrational love was indulgent. The only love worthy of respect was love for one's fellow man, the love that made him slave every day in the face of ignorance and greed. *Leave your home*, Christ, the first true Marxist, had said. *Give up your family and your possessions, put away childish things and follow me*. Art had tried to follow this call. He would never have set foot here again were it not for the key in his wallet.

Donegal was poor when he left and this war had not helped. A quarter-century of alleged freedom had yielded nothing for the disorganised serfs clinging to smallholdings and superstition in these glens. The only money ever spent was whenever American GIs stationed in Northern Ireland clandestinely crossed the border on drinking expeditions.

Bruckless station was in total darkness. Art dismounted with his suitcase. The carriage wheels creaked as the horse plodded away. It was late, with frost starting to form. He crossed the small hump-backed bridge leading to the gates of Bruckless House. A light burned in the library window as Art walked up the dark avenue. He did not know who lived here now – some distant relation of Ffrench's. Art felt tempted to creep up to the window and gaze in at the fireside where he had first learned the truths that sustained him in the decades since. But he kept to the shadow of the trees because he had come here not to visit the living but the dead. He knew the location, by the small pier he had loved as a boy. Ffrench had often discussed his plans, laughing in advance at the outrage that his burial would cause. Here it stood in the moonlight, a plain stone slab unadorned by religious shibboleths or the comfort of pious untruths. Mrs Ffrench had chosen to share this unconsecrated grave, close to the water and within sight of their old home. Art traced the inscription with his fingers, then lit a match to read it: '*Thomas Roderick Ffrench: The Immortality of the Dead Exists Only in the Minds of the Living*'. The match spluttered out and Art hunched down, aware of how cold he was. He had not anticipated such grief. He had felt differently at Father's funeral, mainly because of the need to steel himself against the unspoken hostility of many mourners who gazed at Art as if he had personally killed him. But here in the dark, grief ambushed him with no witnesses. For Father, for the Ffrenches, for those whom he did not know to be alive or dead. Among the living only Mother refused to judge him. She understood that he had not chosen this path: it had chosen Art to do penance for the sins of previous generations.

484

Walking out onto the pier, he recalled the sound of laughing bodies running down these stones in swimsuits. It had been wrong not to get off at Dunkineely, wrong to allow nostalgia to distract him from the work to be done. Art had come here not to remember the past but to help build the future. Finding it impossible to ignore his legacy, he must confront it. Picking up his suitcase he left the grave and commenced the long walk to Dunkineely. By next spring the Manor House would echo again with young laughter. It would not be a home for one family, but a home from home for dozens of families who, in the past, had only ever entered such houses through the servants' door. Whole generations born in the Dublin slums had never known a holiday, but Art would ensure that at least some of them would enjoy the same privileges enshrined for honest workers under Soviet law. Western saboteurs had managed to prevent this system from functioning fully while Art was in Russia. But he had once visited a workers' rest home on the Baltic Sea and Brendan had spoken about even finer sanatoria, run by the NKVD, where the traitor Polevoy had taken him to stay.

This final solution to the Manor House problem had occurred to him while studying an appraisal of the extraordinary success of rest homes in a Soviet magazine he procured for the library of the newly established Irish Workers' League. It had taken time over the past two years to re-establish contact with loyal communists in Dublin who, like him, were outraged at the liquidation of the Irish Communist Party by Trotskyite opportunists. But the newly formed Irish Workers' League was the true voice of Irish communism, resolutely obedient to the wisdom of Moscow. Without the Raglan Road house which Art had inherited from Father it might have been difficult to provide a forum for this party. But once word spread that Art possessed such a large house on an exclusive Dublin thoroughfare which he wanted to give away to be used as a headquarters, comrades had emerged to form a committee to assume responsibility for the property once Art signed over the deeds. For the past year Art had lived in an attic flat in that house, working on the renovations to turn it into offices and lecture rooms. Jim Gralton had been deported from Ireland for trying to give ordinary people in Leitrim such a meeting place. Art had arranged for the committee to pay him the wages of an ordinary Dublin carpenter, with a deduction for his rent. Funds were low and they could only pay him this wage when he also donated most of the small bequests that Father left him.

Still it had been his own fault not to clarify in advance his exact position within the Workers' League once the building work was completed. He had imagined being employed as a caretaker, somebody who modestly excluded himself from power but was on hand to offer guidance when complex ideological issues arose. In retrospect he realised that his expectation had been a reactionary stance, because it implied that the Workers' League owed him something. To stake any claim on the Raglan Road headquarters would be to validate the bourgeois concept of inherited wealth. Perhaps he might have tried harder to make small talk with his new comrades, but he utterly disputed the contention that he – of all people – was overtly dogmatic. He had simply exercised the freedom to speak his mind, whether people liked it or not. Similarly they had now exercised their freedom to employ a different caretaker, making it clear that while they were not evicting Art from his attic flat, there were better ways in which his room could be utilised to the maximum benefit of the party.

Two days ago while packing to leave, he remembered a story that Madame Despard once told him. Before she bought Eccles Street, she had owned a house in Dublin, which she invited Maud Gonne MacBride to share. Maud Gonne in turn had invited other Diehard Republicans until every room was packed. One day, sensing an atmosphere of discord within the house, she asked Maud Gonne if there might be anyone present who did not belong. Gently Maud Gonne had explained that indeed there was, but people had been too polite to tell Madame Despard how she in fact was the intruder. Art had left Raglan Road, aware that some comrades were relieved to see him go. But he had achieved his ambition and defeated the traitors by helping to start a new party. Budapest and Warsaw were in Soviet hands, with the Red Army nearing the German border. They would reach Berlin before the imperialists, with this new clandestine Irish communist party positioned to reap the avalanche of recruits unleashed by a Soviet victory.

All that remained in Ireland for him to do was liberate the Manor House from its past. Having sold Father's final two bequests he would need to be frugal in his personal needs and do all the physical labour himself. But by Easter the house would be packed with Dublin slum families. This would also be good for Dunkineely, with outsiders spending money and spreading ideas.

Eventually he reached the main street of Dunkineely. There was no street lighting, but here and there lights shone in windows. Some bicycles were parked outside MacShane's pub. A man emerged from the doorway and stared at Art, then ducked back inside. Art walked on, guessing that a small knot of drinkers would come to the door to stare after him. Passing the Methodist Hall he reached his old home. But he could not look up because he was convinced that figures stood in the darkness at every unlit window, staring down.

Art was freezing. For a moment he panicked, thinking that he had misplaced the key. He did not know if Father had left any furniture behind or if the house had been looted during the years when it stood empty. The sense of being watched was overwhelming. Slowly he inserted the key and slowly it turned.

Pushing open the door he stared into the dark hall before he entered. It smelt of damp and stale air. He needed to brush aside cobwebs. A boy in a comic hat was watching from the top of the stairs. Art knew that he was there, although he could not see him. The door to Father's study was open. Art walked in and stared at the accusatorial eyes of Martin Luther. For ten minutes he remained frozen, forced to appraise every deed in his life since he last stood there. Then finally, breaking the spell, he crossed the room and removed that portrait from the wall.

# THIRTY-SIX

# The Former People

## Easter 1945

The three Dublin families – chosen by Art for having never previously known a holiday, beyond day trips to Skerries – would share her slow journey up to Donegal. The route through Northern Ireland was simpler, but Eva knew that – with one husband wanted there for Republican activities – the families were reluctant to cross the border. Standing in Dublin's Broadstone Station Eva enjoyed watching the excited children clamber in and out of the carriages. Curiosity made her wish to travel alongside them. The three mothers anxiously glanced back along the platform for any sight of their husbands. The guard had appeared with his flag before three men emerged from the public bar to vault the barrier and join their families, joking that they would feel homesick by the time the train passed the Cabra siding.

Climbing into her carriage, Eva leaned out to watch the last man board the train as it slowly began to move. She was right not to introduce herself. They might plague her with questions about the Manor House that she couldn't answer. The size of the families concerned her, but Art knew what he was doing, having told Eva about his study of Soviet sanatoria. It would be intrusive for her to tell the travelling children how some of them would sleep tonight in the room where she once slept as a child. Their mothers might misunderstand and think that she resented their arrival. But Eva felt no regrets and was simply pleased that Art had found a role for himself. Unexpectedly writing to her some months ago, he had radiated a crusading enthusiasm when outlining his plans to renovate the Manor House as a rest home where slum families might experience the sort of holiday enjoyed as a right by Soviet citizens.

Eva was not sure what intrigued Francis and Hazel about Art's letter but they had persuaded her to let them spend their Easter holidays working with him in Donegal before the Manor House received its first guests. Now she would join them for the opening, returning to her village after eighteen years.

During this time she often longed to revisit Dunkineely and see the faces that populated her dreams. But she could not have borne to see the Manor House lying empty, with nobody to repair the roof tiles or stop rain splashing through the broken windows. It would have felt like a fairy tale gone wrong. The bewitched castle, not hidden by an enchanted forest but simply abandoned by the prince with the only key who refused to return. Sometimes she still dreamt that her younger self was trapped in those rooms, with neighbours unable to see her banging on the windows as they passed.

Now at last the house would come alive, with laughter again on the stairwell. Francis's postcard had mentioned rigging up a tent beside the tennis court where Maud and Eva had often slept out in summer in long cotton nightgowns. Tonight she would sleep out there with her daughter and son and tomorrow they would bathe at Paradise Pier.

The old pet name for the pier excited her, with memories flooding in as the train slowly journeyed across Ireland.

When they eventually reached Boyle there was a long delay as more fuel was sought before the train crawled past Ballymote and Collooney to terminate at Sligo where Eva was glad to step onto the platform. She could smell the sea and her heart thrilled at being in the west. The Dublin mothers looked apprehensive, surveying this foreign world but their children were ecstatic to be liberated from the cramped carriages. As they raced around the crowded platform, one small girl bumped into Eva. She stepped back and Eva smiled, bending slightly down to the child's eye level.

'What's your name?'

'Theresa. What's yours?'

'Eva.'

'You're very small, missus. Why did you stop growing?'

'I just did. Are you excited?'

'I'm hungry.'

'I'm sure there'll be lovely food in Dunkineely.'

The child ran back to whisper something to her mother who glanced sharply at Eva. The husbands were unloading suitcases tied with twine, though one family's possessions were in flour sacks. Art had supplied tickets for the unreliable bus service to Donegal town, which, Eva knew, might not depart for hours. The way the families clustered together for protection filled her with foreboding. She should not have mentioned Dunkineely because all the adults were staring at her now. Eva smiled at Theresa who glanced up at her mother for permission before waving back shyly. Walking out through the station forecourt, Eva claimed a window seat on the bus so as to be able to look out at Donegal Bay.

Finally the vehicle chugged into life, with the children crushed into the back seats, complaining of feeling sick. The vehicle was slow and the road badly-surfaced, but every bend drew her closer to home. Rosses Point was visible before they turned inland. Then, after a long wait, came the first view across Donegal Bay, with Slieve League rising up from the vast expanse of sea. There was Kilcar and Killybegs where the fishing fleet would be out and – at the base of the jutting finger of St John's Point – stood Dunkineely. From here it was only a speck, but she could picture it clearly in her mind.

The bus reached Bundoran, where a sign outside the Atlantic Hotel boasted of every modern convenience, including hot and cold water in the bedrooms. The Corner Teashop retained its handpainted slogan for *Dainty teas at moderate prices*.

The Dublin children stared excitedly at the holidaymakers along the promenade. The sands stretched for miles, packed with bathers. Cordoned-off sections were equipped with changing huts for women and children, with mixed bathing allowed in some areas. A deputation from the back of the bus asked the driver if this was Dunkineely. The man laughed.

'You see the priests' bathing pool out among the rocks? You could drown all of Dunkineely in that puddle without a soul noticing. You need to get another train from Donegal town.'

The two women began to walk back to their disappointed children. Theresa's mother stopped as they passed Eva.

'Are you following us, missus? My daughter says you knew where we're going. Are you from the church?'

'I beg your pardon?'

'Me and me sister were snatched off a boat by priests when a Liverpool family offered to feed us during the 1913 Lock-Out. It was the sight of us starving that drove my father back to work. But I'll not see my chislers denied a holiday because it doesn't have your blessing.'

'I'm not Roman Catholic. Art Goold is my brother.' Eva

reached into her bag for two nut roasts she had brought to eat herself. 'Share these among the children, they must be hungry.'

Both women suspiciously examined the offering.

'What are these yokes?' the other mother asked.

'There's no meat in it. I don't eat meat.'

'No more than ourselves. Sure, who can afford it, missus? But I've two pigs' heads wrapped up in a cloth and we won't see you stuck tonight.'

The women returned to their seats to share out the food among the children who were too hungry to grumble at the unusual taste. At Ballyshannon, Theresa was sent up with an older girl to say thanks. Eva quoted for them lines written by the town's poet, William Allingham, about Donegal.

> *'Up the airy mountain,*
> *Down the rushy glen,*
> *We daren't go a-hunting*
> *For fear of little men:*
> *Wee folk, good folk,*
> *Trooping all together;*
> *Green jacket, red cap,*
> *And white owl's feather!'*

The older girl was inhibited and keen to retreat, but Theresa laughed at the poem, with her open face reminding Eva about the paints and brushes in her bag. In recent years Eva had only ever painted walls and ceilings, often working all night, caught up in the hypnotic rhythm with a meditative quality in the strokes letting her open her soul to prayer. It always felt like brushing away the past, making every surface new. Eva knew by now that she would never be an artist, but lately she had started to wonder if she might possibly have a vocation to teach. This evening she planned to erect an easel in the garden in Dunkineely. If children gathered around with their natural fascination, she would pin up a clean sheet and let each child paint whatever possessed their imaginations. She would encourage the others to leave the working child alone, with neither jeers nor comments allowed to interrupt the joy of creation.

'Give us more of them words.' Theresa resisted the older girl's efforts to drag her away.

> *'High on the hill-top*
> *The old King sits;*
> *He is now so old and grey*
> *He's nigh lost his wits.*
> *With a bridge of white mist*
> *Columbkill he crosses,*
> *On his stately journeys*
> *From Slieve League to Rosses.'*

'Are there really fairies in Donegal?' Theresa asked.

'Don't be silly.' The older girl finally managed to drag her away. 'There's only cow shite and bogmen.'

Eva smiled and stared out as the bus neared Donegal town. Francis and Hazel had promised to collect her by pony and trap, but Art would be unable to transport the Dublin families except by the irregular CDRJC train that meandered towards Killybegs. Exhausted babies cried from the back seat as faces peered out desperate for this journey to end. The bus chugged into the Diamond and everyone clambered off. Hazel and Francis were waiting, bronzed after their week in the sun. Her heart thrilled to see them. Francis could have been Brendan at the same age, good-looking and good-natured, brimming with zest. He kissed her and bowed, pointing to a pony and trap outside Flood's Garage.

'Your chariot awaits,' he said, 'and darn difficult it was to get.'

Hazel laughed as she kissed Eva. 'Hello, Mummy. We would never have managed to steal it except that Francis unveiled his Goold Verschoyle cloven hoof and the owner ran off blessing himself.'

Francis gave Eva a gentle squeeze. 'It's not that bad. When Mr Floyd in the shop heard you were coming he was thrilled. He harnessed his pony up for you himself.'

Hazel gazed across at the Dublin families. 'Don't tell me all those are Uncle Art's brood. Uncle Art has no faith in Christ, but I hope that Marx is as dab a hand at the loaves and fishes miracle.'

'Is the house that bad?' Eva asked anxiously.

'On the contrary,' Francis said. 'It's so shipshape that a People's Commissar could eat off the floorboards.'

'Or even eat the floorboards,' Hazel added. This physical work had suited them, their eyes tired but happy. Being in Donegal made Eva feel like a girl again, but the plight of the Dublin families troubled her. The Killybegs train was not due for an hour and a stand-off was developing between the children and local youths who taunted them. Eva climbed into the trap and they headed out the road with every bend familiar. Hazel held the reins, though the pony knew his own way. Francis presented Eva with a bar of dark chocolate and two packs of her favourite cigarettes. She scolded him for spending what little money he had.

'We're loaded,' he told her. 'Uncle Art insisted upon paying us. At the same *trudoden* as himself.'

'The same what?' Eva asked.

'It's a labour Day Unit,' Hazel explained with an edge of good-humoured exasperation. 'What a peasant on a *kolkhoz* earns. But collective farms being thin on the ground in

Donegal, he based it on the rate that a farm labourer gets. Not that we qualify as peasants, of course.'

'Or, worse still, *kulaks*,' Francis said.

'Heaven forbid.' Hazel rolled her eyes. Eva knew that she was dying to regale schoolfriends with stories about her uncle, though in certain circles Hazel was careful not to betray any connection to Art Goold. 'We're *Byvshie Liudi*.'

'We've had long chats on this subject,' Francis explained, 'seeing as we had every evening to debate the issue. At first the locals didn't make us over welcome.'

'Some villagers hurry their children into their cottages and bless themselves if they see Art coming,' Hazel said.

'Not the old men though,' Francis added. 'Some still touch their cap to him, out of respect for Grandfather, but their servitude infuriates Art more than the others sprinkling holy water after him.'

'A brick came through the window the first night we stayed there,' Hazel said. 'Glass everywhere. People thought we were two more of his Dublin aficionados. But when they discovered that we were your children their attitude changed. Yesterday people told us about your wedding day.'

That was the last time Eva had travelled along this road, gazing back from the huge car as the crowd ran to the bend of the road to wave her off. She took Francis's hand as the miles passed. Every bush and stone wall was sacred, every gap where honeysuckle or wild roses grew. This was her dream landscape. Walking with Father past green banks while he recited Walt Whitman poems. Running behind Brendan to hold his bicycle steady as he pedalled furiously before telling her to let go, thrilled to travel thirty yards on his own before tumbling into the ditch. Those were her good dreams. In the bad ones she ran through the dark here in search of Brendan, knowing that a terrifying creature was loose on this road and only she could save him.

'What was that Russian expression Art had for you?' Eva asked.

'*Byvshie Liudi.*' Francis pronounced the words carefully. 'The remnants of the despised tsarist class who refused to play their part in the revolution.'

'What it means literally is *former people*,' Hazel explained. 'We are former people. Or formerly we were people.'

'What are we now?'

Francis watched two men working on the bog and laughed. 'Whatever we are, we're earning those fellows' wages and are in dire need of a bath.'

Hazel laughed and spoke of her plans to spend hours soaping in the tub when they got back home to the small house that Eva currently rented during term time in Dublin. But neither that nor Glanmire House or indeed any other address lived in had ever truly felt like home to Eva. For her there had only ever been one true home and she was finally returning there. A childish song entered her mind, composed by her and Maud as girls. Eva could still see herself banging out the notes on Father's piano while Maud chewed a pencil and strove to find the words.

'*Dunkineely, Dunkineely, Dunkineely wondrous fair,*
*Many visitors this summer your many joys did share.*
*First came the Hawkins family, brother, sisters, Ma and*
*Pa,*
*Then Eric, Percy and Cecil from the Royal School,*
*Armagh . . .*'

Dunkineely, wondrously fair. They were getting close now. First she would spy the slated roofs that never knew thatch and then, climbing the hill, the shaky village pump where children constantly queued during her childhood. Would ducks still splash in rain-filled potholes along the street? Had anyone bothered to tend the wealth of sweet peas beneath Father's window – the smell of which, after rain, always made his heart swell with life's ever-budding freshness? They were finally here now, mounting the hill with everything the same and everything different. Mr Floyd must have been watching out because he rushed from his shop to halt the pony and present Eva with a white twist of paper brimming with sweets.

'Welcome home, Miss Eva.' She had not been called that in decades. Other faces congregated around before she could finish thanking him. Mr MacShane and his son from the pub, Lizzie Cunningham and Kathleen Lynch whom Eva had held on the day she was born. Hazel and Francis stayed back, letting her savour the euphoria of homecoming. She was momentarily too preoccupied with embracing childhood friends to turn around and see the Manor House. A slight silence occurred when she did so, with people letting the sight speak for itself. The knot of neighbours drifted away as Art appeared in the doorway. The garden had obviously become a wilderness, which he had mown with a scythe. Broken panes were replaced and the windowframes painted, but the walls seemed scarred and desolate. Still it radiated the aura of home as she ran towards it.

'Welcome back.' Art stepped aside to let her enter the hall. The carpets were gone, the bare floorboards unvarnished. The walls were freshly painted, but the paint was the colour of amnesia. The drawing room door was open. Father's piano was there, discoloured, with the keys yellow. It seemed small. The only other recognisable features were the fireplace and the window.

Art had assembled an assortment of furniture, with chairs crammed into every space and a long table piled with leaflets and magazines about the Soviet Union. He had also acquired a wind-up gramophone. Eva flicked through a selection of symphonies by unfamiliar composers like Tikhon Khrennikov. She imagined the Dublin families here, men sweeping these books aside to play cards, children still dreaming of Bundoran. Art watched her.

'The records ate into my budget,' he said. 'I had to cut back on other things, but music is so important.'

'Do you know how many are coming?' she asked.

'By Soviet standards this will be quite uncrowded.'

'We're not in the Soviet Union,' Hazel reminded him from the doorway.

Art smiled. 'We've had good discourse,' he told Eva. 'You reared them as Father reared us, to be independent thinkers. The important thing is not to agree but to be able to discuss issues openly.'

'And is that what you get in the Soviet Union?' Hazel taunted. 'Try discussing something there and you wind up in a salt mine.'

Art shrugged indulgently. 'How can I blame you for parroting lies when you only know Western propaganda? Stay another week and you'll see that to Dublin slum dwellers this is paradise.'

Hazel snorted and went to help Francis unharness the pony. The visitors would arrive soon, these rooms crammed with people. Eva welcomed life returning to the Manor House, but she coveted one quiet moment to confront each room again. Father's study had become Art's makeshift office, with the word *Caretaker* painted on the door. A picture of Stalin displaced Father's portrait of Martin Luther.

Her shoes were loud as she climbed the bare stairs to open her old bedroom door. Only the windowframe looked the same and the slope of the ceiling meeting the eaves. The room was spotlessly clean, but in a militaristic functional way. Art had obviously built the five tightly cramped wooden bunks. Two tiers of rough canvas were tacked across each frame. A child rolling off the top tier would face a terrifying drop. The walls were the same antiseptic colour as the hallway, reminding Eva of an army barracks. She approached the window and heard Art enter behind her. For a moment Eva imagined that he was Mother on that distant evening when mackerel swarmed to their death and her perfect childhood seemed turned upside-down. She could almost feel Mother's hand inches from her hair.

'It has been difficult,' Art said. 'Local people are not keen to co-operate. The priests poison their minds. I should have brought more supplies from Dublin.'

'Are you nervous?'

'Once we co-operate as a collective everything will go smoothly. I don't mean you, of course. You must go visiting with your children. Those neighbours who speak to me ask always about you and Brendan.'

'What do you tell them?'

Art was silent. They had learnt not to discuss Brendan. Eva looked down, imagining Mother tending the flowering beds of sweet peas, with the sound of Father's piano and the thud of tennis balls from the back garden.

'Do you remember a sandy-haired boy herding sheep with bruises down his legs?' Eva asked.

'What boy?'

'Grandpappy let you drive the trap. We were returning from a picnic when sheep blocked the road. You wanted to give him your shoes.'

'I don't remember.'

Eva turned, shocked. 'You must remember. That was the moment which led to all this.'

Art shrugged. 'Maybe I've forgotten. I recall no interest in *all this*, as you call it, till poor Ffrench educated me. You should visit his grave. He was a good man, stuck to his beliefs, yet people here accepted him in a way they can't seem to accept me.'

Eva knew that local people had seen Mr Ffrench more as a likeable eccentric than a threat. Art's intensity was different and as dangerous as a Christian actually trying to live like Christ.

'Do people ignore you?'

'They're civil, generally. Two evenings a week I go down to MacShane's pub for a bottle of Swithwicks and a quiet talk with Mr MacShane about the old days. But mostly I'm too busy with my work.'

A babble of Dublin voices filled the street below. The pump went silent. Eva knew that every door in the village was closed, with locals standing behind lace curtains to watch the families arrive.

'You should meet your guests,' Eva suggested.

Art surveyed the room for dirt and then, as a last touch, hung a silver picture frame from the nail in the wall. It was the same nail that once held Eva's picture of a girl kneeling in prayer. She recognised the frame as having previously held a family photograph. It now contained a quotation, typed in capital letters.

'WE DEMAND THAT OUR COMRADES BE GUIDED BY THE VITAL FORCE OF THE SOVIET ORDER – ITS POLITICS. ONLY THUS CAN OUR YOUTH BE REARED, NOT IN A DEVIL-MAY-CARE ATTITUDE BUT IN A STRONG AND VIGOROUS REVOLUTIONARY SPIRIT.' *ANDREI ZHDANOV*

Eva read the slogan, then had to leave the room. Art's old bedroom was similarly rigged out as a cramped boys' dormitory with iron beds set up in the remaining three bedrooms for the adult couples. Eva looked out of the back window. No clue remained that a tennis court ever stood in the mown meadow of the garden. But a tent was pitched beside the slope. Hazel appeared at the top of the stairs.

'Did he not think that the children might want to sleep in with their parents?' Eva asked.

'Art claims that communal sleeping will foster closer comradeship among the children. He threw out all kinds of old family documents and books before we came. They're piled in the yard. I don't know if there's anything you might want to keep.'

Eva carried her case down the back stairs to avoid the families crowding into the hall. Children's boots stomped on the bare floorboards. A child tunelessly banged the piano keys. The kitchen was stark and spotless but contained little food. It was the first time Eva had entered this room without some cat raising its eyes to observe her. Out in the yard Art had dumped what he regarded as rubbish: mildewed novels more likely to be read than the political tracts inside, and gramophone records like *Yes, We Have No Bananas* – out of date but with more chance of being played than Khrennikov's symphonies. Old family snapshots had become stuck together among Father's papers, illegible after the rain. The remnants of *Byvshie Liudi*, former people.

Eva wanted to turn away from this ugly rubbish tip. But she kept sifting through the past, searching for something to hold onto. Some books near the bottom were unsoiled, but it was two sheaves of pages typed in crude columns and sewn with thread that she extracted with a surge of excitement. Maud's photograph was on the cover, with the legend, 'The

Editor at her residence'. Above it was the letterhead that Eva had designed: *The Dunkineely News, summer issue. Price 4d.* There had only been summer issues. Eva remembered the hours Maud spent compiling this family newspaper. Father had written an essay for each one, with poems coaxed from Brendan and Art. Eva had provided the illustrations while Maud as editor recorded every tiny event:

> *The Goold Verschoyle staff reporter has made careful notes about the behaviour of our English visitor, Mr Oliver Hawkins. Reports indicate that he plays tennis smartly and wets his hair on Sundays. He started smoking cigarettes at the age of seven and is rumoured to wear pink pyjamas. While watching the ladies' tennis, Mr Oliver Hawkins was seen – at a crucial moment – to wipe his nose with his green handkerchief which matches his socks . . .*

Eva's hand shook as she read these pages that had somehow survived. No issues were ever as carefree after news of Oliver Hawkins's death at Ypres. Maud had been changed by her first encounter with death. They all had. A dress rehearsal for the deaths to come.

Voices were raised inside the house as Art argued with the exhausted travellers.

'If I wanted my son to share a prison cell I'd have stuck him in Mountjoy. St Joseph himself couldn't stop those bunks collapsing if a child bounced on them.'

'This is no prison,' Art retorted. 'Anyone can walk out the door at any time.'

'Walk where?' a woman said. 'There's nothing here.'

'There's fresh air and sand.'

'If we wanted them we could have walked to Dollymount

and got a few chips at least. You promised us things for the kids.'

'There are books and . . .'

'Fuck your books,' another man interrupted. 'You'd want a few amusements. Somewhere like Bray. I mean is there even a bookie's in this kip?'

'There's a bookmaker's in Donegal town.'

'What use is that if I want to stick on a bet? You'd need Hannibal's shagging elephants to make that trip.'

'Never mind the bookie's,' some woman said. 'I'm not sticking my kids in with strangers we don't know.'

'I'd mind you not to cast accusations on my kids,' the man retorted. 'Especially as your sons nearly wore their fingers to stumps scratching their scalps all the way here.'

'Please, comrades,' Art interrupted. 'Nothing is achieved by arguing. We can vote on sleeping arrangements in council. Remember this rest home is a collective. Now I have a rota of duties for us all drawn up.'

'Hold your horses, pal,' the first man said. 'My wife is not skivvying for strangers. We look after our own brood and that's it.'

Eva moved off, not wanting to hear the arguments. Further down the garden it was possible to ignore the voices. She closed her eyes and recalled holding her pet rabbit while watching Father practise at the window with a black cat motionless on the piano. That was the room where Father had written his essays for *The Dunkineely News*, delighted when he occasionally managed to later place one as *An Irishman's Diary* in the *Irish Times*. She sat on the slope to read his words in the family newspaper:

*How our idle moments bring us closer to the wider truths of the universe. These truths buried within us all.*

*Take our gardener, a man of few words, yet I have heard him set forth the beauties of cliff and bay with a clarity quite worthy of one trained in word-painting. The pity is that in a country so fair there should be room for fancied differences of caste and creed . . .*

Perhaps this last line had been a spark to Art's rebellion. He did not recall encountering the sandy-haired boy on the road, just like Eva in turn could not remember reading this essay before. Maybe Maud and Thomas and Brendan also had completely different memories of childhood in this paradise which none of them had ever recaptured. However perhaps on this trip she might recapture the magic of painting at least. Opening her case she erected the portable easel, pinned up a sheet and took out brushes and paints. She sat on the slope to mix the paints and raised the brush, but an invisible force prevented her touching the sheet. Painting had been instinctive once, a world of lines begging to be drawn. She remembered Father's phrase about the ever-budding freshness of life and realised that she no longer knew how to capture it.

A sound made her turn. Theresa and the older girl from the bus were observing her, along with a tiny child whose hands they both held.

'What are you writing?' Theresa asked.

'I'm painting.'

'We're going home tomorrow,' the older girl announced. 'This is an awful Godforsaken kip. Bundoran looked like a bit of gas but the silence here would drive you daft.'

Theresa ignored her companion, her eyes fixed on the sheet of paper.

'Well, go on then,' she said, 'show us how you do this painting stuff.'

Eva held out the brush. 'You have a go.'

'Don't be stupid, missus, sure I can't paint nothing.'

'Try. It's fun.'

Theresa laughed nervously.

'Come away, Theresa,' her companion urged. 'She's making a cod of you.' The girl went to move off but Theresa held her ground, although still refusing to accept the brush that Eva held out. 'Stop being thick, Theresa,' the older girl snapped. 'They're all mad Protestants in this dump. I'll leave you here for them to snatch your soul if you're not careful.'

Theresa reached out to take the brush. 'Can you teach me?'

'I can help you to teach yourself.'

'Jaysus, Theresa!' The older girl stormed off in disgust, dragging the tiny child behind her. Theresa stared at the sheet, terrified to dirty it.

'Me teacher in school is always jeering that I can't draw a straight line.'

'You don't have to only draw what's outside. Draw what's inside your mind, draw your emotions. They don't have straight lines, do they?'

'I don't know. How much do the sheets cost? Me Ma will kill me.'

'Why?'

'I don't know. What were them words you said on the bus?'

'*Up the airy mountain . . . ?*'

'Yeah.'

> '*. . . Down the rushy glen,*
> *We daren't go a-hunting,*
> *For fear of little men.*'

Theresa dipped the brush in the green paint. It came out smeared with too much paint and a blob landed on the grass. Eva showed her how to regulate the amount of paint and create a brush stroke instead of just smudging the paint on. Other than that she remained silent and simply watched. This was where a teacher belonged, not up on a platform but at the child's shoulder. And even the term *teacher* was wrong. Rather it should be *evoker*, someone willing to be a silent instrument drawing out what already resided within the inner radiance of a child's imagination.

Theresa progressed laboriously at first but gradually gained confidence. Her eyes were fixed on the sheet, oblivious to the children who came to gape but were reluctant to approach too closely. The adult voices went silent in the house, with a temporary truce negotiated. Smells of cooking came from the kitchen and Eva imagined the two pigs' heads boiling away. She wanted to ask if people were really leaving tomorrow, but didn't wish to interrupt her first ever pupil. The thrill she had known as a child, the limitless possibility of every brush stroke, was back – only now Eva was experiencing it through Theresa's excitement. She didn't know who was more apprehensive when the girl stepped back with uncertainty in her eyes.

'It's the airy mountain,' she explained.

Eva examined the sheet, saturated from corner to corner with streaks of green paint. She had never seen anything so tangibly and visibly green.

'It's beautiful,' she said.

The small girl's eyes shone with pride. 'Can I do another then? Will you pin up a sheet?'

'Put it up yourself,' Eva said. 'That's what artists do.'

'Am I an artist?'

'You are what you want to be. What will you draw next?'

'The sky over the airy mountain, teacher.'

Eva taught her how to clean the brush, then watched the child work with renewed energy. She was quicker now, singing as she painted. It was the first time anyone had called Eva 'teacher', but Eva knew that the child was teaching *her*. Not to interfere or judge or suggest. Mother had known this, never trying to improve Eva's sketches as a child, letting what was inside find its own way out.

Art stood at the window, looking utterly alone. Francis appeared behind him, talking kindly as Art shook his head. The Dubliners were wrong about the bunks. They were strong and when this experiment collapsed and Art returned to Dublin, one day Eva would hire him to build twelve miniature easels, paying him the daily rate of a jobbing carpenter. Tonight she would cross Dunkineely to visit old friends. But after that she would be glad to return to Dublin and find the courage to start planning her freedom, the chance to live her own life in her own way.

Theresa stepped back, smearing a thick trail of blue paint down the wooden easel. The child was so excited that Eva knew she wanted to dance. The sheet was soaked in blue, her fingers were blue and there were blue streaks in her hair as she called out in triumph: 'Would you just have a gawk at the blueness of that blue sky!'

# THIRTY-SEVEN

# *The Flag*

### *Dublin, 8 May 1945*

All evening the mood among much of the crowd had grown more outraged as people stopped in College Green to stare up at the flagpoles above the locked gates of Trinity College. Art sensed that the majority of Dubliners wished to celebrate Victory in Europe Day, but this effrontery was too pronounced. People were annoyed enough that the censorship laws – forbidding any expressed opinion on the war – had been bypassed this morning by the Protestant *Irish Times* who laid out the censored news on its front page in the shape of a massive V for Victory. But an hour ago when Trinity College students climbed onto the roof to raise the Union Jack on the main flagstaff, higher than the nearby Irish tricolour, this had proved too much for ardent nationalists who tried to storm the main gate and remove the flag.

The Trinity students had either been drunk or dangerously high-spirited because, in response to abuse shouted up from the street, one student had lowered the tricolour and tried to set it alight. His companions remonstrated and quickly stamped out the flames, but by now reports had reached every public house nearby from which angry drinkers were emerging. Ireland had sat out this war, maintaining such a strict code of neutrality that, with the victorious Red Flag already flying over the Reichstag, de Valera had still followed protocol by officially visiting the German Legation to express condolence on Hitler's death.

Tonight in London and Moscow and Paris and amidst the ruins of Stalingrad people were cheering, but in Dublin there was a sense that nobody knew how to react. The risk of invasion was gone and with it hopefully a gradual reduction in rationing and censorship. But the Irish were neither victors nor vanquished. Any sense of idealism was dead. Ireland had threaded a safe passage through this war by taking decisions for cold and pragmatic reasons. To de Valera's credit he remained his own man to the end, not joining the last-minute rush of countries like Saudi Arabia and Argentina who, with the battle won, felt it opportune to declare war on Germany. But during the past hour the crowds in College Green had remained angry and deflated, as if their noses were being rubbed in the dirt by the Trinity students who remained on the roof beside the Union Jack.

Tomorrow Art was leaving for London where an election would soon be called and he could canvass for communist candidates. But tonight he had one final duty to do because while Irish people wanted to celebrate the end of fascist tyranny, they could not be expected to do so beneath the British flag. Art could see American flags in the crowd and therefore felt it important that the true victors be represented by the Soviet flag he held folded inside his jacket.

Last week he had left Dunkineely, two days after communist partisans strung up Mussolini's corpse from the façade of a Milan petrol station. Ignorance and prejudice had thwarted Art's plans for a Workers' Rest Home after the first Dublin families left early. Because of whatever slander they spread on their return, the second consignment of families never arrived in Donegal, despite Art sending money for their fares. He had spent days keeping the empty Manor House spotless while awaiting them. Long nights walking from room to room, unable to surrender his dream even though he sensed the whole village laughing at him. All that arrived were poorly written cancellations from families who had booked free holidays for the summer, so similarly worded that he wondered if Trotskyites had poisoned their minds. He had lost the will to cook for himself as the vegetables stored up for his guests began to rot in the kitchen. Art might not have eaten except that Samuel Trench's daughter, now married, had taken pity and sent over her daughter with hot stews each evening which Art ate alone in Father's study. On the evening when reports were announced on his wireless about the Americans liberating Dachau, Art was so sickened by the details that he had been unable to touch his stew. When the child called back for the plate, Art had returned it along with the key to the Manor House. Telling the child to instruct her mother to do whatever she wished with the house, he had closed the door behind him and walked through the night towards Donegal town, knowing that, once he caught a train next morning, he would never return.

There was a stir now among the College Green crowd as a party of students from the nearby National University marched down Grafton Street. Art had noticed them an hour ago for being the most vociferous hecklers of the Trinity students. He climbed onto the railings to wave the Red Flag, but few people noticed at first because their attention was focused on this group of students. Two students at the very rear had acquired Nazi swastikas, which they waved defiantly at the Trinity students on the roof. Some people among the crowd roared their approval at this bravado while others

511

shouted for the swastikas to be torn up. The cultivated ignorance and tomfoolery of the Catholic students sickened Art. Millions of deaths meant nothing to them compared to the chance to taunt a few Anglophiles on the roof of Trinity.

Art lifted the Red Flag higher and shouted: 'Long live Comrade Stalin. Salute the victorious Red Army.' But nobody turned because a young Nationalist student at the front of the group had stopped outside the closed gates to make a speech. He seemed a natural public speaker, conveying his indignation at this affront to Irish sensibilities by Trinity College with an aura of self-possessed mocking braggadocio.

'Good man, Charlie!' a fellow student shouted. 'If there's one man to show the Brits, it's Charlie Haughey.'

'Do it, Haughey, do it!' others urged and Art watched the young Haughey fellow produce a Union Jack which he hung from the college gates and proceeded to set alight. A cheer arose with other students urging people to storm the British Embassy. Dissenting voices shouted back and fistfights broke out. Scanning the crowd Art recognised two of the committee to whom he had ceded control of the Raglan Road house. To his amazement they were cheering the burning flag when they had a duty to show example by publicly celebrating Stalin's victory. Art shouted in their direction and waved the Red Flag higher, but although he was sure they spied him they made no effort to join his demonstration. Instead they pushed further back into the crowd as people started to take notice of his flag.

'Get that rag down, you godless communist bastard,' a man shouted.

Art ignored him and shouted: 'Long live Comrade Stalin. Rejoice at the victory of Comrade Stalin!'

People were torn between wishing to watch the Union Jack burn and wanting to attack Art. A hand grabbed his elbow and, looking down, he recognised Kathleen Behan's son Brendan, the one who had gone to borstal for trying to bomb Liverpool.

'Goold, you daft fucker, get down out of that or they'll kill you altogether,' Behan urged.

'I'm celebrating,' Art replied. 'Tomorrow I leave for London, and Ireland can go to hell. But my country has won a victory costing millions of lives and I defy any man to stop me celebrating.'

'Listen,' Behan coaxed, 'the best way to enjoy celebrations is to be fecking alive for them. Get down from there and we'll have a drink. My ma thinks you're a saint, but she'd sooner not be praying to you in heaven just yet.'

However, even if Art wanted to move there was no escape from the hostile crowd. Two men grabbed the Red Flag from Art's hand although he struggled to hold on, losing his grip on the railings. Others joined in, spitting on the flag and spitting at him. Art saw it being tossed further into the mob where a man managed to set it alight. Behan was trying to drag him away, kicking out at people to clear a path. There was commotion at the college gates as riot police arrived with batons. One man threw a punch at Art who squared up to him, raising his fists in a classic fighting stance. Behan climbed onto the railings from where he could kick out at people.

'Jaysus, Goold,' he shouted, 'you're not in a boxing ring in Marlborough College. Never mind your fists. Fuck the Marquess of Queensberry. Remember poor Oscar Wilde and kick them in the balls.'

There was a flash of raised batons and the crowd scattered, with Behan jumping down to grab Art as he tried to retrieve the burning Red Flag. Dragging Art down Dame Street, Behan ducked into a cobbled alley, raising a finger to the blood on his face.

'Where are you bleeding from?' Art asked.

'Russell Street. But at least I know where I'm bleeding from.' Behan laughed and scrutinised Art. 'Are you really heading for the Big Smoke?'

'There's nothing to keep me here.'

'The Ma will miss you. You should go back to Russia.'

'I will one day, if it's the last thing I ever do.'

'We'll have a jar on the strength of that and see you onto the boat in style.' Behan wiped the blood from his face with his sleeve. 'I've been going to American wakes since I was a chisler, sure it's about time I attended a Russian one.'

# THIRTY-EIGHT

# A Darkened Room in Oxfordshire

*September 1946*

Heavy full-length drapes drawn across the window gave the bedroom an appearance of twilight, though it was only early afternoon. The door was ajar and Eva knew that Mother was patiently waiting to say goodbye in the bed by the window. Leaving her bag in the hall, Eva walked back upstairs, stung by an aching familiarity. This might be Donegal except that their roles were reversed. Back then Eva had been the figure in bed, the aftertaste of hot milk staining her tongue as she waited for Mother to stroke her hair. Now at forty-three, Eva realised that she was older than Mother had been on those childhood nights when even the crickets outside the window seemed hushed in expectation of her arrival. And Mother . . . ? For a moment Eva half expected a nine-year-old girl to greet her when she entered the room.

The hired nurse crept out onto the landing and placed one finger to her lips to indicate that Mother had drifted off to sleep. She held open the door, anxious to slip downstairs and savour more of the butter that Eva had brought over from Ireland two weeks ago. Mother's tea ration in the kitchen was unused and Eva had told the nurse to take it for her children. Since Father's death Mother had gradually lost interest in everything except the fate of her youngest son.

The nurse's cigarette smoke lingered in the sick room but could not cloak the musty odours surrounding a dying woman. Eva approached the bed on tiptoes. Mother had shrunk even in the last few days, leaving Eva with severe reservations about venturing into London. Her features were creased with pain but her hair was soft and fine like a child's. Through the open wardrobe door Eva glimpsed the scarves that Francis had once dressed up in. They were folded beside the dusty hatboxes and mothballed dresses Mother used to wear in Donegal. Maud had inherited Mother's fashion sense, which had bypassed Eva. Yet Maud – who, home at last from her family's enforced exile in South Africa, would arrive this evening to take over this vigil – was like their brothers in being immersed in politics.

It was Eva who inherited many of Mother's 'beliefs' – though '*intimations*' might be a better word. The sense that there might be other states and truths, tantalisingly close yet impossible to grasp, revelations you had to patiently await in the hope that one day they might reveal themselves, those signposts that Mother had sought through spirit messages during planchette. Eva had sought them too as a child by spinning around until dizzy, half expecting – as the shaky world sorted itself to rights – to glimpse a minute crack in reality, a peep into a parallel existence.

However, despite what people termed her unworldliness, Mother had managed her life well, perpetually keeping one foot in reality. Finding a perfect partner in love, maintaining a fine house until her son destroyed it, being always able to hold up her head. This thought increased Eva's sense of failure. So much of Eva's life had already occurred, yet there was a sense that she was still only waiting for it to start. Eva moved softly about the sickroom, disturbed by the pervasive odour of oncoming death. *The Great Outlaw* – Mother's favourite book about Christ – lay on the bedside locker beside Sir Arthur Eddington's *The Expanding Universe*. Opening the drawer she examined the small bottles of perfume that Mother had nursed through the war. But she could not find the hand lotion which Mother had always used after gardening, a fragrance that summoned up the certainty of childhood nights.

How long was it since Mother had been able to garden? Her arthritis had grown so acute that even holding a pen was torture. Eva could sense the first canker of it within her own bones, a legacy of the damp basement in Glanmire House. It was a mystery how Mother had managed to keep writing to British and Russian officials since Father died. Every line must have represented physical agony, yet she had been kept going by the need to quench the greater anguish in her heart. Years of curt replies were filed in the bedside drawer, expressing regret at being unable to supply information. Eva picked up Mother's most precious perfume and spilt several drops on the pillow. The scent roused her. Mother's head twitched, a small moan escaping her lips before she opened her eyes to look at her daughter.

'I thought you were someone else.'

'I know.'

'I dreamt he came to see me . . . only he was an old man like Grandpappy. A white beard and dead eyes . . . but I knew him . . . my baby . . . trying to tell me something.' Mother lips were so cracked she could barely talk. Eva soaked a face cloth to moisten them and took her hand that felt cold and bony, the fingers permanently contorted.

'I won't go to London,' Eva said. 'It's more important to stay with you.'

'You will go, like we agreed.' Mother's eyes were determined. 'It's the biggest night of your husband's life. He needs you beside him when he gets his MBE. Do this for him, then afterwards you must tell him your plans.'

'I'm afraid.'

'Of what?' Mother closed her eyes and Eva knew that the pain had come for her. 'I'll still be here when you get back.'

'Maud will arrive soon. She can phone . . . if I'm needed.'

'I need you to see this through.' Every word was difficult, with the doctor's injection still two hours away. 'I should never have let you marry that man. You have the right to be happy. Am I leaving you enough money?'

'Don't talk about money.'

'I have to. I must at least set one thing right. The auctioneer . . . he'll wait for the balance until after probate?'

'Yes. Now try to rest and don't stress yourself.'

'How can I rest?' Mother pulled her hand away and closed her eyes, drained by the effort to talk. The uncharacteristic anger in her whisper surprised Eva. But, as this vigil was unfolding it felt as if a buried seam of pain was gradually seeping out from Mother. She gave a muffled groan, though Eva couldn't tell if her distress arose from a dream or from the physical pain that she was enduring. These two worlds seemed blurred. Some afternoons with her pain at its apex and the doctor trying to fathom how much of the precious ration of painkiller he could afford to give her, Mother called out to people no longer living. Not just to Father but to her own parents and others whose names Eva barely knew. The one name she never called for was Art who – as Freddie phrased it – was still playing at being Christ in the desert. Mother never criticised Art, but Eva felt that he should be given the chance to be here.

Eva picked up her handbag, undid the clasp and fingered

the envelope inside. Mother's breathing settled into a regular pattern, allowing Eva time to ponder her dilemma. Mother had a right to know about this envelope addressed to her, but only if Eva could be sure that the contents were true. On paper it appeared to answer the question that had plagued their lives for years. This perfunctory death certificate had arrived from the Soviet authorities yesterday without explanation. Brendan did not merit a first name. He was listed as Prisoner Verschoyle B., with a long identification number. The certificate indicated that he had been killed in a Nazi bombing raid on a prisoner train. At one time Eva would have believed the official document and succumbed to grief, mingled with relief that at least they could no longer hurt her brother. But the newsreels of liberated concentration camps made her doubt everything now. There seemed no cruelty or duplicity that mankind was incapable of.

The euphoria of VE Day had dissipated on these Oxford streets where women queued outside shops all night if a delivery of potatoes was rumoured while their half-starved children played in bomb craters. The Allies had splintered apart, with stories appearing about Soviet prison camps that no paper would have printed a year ago. Truth was lost in a fog of propaganda, with nobody sure what words meant any more. Eva had joined the campaign for the release of Raoul Wallenberg, the Swedish diplomat who saved thousands of Jews until he disappeared at a checkpoint manned by the advancing Soviet army. With the furore over Wallenberg, it might suit the Soviets to fob off minor cases with a bogus death certificate.

The nurse re-entered the room and sat by the window, moving the curtain slightly to gaze out at the distant view of Magdalen College, while awaiting the doctor whose magic injection would get Mother through another night of muted pain. Being able to lift a curtain without a shout from an air raid warden still felt strange. Eva wondered what the nurse made of Mother. How could you explain the totality of a life to someone who encounters a patient only when she is dying? The nurse had lost her husband at Aden and an eight-year-old daughter in a bombing raid. She had four other children, the eldest girl minding the others now while she worked shifts to let Eva sleep. She once told Eva about her daughter's death, an account made more harrowing for being focused on the factual problems of queuing to get her ration book altered, then walking miles to procure a death certificate in a makeshift office.

Eva examined the date on Brendan's death certificate again, trying to recall what she had been doing on that day in 1941. She possessed no definite recollection of it amid the seamless blur of an Irish summer. The children had probably explored the woods, with the dog barking and Eva reading poetry on the lawn while Brendan was penned in a burning railway carriage. Skeletal figures fighting to claw their way out to where bombs were falling. Afterwards, when the plane moved away, the dead eyes would have gazed up like slaughtered mackerel. Would Eva ever know if this was another Soviet lie? Replacing the envelope in her bag, Eva touched her mother's hand, then tiptoed from the room.

This morning Hazel and Francis had made the crossing from Dublin with Maud. While Maud travelled on to Oxford, they would meet Eva in Paddington Station. Hazel loved Dublin where she was in her final year as a day girl in the school she had previously attended as a boarder and Francis had just entered Trinity. They had occasionally met Maud's children before the war, but there was great excitement in starting friendships anew after six years of enforced separation from their cousins. Hazel had talked so openly about her trip to London that Eva had needed to warn her how not everyone in Dublin might approve of her father being made a Member of the Order of the British Empire. Hazel dismissed such caution as another of Eva's eccentricities, replying '*Obviously not everyone, but everybody important will be chuffed.*' Every important young Dublin man already seemed to know Hazel who relished the freedom of being a day girl able to cycle everywhere. Every Saturday she bicycled to a riding stables near the Dublin mountains to rub down horses, then freewheeled back at dusk to their rented house to meet some young man waiting to take her to a rugby club dance. She could hardly wait to discard her school uniform and embrace the new world which Eva could not hold her back from. Freddie might not approve of such freedom, but Hazel was more than a match for the young men who flocked around. Her tempestuousness scared most of them. She had the looks of a young Ingrid Bergman but would never pass for an innocent Swedish milkmaid, possessing an inherent poise and sophistication that had bypassed Eva.

When the Oxford train pulled into Paddington the children were already waiting, having found her platform with ease. They would stay in the married quarters at the barracks, but neither wished to go there yet. They had deposited their cases at the left luggage hatch and, after enquiring about their grandmother, Hazel was desperate to drag Eva around the shops. Eva wished to avoid the barracks too, which seemed deserted with so many soldiers demobbed. Freddie was currently among the officers supervising security at Buckingham Palace while the damaged wings were rebuilt, but Eva knew that his duties were mainly illusory. The war had been good for him, but lately his bloodshot eyes suggested that the limbo of peace was more dangerous. Eva suggested that the children might have more fun visiting the shops without her. They arranged to meet at six-thirty and as she watched them stroll off to catch a tube to Oxford Circus, Eva felt an inexpressible grief. In the last year they had grown up so fast. They still needed her but not like before. She had surrendered her own happiness to be their mother and now her role was almost finished.

Most young men might be bored accompanying Hazel around the expensive stores, but Francis would happily comment on each shoe Hazel tried on, suggesting that she try just one more pair as they sat besieged by assistants. Both would savour the joke of barely being able to afford a coffee and a Lyon's bun, never mind the new soft-shouldered Christian Dior hourglass outfits in the windows, which were condemned in parliament for wasting precious fabric with their full-length billowing skirts.

Eva was relieved to let them explore London alone, because it gave her time to try and locate her brother. Eva knew that Art had moved to London last year. He had a right to be left alone, but also the right to know about his mother's condition. More importantly he was the only person Eva trusted enough to verify the death certificate in her handbag.

She decided to call at the offices of the *Morning Star* where a young man curtly denied that Art had any connection with that newspaper. The British Communist Party was equally unforthcoming, though the belligerent attitude of the woman there with a slight limp made Eva suspect that she knew who Art was. At a loss, she sought out an afternoon drinking club on the Strand near the BBC studios, rumoured to be frequented by Irish poets, political activists and contributors to *The Third Programme*.

An Ulsterman descending the narrow staircase heard Eva's accent and offered to sign her in as a guest. Once inside she felt uncomfortable in the smoky atmosphere which seemed more bitchy than bohemian. No daylight penetrated the cramped cellar where small groups drank. A wireless played behind the counter and Eva was shocked and fascinated when two men began to dance together in what at first seemed a parody but then became a genuine embrace. The other drinkers appeared indifferent but Eva could not stop watching. Was this where Francis would end up, risking a furtive dance to a crackling radio set? These men were the first homosexuals she had knowingly encountered, apart from her son and poor Harry Bennett who had reportedly died during one of the last air raids on London. She didn't know if Freddie suspected anything about Francis's brief relationship with his tutor but when discussing the liberated camps Freddie had once expressed satisfaction that while the Jews and Gypsies were freed, the homosexuals were simply transferred to Allied jails.

The two men broke free as the tune ended. One gave a mocking bow, carefully reducing their dance to the camouflage of farce.

The Ulsterman bought Eva a gin that she didn't want. A poet, whose name was familiar to her from the radio, he knew of Art by reputation but had no idea where he lived. However once the pubs officially opened he offered to take Eva to a nearby bar where Irish labourers drank, because some regulars there had been interned in the Curragh. He insisted on buying a second gin while they waited so that Eva was tipsy by the time they reached the pub which stood alone – the buildings on both sides lying in ruins. The atmosphere here was different, the type of establishment where a woman's intrusion was unwelcome. Leaving Eva at the door, the poet pushed through the crush, addressing various men who turned to scrutinise her. Finally he returned with a man who had been studying the racing page of a newspaper.

'This is Murray Bolger from Wexford,' the poet said. 'He remembers your brother from the Curragh.'

'Not well,' the Wexford man said. 'But I never approved of him being court-martialled for making crazy speeches. Not that I ever attended his meetings. Life is too short for all that yap-yapping. I just wanted the Brits out.'

'Do you know where he's living?' Eva asked, sensing something familiar about his face.

'No.' Murray paused. 'But I heard that he sells the *Irish Democrat* around pubs in Whitechapel at closing time, though he gets chased out of most of them.'

Eva wanted to go to Whitechapel immediately, but she was already late for meeting her children in the barracks. When she got there, an orderly had let Hazel and Francis into Freddie's quarters. Freddie had left a note to say that he would go straight to the Dorchester Hotel where tonight's banquet was being held for families of officers mentioned on the Honours List. Maud would be in Oxford by now, so at least Mother was being looked after. Eva tried to focus on helping to get Hazel ready for the banquet and on making herself respectable too. Francis fussed around them both, at ease with women in a way that few men were. Eventually they made it into the waiting taxi.

Freddie stood alone in the bustling hotel foyer. From the neck down Eva would have hardly recognised him. His dress uniform was impeccably presented, the attire of a confident man who had made a success of life. But his shoulders were hunched, reminding her of that young boy who must have sat alone in the kitchens in Glanmire House after his father died. A boy who never contemplated surrendering to tears at the grief he could not articulate, with the only visible sign of suffering being his shoulders hunched up like this. Freddie straightened up, seeing his family amid the crowd. Hazel ran ahead to greet him, savouring this glamorous occasion, with every detail to be relayed to her chums back at school.

'Hello, Daddy,' she said. 'You do look smart.'

As Hazel kissed him, Eva saw Freddie thrill at having such a beautiful sixteen-year-old daughter. Francis was less forthcoming, formally shaking his father's hand. Three weeks into his first term at Trinity College, he towered over Freddie.

'Congratulations, Father. Give the king my regards tomorrow.'

'I'm sure he will be chuffed to receive them.' Freddie laughed, looking past the children at Eva. His whole face suggested happiness except his eyes. 'Hello, old pet.'

Eva longed to take him into a corner and discover the problem. But she had no time. An officer named Templeton approached, his wife steering him towards them like a decorative tugboat. Eva remembered her piercing laughter from wartime barracks parties and knew that her son was attending the English boarding school where Francis had his troubles.

'Is it really Eva?' she gushed. 'How *marvellous* to see you, and to see Francis looking so recovered.'

Eva tried to chat back while Freddie clicked his fingers for a waiter to fetch wine and sherry for Francis and Hazel. Hazel was attracting attention as Freddie introduced his children to fellow officers, getting ribbed about keeping such a young beauty hidden away. Less was said about Francis, with several officers aware of his ignominious departure from Castlebridge College. But Eva was pleased to see Francis hold his own in conversation, his gaiety and grace evident as he laughed. Nobody would openly comment on his good looks but every girl in the foyer was acutely aware of him.

Any sadness left Freddie's eyes as he revelled in the attention his children were receiving. Eva was pleased for him.

Most officers of his rank – those who had attended the right schools and drank in the best clubs – would receive the more prestigious OBE tomorrow, but none could boast of such striking children.

'I imagine you have done nothing except shop since arriving,' Mrs Templeton was saying. 'Ireland may be awash in meat and butter, but it must be a relief to encounter stores with a sense of style.'

The woman was half correct in that Eva had spent any free time away from Mother looking in shops. But not for clothes. She had searched secondhand bookshops on Charing Cross Road to find books on child art by Herbert Read and the Austrian pioneer, Professor Cizek. These were two more pieces in the jigsaw of a secret new life forming in her mind. Freddie had reinvented himself in the army and now – with the children almost grown – it was Eva's turn to grasp at freedom. She had made her last winter plans when the children returned to boarding school and she retreated to spend time alone in Glanmire House. Moving from room to room as shifting winds chased rain through the house, she had finally despaired of the chore of arranging enamel jugs to catch the drops and brought her bed down to the kitchen.

Some abandoned Big Houses in Mayo were starting to be reoccupied as old families returned, horrified at the advent of a British Labour government, in what one Mayo Protestant called 'the retreat from Moscow'. For Eva, last winter had been the start of the process of letting go of her old life. Snowed in and burning woodwormed furniture, she had re-read Rudolf Steiner's *Way of Initiation*, slowly absorbing its layers of meaning about how the slow path to inner tranquillity led to a knowledge of higher worlds. She had memorised each initiation stage from preparation and enlightenment to control of feelings. Sensing the companionship of a familiar presence in the wine cellar, some nights she had sung Francis's favourite hymn from the doorway:

> 'Blessed are the pure in heart,
> For they shall see our God;
> The secret of the Lord is theirs,
> Their soul is Christ's abode.'

One weekend Francis had arrived from his Quaker boarding school in Waterford, concerned both for her and for a young beech tree he had noticed the previous summer hemmed in by dead wood. Eva had helped him to clear a path for it up into the light and, after he left, realised that this was what she needed to do for herself. Maureen had known it was time to leave their cocoon at Glanmire when she emigrated three weeks after the war ended. There was little prospect of meeting eligible men in Mayo as they flocked to Britain to rebuild its cities. But Eva wondered if Maureen was spurred to choose New York after a postcard of strolling couples on Coney Island arrived, addressed to '*Any remaining staff, Glanmire House*'. There was no message, just the signature of the Foxford maid who quit when Jim Gralton was hiding there.

Mrs Templeton was still addressing Eva in a torrent of words that only required her to nod occasionally. Freddie rescued her and the officer's wife released Eva reluctantly, like a child not quite finished inspecting an exotic creature in a zoo. Making his way into the ballroom, he commiserated: 'That woman is a frightful snob, always waiting to stick in the knife. She said nothing, did she?'

'About what?'

Freddie shrugged. 'Anything really. Let's take our places. Hazel has cut quite a dash, you know.'

They were seated down the main table, with Francis and

Hazel at a side table where the young people created such chatter that Eva longed to be among them. Still, she liked the old brigadier on her left who had been informed by Freddie about Mother's condition. When he expressed his sympathy Eva told him how Mother wanted Tennyson's *Crossing the Bar* read at her funeral. The old man nodded his approval, closing his eyes to recite:

> '*Sunset and evening star,*
> *And one clear call for me!*
> *And may there be no moaning of the bar,*
> *When I put out to sea . . .*'

Eva was moved by the lines, wishing that she was still in Oxford as a clink of glasses heralded the first speaker. There were six courses, four containing meat. Freddie glanced at her as the first one arrived, anxious lest she show him up by insisting on what he termed her oddball vegetarian beliefs. With the meat ration in Britain reduced yet again in the latest austerity cuts, any seeming ingratitude at this feast would be frowned upon. Nausea swamped her as she forced herself to swallow the first bite, determined to support Freddie this final time by playing the obedient officer's wife. After tomorrow's ceremony she would tell him about her plans. Conversation at the table turned to politics, with the turmoil in the Empire being discussed.

'I consider it a shame to abandon India to slaughter just because Gandhi has whipped them up,' a young officer named Cooper stated.

'Slaughter is too mild a term,' insisted Templeton. 'Four thousand were hacked to death after the Muslim Direct Action Day. For all Gandhi's balderdash the next atrocity will probably top that.'

'I don't think Gandhi speaks balderdash,' Eva said quietly.

Templeton bristled. 'Do you not? And what has the daft beggar got to stop millions from killing each other?'

'A vision.'

'*A vision?*' He suppressed a laugh. 'God help any country where public order is maintained by a vision.'

'The government is talking of sending Mountbatten,' Freddie interjected for her sake. 'He will make a difference.'

'*You* might think so, Fitzgerald,' Templeton replied, 'but have *you* actually been to India? Those of us who served there and know what we're talking about know that the Congress Party are criminals. People will be at each other's throats within days of our pull-out and it will be left to the army to return and rescue the situation.'

The old brigadier snorted. 'Thirty years ago your father said the same about Ireland, Templeton, and they have done fine without us.'

'Even the fish off Ireland are fat,' Cooper sneered. 'From feasting on the carcasses of British seamen.'

'Enough Irish seamen drowned for them to feed off,' Freddie replied hotly. 'Irish lads who willingly gave their lives in your uniform. Thousands more from my Free State, Cooper, than from the loyal Ulster province where your cousins sat on their hands. And not one man I ever met felt that de Valera should have joined the war.'

'So why did your sort fight then?'

'Gentlemen,' the brigadier interrupted, with the prerogative of old age, 'tonight is for celebration, not politics. All I can say is thank God that decent chaps like Fitzgerald did join us. Now were any of you at the MCC when Denis Compton was batting last week? I never saw such cavalier cricket . . .'

Others agreed, keen to brush over the argument. It was

typical of Freddie – while criticising de Valera in private – to publicly defend Ireland. He had been defending Eva too, but she sensed that he seemed outside things at the table. Normally he was in demand for what people termed his *Blarney*. Officers were avoiding her eye. Freddie touched her hand as the next course arrived. 'Stick to your guns,' he whispered. 'Only eat what you like.'

This evening was not working out as planned, with Freddie's malaise increasing as the banquet crawled by. Eva picked at the vegetables and wondered how to tell Freddie about the house she saw in Dublin's Frankfurt Avenue last month, with leaded glass in the fanlight above the door. She had known, with every nerve-end of what Steiner called the 'faculties slumbering in the human soul', that this was the house in which to commence her new life. The light-filled kitchen was perfect for children to come and open their imaginations.

Mr Ffrench had been wrong to predict that Eva would be a great artist. What seemed glorious in her mind's eye was inconsequential to others who dismissed her work as possessing the mere vision of a child. But children should be allowed to express their unselfconscious vision without being corralled by adult expectation. She longed to create a haven where children could realise that vision. Frankfurt Avenue would cost every penny that Mother was leaving her, but Eva's needs were simple and the art classes would help pay her way. She would not be a burden on Freddie who, once he supported the children, could get on with army life in London. For years they had prevaricated, maintaining this pretence of marriage. But Eva hoped to make him understand that by choosing separate paths they might both be fulfilled.

The banquet finished with a speech in praise of the officers being decorated and a final toast to the King. The young people were impatient for the music to commence. Francis so adored dancing with girls that Eva had briefly allowed herself to hope that his homosexuality was a passing phase. He had laughed when she expressed this hope, saying, '*You know, Mummy, I love dancing with girls. They're like rose petals, but I feel nothing else. I don't fall in love with them.*' Nothing about his appearance suggested the hidden life which he often confided to her. For a second she imagined the scene in this ballroom if Francis's secret was known. An image of officers in dress uniforms transformed into baying hounds made her shiver. Freddie touched her shoulder as couples left the main table to regroup in tight-knit circles.

'Are you cold?'

'Just worried about Mother.' She smiled. 'Is there a table you want to join?'

Freddie pointed to an empty table near the dance floor. 'We'll keep our own company.'

He led the way, his limp somehow more pronounced in this dress uniform. She knew that many in the ballroom mistook it for a war wound. He ordered fresh drinks, lit the cigar he had chosen when the waiter carried around the box and puffed slowly, casting a disdainful eye over his colleagues.

'What's the matter, Freddie?'

'Nothing that won't keep, old pet.'

'Please,' she pressed. 'I'd sooner know now.'

Freddie waited until the waiter brought their drinks and moved away. 'It was decent of you to come with your mother so ill.'

'She insisted. She didn't want me to miss your big day.'

'Aye.' Freddie sipped his whiskey. 'When I get my medal and some initials after my name. Other men only get a watch and chain.'

'You sound like an old man at the end of his working life.' Eva tried to disguise her apprehension.

531

'Forty-six is hardly old, is it?'

'Of course not.'

'Life is just starting, what?'

'What are you saying, Freddie?'

'I planned to say nothing till tomorrow, but you'd best hear it from me rather than from some frightful gossip. It's cheerio time.' Freddie affected an English accent. '"*Do pop back for regimental dinners. We love your 'Oirish' stories"*.'

'You're leaving the army?'

'Being kicked out without a pension, though they'd use a politer term.'

'But they know you want to stay?'

'For so long as a war was on I could be one of them, as British as the next man. Irish first, of course, but still British. Times have changed. They don't need half-breeds clogging up the system for their sons coming in. It appears that a detailed report about me was posted.'

'What type of report?'

'One that claimed me incapable of fulfilling routine tasks by arriving on duty in an intoxicated condition.' He took a sip of whiskey. 'It detailed excessive drinking in the mess, disorderly behaviour. There may have been some letting off steam. But how, in all conscience, could anyone present in the mess make such a report when every man jack of us was equally smashed? Whoever reported me lacked the decency to report themselves.' Freddie looked at her, unable to hide his bitterness. 'My MBE is a pay-off. I wanted to let you enjoy tonight, but this is as good as it gets. Surrounded by chums with knives behind their backs. I gave them six years and what do I have? What home have I to return to?'

'Glanmire was always your home.' A chill gripped Eva, imagining the tiny easels in her new kitchen blighted by Freddie's uncomprehending presence. The army had been a bulwark for them both. With his excuse gone for staying in London they were stranded in the glare of truth.

'It didn't feel like my home these last times I went back,' Freddie said quietly. 'I felt an intruder with you all there. Home has become whatever room I'm billeted in.'

'What will you do?'

Freddie downed his whiskey and watched the first dancers take to the floor. 'You tell me,' he said quietly.

Eva lit a cigarette, trying to stop her hand shaking. 'The thing is, Freddie, with the money Mother is leaving she has encouraged me to buy a house in Dublin.'

'A wise move. I can help you look.'

'I've looked already. I paid a deposit on one for the children and myself. I thought you were staying in London.'

'So did I.' Freddie considered the implication that Eva had not consulted him. 'You did okay on the price?'

'I think so. I thought I might teach.'

'Teach what?'

'Painting to children.'

'Teach them to draw?'

'To express themselves freely. I could be good at it.'

'What would you think of my chances?'

'Of painting?' Eva was surprised.

'No.' Freddie smiled. 'Of teaching again.'

She imagined Freddie stalking between the tiny easels, barking at children to buck up.

'The thing is, Freddie, I thought I'd teach them alone.'

Freddie looked away, unable to contain a mirthless laugh. 'Me with a paint brush? I don't think so.' He clicked his fingers at a waiter for another whiskey. 'That's not what I meant. There is a position which I'm told is mine should I care to accept it.'

'Where?'

'A prep school in Wicklow. They want someone to double as a mathematics and games master, a disciplined chap not scared by a few drops of rain. It's not compulsory to live in, but I get the impression they'd prefer if I did. They need a man on the spot to organise the young chaps. It's where military experience comes in, you see.'

The waiter brought his drink. Eva wasn't sure whose feelings he was trying to spare with this face-saving enthusiasm for his new job. 'Therefore a house in Dublin would be awkward for me, though it sounds perfect for you. Naturally the school would welcome you, but my cottage sounds pretty compact . . . a gate lodge really. Not that I mind, but I mean you're used to more space . . .'

Freddie's jovial tone could not disguise his hurt. The chatter around them grew louder, making him raise his voice and drown out any last vestige of intimacy. The band struck up Hazel's favourite tune, *A Gal in Calico*, and on cue she took to the floor.

'Not that you won't be a welcome guest,' Freddie added. 'Any weekend you wished to pop up.'

His pause allowed her the chance to say that he would be equally welcome in Frankfurt Avenue. It was cruel not to reply, but while Freddie hadn't scoffed at the notion of her teaching, even if he didn't interfere, his sense of unspoken ridicule would pervade the house, crippling her dreams as surely as arthritis had crippled Mother.

'Of course I'll come to see you,' she said. 'The children too. When do you start?'

'January. I'll be a new boy, like Francis in Trinity. I have of course made provision for his fees.'

Freddie approvingly watched Hazel swirl about the dance floor with her young man.

'The thing is, Freddie,' Eva said. 'Hazel is talking about wanting to go there too.'

'Hazel attend Trinity?' Freddie looked surprised. 'With her looks? That seems a tad unnecessary.'

'She has a good brain.'

'Undoubtedly she'll use it to find a good man.' He lowered his voice. 'The fact is this damned prep school doesn't pay well. There's rather a surfeit of retired officers. MBE doesn't stand for Mayo Before Eton. The old boys' network have all the good Civvy Street jobs collared. Surely you can make Hazel understand the need to prioritise. Francis will have to earn his own way in time. He'll have no one to support him. Hazel has her love of horses.'

'That's hardly the same thing.'

'It's as good a way as any to meet a decent young man. What about the *Irish Times* photograph you sent me of her jumping at the Horse Show? Hazel stands out. She's still at school, yet she's the finest looking woman in this ballroom. She knows it too, she has the poise and confidence to hold her own with anyone. She won't be slow getting invited to the Trinity Ball and we'll let her if a decent class of chap invites her. Let's see if Francis is as quick to find a partner to invite along.'

'Young women flock around Francis,' Eva said. 'He's like a bosom pal to them.'

'That's a new word for it,' Freddie replied scornfully. 'I've heard Clark Gable called many things but never a bosom pal. Trinity should knock the soft focus out of him, once he avoids those Yankee ex-servicemen on the GI bill.' Freddie watched his daughter dance. 'Will she be frightfully upset not to go?'

'She'll understand.'

Freddie nodded, aware that Eva was lying for his sake. Tomorrow in Buckingham Palace he would receive his bauble, a pay-off for the years which cemented their slow separation. Eva would take appropriate snaps with her Brownie camera, playing the role of an officer's wife. Such memories were all he would have to sustain him when he placed his dress uniform in a trunk and donned the dull garb of a teacher in his native country where few wanted reminders of having sat out the war.

Silently they watched Francis lead a partner out among the couples. He danced with rare grace and the girl in his arms knew it. The dance floor was crowded, though it lacked the frantic gaiety that Eva recalled from the war. These young people did not need to treat each dance like it might be their last. Freddie leaned forward.

'Since we've exhausted our range of excuses for not living together, can I ask one question? Why did you ever marry me?'

'You know why.'

'I don't because I never thought about it back then. I loved you and presumed you loved me.'

'I did.'

'You probably actually did, because people like you – God bless them – love the entire world. Trees, birds, bunny rabbits in the fields. Love is easy because you splash it around like rainfall. I loved you differently, I didn't love anything else. I would have picked you out from a thousand people. You were my favourite living being. I was never even your favourite Freddie.'

'That's not true,' she protested.

'It is.'

Eva was hurt by the truth in his accusation. The two Fredericks journeying to Donegal twenty years ago as rivals and friends. She had let herself be ensnared in the excitement, imagining that once she had exchanged vows with Freddie all doubts would disappear. It took her two decades to fully wake up. But if Freddie loved her so much, why did it take so long to hammer out a marriage settlement in Father's study while she had paced upstairs, feeling like a heifer at mart? Freddie might not have spat on his palm to seal the bargain, but pragmatism had guided his love, clinching the best deal between a clubfooted man and a dowered woman edging towards spinsterhood. Still they had done their duty by the children and while the future would be difficult, at least she could now make her own mistakes without being impeded by his disapproval and could stop seeing herself reflected in his eyes as an irredeemable dreamer.

'Perhaps tomorrow we might talk to the children and work out a civilised arrangement,' she said. 'Come down from Wicklow some evening when you're settled into the new job. Inspect the house. I'd value your opinion.'

'At least it will be warmer than Glanmire House. I hope to visit Mayo over Christmas for some shooting. I'll enjoy rattling around the old place on my own.'

Eva could see him calling into his uncle in Turlough Park, drinking in the Imperial Hotel, stopping at Durcan's shop for cheap Skylark whiskey. He would not mention his MBE, but the news would have gone before him. Everyone would acknowledge it by their comments or their silence. Freddie had fought to keep his neighbours free from war, a truth too uncomfortable to mention. Despite sly remarks about him bowing before a foreign king, there would be local pride in his success.

The band swung into *It's a Pity to Say Goodnight*. Freddie watched his children who were flushed with vitality and excitement and who wanted this evening to never end. They were unaware that it was their father's final encore. He would spend his last weeks in the army as an outsider, knowing that somebody had betrayed him. Perhaps it was planned for months with tabs kept on him, loose remark after remark, last drink after last drink. The war was over and ranks were closing. He would be resolute with his new pupils, teaching them values they would grow to laugh at. Occasionally he would visit her, the homeliness of Frankfurt Avenue increasing his sense of failure. He would make new friends, not all in a bottle. But tomorrow would remain the bitter apex of his life, while Eva was poised on the cusp of both orphanhood and freedom. They would never be as close as this again. Seeing Mrs Templeton watching them, Eva deliberately took Freddie's hand in hers. He looked down, surprised and pleased, as he grew aware of being watched. A waiter approached, paging Eva who was wanted on the telephone. Freddie accompanied her to the porter's desk. It was Maud, saying that she had called the doctor again because the pain was worse, with Mother slipping in and out of consciousness. It was probably impossible to reach Oxford tonight, but Mother might be gone by the time Eva got there tomorrow.

'I'd drive you if I could,' Freddie said when Eva replaced the receiver. 'At one time chaps here would loan me a car with petrol but people don't want to know me now.'

'I shouldn't have left Mother,' Eva said, 'but she insisted that I come.'

'You belong with her really. I should never have taken you away from Donegal. You must get the first train in the morning. I'd like the children to stay, see their father in a good light. The thing is that I'd feel bad asking you to return to the barracks tonight, with only one bed and whatnot. I think you would be better off in a hotel. I'll pay, naturally. Let the children enjoy the rest of the night but there's no need for you to stay. There's nothing more to say, is there? I'll tell them you were called away to Oxford and are trying to get there tonight. I'll put them on a train to you straight from Buckingham Palace.' He surveyed his former comrades and added, with such force that she almost believed him: 'I'll be glad to get away from this.'

In the end she agreed to slip away without spoiling the children's evening. But firstly she showed him the Russian death certificate. He snorted, like she knew he would.

'Oddly enough, this could be good news. The Russians are masters at twisting facts. They may say he is dead to hide the fact that he's alive. You might as well try to eat mercury with a fork as understand how they operate. I don't know anyone who could tell you whether to believe this or not.'

But Freddie was wrong in that and wrong to believe that she was going directly to a hotel to await the first train. The porter hailed a taxi outside the Dorchester, with the driver reluctant to let her out on a corner in Whitechapel, where just one terrace of uninhabitable houses remained standing against a flattened streetscape. But Eva wanted to walk from here.

Finally it was done, she had left Freddie and after tonight her world would be different and uncertain. Like the citizens of these bombed streets, she needed to start a new life. Mother's life was ending and Eva had one last duty to attempt. She reached a street with sounds of life. Turning a corner she found a crossroads miraculously unscarred, with public houses on two corners. Making herself an object of curiosity, she hovered outside an unlit shop, reluctant to venture unaccompanied into either pub. Despite trying to remain unobtrusive, a policeman approached after a time, his voice suggesting that he mistook her for a streetwalker. When her clothes and identity papers revealed her as a lieutenant colonel's wife his tone grew respectful. He seemed reluctant to leave her standing alone after she explained how she was waiting for someone. But his attitude changed when Art emerged from a side street, carrying a satchel of newspapers. Perplexed, he shook his head and walked away.

Art stopped when she approached, anxiously scanning her face for news of Mother. He was losing the public school accent so at odds with his shabby appearance. Neither of them wanted to enter a smoky pub. Art had a one-room flat nearby on Hungerford Street, with an entire corner devoted to a stack of pamphlets condemning *Animal Farm*. Apart from a portrait of Stalin, the room was otherwise spartan as a prison cell.

Eva showed him Brendan's death certificate, which he studied carefully. Art could never utter the heresy that a Soviet document might be a fake, but Eva noted his reluctance to positively authenticate the certificate.

'He should never have gone to Spain,' Art said. 'Enthusiasm is no substitute for discipline.'

'Is he dead?'

'This appears to state so.'

'Conveniently killed by the Germans, with no offer to repatriate the body, no proof of anything.'

'Proof would be impossible. Do you know how many patriotic comrades died in the war, never mind . . . ?' Art hesitated.

'Never mind *what*?' Eva asked angrily. 'Your brother was an innocent man. Did you betray him?'

'What do you mean?'

'I don't know what I mean,' Eva said. 'You're the one of us who always knew everything. You were the shining light, so you explain it. Mother is dying. Will you travel with me in the morning and face her?'

'I've told you before, my life as a Verschoyle is over.'

'Then, as a Russian, tell me whether to show her this death certificate if she is still alive when I get there?'

Art spread his hands. 'Bureaucratic mistakes may occur. We lost millions in the Great Patriotic War. England thinks she won the war because London suffered. But not like in Russia. I can't say if every prisoner on the train was killed or just marked down as dead after fleeing in the confusion. All I can offer you is my bed for the night. I don't mind the floor.'

'There's a bed for you in Oxford and a house in Donegal falling asunder. Why won't you face Mother?'

'She blames me for what happened. I blame myself.' He rose. 'I have some customers – not many – here. If I don't catch them leaving the pubs they'll be gone.'

'Sit down,' Eva pleaded. 'Stop always running from us.'

Art lowered his satchel reluctantly. 'In my dreams I often see you and Maud and Beatrice Hawkins laughing in sun hats, sitting up on Mr Ffrench's cart. I don't know if my wife and child starved to death. Maybe I dream of Donegal to avoid dreaming about them.' He hesitated, unsure whether to confide in her. His sudden boyish look reminded her of when he would enter the kitchen in Dunkineely, excited at having discovered wreckage on the Bunlacky shore. 'That's why I'm finally going home.'

Mother always claimed that Dunkineely was in his blood.

'I'm pleased,' Eva said. 'But what about Samuel Trench's daughter. Will you share it with her family or . . . ?'

She stopped as Art stared at her like she was a retarded child.

'I'm going home to Russia. They have finally issued a visa. They know I never broke faith. I kept the flame alive and they have recognised that.' His tone held the fervour of a true believer who would calmly confront savage beasts in a coliseum. His gaze recalled Martin Luther's piercing eyes. 'The British Empire is finished, with just the fag-ends ready to be swept away. New nations will look to the Soviet Union. That's why I must be there. I know my place. I hope one day you find yours.'

'Your place?' Eva felt a sudden fury. 'After what they did to your brother?'

'Your certificate shows that he was a victim of Nazi aggression. The Soviet Union never harmed him.'

'They kidnapped him in Barcelona.'

'How do you know that is the true version of events?'

'Will you promise to find out the truth when you go there?'

'Brendan may not wish us to find him. He may have requested the Soviet authorities to produce this certificate so that we will give him the freedom to be left alone. I am going to Russia to try and find my wife and child.'

'And what if the secret police are waiting to put you into a camp too?'

'There is more than one kind of prison. If a labour camp is the work that Stalin has earmarked for me I will take it, because it is better to be the smallest cog in a great mosaic than to stand alone in exile and know that your life means nothing.'

'You asked me a favour in Mayo once,' Eva said. 'I hid Jim Gralton. Now I'm asking you for the favour back. Come to Oxford.'

'No.'

'Are you so proud that you cannot even say goodbye?'

'I was never proud. I live by the sweat of my hands. There is no work I ever refused.'

'Watching a mother die is work too,' Eva said. 'It's slow and painful but it must be done because we are only asked to do it once. If you're brave enough to face a Soviet prison, then surely you can face a darkened bedroom in Oxfordshire?'

Eva had thought it impossible to reach Oxford at this late hour. But Art knew a night mail porter at Paddington Station. The station looked deserted when they got there, with the public entrances closed. Art cut down a side street however and soon Eva heard voices and the trundle of barrows behind the station wall. Art knocked repeatedly on a small door until it was opened. He mentioned a name and the door closed again, only to be reopened moments later by a bearded figure who shook Art's hand and called him *comrade*. It was the first time that she heard anyone address Art by this term. For once it made him not seem a solitary figure. Art explained their dilemma and the bearded man shook Eva's hand. He motioned them in to wait in a shed crammed with mail sacks. It was quiet there in the heart of the city, with the platform deserted except for the occasional mail train arriving with no passengers and just the sound of sacks being loaded. An hour passed before the bearded man returned as a Western Region mail train pulled in. Art's comrade tapped on a window, which was opened by a sorter clutching a sheaf of letters. After a short conversation he welcomed them surreptitiously on board. Eva knew she looked incongruous in her evening dress, sitting on a mail sack and listening to Art and the sorter discuss *The Ragged Trousered Philanthropists*. But she didn't care because this journey reminded her of long train trips home to Dunkineely. All that now awaited them was a deathbed, but finally – even if only briefly – they would be a family together.

The Oxford streets were empty, the house in darkness except for a faint glow behind the curtains in Mother's room. Eva had a key.

Mother appeared to be in a coma or a deep sleep, with the doctor's injection keeping pain at bay. Maud looked up as they entered the bedroom, surprised by Art's presence. But the circumstances of this meeting prevented all arguments or recriminations, anything that might drag Mother back into the grip of conscious pain. In sleep she ruled her unruly children, reducing them to whispers as Art took a chair between his two sisters. The only sounds came from Mother's irregular breath and the ticking clock. No outside world might exist beyond those thick curtains. Maud looked jaded after her trip from Ireland, but Eva knew that they all felt exhausted as if they had spent decades travelling towards this moment of being reunited.

It was impossible to know if Mother would ever reawaken. From the size of the rationed injection Eva knew that the doctor expected only to be called again to sign her death certificate.

Eva decided against showing Maud the Russian death certificate just yet. Let her grieve for the passing of one life at a time. Eva's wedding day had been the last time when Mother's three eldest children sat together. Back when they still knew who they were, when their world was still recognisable. Who were they now? She remembered Art's phrase: *Byvshie Liudi,* the former people of a former world. How many former people were scattered across this continent blinking in the light of change, people trying too hard to cling to the past or to let it go. Memories returned from across the broken decades: the excited laughter of children playing musical bumps in the drawing room at Dunkineely, the weekly race to Phil Floyd's shop for sweets to be shared out. Back then the entire world – from its extremities of Mountcharles to Killybegs – knew and viewed them as special. The golden Goold Verschoyle children. Five children lying in a hayrick to imagine their futures, five children picnicking in the rain, five dolphins in the waters off what she once called Paradise Pier, five eaglets poised for flight on a ledge of Slieve League, ready to swoop up towards the sun, swooning and dazzling each other.

Eva knew that the others must share at least some of these

memories from the time when they had a world in common. Art and Maud might remember some moments differently, but this did not make her memories any less true. The one truth they could not differ on was the absolute love of the dying woman in this bed. It awed Eva to have known her parents and borne witness to their love. Perhaps this was what had ill prepared their children for the world, the notion that life could be perfect. The stances taken by Art and the others had shocked many, but while growing up none of them had ever been checked for expressing a thought or an opinion that truly came from within. There had been no bars placed around their minds, no notion that the outside world disallowed such freedom.

When Mother died they would leave this room, quarrel and go their separate ways. But for now they were united by what they were about to become. Orphans. Eva felt certain that Brendan was somewhere in their midst, a small boy in a comical hat, and that Thomas in South Africa could sense what was occurring. The one great love which each of them always knew that they could turn to was being extinguished from this world.

Eva felt more grief for herself than for Mother. Mother was ready for death because all her life she had been preparing for this final adventure to which all stepping stones led. Mother moaned slightly and Eva was torn between a desire that Mother might see Art one more time and a wish for her to be spared more conscious pain. Her lips formed words that were impossible to discern, although Art leaned across to try and hear and then took her hand. Eva clasped Art's other hand and Maud placed her hand over his fingers that were entwined with Mother's. Eva's eyes were closed and she did not remark upon the scent, knowing that the words did not need to be said. Because she knew that the others could smell the familiar hand lotion, the cream that Mother had used after gardening on those evenings when they lay in bed awaiting her step on the stairs and knowing, as they still knew, that they were truly and unconditionally loved.

# AUTHOR'S NOTE

I first met Sheila Fitzgerald in 1977 when she lived in a small caravan in Turlough in Mayo, close to her former – and by then derelict – house in the small woodland which she had turned into an animal sanctuary. Her caravan – the Ark – was a true sanctuary for both humans and adults. *The Family on Paradise Pier* originated from taped conversations made in 1992, when Sheila was almost ninety years of age and still enjoying her alternative lifestyle, with her caravan by then parked beside an independent hostel and workspace for local artists in County Wexford. We discussed the idea of my writing a book based on her life and Sheila preferred the form of a series of interlinking vignettes, with some name changes and deliberate blurring of facts.

To write a book like this is to feel yourself being judged not just by the living but by the dead. For years I hesitated to write this novel, knowing that I could never capture the essence of this unique and joyous woman who quietly inspired many who encountered her. But, sorting through her papers, I found a line that she had written in the 1960s (not long before the tragic deaths of both her children) about how she admired artists with the courage to take reality and shape it into something new.

Fiction can never tell the full truth, yet perhaps it can tell altered but equally important truths. Biographies or even auto-biographies cannot reveal the full truth either. Our lives are invariably viewed through the prism of whatever version of reality we construct from selected memories so that our pasts begin to consist not of what has happened but what we remember happening.

Rather than pretend to be able to tell the full truth, this book deliberately plays with many aspects of reality. I changed the first names to show that Eva, Maud, Thomas, Art and Brendan are re-creations shaped by my own imagination. I retained the family name because the Goold Verschoyle children were too unique to be any other family. My wilful blurring of reality (where, for example, Madame Despard loses her house several years too soon but Jim Gralton enjoys his native Leitrim for longer than de Valera allowed) may frustrate historians. But it allowed me to create a parallel and condensed fictional universe that, hopefully, still reflects the essence of Sheila's experience while allowing me to explore certain aspects of her family's life and many of the political and social tensions of the period.

Readers wishing to know more about the person on whom Art is loosely based should seek out pamphlets by Neil Goold like *Trotskyism: Its Roots and Fruits* and *The Twentieth Congress and After: A Vindication of J.V. Stalin and His Policy.* They capture his beliefs and personality in a way that I cannot claim to. Brendan is based on Brian Goold Verschoyle, who became disillusioned and disappeared after being kidnapped by the Soviets during the Spanish Civil War. He died in 1941 on a prisoner train that was bombed by the Nazis. The experiences ascribed to him during the years of his disappearance are chosen to be representative of the many who shared his fate.

Like many others in this novel – not least Eva herself – the characters of Mr and Mrs Ffrench are very much my own interpretations, loosely inspired by a married couple with communist beliefs who occupied Bruckless House at the time this book is set, who spent time in Moscow and who lie buried beside the small pier at the end of their former garden, under the fine epitaph in this book. In 1984 I helped to edit a collection of drawings by Sheila Fitzgerald from the sketchbook which she kept as a girl in Donegal, entitled *A Donegal Summer* (Raven Arts Press). The illustrations on the endpapers of this book are taken from that sketchbook.

Sheila did open her highly innovative children's art studio in Frankfurt Avenue in Dublin, delighting in her students while often working under such financial constraints that she had to sometimes whitewash old newspapers for the children to paint on. In his collection of poems, *Crazy About Women*, one of her pupils, Paul Durcan, stated how the origins of that book, inspired by his love of paintings, went 'back to winter nights in Dublin in the early 1950s when my mother used to take me one night a week for yet another magic assignation with Sheila Fitzgerald'.

I am deeply indebted to many of her friends who helped with recollections. None of them is responsible for factual errors or falsifications. Particular thanks are due to Derek Johns, Clare Reihill, Catherine Heaney, Mandy Kirkby and Philip Gwyn Jones for their faith in my work, and to Trinity College, Dublin and All Hallows College, Dublin, where at stages during the writing of this book I was respectively the Writing Fellow and the fellow who writes. Sheila died in 2000 in Wexford. At her request her body was taken to Dublin by young friends not in a hearse but in a plain wooden box lovingly painted in bright colours. In Glasnevin crematorium no clergyman spoke but Tennyson's *Crossing the Bar* was recited before the body she had finally outgrown entered the flames to her chosen music, the joyous final chorus of Beethoven's Ninth Symphony. Sheila's tiny handmade coffin looked like a small boat that would cause only the barest ripple. Only afterwards did her friends realise how that ripple had spread out across her lifetime to touch distant shores and how it still keeps moving on its own course long after many of the seemingly great waves of her time have died away.

In remembrance,

Dermot Bolger
*Dublin, August 2004*